SLEEPWALKER

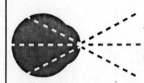

This Large Print Book carries the
Seal of Approval of N.A.V.H.

SLEEPWALKER

WENDY CORSI STAUB

KENNEBEC LARGE PRINT
A part of Gale, Cengage Learning

GALE
CENGAGE Learning

Detroit • New York • San Francisco • New Haven, Conn • Waterville, Maine • London

GALE
CENGAGE Learning·

LIBRARY OF CONGRESS CATALOGING-IN-PUBLICATION DATA

Staub, Wendy Corsi.
    Sleepwalker / by Wendy Corsi Staub. — Large Print edition.
        pages cm. — (Kennebec Large Print Superior Collection)
    ISBN 978-1-4104-5732-5 (softcover) — ISBN 1-4104-5732-X (softcover)
    1. Serial murders—Fiction. 2. Large type books. I. Title.
PS3569.T336456S54 2013
813'.54—dc23
                                                              2013007294

Published in 2013 by arrangement with Harper, an imprint of HarperCollins Publishers.

Printed in the United States of America
    1 2 3 4 5   17 16 15 14 13

For Morgan, Brody, and Mark
And in loving memory of my dear friend
Beverly (Beaver) Barton, gone much too
soon, mourned by so many.

Loveliest of lovely things are they
On earth that soonest pass away.
The rose that lives its little hour
Is prized beyond the sculptured flower.
WILLIAM CULLEN BRYANT

ACKNOWLEDGMENTS

Special thanks to John McNamara, Theresa Gottlieb, Linda Fairstein, Ken Isaacson, Jamie Freveletti, and Alafair Burke; to my agent, Laura Blake Peterson, and the gang at Curtis Brown; to my editor, Lucia Macro, and the gang at Avon Books/HarperCollins; to my friends and family, who endured my deadline-induced reclusiveness; to my husband, Mark Staub, who is always there to read, to listen, to brainstorm, to help make the book — and *me* — better and stronger; and, most of all, to my son, Brody Staub, for his title.

Please note: this is a work of fiction. While certain names, places, and events are real and/or based on historical fact, the plot and narrative action depicted within are strictly products of the author's imagination.

■ ■ ■ ■

Part I

■ ■ ■ ■

The worst thing in the world
is to try to sleep and not to.
F. Scott Fitzgerald

CHAPTER ONE

Glenhaven Park, Westchester County, New York
Sunday, September 11, 2011

Her husband has suffered from insomnia all his life, but tonight, Allison MacKenna is the one who can't sleep.

Lying on her side of the king-sized bed in their master bedroom, she listens to the quiet rhythm of her own breathing, the summery chatter of crickets and night birds beyond the window screen, and the faint hum of the television in the living room downstairs.

Mack is down there, stretched out on the couch. When she stuck her head in about an hour ago to tell him she was going to bed, he was watching *Animal House* on cable.

"What happened to the Jets game?" she asked.

"They were down fourteen at the half so I

turned the channel. Want to watch the movie? It's just starting."

"Seen it," she said dryly. As in, *Who hasn't?*

"Yeah? Is it any good?" he returned, just as dryly.

"As a former fraternity boy, you'll love it, I'm sure." She hesitated, wondering if she should tell him.

Might as well: "And you might want to revisit that Jets game."

"Really? Why's that?"

"They're in the middle of a historic comeback. I just read about it online. You should watch."

"I'm not in the mood. The Giants are my team, not the Jets."

Determined to make light of it, she said, "Um, excuse me, aren't you the man who asked my OB-GYN to preschedule a C-section last winter because you were worried I might go into labor while the Jets were playing?"

"That was for the AFC Championship!"

She just shook her head and bent to kiss him in the spot where his dark hair, cut almost buzz-short, has begun the inevitable retreat from his forehead.

When she met Mack, he was in his mid-thirties and looked a decade younger, her

12

own age. Now he owns his forty-four years, with a sprinkling of gray at his temples and wrinkles that frond the corners of his green eyes. His is the rare Irish complexion that tans, rather than burns, thanks to a rumored splash of Mediterranean blood somewhere in his genetic pool. But this summer, his skin has been white as January, and the pallor adds to the overall aura of world-weariness.

Tonight, neither of them was willing to discuss why Mack, a die-hard sports fan, preferred an old movie he'd seen a hundred times to an exciting football game on opening day of the NFL season — which also happens to coincide with the milestone tenth anniversary of the September 11 attacks.

The networks and most of the cable channels have provided a barrage of special programming all weekend. You couldn't escape it, not even with football.

Allison had seen her husband abruptly switch off the Giants game this afternoon right before the kickoff, as the National Anthem played and an enormous flag was unfurled on the field by people who had lost loved ones ten years ago today.

It's been a long day. It might be a long night, too.

13

She opens her eyes abruptly, hearing a car slowing on the street out front. Reflected headlights arc across the ceiling of the master bedroom, filtering in through the sheer curtains. Moments later, the engine turns off, car doors slam, faint voices and laughter float up to the screened windows: the neighbors returning from their weekend house in Vermont.

Every Friday, the Lewises drive away from the four-thousand-square-foot Colonial next door that has a home gym over the three-car garage, saltwater swimming pool, and sunken patio with a massive outdoor stone fireplace, hot tub, and wet bar. Allison, who takes in their mail and feeds Marnie, the world's most lovable black cat, while they're gone, is well aware that the inside of their house is as spectacular as the outside.

She always assumed that their country home must be pretty grand for them to leave all that behind every weekend, particularly since Bob Lewis spends a few nights every week away on business travel as it is.

But then a few months ago, when she and Phyllis were having a neighborly chat, Phyllis mentioned that it's an old lakeside home that's been in Bob's family for a hundred years.

Allison pictured a rambling waterfront mansion. "It sounds beautiful."

"Well, I don't know about *beautiful,*" Phyllis told her with a laugh. "It's just a farmhouse, with claw-foot bathtubs instead of showers, holes in the screens, bats in the attic . . ."

"Really?"

"Really. And it's in the middle of nowhere. That's why we love it. It's completely relaxing. Living around here — it's more and more like a pressure cooker. Sometimes you just need to get away from it all. You know?"

Yeah. Allison knows.

Every Fourth of July, the MacKennas spend a week at the Jersey Shore, staying with Mack's divorced sister, Lynn, and her three kids at their Salt Breeze Pointe beach house.

This year, Mack drove down with the family for the holiday weekend. Early Tuesday morning, he hastily packed his bag to go — no, to *flee* — back to the city, claiming something had come up at the office.

Not necessarily a far-fetched excuse.

Last January, the same week Allison had given birth to their third child (on a Wednesday, and not by scheduled C-section), Mack was promoted to vice president of television advertising sales. Now he works longer

15

hours than ever before. Even when he's physically present with Allison and the kids, he's often attached — reluctantly, even grudgingly, but nevertheless inseparably — to his BlackBerry.

"I can't believe I've become one of those men," he told her once in bed, belatedly contrite after he'd rolled over — and off her — to intercept a buzzing message.

She knew which men he was talking about. And she, in turn, seems to have become one of *those* women: the well-off suburban housewives whose husbands ride commuter trains in shirtsleeves and ties at dawn and dusk, caught up in city business, squeezing in fleeting family time on weekends and holidays and vacations . . .

If then.

So, no, his having to rush back to the city at dawn on July 5 wasn't necessarily a far-fetched excuse. But it was, Allison was certain — given the circumstances — an excuse.

After a whirlwind courtship, his sister, Lynn, had recently remarried to Daryl, a widower with three daughters. Like dozens of other people in Middleton, the town where he and Lynn live, Daryl had lost his spouse on September 11.

"He and Mack have so much in common," Lynn had told Allison the first morning they all arrived at the beach house. "I'm so glad they'll finally get to spend some time together. I was hoping they'd have gotten to know each other better by now, but Mack has been so busy lately . . ."

He *was* busy. Too busy, apparently, to stick around the beach house with a man who understood what it was like to have lost his wife in the twin towers.

There were other things, though, that Daryl couldn't possibly understand. Things Mack didn't want to talk about, ever — not even with Allison.

At his insistence, she and the kids stayed at the beach with Lynn and Daryl and their newly blended family while Mack went home to work. She tried to make the best of it, but it wasn't the same.

She wondered then — and continues to wonder now — if anything ever will be the same again.

Earlier, before heading up the stairs, Allison had rested a hand on Mack's shoulder. "Don't stay up too late, okay?"

"I'm off tomorrow, remember?"

Yes. She remembered. He'd dropped the news of his impromptu mini stay-cation when he came home from work late Friday night.

"Guess what? I'm taking some vacation days."

She lit up. "Really? When?"

"Now."

"Now?"

"This coming week. Monday, Tuesday, maybe Wednesday, too."

"Maybe you should wait," she suggested, "so that we can actually plan something. Our anniversary's coming up next month. You can take time off then instead, and we can get away for a few days. Phyllis is always talking about how beautiful Vermont is at that time of —"

"Things will be too busy at the office by then," he cut in. "It's quiet now, and I want to get the sunroom painted while the weather is still nice enough to keep the windows open. I checked and it's finally going to be dry and sunny for a few days."

That was true, she knew — she, too, had checked the forecast. Last week had been a washout, and she was hoping to get the kids outside a bit in the days ahead.

But Mack's true motive, she suspects, is a bit more complicated than perfect painting weather.

Just as grieving families and images of burning skyscrapers are the last thing Mack wanted to see on TV today, the streets of

Manhattan are the last place he wants to be tomorrow, invaded as they are by a barrage of curiosity seekers, survivors, reporters and camera crews, makeshift memorials and the ubiquitous protesters — not to mention all that extra security due to the latest terror threat.

Allison doesn't blame her husband for avoiding reminders. For him, September 11 wasn't just a horrific day of historic infamy; it marked a devastating personal loss. Nearly three thousand New Yorkers died in the attack.

Mack's first wife was among them.

When it happened, he and Carrie were Allison's across-the-hall neighbors. Their paths occasionally crossed hers in the elevator or laundry room or on the front stoop of the Hudson Street building, but she rarely gave them a second thought until tragedy struck.

In the immediate aftermath of the attacks, when she found out Carrie was missing at the World Trade Center, Allison reached out to Mack. Their friendship didn't blossom into romance for over a year, and yet . . .

The guilt is always there.

Especially on this milestone night.

Allison tosses and turns in bed, wrestling the reminder that her own happily-ever-after

19

was born in tragedy; that she wouldn't be where she is now if Carrie hadn't talked Mack into moving from Washington Heights to Hudson Street, so much closer to her job as an executive assistant at Cantor Fitzgerald; if Carrie hadn't been killed ten years ago today.

In the most literal sense, she wouldn't be where she is now — the money Mack received from various relief funds and insurance policies after Carrie's death paid for this house, as well as college investment funds for their children.

Yes, there are daily stresses, but it's a good life Allison is living. Too good to be true, she sometimes thinks even now: three healthy children, a comfortable suburban home, a BMW and a Lexus SUV in the driveway, the luxury of being a stay-at-home-mom . . .

The knowledge that Carrie wasn't able to conceive the child Mack longed for is just one more reason for Allison to feel sorry for her — for what she lost, and Allison gained.

But it's not as though I don't deserve happiness. I'm thirty-four years old. And my life was certainly no picnic before Mack came along.

Her father walked out on her childhood when she was nine and never looked back; her mother died of an overdose before she graduated high school. She put herself through the Art Institute of Pittsburgh, moved alone to New York with a degree in fashion, and worked her ass off to establish her career at *7th Avenue* magazine.

On September 11, the attack on the World Trade Center turned her life upside down, but what happened the next day almost destroyed it.

Kristina Haines, the young woman who lived upstairs from her, was brutally murdered by Jerry Thompson, the building's handyman.

Allison was the sole witness who could place him at the scene of the crime. By the time he was apprehended, he had killed three more people — and Allison had narrowly escaped becoming another of his victims.

Whenever she remembers that incident, how a figure lurched at her from the shadows of her own bedroom . . .

You don't just put something like that behind you.

And so, on this night of bitter memories, Jerry Thompson is part of the reason she's having trouble sleeping.

It was ten years ago tonight that he crept into Kristina's open bedroom window.

Ten years ago that he stabbed her to death

in her own bed, callously robbing the burning, devastated city of one more innocent life.

He's been in prison ever since.

Allison's testimony at his trial was the final nail in the coffin — that was how the prosecuting attorney put it, a phrase that was oft-quoted in the press.

"I just hope it wasn't my own," she recalls telling Mack afterward.

"Your own what?" he asked, and she knew he was feigning confusion.

"Coffin."

"Don't be ridiculous."

But it *wasn't* ridiculous.

She remembers feeling Jerry's eyes on her as she told the court that he had been at the murder scene that night. Describing how she'd seen him coming out of a stairwell and slipping into the alleyway, she wondered what would happen if the defense won the case and Jerry somehow wound up back out on the street.

Would he come after her?

Would he do to her what he had done to the others?

Sometimes — like tonight — Allison still thinks about that.

It isn't likely. He's serving a life sentence. But still . . .

Things happen. Parole hearings. Prison breaks.

What if . . . ?

No. Stop thinking that way. Close your eyes and go to sleep. The kids will be up early, as usual.

She closes her eyes, but she can't stop imagining what it would be like to open them and find Jerry Thompson standing over her with a knife, like her friend Kristina did.

Sullivan Correctional Facility
Fallsburg, New York

One hour of television.

That's it. That's all Jerry is allowed per day, and he has to share it with a roomful of other inmates, so he never gets to choose what he wants to watch. Not that he even knows what that might be, because it's been ten years since he held a remote control.

Back then — when he was living in the Hell's Kitchen apartment that was a palace compared to his prison cell — he liked the show *Cops.* He always sang along with the catchy opening song, *Bad boys, bad boys . . . whatcha gonna do when they come for you?*

It was so exciting to watch the cops turn on the sirens and chase down the bad guys and arrest them. Then one night, they came

23

— in real life, the cops did — and they arrested Jerry because Mama was dead in the bedroom and they thought *he* was a bad boy. They thought he had killed her, and two other ladies, too.

"Admit it, Jerry!" they kept saying. "Admit it! Tell us what happened!" They said it over and over again, for hours and hours, until he started crying. Finally, when he just couldn't take it anymore, he did exactly what they were telling them to do: he admitted it. He said that he had killed his mother and Kristina Haines and Marianne Apostolos, and then he signed the papers they gave him.

He did that because you have to do what the police tell you to do, and also because maybe he really had killed the women. Maybe he just didn't remember.

He doesn't remember a lot of things, because his brain hasn't been right for years, not since the accident.

Well, it wasn't really an *accident*.

Someone doesn't *accidentally* bash a person's head in with a cast-iron skillet. But that's what Mama always called it, an accident, and that's what Jerry always thought it was, because the truth about his injury was, of course, just one more thing he didn't remember.

that's what she told the judge, too, and the jury, and everyone else in the courtroom during the trial. She said Jerry shouldn't worry, even though he had admitted to killing people and signed the papers, too.

"You were not responsible for your actions, Jerry," his lawyer would say, and she would pat Jerry's hand with fingers that were cold and bony, the fingernails bitten all the way down so that they bled on the notebook paper she was always scribbling on.

"You're going to be found not guilty by reason of insanity," she said. "You're not going to go to prison. Don't worry."

"I won't," Jerry said, and he didn't.

But then came the day when the judge asked the lady in charge of the jury — the tall, skinny lady with the mean-looking face — "Have you reached your verdict?"

The lady said, "We have, Your Honor."

The verdict was guilty.

The courtroom exploded with noise. Some people were cheering, others crying. Jerry's lawyer put her forehead down on the table for a long time.

Jerry was confused. "What happened? What does that mean? Is it over? Can I go home now?"

No one would answer his questions. Not

even his lawyer. When she finally looked up, her eyes were sad — and mad, too — and she said only, "I'm so sorry, Jerry," before the judge banged his gavel and called for order.

Jerry soon found out why she was sorry. It was because she had lied. Jerry *did* go to prison.

And he's never going to get out. That's one of the things Doobie says to him, late at night.

He scares Jerry. He scares everyone. His tattooed neck is almost as thick as his head, and he's missing a couple of teeth so that the ones he has remind Jerry of fangs.

He's in charge of the cell block. Well, the guards are really supposed to be in charge, but Doobie is the one who runs things around here. He decides what everyone else gets to say, and do, and watch on TV.

Tonight, though, the same thing is on every channel as Doobie flips from one to the next: a special news report about the tenth anniversary of the September 11 attacks.

After shouting a string of curses at the television, Doobie throws the remote control at the wall. When it hits the floor, the batteries fall out. One rolls all the way over to Jerry's feet. He looks down.

"Touch that, and you're a dead man," Doobie warns.

Jerry doesn't touch it.

He's sure — pretty sure, anyway — that he doesn't want to be a dead man, no matter what Doobie says.

Doobie is always telling him that he'd be better off dead than in here. He tells Jerry all the things he'd be able to do in heaven that he can't do here, or even back at home in New York. He says there's cake in heaven — as much cake as you want, every day and every night.

He knows Jerry's favorite thing in the whole world is cake. He knows a lot of things about Jerry, because there's not much else to do here besides talk, and there aren't many people to talk to.

"Just think, Jerry," Doobie says, late at night, when the lights are out. "If you were in heaven right now, you would be eating cake and sleeping on a big, soft bed with piles of quilts, and if you wanted to, you could get up and walk right outside and look at the stars."

Stars — Jerry hasn't seen them in years. He misses them, but not as much as he misses seeing the lights that *look* like stars. A million of them, twinkling all around him in the sky . . .

Home. New York City at night.

The thought of it makes him want to cry.

But the New York City they're showing on television right now doesn't bring back good memories at all.

He remembers that day, the terrible day when the bad guys drove the planes into the towers and knocked them down. He remembers the fire and the people falling and jumping from the top floors, and the big, dusty, burning pile after the buildings fell, one right after the other.

"Sheee-it," Rollins, one of the inmates, says as he stares at the footage of people running for their lives up Broadway, chased by the fire-breathing cloud of dust.

"I was there."

All of them, even Doobie, even Jerry, who had the exact same thought in his head, turn to look at B.S., who uttered it aloud.

B.S. is small and dark and antsy, with a twitch in his eye that makes him look like he's winking — like he's kidding around. But he's not. He told Jerry that he always means what he says, even when everyone else claims he's lying.

"I don't care what they say, because I know I'm telling the truth," he told Jerry one night after lights-out. "You do, too, don't you?"

"I do what?"

"You know I'm telling the truth, right, Slow Boy?"

That's what they call him. Slow Boy. It's just a nickname, like B.S. and Doobie.

Doobie says nicknames are fun. Jerry doesn't think they are, but of course, he doesn't ever want to tell Doobie that.

As nicknames go, that's not the worst Jerry has had. Back in New York, a lot of people called him Retard. And in the courtroom, during his trial, everyone called him The Defendant.

"That's a big ol' pile of bull," Doobie tells B.S. now. "Just like your name."

"No!" B.S. protests. "I was. I was there. I was a fireman."

"You wasn't no fireman in New York City," Rollins tells him. "*Sheee-it.* You from Delaware. Everyone know dat."

B.S. is shaking his head so rapidly Jerry thinks his brains must be rattling around in his head. "I climbed up miles of stairs dragging my fire hose, and —"

"Your fire hose was *miles* long?"

"Yeah, yeah, it was long, like miles long, and I got to the top floor right before the building collapsed —"

"If you were up there," one of the other inmates cuts in, "then how the hell are you sitting here right now? How'd you get out alive, you lying mother— ?"

"I jumped. That's how. I jumped, yeah, and the other firemen, they caught me in one of those big nets."

Jerry regards him with interest as the others shake their heads and roll their eyes because they're thinking B.S. makes things up all the time.

Jerry usually doesn't know if B.S. is telling the truth or not, and he doesn't really care. He talks all the time, especially at night, and Jerry usually has no choice but to listen. Like Doobie, B.S. lives in the cell next to Jerry's, but on the opposite side.

But this time, for a change, he's interested in what B.S. is saying.

"I was there, too," Jerry says, and they all turn to him. "When the terrorist attack happened."

"Yeah? Did you jump out the window too, Slow Boy?" someone asks.

"I wasn't in the building. But I was near it. I saw it burning. I saw . . ." Jerry's voice breaks and he swallows hard.

He squeezes his eyes closed and there are the red-orange flames shooting out of white buildings, gray smoke reaching into a deep blue sky, black specks with flailing limbs, falling, falling, falling . . .

There are some terrible things that, despite his brain injury, he has no problem remembering.

September 11 is one of them.

That was the day before he killed Kristina Haines, the other lawyer, the one who didn't like Jerry, said at the trial.

"On the morning of September eleventh, The Defendant was teetering on the edge . . ."

At first, Jerry thought the lawyer was confused. He tried to speak up and tell everyone that he wasn't in the towers on that morning. A lot of people were teetering on the edge up there, but he wasn't one of them.

But he found out that you aren't allowed to just talk in the middle of a trial, even if you're The Defendant and what they're saying about you is wrong.

Anyway, Jerry soon discovered that the lawyer wasn't talking about teetering on the edge of a building.

Sanity: that's the word he kept saying. Teetering on the edge of sanity.

"When those towers fell," he told the courtroom, "a lot of people lost their already tenuous grip on sanity. Jerry Thompson was one of them."

He told everyone that Jerry stabbed Kristina Haines to death in her own bed because he was angry with her for turning him down when he asked her out.

The lawyer was right about that.

Jerry *did* ask Kristina to go eat cake with him.

He *was* angry with her when she said no, especially because she gave him the finger as she walked away, and —

"Tell us more, Slow Boy."

Doobie's voice shoves the memory of Kristina from Jerry's mind. "What?"

"Tell us what happened in New York that day."

He doesn't want to look at Doobie, or at anyone else, either. He can feel their eyes on him, burning into him, and he turns away, toward the television. He stares at the pictures of the mess the bad guys made when they flew the planes into the buildings. He takes a deep breath and his nose is full of the smell of burning rubber and smoke and death.

Jerry shakes his head. "I don't know why they did that."

"Why who did what?"

"Why the bad guys made that mess. Why they killed all those people. They even killed themselves. Why would they do that?"

"Because they knew the secret, Slow Boy,"

Doobie says, leaning closer so that the only way Jerry won't be able to look at him is to close his eyes. He doesn't do that, though, because he thinks it might make Doobie mad.

"What secret?"

"The one I told you. Remember?"

"No." Jerry doesn't remember Doobie telling him any secrets.

Doobie's face is close to Jerry's, and his black eyes are blacker than black. "The bad guys knew that heaven is the best place to be. They wanted to go there. They chose to go there. It's better than anywhere on earth. A hell of a lot better than here. Hell . . . Heaven . . . get it?"

He grins, and Jerry can see that his teeth are black in the back.

"So . . ." Doobie shrugs and pulls back. "You should go. That's all I'm saying."

"Go where?"

"Heaven."

"Heaven?" Rollins echoes. "Ain't none of us goin' to heaven, brother. We all goin' straight to —"

"Not Slow Boy," Doobie cuts in, turning to look at Rollins.

Jerry can't see his face, but it must be a dirty look because Rollins quickly shuts his mouth and turns away.

"You . . . you're going straight to Heaven," Doobie whispers, turning back to Jerry. "You can go now, if you want to."

"Why would I want to do that?"

"I told you. It's better than being stuck here for another fifty years, or longer. You can have cake there."

Jerry's mouth waters at the thought of it.

He hasn't had cake in years. Ten years.

"But I . . . I can't fly a plane into a —"

"You don't have to." Doobie's voice is low. So low only Jerry can hear it. "There are other ways to get there, you know? There are easy ways to get yourself out of here, Jerry."

Jerry.

Not Slow Boy.

"I could help you," Doobie says. "I'm your friend. You know that, don't you?"

Jerry swallows hard, suddenly feeling like he wants to cry. A friend — he hasn't had a friend in a long time.

He thinks of Jamie . . .

No. Jamie wasn't your friend. Jamie was your sister, and she died when you were kids. She didn't come back to you all those years later, like you thought. That wasn't real.

"Jerry," Doobie is saying, and Jerry blinks and looks up at him.

"What?"

"We'll talk about this later, okay? After the lights go out. I'll help you. Okay?"

Jerry doesn't even remember what they were talking about, but he doesn't want to tell Doobie that, so he says, "Okay."

CHAPTER TWO

Glenhaven Park, Westchester County, New York
Tuesday, September 13, 2011

"Mommy!"

"Shh!" Allison hurries to the foot of the stairs and looks up to see her older daughter leaning over the railing at the top. "Daddy's still sleeping, honey, and I don't want —"

"No, he's not." Mack appears behind their daughter, having just come out of the master bedroom, looking like he just rolled out of bed. Unshaven, barefoot, and wearing only a pair of boxer shorts, he tells Allison, "I sent her to come get you."

"Why?"

"Daddy wants you to watch TV with him," Hudson informs Allison matter-of-factly, and turns briskly away as if to announce, *My work here is done.*

A moment later, the door to her bedroom closes, and Allison knows that the world's most efficient six-year-old has resumed getting ready for school, even though the bus won't be here for over an hour.

Allison scoops up J.J. as he crawls rapidly past her.

"Al," Mack says from the top of the stairs, above J.J.'s bellowed protest. "Come up here."

"Gee, honey, as much as I'd love to lie around in bed and watch TV with you" — Allison lifts the wriggling baby's pajama-clad butt to her nose, sniffs, makes a face — "he needs to be changed, and I'm heating the griddle for pancakes, and —"

"That stuff can wait. You have to see this."

"See what?" Something about his tone makes her doubt that it's just one of the commercial spots on his network, which is usually the case when he summons her to the television.

"Come up and I'll show you."

"Everything okay?"

"Just come here," Mack tells her. "I have the TV paused."

Ah, the beauty of the bedroom DVR. After Mack got the new job, he went out and bought three new plasma televisions and TiVos for all of them — one for the living room; one, still sitting in a box, designated for the about-to-be-painted sunroom; and one for the master bedroom.

Allison initially protested. "Dr. Cuthbert" — he's the sleep specialist Mack recently started seeing at her insistence — "said you're supposed to use the room only for sleeping and sex, remember?"

"Well, lately, I haven't been using it for either of those things, so . . ."

Point taken. She's been too tired at night for anything more strenuous than falling asleep.

"Anyway, the bedroom TV is for you," Mack told her at the time. "This way, you can tape all those reality shows you like to watch up here, and I won't have to sit through them downstairs."

That sounded good in theory. But Mack's the one who spent the whole day yesterday in front of the bedroom TV, moping around and channel surfing when he was supposed to be painting.

She didn't nag him about it, though. She knew he hadn't slept a wink the night before. When she got up with the baby before six, she found her husband still on the couch, watching another old comedy — but not laughing.

"Why don't you go up to bed?" she suggested.

"Because I won't be able to fall asleep.

40

What's the point?"

"The girls will be down here soon, and if they see you, they'll want to play. If you're not in the mood, you'd better make yourself scarce."

He did.

It was a little better this morning. When he climbed into bed, she stirred enough to see that the bedside clock read 4:30, and when she got up an hour later, he was snoring.

Now, Allison starts up the stairs with J.J. balanced on her hip. He squirms, not happy to have been interrupted on his journey across the hardwoods, undoubtedly toward some kind of mischief. But he quickly switches gears, deciding to indulge his favorite new habit: pulling his mother's long hair.

She hasn't had time yet this morning to pull it back into a ponytail, her daily hairstyle these days — not because it's flattering, by any means, but to spare herself endless tugging by J.J.'s chubby fingers, perpetually wet from teething drool.

He delights in pulling his sisters' hair, too, leaving them much less eager to "babysit" their little brother lately.

It's just as well. When he was immobile, the girls loved to keep an eye on him as he lounged in his bouncy seat or swing while Allison bustled around the house. Now she wouldn't dare leave them alone in a room with J.J.-the-human-monkey.

Hudson, six, and Madison, almost four, were much more laid back at this age. Either that, or Allison has simply forgotten how challenging it is to keep a baby-on-the-move out of trouble. J.J.'s had too many close calls for comfort. Just yesterday, she found him pulling on a cord, Mack's heavy desktop computer teetering just above his fragile little head. She caught it just in time.

"You're a handful, you know that, J.J.? And you've *got* a handful. Ouch!"

The baby affectionately tightens his grip, laughing in such delight that Allison can't help but smile through her grimace.

Sometimes she wonders whether this child would even exist had Mack been promoted last January instead of this past one.

On New Year's Day 2010, they'd started discussing having a third child, torn between expanding their family and upsetting the already delicate balance. Their daughters were just becoming old enough to be more flexible and portable; less needy. Neither Allison nor Mack relished the idea of going back to diapers and schedules and wee-hour feedings.

In the end, they realized that parenthood has been the most rewarding thing in their world, and their desire for another child to love won out. By April, she was expecting.

The third pregnancy was more exhausting than the others had been. She had morning sickness all day, every day, for the entire nine months — boy hormones, predicted her closest friend, Randi Weber. Neither Allison nor Mack wanted to know the baby's gender in advance, though. Everyone assumed they were "trying for a son," but that wasn't the case. They'd have been just as happy with another daughter, as long as the baby was healthy.

Please let this baby be healthy, Allison prayed frequently throughout the pregnancy, worried that her life was already too good to be true.

The baby *was* healthy — though the breech delivery was excruciating. But it quickly became apparent that J.J. was a colicky infant. Now, on the verge of toddlerhood, he remains far more demanding than his sisters ever were.

It's all worthwhile, of course, every exhausting maternal moment, but still . . .

Between the baby and the girls' needs and Mack's new job and the ever-challenging treadmill of life in suburban New York, Allison sometimes finds herself thinking, *It isn't supposed to be like this.*

But of course, that isn't really true. This is exactly how it's supposed to be; it was part of her master plan in another lifetime. She'd not only longed to one day become a wife and mother, but she'd hungered for the breakneck velocity of New York, with its vast population of ever-striving over-achievers, a welcome world away from the lazy pace and status-quo lifestyle of her rural Midwestern hometown.

Her dream became reality: she transformed herself from impoverished Nebraska schoolgirl to Manhattan fashion editor with dozens of pairs of Christian Louboutins in her closet.

But after the September 11 attacks, the things that had once mattered so much — the designer status symbols she had coveted all her life and worked so hard to eventually own — seemed frivolous.

Not only that, but she realized that she lived in a city that lay squarely in terrorism's crosshairs. She felt as though she were taking her life in her hands every time she rode the elevator up to her office, or got on a subway, or even walked down the street.

Yes, she considered moving away in those months following the attacks. Even now, it bothers her to admit that, even to herself. After all she had survived in her childhood, she almost let fear get the better of her as an adult.

In the end, it came down to the same choice she'd faced all her life.

You can run scared, or you can dig deep for inner strength, hold your head high, and fight for what you deserve.

She'd stayed in New York, and thank goodness for that. If she hadn't, she wouldn't be —

"Al?" Mack calls from the bedroom. "You coming?"

"I'm coming, I'm coming." She reaches the second floor and detours down to Hudson's room to make sure she's getting ready for school. She needn't have bothered. The bed is neatly made — her daughter takes care of that the moment she climbs out of it — and Hudson is sitting on it, busy transferring things from her well-organized desk to her open backpack.

Looking into the room next door, Allison sees Madison curled up on her rumpled purple bedspread with one of her favorite books, a dog-eared copy of *Tikki Tikki Tembo* that had once belonged to — and been equally cherished by — Allison. Twirling a long strand of honey-colored hair around

45

her index finger, Maddy is so lost in the pages she doesn't notice her mom in the doorway.

A faint smile plays at Allison's lips as she heads back down the hall, thinking about her budding bookworm. Maddy was thrilled to start a Monday-Wednesday-Friday preschool program last week, and the teacher was impressed that she was already reading.

The conversation reminded Allison of one she'd once overheard between Mrs. Barnes, her own kindergarten teacher, and her mother.

"Allison is already reading, Mrs. Taylor. It's really quite impressive. Did you teach her at home?"

Naturally, her mother took credit for it — but in truth, it had been Allison's father who taught her to read. He was the one who had bought her that cherished copy of *Tikki Tikki Tembo* and all the other books she'd loved; the one who read her bedtime stories and had her sound out the words on the pages.

Allison's smile fades, as it always does when unwelcome memories of her father drift back to her.

But he's completely forgotten the moment she crosses the threshold into the master bedroom and sees the image frozen on the television screen.

46

It's not a television commercial, as she expected.

It's a face. A mug shot. One she's seen many times.

"What's going on?" she asks Mack, heart pounding.

"I was watching the news, and — here, just sit down." Her husband, sitting on the foot of the unmade bed, pats the mattress beside him. "I rewound it to the beginning of the story."

She sits.

J.J. emits an ear-splitting objection.

"Shh, sweetie." She bounces him a little on her knee, already wobbly-weak from the mug shot shock.

But J.J. has fixated on the BlackBerry that is a regular fixture in Mack's hand. He covets it, and Allison's iPhone, too — not that they ever let him get his sticky little fingers on their electronic devices if they can help it.

J.J. wails and strains for Mack's Black-Berry, which Mack quickly tucks out of his son's view. He reaches toward the pair of yesterday's jeans that are dangling from the bedpost, pulls his key ring from the pocket, and jingles it. "Here, J.J., look! J.J.!"

Delighted, J.J. reaches for it, the Black-Berry instantly forgotten.

Hoping he'll be kept occupied for a minute, maybe even two, Allison sets him down in a rectangle of sunlight that falls across the rug at her feet. She gently pats the tufts of fine dark hair that cover his head and he babbles happily, inspecting the keys.

"Are you ready for this?" Mack is poised with the remote aimed at the television.

"I don't know . . . am I?"

No reply from Mack. He simply presses play.

"They called him the Nightwatcher," a female reporter's voiceover begins, and a chill runs down Allison's spine.

It's not as if she hasn't thought about him every day for the past ten years, about her own role in putting him behind bars, but still . . .

"In the waning hours of September 11, 2001, as the shell-shocked citizens of New York City were grappling with the horrific terrorist attack on the World Trade Center, a serial killer was launching a deadly spree. By the time the NYPD arrested handyman Jerry Thompson a few days later, four people, including Thompson's own mother, lay dead."

The mug shot gives way to footage of Jerry Thompson being led in handcuffs up the steps of the courthouse.

"During the trial, the defense team argued that he was mentally impaired due in part to a childhood brain injury inflicted by the defendant's own twin sister, Jamie Thompson — who in a bizarre twist was killed in an apparent random mugging in December 1991, just days after she attacked her brother."

The scene shifts to show a school portrait of an eighth-grade girl with pigtails, her crooked front teeth revealed by a smile that doesn't reach her eyes.

Allison knows the terrible story: how one night, Jamie Thompson snapped and attacked her brother with a cast-iron skillet. As the ambulance and police rushed to the scene, Jamie ran away — not seen again until her stabbed, mutilated body was found in an alleyway a few days later.

When Allison thinks about a girl that age trying to survive alone on the mean city streets . . . well, is it any wonder she didn't?

One tragedy triggered another, and so the dominoes began to topple.

"The jury rejected the insanity defense," the reporter continues, "convicting Thompson on four counts of second-degree murder."

The scene has shifted again, showing footage of a handcuffed Jerry Thompson being led down the courthouse steps past a media mob.

Allison wasn't there the day the verdict came in. She had done her part, testifying when she was called as a key witness, but she had no interest in reporting daily to the trial of her friend Kristina's murderer.

No, she was trying to lose herself in other things: working as a fashion editor at *7th Avenue* magazine, hunting for a new apartment far from the shadow of the fallen towers and her murdered friend, establishing a friendship with the newly widowed Mack.

Carrie had been in her office high in the south tower when the first plane struck below her floor. She never had a chance.

Nor did Kristina, who was most likely sound asleep that very night when Jerry crept into her apartment — dressed as a woman, believing he was his alter ego, his dead sister, Jamie — and slaughtered her in her bed.

Allison and Mack became two more New Yorkers trying to pick up the pieces of shattered lives that September. Two more New Yorkers drawn together by unspeakable tragedy . . .

And somehow, we fell in love.

But not right away. No, that would have been wrong. Though Mack had confessed to Allison that his marriage to Carrie was crumbling before she died, he had a lot of grief and guilt to work through before he was ready to move on.

Earlier that year, Allison had endured a bitter breakup with Justin, a biologist, for whom she'd fallen hard. Bruised, regretting that she'd let someone into her life despite having promised herself that she never would, she wasn't interested in another relationship. Ever.

She was there for Mack when he needed her; when he didn't, she steered clear for her own sake as well as his. She knew she was attracted to him long before anything romantic happened between them, but it felt wrong.

Then one December night more than a year later, he kissed her — and suddenly, it felt right.

She tries not to look back at the tragic circumstances that brought them together.

Sometimes, though, she just can't help it.

She stares at the televised photo of Sullivan Correctional Facility, where Jerry Thompson is serving a life sentence. Why is the media dredging all this up again? Is it just another dismal footnote on the heels of the wall-to-wall retrospective September 11 coverage?

Or is it something much more ominous?

How many nights has she lain awake — thanks, in part, to her husband's chronic tossing and turning — and imagined what would happen if Jerry were to somehow escape from the maximum security prison? How many times has she imagined him creeping into her bedroom the way he did the others?

The great irony in all of this is that she never would have believed — even though she saw him at the murder scene that night — that he was capable of murder. She didn't know him well, but her gut instinct told her he was innocent.

Then he confessed.

So much for my gut instinct.

That same *undependable* gut instinct had also made her wary of Mack in the beginning. She'd actually entertained the fleeting notion that he might have been having an affair with Kristina, and that he'd killed her in a fit of violent passion or passionate violence or . . .

God only knows what I was thinking. But I couldn't have been more wrong about Mack.

Or about Jerry.

He's a cold-blooded murderer, and now he's back in the news. Why? Did he break out of prison?

But there's a witness notification program. She would have been told immediately if Jerry were back out on the street.

Then again, no system is foolproof.

She looks at Mack, watching the screen intently, and asks, "What if —"

"Shh, wait, listen!"

Allison clamps her mouth shut.

"This past weekend marked ten years not just since the worst terror attack in our nation's history," the reporter is saying, "but ten years since Jerry Thompson's murderous rampage through a scarred, burning city. Sometime in the wee hours of September 12, however — perhaps to exactly the hour, the very minute, that he murdered aspiring Broadway dancer Kristina Haines ten years ago — Jerry Thompson took his own life."

Allison clasps a hand over her mouth, her blue eyes wide.

Again, she looks at Mack. This time, he meets her gaze, nods slowly.

"He's dead." For some reason, she finds it necessary to say it aloud.

"Yeah." Mack's expression is so relieved that she knows she wasn't the only one who's always worried that Jerry might escape one day and come after her again.

But they don't have to worry anymore.

Thank God. Thank God.

It's over at last.

And so it begins . . . again.

The need — the overpowering need, consuming every waking moment, every thought, every breath . . .

The need is back. And so is Jamie.

After all these years.

Ten, to be exact.

Funny how it happens. One morning, you wake up and everything is great, and then the next . . .

Wait a minute, great? Your life was never great.

All right, no, it wasn't.

But it was manageable.

For almost ten years now you've been functioning, going to work, paying bills, taking meds, and Jamie was nowhere to be found . . .

Then, out of nowhere, came the news that Jerry was dead.

Dead, and you had to find out on television.

Well, what did you expect? No one even knows you exist — not in Jerry's world, anyway.

If it weren't for the media, you wouldn't even have a clue what happened to Jerry after you left him there that night ten years ago, helpless and alone, with his mother's stinking corpse in the bedroom and the cops closing in.

But what were you supposed to do? You tried to make him run, too. He wouldn't budge. He wouldn't go with you. You had no choice but to leave him there.

You didn't even go far. Just took the train north to Albany — a safe distance, but close enough to keep tabs on the trial.

Serial killers are big news. The Nightwatcher trial was covered blow-by-blow in the newspapers, on the radio, on the TV news.

When it was over, Jerry went to prison for crimes he'd confessed to committing.

But you knew better.

You knew he wasn't guilty — because you knew who was.

You knew that Jamie's soul had taken over your body and killed those four people, including her own mother — hers and Jerry's.

Yet you let Jerry take the fall.

But what were you supposed to do? Come forward and admit that you thought you might have done it? That someone else — your own dead daughter — was living inside of you, making you do terrible things? That you had let your own son take the fall?

No. No way. You'd have been hauled off to the loony bin for the rest of your life, just like your crazy old man was when you were a kid.

It's just like that Old Testament quote, the one that's resonated for so many years.

There's not much to do when you're stuck behind bars; sometimes, you read the Bible they give you. Sometimes, you actually learn something from it.

The sins of the father shall be visited upon the son.

Those words couldn't be more true.

You paid for the sins of your father — and now your son is paying for yours.

After Jerry was convicted — well, it wasn't easy to live with the anger. The guilt. The injustice of it all.

Things got a little crazy . . .

You got a little crazy. A lot crazy — and it wasn't the first time.

Suddenly, Jerry wasn't the only one behind bars.

For me, though, it was just for aggravated assault. Nothing so bad.

No one had died . . . this time.

During that last jail sentence, Dr. Patricia Brady came into the picture. And at last, everything changed.

For the first time ever, someone was willing to listen. Dr. Brady was young, new at her job, so eager to help . . .

She didn't know the whole story, of course.

She knew nothing about the twins, Jamie and Jerry, whose teenage father, Samuel Shields, walked away from their pregnant mother many years ago, denying that they were his.

Denial is so easy until you get your first glimpse of a fourteen-year-old child and see your own face looking back at you.

Dr. Brady knew the rest, though — about the childhood beatings by a mentally ill father, and all the years in and out of juvy and then jail, and one state pen after another. . . .

She said that all those bad things that happened could be partly due to illness. Not physical, but mental illness. She said it runs in families. If your father has it, chances are you might, too.

She said that when people are mentally ill, they can't help what they do, because they're only following the commands of the voices that never stop talking, never, never, never, never, *never* . . .

Dr. Brady said the medicine would make the voices go away.

"All of them? Even Jamie's?"

"Even Jamie's," Dr. Brady said, not realizing that Jamie had ever been real, an actual person who lived — and died. His own daughter.

She was my child, just like Jerry was. And I failed her when I walked away from their pregnant mother, just like I failed Jerry.

"I don't want Jamie to go away, Dr. Brady. She's a part of me."

No. It was more than that.

Jamie is me, and I am Jamie . . .

But Dr. Brady couldn't possibly understand.

She said, "Look, Sam, I know you don't want Jamie to leave. But you have to trust me. You have to try it. Please. For me."

She had such kind eyes. The kindest eyes anyone could ever have.

"All right. I'll try it."

Dr. Brady was right: it worked.

Jamie was gone, but somehow, that was okay. Everything was okay — especially when that final sentence had been served and handcuffs and inmate jumpsuits became relics of the past.

"You'll never go to jail again, Sam," Dr. Brady promised on that last day. "You've got your life back."

Back? I never had a life, never thought I could.

A normal life, the kind of life other people — normal people — get to live. A life spent working hard and hoarding every spare cent, saving up to hire the best lawyer in the world to get Jerry out of prison . . .

And now . . .

It was all for nothing.

Jerry is gone. He never even realized he had a chance — that he hadn't been abandoned by his father to waste away the rest of his life behind bars.

I was going to surprise him, one day soon. Go visit him. Remind him I promised to take care of him, and that I didn't forget. I was going to get him out of there . . .

But it's too late now.

Jerry took his own life before he could be rescued.

The news was devastating, and in its wake, the whole world came crashing down. Suddenly, it was all so pointless. Work, money, medicine . . .

For years, there had been regular visits to the Albany mental health clinic that wrote prescriptions and set up the obligatory follow-up appointments. But the doctors there weren't nearly as engaging as Dr. Brady had been; not nearly as invested in their patients' treatment. There was a lot of turnover at the clinic; you couldn't really count on seeing the same shrink from one visit to the next.

For a long time, though, that didn't matter. Nothing mattered in all those years except that the medicine helped. Now, with Jerry dead, nothing mattered at all.

The big blue capsules went swirling down the toilet in an impulsive flush, and Jamie came back shortly after, whispering, taunting, teasing, wanting to take over again.

Now Jamie is all I have.

She's inside me again, and she's becoming me again and I'm becoming her, and that's okay. That's how it used to be. That's how it's supposed to be.

And this time, I don't need any medicine and I don't need Dr. Brady to tell me that none of this is my fault.

No, because there are two other people who are to blame for destroying Jerry: Rocky Manzillo, the homicide detective who got him to confess, and the prosecution's star witness, Allison Taylor — now Allison MacKenna.

She was supposed to die, too, ten years ago. Remember?

I know, Jamie. I know she was.

We were close, so incredibly close . . .

I know. We almost had her. But somehow, she got away.

At the trial, Allison told the court that she had seen Jerry furtively leaving the Hudson

60

Street apartment building the night Kristina Haines died.

There should have been video evidence, too, from the building's hallway surveillance cameras. But the footage for that particular time frame was mysteriously missing.

The prosecution implied that Jerry obviously took it and destroyed it in an effort to cover his tracks. After all, he had the keys to the office where the videotape was kept.

But Jerry wasn't the only person in the world who had access.

I did, too.

No one, though, not even the defense, wasted much time considering that someone other than Jerry might have stolen the incriminating tape. Jerry had confessed; there was a witness; there were no other viable suspects; he had a clear motive for every one of those murders.

Well, for three of them, anyway.

Kristina Haines and Marianne Apostolos had spurned his advances.

Lenore Thompson, Jerry's mother, had been cold and abusive.

As for the fourth victim . . . Hector Alveda was a street punk, found stabbed to death in a Hell's Kitchen alleyway a few hours after Jerry's arrest. It was only the timing, and the proximity to Jerry's apartment building, that caused the cops to consider a possible link. Sure enough, Alveda's blood turned up on the knife that was found in Jerry's apartment.

There was plenty of speculation during the trial about how Jerry's path might have crossed Hector's.

But it didn't. It crossed mine. Mine and Jamie's.

"Please don't hurt me. Take my wallet. Please. Just don't hurt me . . ."

Those were Hector Alveda's last words.

Ah, last words. I've had the pleasure of hearing them from quite a few people, and they're always the same, begging for mercy . . .

It's been a while, though.

Too long.

But now it's back: the urge, the overpowering urge, to kill. For Jerry's sake. To make things right.

Because the thought of an innocent soul like Jerry killing himself in a lonely prison cell when he never should have been there in the first place . . .

Someone has to pay.

There they are, pictured in newsprint photographs lain out on the table, spotlighted in a rectangular patch of bright sunlight that falls through the window above the sink.

Beautiful days like this one are rare here in Albany. Maybe the blue skies and sunshine are a good omen for what lies ahead.

The photos were clipped from media accounts during the trial, and later painstakingly laminated to keep them from yellowing and tearing.

Ordinarily, they're tucked away in a big box, along with some of Jamie's old clothing. The box is kept in the crawlspace beneath the rented duplex; a crawl space that — come to think of it — might just come in handy for other things in the weeks ahead.

But don't get ahead of yourself. You don't know yet how you're going to do what has to be done, you only know that it's time to begin.

Now the box, with clothes inside, sits open on the floor beside the table littered with photographs of Rocky Manzillo and Allison MacKenna.

And what about the prison guard on duty that night on the cell block, the one who should have been watching over Jerry, making sure he didn't harm himself?

No photos of him; no idea who he is.

But it won't be hard to find out.

Meanwhile . . .

The faces staring up from the table seem expectant, as if they're waiting for their fates to be decided.

"You're going to *pay!*" With a furious shove, Jamie sends the table over onto its side, where it teeters, then falls flat on the top with a resounding bang.

Almost immediately, there's a thumping sound overhead.

The dour old man who rents the apartment upstairs, the man who complains about the slightest thing, is banging on the floor — the ceiling — with something, probably his stupid old shoe.

He's never going to let this go by without further confrontation.

Dammit, dammit, dam—

Then again . . .

Hmm.

Maybe a confrontation with the old son of a bitch is just the thing to get the ball rolling again after all these years.

"Daddy?"

Startled, Mack looks up from the paint can he's been staring at for, what . . . five minutes now? Ten?

His older daughter is standing in the doorway of the sunroom.

Hudson has long, straight blond hair that people always assume she got from her mother, unaware that Allison's natural hair color is brunette. Their daughter's fair coloring comes from Mack's mother's side of the family — though he himself has dark hair — and so do the light green eyes that are a mirror image of his.

But that's where the resemblance to her dad stops. Hudson has elfin features, a sprinkling of freckles, and is small for her age. She also has an air of precocious confidence she didn't inherit from either of her parents.

"I don't know where she gets it," Allison frequently says, shaking her head over something their firstborn has said or done.

Mack has a pretty good idea. His own mother, Maggie, had the same strong-willed flash in her Irish eyes that he so often sees in Hudson's.

But of course, Allison wouldn't recognize it because she never knew his mother, who died the year before they met.

His first wife met her a few times. That was enough for a terminally ill Maggie MacKenna to decide Carrie was wrong for her son.

You were right, Mom. You were so right.

Back then, though, I kept thinking that if you just got to know Carrie, just got to know what she had been through in the past . . .

But Mack never had the chance to bridge

65

the gap between the two women in his life, and he never got the chance to tell his mother that he regretted not having talked to her before he eloped with Carrie after a whirlwind courtship. His mother died a few months later.

Now, looking back, he knows it's no accident that after preserving his bachelorhood well into his thirties, he quite literally married the first woman who came along on the very day he got the shocking news that Mom had just six months to live. He was in no frame of mind, at that time, to begin a relationship, let alone take marriage vows.

He also understands now that he avoided discussing Carrie with Maggie because he was afraid his mother would tell him he was making the wrong choice. He didn't want to hear that, didn't want to face it. Somewhere deep down inside, terrified of the looming loss, he was attempting to replace a mother with a wife.

No, not even just a wife — a family. He and Carrie started trying to get pregnant right away, even before they'd exchanged vows and rings. Why waste time, they asked each other. Life was too short.

That was for damned sure.

Later, Mack would look back and wonder

what might have happened if only he'd asked Maggie's advice before eloping; if only she'd noticed he was faltering and reached out . . .

But that wasn't their style, either of them. They were descended from a proud, unflinching clan who'd fled the poor-houses and famine of mid-nineteenth-century Galway in search of a better life in America. Their legacy: everything they'd struggled to earn — food, money, time, privacy — was far too precious to squander. Thus, Mack was raised with plenty of love, but in a family that, above all, got things done, without benefit of much soul-searching or heart-to-heart discussion.

Maggie MacKenna faced her own death as she'd faced every other challenge life had tossed her way: with grim acceptance. Mack didn't realize until later, looking back, that he'd adopted the exact same attitude with his first marriage, determined to make the best of it.

Things are so different the second time around. How he wishes his mother had had the chance to meet Allison. Maggie would have loved her; probably would have declared that he and Allison were as right for each other as two peas in a pod, a favorite saying of hers.

Although lately . . .

It's not that anything's wrong between them. It's just that they haven't had time for each other, what with his job, the kids, all the little details involved in daily life — and they're both always so exhausted. . . .

"Shouldn't you have some paint on that wall by now?" Again, his daughter's voice jars Mack back to the moment. He looks up to see Hudson gazing around the room at the stepladder, paint cans, tray, brushes, rollers, tape, drop cloths draped over the furniture and across the slate floor tiles.

"I'm about to get started," he tells her. "It just takes a long time to do the prep work."

Longer than it should, today, Mack realizes, noticing the angle of the sunlight falling through the glass. He rubs the burning spot between his shoulder blades. He's operating on an hour's sleep — so what else is new? — and his weary brain keeps drifting to the past. To Jerry Thompson, and Kristina Haines, and . . .

Carrie.

Always Carrie.

She's been dead ten years now, but dammit, she's going to haunt him forever.

"I can't wait to see how the color looks on the wall," Hudson chatters on. "I'm the one who chose it, remember?"

"How could I forget?" He smiles, thinking back to that day in the paint store. He was leaning toward plain old white, and Allison was trying to talk him into a mossy green, and then along came Hudson, the artist in the family, waving a paper swatch in a creamy shade called Buttered Popcorn.

"It should be a happy color like this," she declared, and she was right. It should be, and it will be.

Happy.

Absolutely.

A happy color for a happy family in a Happy House.

That's what the Realtor called this center hall Colonial on Orchard Terrace when she pulled them up to the curb out front six years ago.

"This is a Happy House," she proclaimed, and Allison, in the front seat of the Mercedes, turned to exchange glances with Mack, sitting in the back.

A Happy House, they'd figured out by that time, was most likely Realtor-speak for *Something is wrong with it.*

After all, the woman had called a Victorian with a leaky roof a "historic architectural masterpiece" and a raised ranch with a moldy first floor a "trove of possibility."

This house — the Happy House, built in

the 1920s, white with dark green shutters — certainly had curb appeal — and a million-dollar-plus price tag.

Allison later pointed out that the same house in Nebraska would have cost five figures instead of seven.

"But you're paying for location. This is Westchester County, New York. Do you want to live in Nebraska?"

"You know the answer to that."

Yes. He sure did. She didn't even want to *visit* Nebraska.

Meanwhile, it turned out they'd bought at the peak of the market, before the economic downturn that sent real estate prices plummeting. Plummeting, as in they could probably get nine hundred thousand for the house if they had to sell it now. Of course, they don't — and they won't.

"I think this is my dream house," Allison whispered to Mack that first day, as the Realtor led them along a brick walk past tall shrubs and stately old trees covered in English ivy that also climbed a white trellis and black wrought-iron lamppost.

Inside, the rooms were inviting, flooded with light. A formal dining room lay to the left of the entry hall with its curved staircase, and a formal living room to the right; fireplaces in both. Off the living room, the charmed sunroom had built-in shelves and cupboards. Across the back of the house, a large kitchen opened to a great room overlooking a sunken brick patio.

Upstairs, there were three family bedrooms, a small study, a hall bath, and the master suite, which took up half the second floor and stretched from the front of the house to the back.

Aesthetics aside, it is truly a Happy House, and that's what Mack and Allison have called it ever since. There's just a nice vibe here. Good energy.

"That's because the owners didn't get divorced or die or go bankrupt like some of the other houses we looked at," Allison said, before they made their offer.

No, the sellers had raised three children here, now grown, and were retiring to play golf in Florida.

Someday, that will be me and Allison, Mack thinks.

Yes, when the kids are grown — and Allison has learned to golf — and his career is behind him, that's exactly what they'll do. Move away, head to someplace warm and sunny, where the living is easy and reminders of the past — not *this* past, but the one that came before — are easily forgotten.

Mack can hear the *Sesame Street* theme

song playing on TV in the living room. Maddy is singing along, *"Sunny day, sweepin' the . . . clouds away . . ."*

Yes, that's it. That's exactly it.

In the background, Allison clatters breakfast dishes in the kitchen. The baby is in there with her, banging something on his plastic high chair tray. From outside, he can hear a lawnmower, a barking dog, chirping birds.

Mack glances at the roll of blue painter's tape on the floor, then at the baseboards and crown moldings and three walls of this room that are virtually made of paned glass. Taping off the trim is going to take hours. But maybe he can at least paint part of the wall first, so that Hudson can see it and he can feel as though he's accomplished something.

"Okay," he tells her, picking up a screwdriver to pry the lid off the nearest paint can, "just give me a little while to get started and you can come back in and see how it looks."

Hudson looks at her watch — a gift she requested for her last birthday and wears daily. "But I have to go right now."

"Go where?"

"Daddy! Where do you think? School!"

"What? Oh — right. Guess I lost track of

time. You know, maybe *I* need to start wearing a watch around the house on my days off. That, or we need a couple more clocks around here. What do you think?"

"I think you should probably stop talking and start *doing*," Hudson says, and he grins. That's one of Allison's favorite phrases.

"Good idea. And when you get home this afternoon, the room will be all finished. How does that sound?"

"All finished?" Hudson looks dubiously from him to the paint can to the walls. "I don't think so, but good luck."

He watches her skip off, then mutters, "Yeah, I don't think so, either."

Why did he have to make such a big deal about getting it done this week?

Because you felt guilty taking off work just because you couldn't deal with all the hoopla in the city.

He's never been able to deal with it. That's why every year, right after Labor Day, he and Allison and the kids have always taken their second annual vacation: not to the Jersey Shore, but to Disney World.

Ah, yes, the happiest place on earth. An amusement park can't completely erase the nightmarish memories of 9/11, but it helps.

They were forced to skip the trip this year, though. Not because Mack couldn't get away — which was questionable — and not because J.J. doesn't travel well — which he doesn't — but because Hudson started elementary school this past week. Pulling her out of her Montessori preschool was never a problem, but other moms had warned Allison that the local school district frowns upon illegal absence.

"In kindergarten?" Mack rolled his eyes when she told him.

"I don't know . . . everyone says it's a bad idea to kick off her entire school career on the wrong foot."

"I think it's a bad idea to listen to what everyone says. People around here can be so uptight. Just ignore them."

"That's easy for you to say. You get to go off to the city every day and leave me to figure out how to raise these kids in a place where no one is ever satisfied and nothing is ever enough."

"Want to trade?"

He saw her weigh her response. Whatever she wanted to say — she didn't say it. Typical Allison. She'd told him once that she'd learned, during her hard-knocks childhood, that saying the first thing that comes to mind often leads to trouble. Anyway, she knows that Mack isn't away from home by choice. If it were up to him, they'd probably

74

be living barefoot on a deserted island, just the five of them, insulated from the rest of the world and the terrible things that happen in it.

When Mack couldn't escape New York this year with his family over September 11, he thought he'd be capable of making the best of things. It was just a day on the calendar, after all. Maybe he could just put that out of his mind; treat it like any other day and try to forget . . . forget . . .

By late last week, though, with the city awash in commemoration and fresh terror threats, he realized that wasn't going to happen. There was no escaping the memories . . . not even at home in the suburbs at night.

No, especially not at night.

That's how it's always been for him. When the rest of the world is asleep, Mack lies awake in bed or prowls restlessly through the wee hours, torturing himself with could haves, should haves, would haves.

Especially lately.

Why can't you just get over it once and for all? You've put all that behind you, moved on. You love Allison in a way that you never loved Carrie.

That, Mack thinks grimly, is part of the problem.

Whenever he thinks he's past the guilt, something comes along to dredge it up again. Why does he let it eat away at him? He has a great life now. Crazy sometimes, exhausting, but happy. Happy family, Happy House . . . paid for by his first wife's death.

Jaunty music is still playing in the next room.

Sunny day . . .

Yes. It is sunny today: it's a beautiful Tuesday morning in September.

Just like . . .

No.

Mack picks up a paint stirrer. He'd better get busy.

"What the hell is going on down there?" Roger Krock calls from the top of the steps, not really expecting the first floor tenant to answer him.

Sure enough, all is silent below . . . *now.*

But a minute ago, there was such a loud banging noise that Roger nearly fell off the kitchen chair he was standing on. At his age, a fall from that height could easily snap a bone.

Who would look after him then?

He's eighty years old, living alone, long retired from his janitorial job at the state capitol building a few miles away, with pen-sions from that and from the navy. Not much to spend his money on, though, so he adds it to the cash he's been stashing away for years, though he's not sure who will even inherit it when his time comes.

His brother has been gone for nearly five years, his sister for seven, and he lost his wife way back in '96.

It's not like he has kids and grandkids to lean on in his so-called golden years. No, he and Alice were childless. They didn't want or expect it to be that way — they were hoping to raise a big family — but things were different back then.

If God didn't want you to have children, you didn't get to have them. Period. There was none of this nonsense with test tubes and women carrying other women's babies and being injected with octuplets and whatever the hell else goes on in this day and age. People adopting from foreign countries, and all those Hollywood movie stars not even bothering to get married . . .

The world is going to hell in a handcart as far as Roger is concerned.

Anyway, being all alone in the world the way he is, he can't afford to have any broken bones.

Yeah, and it's not like that inconsiderate tenant downstairs ever thinks to look in on him, even when the weather is bad — which it was more often than not this past winter. His neighbor is a good thirty, forty years younger than Roger, but he doesn't even bother to shovel the front steps and walk when it snows. He just waits for the landlord to come around and do it, and half the time that's not until a day later.

Meals on Wheels can't deliver when they can't get up to the door. That means Roger resorted to canned beans on quite a few stormy days, all because of his lazy neighbor.

And now I almost fell off my damned chair because of him slamming something around down there. Well, I'm going to go down and give that jerk a piece of my mind.

Roger leaves the chair right where it is, beneath the trap door he'd just opened. He'll get back to that later.

The trap door leads to the low attic tucked beneath the roof. This apartment comes with access to the storage area there; the one downstairs gets the basement crawl space.

The attic is better, as far as Roger is concerned. It's a lot drier up there. God only knows what the underground dampness would do to the cash he has stashed away, much less to his magazine collection.

He's been collecting since he was in

Guantanamo sixty years ago; some of those vintage issues of *Hustler* and *Penthouse* are worth a fortune. Not that he'd sell them off, unless he absolutely had to part with them. But it's nice to know that he has his own little nest egg up there. Of course, Alice never knew the trove existed.

If she had ever found out . . .

Roger shudders to think of her reaction.

But she never did, and now that he's all alone, he sometimes feels like those old magazines are his only pleasure in life. Yes, and if he breaks a leg, God only knows when he'd be able to get to them again.

Grumbling to himself, he goes out into the hall, leaving the door propped open, and hits the light switch.

Nothing happens.

The damned overhead bulb is burned out again. It's bright as a Havana beach outside, but you'd never know it if you were stuck in the hallway of this dark old building.

Depressing, that's what it is. But Roger has lived here for years, and though he can afford to move, at his age, he doesn't like change. Hell, he's never liked change.

The neighborhood has gone downhill over the past decade or two, and the house has changed ownership a few times. The latest landlord doesn't keep up with things the way the others have, but at least he hasn't raised the rent.

Clinging to the banister, Roger clumps slowly down the steep, creaky flight of stairs, making sure his shoes land good and hard on every tread.

On the first floor, he crosses the small, shadowy vestibule and knocks on the apartment door marked 1.

No answer.

He knocks again.

"Coming," a faint, muffled voice calls.

Footsteps inside. Odd — they sound like heels tapping on hardwoods, reminding him, with a familiar pang, of Alice.

The door opens.

Roger is taken aback — and pleasantly surprised — to see a woman standing there in the dimly lit entry hall. She's tall, taller than Roger, who's almost six foot, and she's stacked, too — he can see that in the tight sweater she's wearing.

"Yes?" she asks, in a low, husky voice.

Roger seems to have forgotten why he's here. He seems to have forgotten how to speak, too.

"I — you — where — ah —"

"Do you want to come in?" she asks.

Roger does. He can't seem to find his tongue to tell her, but words don't seem necessary, because she opens the door wide.

He crosses the threshold, and she closes it behind him. Hearing her slide the dead bolt, he feels a tightening in his groin, realizing what's about to happen. It's been so long since he's been intimate with a woman — for the last few years of Alice's life she was so sick, wasting away . . .

It isn't until he's followed her into the next room — a room with windows, and light, where he can see her — that he realizes he was wrong about what's going to happen.

He was wrong about a lot of things.

She's not a woman after all.

She's a man, and she — *he* — is holding a butcher knife.

With the baby down for his nap, two more loads of laundry spinning in the washer and dryer, and Madison settled at the kitchen table with a peanut butter sandwich and a Berenstain Bears book, Allison heads for the sunroom at last.

She's been meaning to check in on Mack all morning, but one thing led to another and she never got the chance.

Now she finds him standing on a ladder pressing a length of blue tape along the bottom edge of the crown molding. There's a splotch of yellowish paint on one wall, but

81

that's it.

"How's it going?" she asks him, and he jumps, startled. "Sorry . . . don't fall."

"It's going," he says with a shrug.

"Want some lunch? I can make you a sandwich."

"Nah . . . I've got to get this finished. The taping is taking forever."

"I can help." She wouldn't mind doing something constructive to take her mind off the news of Jerry Thompson's suicide. She's been troubled by it all morning.

"I don't need help."

"Mack . . ." Allison stands at the foot of the ladder. "Come on down. You can paint and I'll finish taping."

"I've got it."

"But I have some time, and —"

"I said I've got it!"

Uh-oh. Major bad mood alert.

"Okay, fine." Allison turns to go.

"Allie —"

She turns back.

Mack climbs down the ladder and rubs the spot between his shoulders. Once again, he didn't bother to shave, and his green eyes are underscored with black circles.

"I'm sorry. I didn't mean to snap at you. I didn't get much sleep again last night, and . . ."

"I figured." She takes the roll of blue tape he hands her. "You need to go see Dr. Cuthbert again."

"Not until November. I have an appointment on the twenty-fifth, remember?"

She remembers. That's the Friday after Thanksgiving, and she's the one who scheduled it for him, well in advance. Mack's office is closed that day, and since the doctor only sees patients on weekdays, there aren't many dates that work.

She'd suggested that he simply call in sick one day, and his response, predictably, was "I'm not going to lie and say I'm sick when I'm not."

No, lying — even the kind of white lie that everyone tells — just doesn't mesh with his moral code. Usually, that's a quality she admires in Mack, so different from her own father, whose whole life was a lie. But sometimes, her husband's sense of honor makes things a lot more challenging than they have to be.

"I mean you should see Dr. Cuthbert sooner than that," Allison tells him now. "You're home this week, and —"

"Why do I need to see him sooner? I did everything he said to do. I stopped drinking coffee after noon, I bought the Tempur-Pedic mattress that cost a fortune, I —"

"I know, but none of that seems to be enough. You can't go on like this, not sleeping at night, grouchy during the day . . ."

"It's been this way all my life, Allie. You know that. I'm sorry I'm grouchy."

"I'm just worried about you."

"I'm okay. Some days — nights — are worse than others, but I'll live."

"There's no reason to for you to suffer, Mack."

Something flashes in his eyes, and then is gone. She recognizes the expression, though.

Guilt.

"Maybe you don't want to help yourself," she hears herself suggesting. "Maybe you're still trying to punish yourself."

"For what?"

"For Carrie going off to work and dying on the very morning you told her you wanted a divorce."

The words are harsh, but true. How many times has she heard him utter them himself?

She knows his story; knows that ten years ago on a rainy Monday night in September, Carrie told Mack she was putting an end to her infertility treatments, no longer interested in trying to conceive a child.

Mack was devastated.

The next morning, he told her their marriage was over. She walked out, and he never saw her again.

That's a hefty burden for anyone to live with. Is it any wonder he can't sleep at night?

"I had insomnia long before that happened, Allison," he says evenly.

"I know, but it's worse than ever."

"It'll get better. This is the anniversary. When everything dies down —"

"But you and I both know that it's never going to go away."

There was always something, it seemed, to bring back the pain.

A few years ago, it had been the death in Iraq of a young soldier named Marcus. Mack had mentored him years ago through his volunteer work with the Big Brother organization, and they'd stayed in touch over the years, though Allison had never met him. Mack took the news that he'd been killed pretty hard.

She had thought he might finally find some measure of closure last spring, when the mastermind behind his wife's murder was killed in Pakistan. But Bin Laden's death only seemed to unexpectedly dredge up the pain again, at a time when Mack was totally unprepared for it.

Looking back, Allison knows that was

when Mack's latest bout with insomnia began.

It only got worse last month when a freak earthquake struck the East Coast. Exactly like the terrorist attack just shy of ten years earlier, it hit out of nowhere on a sunny summer Tuesday. In the midst of a sales call on a high floor of the Empire State Building, Mack had — like countless other Manhattanites — flashed back to September 11. For a nerve-rattling couple of minutes, he was sure the skyscraper beneath his feet had been hit by a plane, or a bomb.

Long after he knew what had really happened, he was up all night, still shell-shocked.

"I don't know why I can't get it out of my head," he told Allison. "It was just . . . I don't know. Maybe if it hadn't been a Tuesday. I hate Tuesdays."

It wasn't the first time he'd said that over the years, prone to noticing the bad things that happened on that particular day of the week. Allison had long since given up trying to convince him that just as many bad things — and good things — happened on other days of the week, but Mack didn't buy it.

He'd met Carrie on a Tuesday, he said, and his mother had died on a Tuesday, and of course, so had Carrie . . .

And now this, today — Jerry Thompson all over the news. Dead.

"You need help, Mack," she tells him. "You need to take care of yourself and get some rest, or the stress is going to kill you. If you won't see Dr. Cuthbert about the sleep issues, then maybe we can find a psychiatrist —"

"No," he cuts in quickly. "No way. I don't need a shrink. I don't have time for a shrink. I can't sleep, okay? That's my only problem."

"It's a big problem. You need to make an appointment to see Dr. Cuthbert again. Look, I'll go call him right now and see if he can get you in this week — later today, or tomorrow, while you're home."

Mack just looks at her.

But he's considering it. She can see it. He's almost reached his breaking point.

She reaches out and touches him on the arm. "Come on. I love you. Let me help you. Do it for me. Okay?"

He shrugs. "Okay."

Hunched over beneath the low ceiling of the crawl space, Jamie throws one last shovelful of dirt over the spot.

There.

Dead and buried — literally.

Jamie stamps over the freshly disturbed earth with the thick soles of her work boots. Just as hastily as she'd changed into the heels and pantyhose, skirt and sweater before the old man came knocking, she'd changed out of them again.

Not just because lugging the old man down to the crawl space and burying him was going to be dirty work, but because everything she was wearing had been spattered with blood. It's probably not going to come out, either. The clothes and shoes will have to be bagged up and thrown in a Dumpster miles from here.

Just like old times.

Jamie retreats to the door and climbs out of the crawl space. Blinking in the sudden glare of sunlight, she realizes that it's a beautiful day. The kind of day when the world is bright and shiny, full of promise . . .

A perfect day to make a fresh start.

Twenty minutes later, Jamie is driving away.

In the car trunk: a garbage bag full of bloody clothes and a hastily packed duffel filled with fresh clothes and toiletries, a laptop, and, of course, the laminated photographs of Rocky Manzillo and Allison MacKenna.

In the glove compartment: several big brown envelopes thick with cash — the money that had been saved to help Jerry, along with the thousands of dollars she'd just found in Roger's attic. The old man had conveniently left a chair beneath the open trap door in the ceiling, igniting Jamie's curiosity as to what might be up there. Nothing but cash — and porn. Sick old bastard. Now Jamie is carrying more than enough money to pay for motel rooms and food for weeks, at least — probably months. However long it takes. She also has two checkbooks — one of which belongs to Roger — and a handful of soon-due bills for both apartments. As long as the rent and utilities are kept up to date, no one is going to come sniffing around the building any time soon.

And on the front seat: a computer printout showing directions to Sullivan Correctional Facility in Fallsburg, New York.

Chapter Three

Friday, September 16

"So things are finally back to normal now, know what I mean?"

"Definitely," Allison tells Randi, who's spent the last ten minutes talking about how relieved she is that her in-laws have gone back to their Florida retirement home after a three-week visit.

Both Mack's parents are deceased, so aside from his sister, Lynn, Allison doesn't have in-laws. But she can certainly relate to life finally being back to normal.

With the sunroom painted at last, Mack got back on his usual 7:19 commuter train yesterday morning, bleary-eyed as always, but at least having promised to start his new sleep medication over the weekend.

"I'm glad you made me go to see Dr. Cuthbert," he said, kissing Allison on the cheek. "You were right."

"I'm always right," she replied with a

smile, trying to hide the vague uneasiness she's felt since Mack came home from his appointment on Wednesday with a prescription for something called Dormipram.

Allison immediately looked it up on the Internet. She wasn't thrilled about some of the side effects, but the good news was that it was supposed to be nonaddictive. Anyway, the last thing she wanted to do was undermine Mack's cooperation with the doctor.

If only she could ignore the troubling ghosts of her own past — a more distant past than the tragic events of September 2001. Her mother was an addict, not just street drugs, but prescription, too — and died of a sleeping pill overdose. It wasn't accidental.

Suicide — that thought segues Allison right back to Jerry Thompson, but she pushes him from her mind. She's been doing it for days now. He's dead. It's over.

Craving normalcy — and some female company — after dropping Madison at preschool on this sunny, unseasonably cool Friday afternoon, she drove with J.J. over to Randi's three-story redbrick mansion for a late lunch.

"Anyway . . ." Randi wraps her perfectly manicured fingers around a baby carrot and dredges it through lemon-artichoke hummus. "Sometimes I wish we hadn't gone all out with that huge guest wing upstairs. It makes it a little too easy for my in-laws to come and stay . . . and stay . . . and stay . . ."

"I can't really blame them." Allison has toured the luxurious guest wing: two large bedrooms, each with its own bath, connected by a large sitting area featuring a state-of-the-art entertainment system and a wet bar.

Until a few years ago, the Webers lived with their two children, Lexi, fourteen, and Josh, nine, in a regular suburban house a few blocks away from the MacKennas'. The two families used to walk back and forth for backyard barbecues and snowstorm game nights. They had a lot in common — parallel lives, Randi used to say.

Ben had launched his career in an ad agency bullpen alongside Mack right out of college. When he moved into the more lucrative sales side of the industry, he recruited Mack and was his boss for years.

Last year, Ben left the network to become executive vice president of sales and marketing at another. The Webers immediately moved to the "estate" side of town, where rambling mansions sit on woodsy lots beyond low fieldstone walls — and security fences and access-control gates.

At first, Allison worried that Ben going from a mid-six-figure yearly income to one that's over seven figures would jeopardize their friendship. But it didn't.

"We're just one step ahead of you," Randi said when it happened. Coming from her, it was somehow not insulting. "We had a head start, but we're right where you guys will be in a couple of years."

Allison isn't sure that's true, and she isn't sure it's what she wants. Ben seems to be home even less often than Mack is. And she loves the house they live in now. It's the first place she's ever lived that truly feels like home, and she envisions herself and Mack growing old together there.

Watching Allison pry a potentially deadly baby carrot from J.J.'s clenched, drool-covered fist, Randi comments, "He's like a little octopus."

"More like a pickpocket. You're lucky your kids are past this stage."

"I won't argue with you."

"That reminds me — can you do me a favor? Do you have your iPhone in your pocket?"

Of course she does. She pulls it out immediately, asking, "Who are we calling?"

"We're not calling, we're using the GPS locator to find my phone. It's not in my pocket and I'm hoping it's either out in the car or that I forgot it at home, because for all I know J.J. grabbed it and threw it on the ground someplace between my house and here."

"What do I do?"

Allison directs her to the application and instructs her to type in the cell phone number.

Randi does, then looks up. "I need your password."

"It's HUMAMA."

"Who-mama? How'd you come up with that? Like, *Who's your mama?*"

Allison laughs. "No — like, Hudson, Madison, Mack. First two letters of each of their names."

"What about J.J.?"

"He wasn't born yet when I got the phone. I remember thinking I'd probably never need to use this locator app, but . . . I pretty much need it every day."

Smiling, Randi punches the password into her own phone, waits for a moment, then shows Allison the screen. It shows a map, with a big, pulsating blue dot sitting over their address on Orchard Terrace.

"Okay, as long as I know it's home. But with this guy, I can never be sure." Allison sighs. "I should probably get going."

"It's still early. Do you want some more salad?" Randi gestures at the bowl.

"No, thanks — I'm full."

Not really. The mix of organic baby arugula, goat cheese, and seared red peppers didn't really hit the spot today. Sometimes lately, when she's feeling low, Allison finds herself craving good old-fashioned, bad-for-you comfort food. Right now, she wouldn't mind a salami sandwich on white bread with yellow mustard — or even a wedge of iceberg lettuce with bottled blue cheese dressing and synthetic bacon bits, which passed for salad in her distant small-town past.

"Are you sure? Did you not like it?" Randi asks. "Because I won't feel bad if you didn't. It's not like I made it."

Allison knows she'd bought the salad mix in a plastic container at David-Anthony's, the gourmet café in town, then tossed it with a shallot vinaigrette — also from David-Anthony's — in an enormous hand-carved wooden salad bowl that probably cost more than Allison had paid for her first car back in Nebraska.

"No, it was great," she assures Randi. "I'm just not that hungry."

"What about dessert? Look what I got!" Randi leaps up and grabs a white bakery box stamped with the gold David-Anthony's seal. She opens the lid to reveal a dozen oversized, frosted sugar cookies that cost seven-fifty each.

Allison knows that because she herself made a rare venture into David-Anthony's on the first day of school last week, thinking it might be nice to pick up a treat for the girls. She picked out two individually cellophane-wrapped cookies, an intricately decorated school bus and a red apple, and was halfway to the register when she noticed the price stickers.

She put them back.

It isn't that she can't afford to spend fifteen dollars — but for two cookies? Given the current state of the economy, she has to draw the line somewhere. Always in the back of her mind is the threat that Mack might lose his job, like so many colleagues in his fickle industry. If that happens, they will be, as Mack recently said and an eavesdropping Hudson later colorfully quoted, up a certain creek without a paddle.

Allison knows only too well what it's like to be laid off without warning. But at least when she lost her job at the magazine, she and Mack were childless newlyweds, and he could support them both on his salary — with a nice cushion in the bank, thanks to his dead wife.

For the first time in her life, someone was taking care of Allison, and it felt good.

Most days, it still does. Stay-at-home motherhood is fulfilling. But once in a while, she longs for something a little more stimulating. Unlike Randi and most of the other women she's met here in the affluent suburbs, she isn't into yoga, golf, manicures, or day spas.

Then again, whenever she's around petite, striking Randi, who has a thick mane of dark red hair and a tanned, Pilates-toned body, Allison wonders if she's let herself go.

She rarely wears makeup these days, and this isn't the first time she's gone too long between dye jobs at the salon, resulting in a streak of dark roots along her part line. Plus, her once-willowy frame isn't quite as taut as it used to be.

This morning, realizing the weather had gone from summer to fall overnight, she'd pulled on a pair of jeans — faded Levi's, as opposed to Randi's dark-wash 7 For All Mankind. After an active summer with the kids — wearing shorts and sundresses that have a lot more give than denim — the jeans feel snugger than she'd expected; the last ten pounds of her third pregnancy weight gain are conspicuously drooping over the top button.

She reinforces her no to the dessert Randi is offering but says yes to a cup of coffee — black — and lingers to sip it as Randi chatters on and J.J. delightedly turns a seven-dollar pumpkin-shaped cookie into sugary sludge.

Interrupting her tale of Lexi's upcoming first high school dance to peer closely at Allison's face, Randi asks, "Are you just quiet today, or am I boring you to tears and not letting you get a word in edgewise?"

Oops — I must have drifted.

Allison shakes her head. "I'm just quiet today."

"Yeah? I think you're just too polite to tell me to please shut up. Most people don't have that problem. Ben sure doesn't."

Allison grins. "Mack doesn't, either. With me, I mean."

"Or with me," Randi says wryly. She and Mack have long had a casual, brother-sister relationship. "Ben said he took a few days off this week. I thought maybe it was to make up for the three vacations he missed out on, but Ben said no."

Three vacations . . . In addition to the curtailed July week at the beach and the September Disney trip they'd had to forgo, Mack and Allison had planned a late August getaway to a charming, family-friendly Vermont inn recommended by Phyllis next door.

But Mother Nature seemed bent on robbing them of any pleasure they might salvage from this all-too-fleeting summer. The day before they were supposed to leave — and just forty-eight hours after the freak earthquake — the unprecedented Hurricane Irene came barreling up the coast with New York in her crosshairs. Not only did the storm leave Glenhaven Park littered with downed trees and wires, but floodwaters swept the New England inn they were to visit.

"Don't bother to come up here," Phyllis Lewis advised over the phone, having driven to Vermont ahead of the storm. "It's like a war zone. You're better off just staying home."

Ah, but the one comfort zone they could always count on — their Happy House — had been cast in perpetual shadow, unnervingly silent in the absence of reassuring electronic hums, with rotting food in the fridge and not even the promise of a hot shower to wash away the tension of a difficult day.

The Webers had a generator and Randi called to invite Allison, Mack, and the kids to come to their house until the power was restored.

"We have plenty of room," she said, "and it'll be fun. We never see enough of each other anymore."

"I thought your in-laws were already staying with you."

"I can always kick them out."

"Randi!"

"I'm kidding. Sort of," Randi added dryly. "Listen, no arguments. You and Mack and the baby can have the master suite, your girls can share Lexi's room, and Ben and I will camp out downstairs."

"We're not going to put you out of your own bed. We're fine at home," Allison told Randi firmly. "I'm sure the power will be back on any second now."

Famous last words. A full week elapsed before electricity was restored; a week Mack opted to spend back at work, leaving a homebound Allison to keep the kids fed and clean and entertained without appliances, lights, electronics, hot water . . .

Those strange, unsettling days had been hard on her. But they were even harder on Mack, she now realized. This year, not only was there no escaping the real world, but even the real world bore little semblance to its usual self. Home didn't feel like home, yet the city wasn't a refuge, either. Not with all the talk of the looming anniversary and the construction of the new Freedom Tower, rising one more story per week above the altered skyline.

Allison had detoured past the site early in the rebuilding stage, when there was little more to see than blue scaffolding, construction equipment, steel girders, and an American flag-bedecked "Never Forget" sign. Predictably, Mack wasn't interested in seeing it then, and he isn't now.

"Mack just couldn't deal with being in the city on the ten-year anniversary, huh?" Randi asks.

"Is that what he told Ben?" Allison is surprised. It isn't like Mack, ever the stoical Irishman, to share his feelings, even with his friends.

Randi shakes her expertly highlighted mane. "That's what Ben and I guessed. I know this is always a hard week for you guys."

"It is. I thought having him around the house would be nice, and the girls were so excited — you know how they are about Mack —"

"Daddy's girls." With a nod, Randi utters the phrase Allison so often uses to describe her daughters.

Randi has one of her own for J.J.: mama's boy. It doesn't sit well with Allison, in part because it's overwhelming to be the only person who can comfort and care for her son so much of the time. Often, when Mack tries to help her out by taking him off her hands, J.J. fusses so much that Allison winds up taking him back.

"That's just how it is — little boys love their mommies," her sister-in-law, Lynn, observed, having two sons of her own.

Yes, but they love their daddies, too — especially when they get to see a lot of them.

This early childhood stage is going to be so different for J.J. than it was for the girls. Mack's job wasn't this demanding when they were little; he had more time to bond with his daughters than he ever will with his son.

Most nights, the baby is in bed long before he comes home, and though J.J. is an early riser, Mack's daily dash out the door to catch the train doesn't allow for father-son interaction.

"So it *wasn't* good having Mack home this week?" Randi prompts.

"Well, he got the sunroom painted, but he was so preoccupied he barely gave them the time of day. He promised he'd take them out for ice cream after dinner one night, and that never happened, which isn't like him."

"Uh-oh — were they upset?"

"They must have been." She sighs, remembering what it was like when her mother broke promises — a frequent occurrence — and her own vow to never break a promise to *anyone.* "But you know how it goes with my girls. In their eyes, Daddy can do no wrong."

"Wait till they turn thirteen," Randi says darkly. "Then nobody — including Daddy, but especially *you* — will be able to do anything right."

"Terrific. Can't wait."

"You know, it's really too bad you guys couldn't go to Disney this year. Or even Vermont. I'm sure not getting a vacation made all of this much harder on Mack."

"That, and . . ." Allison trails off, not sure whether she should even bring it up.

"What?"

"It's nothing, really."

"When people say that, it's always something, really." Randi leans forward and props her chin in her hand. "I'm an expert bullshit detector, you know. It's my favorite claim to fame."

Allison smiles briefly. "So I've heard."

"Tell me what's on your mind."

"Did you by any chance hear about Jerry Thompson?"

Randi, of course, knows who he is. She frowns. "What about him?"

"He killed himself in prison last weekend."

"Really? Well, good riddance, right? You must be so relieved."

"I am." Allison absently uses a napkin to wipe a smudge of crumby paste, courtesy of J.J., from her hand.

"You don't seem convinced."

"It's just . . . I don't know, I guess I expected to find some kind of peace knowing he's dead, but . . . it's kind of the opposite."

"What do you mean?"

She hesitates, not wanting to admit that the news seems to have dredged up a whole new wave of paranoia, leaving her jumpy and uneasy the last few days — and for no conceivable reason.

Now, more than ever, she should finally be able to put the whole nightmare behind her.

"I guess it just brought back a lot of bad memories," she tells Randi. "And I keep remembering how wrong I was about him. Kristina herself said he gave her the creeps, and I told her he was harmless. The next thing I knew, she was dead. How could I

have been such a terrible judge of character?"

"Don't be so hard on yourself, Allie. You
barely knew the guy. We can never really be
sure what's going on in someone else's
head, even someone we think we know well,
let alone a virtual stranger."

"I know, but . . . even after she died —
after I saw him there that night — there was
some little piece of my brain that wouldn't
accept that he was the one."

"Until he attacked you in your apartment
and almost killed you." Randi shakes her
head grimly.

"No — not even then. I never saw his face,
and I was so sure it was someone else . . .
Right up until the police arrested him and
he confessed."

"Serial killers are cunning. They fool
people. Look at Ted Bundy. My cousin
Mindy was at Florida State back in the
seventies when he killed those sorority girls.
She'd seen him hanging around campus,
and he seemed totally normal."

This isn't the first time Randi has brought
that up.

Allison shudders, remembering the horrific details of how Bundy crept into the Chi
Omega house in the middle of the night to
rape and murder sleeping young women. It

was eerily similar to what Jerry did to Kristina Haines and that other woman, Marianne Apostolos.

"Mindy said no one ever would have guessed in a million years that the guy was a homicidal maniac," Randi goes on.

"I know, but . . . Jerry wasn't like that. He was kind of bumbling and dim-witted and . . . I don't know. What's the point of even talking about it? It's over."

"Exactly. You can't beat yourself up over one lapse in character judgment. You've had a great track record ever since, right? I mean, you married Mack, and you have *me* for a best friend . . ." Randi offers her most charming smile.

Allison has to laugh, but she's still feeling inexplicably uneasy inside, remembering what it was like to see a figure looming in her bedroom in the dead of night.

She just prays she'll never experience sheer terror like that again.

But of course you won't, because Jerry Thompson is dead and no one else in this world has any reason to harm you.

It's strictly by choice that Chuck Nowak has worked the third shift for most of his seventeen-year career as a corrections officer at Sullivan Correctional. He's always been a night owl; he'd much rather work until seven in the morning than get up at that ungodly hour to start the day.

Not only that, but if you're going to be locked up with a few hundred dangerous felons, you're better off doing it after lights out, when the vast majority of them are asleep.

The only drawback to the night shift: the love of his life — his wife, Cora, whom he married a few years ago — is a nine-to-five medical receptionist across the river in Beacon. Five days every week, they're ships passing.

But the other two days make it all worthwhile. Chuck likes nothing better, weekend afternoons, than to strap on his helmet and ride off into the Catskills on his Harley with Cora's arms — one of which is tattooed with a "CN^2" inside a heart, to symbolize their identical initials — wrapped around his waist.

Unfortunately, this isn't one of those days.

The Harley is sitting in the garage and the keys to his pickup are in his pocket as he enjoys a last smoke on the small back deck of the house he and Cora rent in Newburgh.

Dusk is falling and he notes the sharp chill in the air that wasn't here yesterday. Off in the distance, the pleasant buzz of a speedboat cruising the Hudson gives way to police sirens, signifying another wave of gang violence.

The neighborhood is sandwiched between the Hudson River and a notorious stretch of dilapidated, drug-infested row houses. Kids kill each other and anyone else who gets in the way — happens every day, every night in this city.

Having grown up here, Chuck didn't plan on ever leaving, but lately, he's been thinking they might have to. Now that the escalating crime from the adjoining neighborhood is creeping into their own, he worries about Cora being home alone every night; worries, too, about her driving through seedy neighborhoods on her way to and from work.

Plus, their commutes are getting longer because there's more traffic around, especially on weekends. On this final Friday night of the summer, throngs of city people will be making their way up to weekend retreats in the Catskills. It will probably take him over an hour to get to work, even on the back roads.

If they lived closer to the prison, he and Cora would have more time together — that's what he told her.

"How so? Closer to the prison means

further from my job."

"You can always get a new job near Falls-burg."

"Or we can move across the river and you can become a CO at the prison in Fishkill," she returned.

She's a strong-willed woman, Cora. That's one of the things he loves about her. Most of the time.

He's not going anywhere. He's been at Sullivan for too long to just start fresh someplace else. He's paid his dues — and then some.

Never a dull moment on the job, that's for damned sure.

He thinks back to last weekend's big excitement. One of the inmates on the block decided to kill himself on Chuck's watch. Son of a bitch gulped down a cup of orange juice laced with cleaning fluid. It wasn't a pretty way to go, that's for damned sure.

The inmate, Jerry Thompson, didn't leave a note or anything. But Doobie Jones, the prisoner who occupies the adjoining cell, claimed that he'd been talking about suicide for a while.

"Guess he just finally gave up," Doobie commented in a tone that made Chuck look sharply at his face.

The guy is a vicious, manipulative psychopath responsible for the deaths of at least a dozen people on the outside. Chuck wouldn't put it past him to commit another murder, just for kicks, while behind bars.

"Wonder where he got the orange juice?" Doobie mused on with an evil gleam in his eye.

Never mind that. Where the hell did Jerry get the cleaning fluid? He wasn't on kitchen or bathroom duty.

But Doobie was.

Yeah, Chuck has his suspicions, but he'll keep them to himself. So the world is rid of one more serial killer. No great loss, right?

He takes one last drag on his Marlboro, stubs it out with his steel-toed boot, and kicks it into the shrubbery beneath the deck.

Time to head to work.

He'd been hoping Cora would show up before he left — once in a while on a Friday, she manages to leave work early enough to see him — but he can't afford to wait any longer.

He closes the slider leading out to the deck and locks it. Then he sets a yardstick into the metal groove to keep the door from opening, an added measure of security, should anyone try to break in.

Cora says it's a joke — "If someone really wanted to get in, he could just break the window next to the door, climb on in, and help himself to our stuff."

She's right. All the more reason to consider moving.

Chuck opens the fridge and looks for the lunch he packed earlier in the insulated bag embossed with a white "CN." Cora ordered it for him this summer, and one for herself, too.

Both are blue. "Mix and match," she told him. "Isn't it nice to have the same initials?"

Yeah, it's nice. Everything about being married to Cora is nice.

He takes the bag from the fridge, turns on a living room lamp so that his wife won't have to walk into a dark house alone, and steps out the front door.

The sirens are still wailing. God knows he's used to the sound, but for some reason it's really getting to him tonight.

Crossing the small, sparse patch of grass, he feels increasingly uneasy, as though something bad is about to happen.

Or maybe it's more a feeling that he's not alone.

His work at the prison has taught him well. You learn, when you're locked behind steel doors with hundreds of depraved, lethal predators, never to ignore your instincts. Frowning, he looks at the windows of the neighboring houses, half expecting to spot someone looking out at him, but there's no evidence of that. Not that he can see, anyway.

Still . . .

Something is off.

He pictures Cora in her little Toyota crossing the Newburgh-Beacon Bridge with all that weaving traffic, and he worries. He can't help it. There are a lot of crazy drivers out there who might have stopped for happy hour to kick off the weekend.

He can't bear the thought of anything happening to her. She's all he has in this world — and all he needs.

His concern evaporates a few moments later when a pair of headlights swing into the driveway just as he's putting the keys into the ignition.

Cora parks her car beside his pickup, jumps out, and scurries toward him with her own insulated lunch bag dangling from her hand. She's wearing a conservative top and slacks and comfort shoes, but five minutes from now, he knows, she'll have changed into slim-fitting jeans, black biker boots, and a short-sleeved shirt that reveals her tattoos. Her glorious dyed-black hair — the same shade as what's left of his own — will be released from its clip to tumble down her shoulders.

God, he loves this woman.

He climbs quickly out of the truck and greets her with a fierce embrace and a passionate kiss.

"Mmmm," she says, "I wish you weren't leaving."

"Me too. But I'll be back, baby."

She sighs and tilts her forehead against his. "I know. I just miss you when you're gone."

"I miss you more. You're my everything."

"You're mine."

It's how they always say good-bye. They smile at each other and exchange one last kiss.

Then Chuck climbs behind the wheel and watches her until she's disappeared inside, safe and sound for the night.

Interesting.

Concealed in the shadows of an overgrown rhododendron, Jamie ponders what just happened.

Ever since a chatty — for a price — prison deliveryman informed her that Charles Nowak was the main guard on Jerry's cell block that fateful night, Jamie has been plotting the man's death. Suddenly, though, the plan seems unnecessarily lackluster.

You're my everything.

Those words had reached Jamie's ears loud and clear.

Food for thought.

Guess life wouldn't be much worth living without your everything, now would it, Charlie?

Sometimes, death isn't the worst punishment a person can endure.

Don't I know it.

A light flicks on inside the house, pooling from the window right above Jamie's head. Standing on tiptoes, she glimpses the room — a bedroom — and Charlie's wife walking right toward the window.

For one hair-raising moment, Jamie is certain she's been spotted.

The woman reaches toward the glass.

But her hand goes to the window lock between the top and bottom panes. She turns it and lifts the sash from the bottom, opening the window a few inches.

Well, how about that? It's like she's inviting you in . . . but of course she can't see you. The light puts a glare on the glass.

No, she has no idea someone is lurking out here in the night, watching her.

Just like the others.

Kristina . . . Marianne . . .

They had no idea that someone was

watching them through the window. They both died because of what they did to Jerry.

This woman . . .

She'll die because her husband helped to kill him.

Yes. *She'll* die. Not him.

She'll die tonight.

And then Charles Nowak will know what it's like to lose someone you love.

"Mack?"

He jumps, startled, and turns to see Allison standing in the doorway of the sunroom.

In her hand is a glass of diet iced tea. She buys it by the gallon and drinks it every night before bed — not the healthiest habit, she admits. But she's been doing it for years, long before they moved to the land of health fanatics who would just as soon lace a drink with strychnine as they would ingest artificial sweeteners and caffeine.

She's changed from jeans, a T-shirt, and sneakers to sweats and slippers. It's harder and harder to recall the fashionista he first met ten years ago — but that's fine with him. She was a little too glamorous, he thought when they first started dating, and that intimidated him. He was, after all, a middle-class kid from Jersey.

Little did he know, back then, that Allison was a welfare kid from the Midwest.

"Sorry," she says, "I didn't mean to scare you. I got the kids down. What are you doing?"

He shrugs. "Just checking out the color. It looks pretty good, doesn't it?"

"The paint?" She smiles. "It looks great. Hudson was right. It *is* a happy shade, you know?"

"Yeah." Mack had been hoping, when he detoured into the sunroom on his way from the living room to the kitchen with an empty glass, that some of this golden happiness would seep into him. But standing here, all he feels is the same monochromatic melancholy that flooded him around Labor Day and refuses to recede.

It will, though, eventually. It always does.

For now, he'll just have to live with it.

"We need to get those back up tomorrow," Allison gestures at the corner where he'd piled the window shades before he started painting.

"I don't know . . . don't you think it's kind of nice to have them uncovered? It lets the sun in."

"During the day. But right now . . ." She indicates the three walls of exposed glass. "Anyone can see in."

"Only if they happen to be standing in our yard. It's not like there's a clear view from the street."

That's one reason this house was so appealing to them when they bought it, having grown weary of the lack of privacy when they lived in the city. Here, dense, tall hedgerows effectively screen the borders of the property.

Catching sight of the expression on his wife's face, Mack sighs. "What?"

She shrugs.

He sighs again.

"The thing is, Mack . . . I mean, you just never know who might be out there looking in."

"Well, I do know that if they're out there, they shouldn't be. It's private property."

She just looks at him.

Okay. So she learned the hard way when Jerry Thompson invaded her bedroom that private property isn't always a safe haven.

Ordinarily, he'd offer her some kind of reassurance. Right now, though, he just doesn't have it in him. He's utterly depleted. Sleepless night after sleepless night will do that to a person.

"I really want the shades back up," she says. "Please?"

"Right *now*?"

The last thing he feels like doing right now is installing — or even discussing — window shades. All he wants is to climb into bed and put this emotionally grueling week behind him.

Such a simple concept: a nightly reprieve from the rigors of this world.

For him, a frustratingly elusive one.

"You can't keep going like this," Dr. Cuthbert cautioned him the other day, "without eventually paying a terrible price."

The physician then ran through a litany of potential problems created by sleep deprivation, from crankiness to a weakened immune system to what might happen to his family — or someone else's — if he continues to get behind the wheel in a state of chronic exhaustion.

"Would you drive your children if you'd had a couple of drinks, James?"

He bristled. "Never. And please call me Mack." No one — not even his mother — has ever called him by his given name.

"Mack, drowsy driving causes over one hundred thousand traffic accidents every year. I could show you horrific photos of accident scenes where —"

"That's okay," Mack cut in. "I believe you. That's why I'm here. I've been doing all the things you suggested and nothing works. I need something else, some kind of serious help with this."

As he had early on, Dr. Cuthbert recommended the kind of help that comes in an orange prescription bottle.

Mack still wasn't crazy about the idea.

"Why are you so opposed to pharmaceutical intervention?" the doctor asked.

There were two reasons, and he didn't really want to get into the first one: that Allison's wariness about any kind of medication — thanks to her mother's deadly habit — has rubbed off on him over the years.

He did tell the doctor his other reservation: that after trying various over-the-counter sleep aids in the past, he always woke up feeling like his brain was swathed in cotton batting, and the grogginess lasted well into the next day.

"This medication isn't like that," Dr. Cuthbert promised. "You'll wake up feeling refreshed."

Mack fervently hopes so. But just in case, he's held off taking it until a night — like tonight — when he doesn't have to set an early alarm.

"Mack." Allison touches his arm, and he looks up to see her watching him, her blue eyes concerned. "Are you feeling okay?"

"I'm fine." He doesn't shake her hand off,

exactly, but he does move his arm to rub his burning eyes with his thumb and forefingers.

Translation: *I'm not fine, and I don't want to be touched.*

To her credit, she doesn't hold it against him, just takes a thoughtful sip of her iced tea.

The best thing about Allison — *one* of the best things — is that she always instinctively gives him plenty of space when he needs it. That, and she doesn't call him an asshole when he probably deserves it.

"Here — give me your glass," she says. "I'm about to start the dishwasher. What was in it?"

"Water. Why?"

"Because you can't mix alcohol with Dormipram, and I know you're planning to take it tonight. I just wanted to make sure."

"It was just water," he says again, piqued at the implication, which is . . . ?

What? It's not like she made any accusation.

Still, he's feeling defensive.

"Sometimes you have a bourbon on Friday night," she points out.

That's true; it's something he looks forward to after a hard week at work.

"So?"

He wants to bite his tongue the moment that word rolls off it.

Carrie used to say it all the time, in just that tone. *So? So?* He couldn't stand it when she did that, and he's always made a point never to do it himself.

Then why am I saying it now?

Probably because he's had Carrie on the brain, thanks to all the reminders, and maybe he's channeling bad energy — *her* bad energy.

Never speak ill of the dead, his Irish grandmother used to say — but she never mentioned that it was wrong to merely *think* ill of them.

Mack attempts — somewhat unsuccessfully — to soften his tone. "What's wrong with having a bourbon once in a while? You drink diet iced tea every night. That's not great for you, either."

No, and it pisses him off that she can glibly ingest caffeine — *which, hello, happens to be a drug!* — right before bed and then sleep like a baby.

"Nothing, Mack. I didn't say anything was wrong with a bourbon."

To be fair to her, not only did she not say it, but she really didn't imply it, either.

"The reason I didn't have a drink tonight," he goes on, not in the mood for fair, "is that

I have to take the damned medicine that the damned doctor you made me see is making me take even though we all know it's not going to help. Okay?"

He can feel his wife's eyes on him, as if she's gauging the pissy-ness of his mood to determine the wisdom of engaging him in further conversation.

"Okay," Allison says after a moment. "Why don't you just go up to bed now and take it?"

"*Now?* It's early."

"It's past nine."

"That's early for me."

"There's nothing wrong with going to bed early, Mack. Trust me — people do it all the time." She smiles gently at him.

He softens. Allison is a good wife. He loves her. He hates himself for acting this way.

He's just worn out by everything . . . *everyone.*

People. They're the problem. He's been surrounded all day, from the moment he boarded the overcrowded commuter train to the city this morning, to this evening when he walked in the door and was instantly bombarded by his daughters, who were bouncing off the walls.

"They're on a sugar high," Allison informed him above the girls' excited chatter.

"I had lunch with Randi today and she sent me home with gigantic cookies for the girls. I didn't want to take them, but, well you know how big-hearted Randi is . . . and how insistent. *'No ahguments,'* " she added in a perfect imitation of Randi's New York accent — and favorite catchphrase. "Anyway, I didn't realize they'd eaten almost all of them until it was too late. Sorry. They're really wired."

In the old days, Mack might have welcomed the household chaos, but tonight, he was too exhausted — mentally, physically, emotionally — to do much more than paste a smile on his face for his daughters' sake.

They were so excited about school, and this weekend's street fair, and Hudson had to sing the song she'd learned in music class, and Maddy, not to be outdone, wanted to read aloud to him . . .

Then the baby bumped his head on a sharp corner and started screaming, and the pasta Allison was cooking boiled over on the stove, and the phone rang a few times, and through it all, Mack's patience wore increasingly thin.

Dinner was a harried affair, as were bath time, story time, bedtime . . .

Mack usually volunteers to tuck in the kids on weekends, but tonight, he made himself scarce and was grateful when Allison carted them all up the stairs.

Yeah. She's pretty amazing.

But he's too exhausted to tell her so, or that he's sorry for being so grouchy, or that he loves her, or to even muster a smile. All he can do is yawn.

"Mack! Please. Go!"

He goes.

CHAPTER FOUR

Stepping out of the shower, humming softly, Cora Nowak reaches for a towel. Her thoughts are on the cold beer that's waiting for her in the fridge, and today's episode of her favorite soap, recorded, as always, on the DVR.

She grabs a bath towel and vigorously rubs it over her dyed-black hair before wrapping it around herself sarong style. Opening the bathroom door, she's hit with a chilly gust.

Wow — time to shut the windows. She opened a couple of them, just a few inches, after Chuck left for work. She's always liked to let in the fresh breeze at night after breathing stale office air all day at work, but Chuck doesn't think it's safe to do that anymore, with the neighborhood going downhill so quickly.

"Anyone could cut the screen and come right in," he tells Cora. "You have to keep the windows closed and locked when you're alone at night."

It's so cute, the way he worries about her.

The truth is, she's one tough cookie. She grew up in a neighborhood as rough as this one has become — even rougher — and she knows how to take care of herself. She never goes to bed with the windows open, and anyway, what Chuck doesn't know can't hurt him.

Shivering, she pads down the short hall to the bedroom and reaches inside the door to flick on the light — then remembers she left the shade up before she went in for her shower.

If she turns on the light, she'll be effectively treating anyone who passes by to a peep show. Grinning at the thought of it, she walks through the darkened room to pull down the shade.

What the . . . ?

She stops short.

The shade *is* down . . . and the window is closed.

But . . . that's strange. She could have sworn she left —

Hearing a floorboard creak behind her, Cora gasps and whirls around.

In the pool of light spilling in from the hall stands a hulking stranger.

In that first frantic instant, taking in the long hair and the clothes, Cora thinks it's a woman.

But then the figure steps closer and she realizes with shock that the hair is a wig. It sits slightly askew atop garishly made-up masculine features.

It's the creepiest spectacle she's ever seen, yet she forces herself to stand her ground as he advances, her thoughts racing wildly.

She'll get herself out of this.

She will.

She always does.

After all, she's a tough coo—

After climbing the stairs, Mack stops at Madison's closed bedroom door.

He opens it a crack. Bathed in the glow of her nightlight, she's already sound asleep, curled on her side, her long blond hair tousled on her pillowcase.

He steals over to her bed, kisses her head gently, and whispers, "Good night, sweetie."

His middle child inherited her mother's fine features and a little-girl face that's softer and rounder and fuller than her sister's. Where Hudson seems old and wise beyond her years, Maddy gives off a sweet naïveté that sometimes makes Mack — and, he knows, Allison as well — fear for her out in the big, bad world.

Ironic, because they named her after the avenue associated with the cutthroat advertising industry. Back when she was born, though, his career had yet to consume him. Business was booming, he was content, and since they'd already named their firstborn after the Manhattan street where they lived when they met, it seemed appropriate to follow suit with their second child. Plus, Mack thought it would be nice if both the girls' names ended in "son," like their mom's.

By the time they were expecting J.J., they were over place names for their children. A sonogram had revealed the baby's gender, and for various reasons, most of them Mack's, they couldn't agree on anything suitable for a boy that ended in "son."

"Jameson," Allison suggested one morning as she flossed her teeth and Mack lathered his face with shaving cream.

"Nah. Too close to James."

"That's the point. James's . . . son."

"No. People will confuse him with me."

She texted him that afternoon: *I've got it. Emerson.*

He texted back moments later: *That's a girl name.*

A few days later, she greeted him at the

door with, "Jackson. It's perfect. It's rugged, and manly, and —"

"And about ten people at work have kids named Jackson."

"How about Anson?" Allison suggested that night in bed, baby name book propped on her rounded belly.

"The kids will call him Potsie."

"What?"

"Potsie. From the TV show *Happy Days.* The actor who played him was named Anson."

"Only you would ever possibly know that in a million years." Allison shook her head with a laugh. "I give up on the 'sons.' He's going to *be* our son. That's enough."

She ultimately convinced Mack that the baby should be named after him. Fittingly, J.J. is the spitting image of his daddy. Mini-Mack, Allison sometimes calls him.

Down the hall in J.J.'s room, he finds his son lying on his back in his crib, snoring softly, his little finger stuck in the corner of his mouth and the blankets kicked off.

He looks so angelic asleep that Mack has to remind himself what a handful J.J. can be — particularly when he's overtired.

Like father, like son, he thinks, tiptoeing out without a kiss. He doesn't want to risk disturbing J.J., and anyway, he can't bend low enough over the bars of the crib.

Peeking into Hudson's room, he assumes that she, too, is out like a light. But her eyes snap open before he's taken two steps across the pink carpet.

"What are you doing, Daddy?" she asks in a loud voice that's not the least bit groggy.

"Shh, just tucking you in."

"Mommy already did that."

"Tonight, you get two tuck-ins. How lucky are you?"

She smiles. "I'm the luckiest."

That's their little ritual, one they've had for months now, every time something nice happens.

How lucky are you? I'm the luckiest.

Tonight, Mack adds a new twist.

"No, you aren't," he tells Hudson, and at the predictable furrowing of her blond eyebrows, he quickly adds, "*I* am. Because I get to be your dad."

The frown is instantly replaced by a grin. Hudson snuggles contentedly into her quilt as he bends over to kiss her good night.

"I love you, Daddy."

"I love you too, Huddy."

Back out in the hallway, he can hear Allison down in the kitchen loading the dishwasher. She'll probably be coming upstairs soon. She's never exactly been a night owl, but she goes to bed earlier than ever thanks to J.J., who rises every morning long before a rooster would ever think to crow.

With a twinge of guilt, Mack hopes his wife will linger downstairs awhile longer tonight.

If she comes up, she's going to want to know what's wrong with me, and I'm not good at talking about my feelings. I really just want to be alone right now.

In the master bedroom, he closes the door behind him and strips down to his boxer shorts. Then he goes into the adjoining bathroom and looks at the prescription bottle.

" 'Take one tablet at bedtime with plenty of water,' " he reads aloud. "Yeah. Here goes nothing."

He swallows a white capsule, returns to the bedroom, climbs into bed, and turns off the light.

Okay, Dormipram . . . hurry up and do your thing.

As he waits for drowsiness to overtake him, he replays the events of the evening, wondering if the kids picked up on his moodiness earlier. Probably.

But I couldn't help it. I felt so overwhelmed by everyone and everything. I just needed a few seconds to myself. Is that so wrong?

Funny. In another lifetime — the one that came to a crashing halt more than a decade ago — it was just the opposite. Mack had more than his share of solitude and often craved human companionship. He was far lonelier during his first marriage than he'd ever been in his single life.

Carrie was not, as he felt obliged to apologetically explain to his family and friends, a "people person." She wanted — *needed* — no one but Mack.

As a red-blooded man with a nurturing soul, he was touched — all right, flattered — by the fact that a fiercely independent woman like Carrie Robinson had chosen to let him into her life.

It was obvious to him from the moment they met that she kept the rest of the world at bay. At the time, he had no idea why. He only knew that, as a man, he was as drawn to Carrie as he had been to stray puppies and kittens as a boy, and to the emotionally bruised children he met through his volunteer work with the Big Brother organization in his early twenties.

He wanted to take her in, look after her, make up for the pain she had endured.

The pain . . .

Sometimes he still thinks about that — about Carrie's past. He thinks about it, and he wonders, God forgive him, if the things she told him were even true.

He managed to keep her secret to himself for the duration of their marriage. But at the very end, when he realized she'd been lost in the burning rubble downtown, his willpower cracked. He told his best friend, Ben, the truth about Carrie.

A few years ago, over a couple of beers, Ben confessed that he had in turn confided Carrie's secret to his wife — and that Randi hadn't bought it.

"What do you mean?" Mack was taken aback, not that Ben hadn't kept the confidence, but that he — rather, Randi — would question the integrity in what Mack had revealed.

Ben took a deep breath. "Look, this has been bothering me for a long time, and I've wanted to say something to you, but it always seemed too soon. Now you have Allison and the girls and you've moved on and I guess it doesn't seem to matter as much . . ."

"What are you trying to say, Ben?"

"When I mentioned to Randi that you'd told me that Carrie spent her childhood in the witness protection program, she basically said that was bullshit."

"What, she actually thought I'd *lie* to you

133

about something like that?"

"No."

"What?" Then, reading the expression on Ben's face, he suddenly got it. "Oh."

Randi — and apparently Ben, too — had concluded that *Carrie* had lied about it — to Mack.

"You've got to admit, it sounded far-fetched," Ben said, and hastily added, "But I'm not saying it wasn't true."

Maybe not — but suddenly, he had Mack thinking it.

I guess it doesn't seem to matter as much, Ben had said.

He was dead wrong.

For some reason, it does matter to Mack. It matters that he'll never know the truth about Carrie's past, if that wasn't it.

It's not as though he can go back and look into a trail that's gone cold, because there never was a trail in the first place. The few details Carrie had provided were murky. She had said — or had she implied, or had he just assumed? — that there was a mob connection; that her father had seen or said or done something he shouldn't have. If Carrie knew what that had been, she wasn't willing to elaborate.

And if she knew what her real name had been, or where she'd lived before her family was swept into oblivion, she wasn't sharing that, either. Not even with her husband. She simply told him that she was so young when it happened that she didn't remember who she or her parents had once been.

"I never asked," she said in response to Mack's gentle probing for the details. "What did it matter? All I knew was that I had a normal, familiar life, and then one day, I didn't."

Yeah. That happens. Mack certainly gets it now, if he didn't back then.

He just wishes he had pressed Carrie for more information. But at the time, he was so relieved that there was a logical — relatively speaking — explanation for her impenetrable walls that it never occurred to him she might have made up the whole story.

Even now, all these years later . . .

Most of the time, he believes what Carrie told him.

But once in a while, ever since Ben planted the seed of doubt, he wonders. That's all. He's just curious. It doesn't make a difference in his life today one way or another.

"If it bothers you that much," Allison said when he told her about Ben's comment and its lingering effect, "then maybe you should see what you can find out. You know — try to trace her path before you met her."

"It doesn't bother me *that* much. Anyway, Carrie's parents died years ago," he pointed out, "and she had no one else."

"No one else that she was *aware* of. Or . . . that *you* were aware of. You never know . . . she might have had a whole family someplace, wondering what ever happened to her. Maybe they deserve to know."

"Maybe they're better off if they don't," he pointed out darkly, and that was that.

Now, lying here in the dark thinking about it all again, he finds himself wondering how he would even go about it if he wanted to find out who Carrie really was.

It's not like he can just call up the government office in charge of the witness protection program and ask them to come clean. That's the whole point: the people who go into the program disappear forever. Carrie and her parents had, in effect, died the day they disappeared from their old lives, and they were reborn on the day they resurfaced under their new identities.

But even then . . .

She never told Mack much about that life, either. Her parents were gone by the time he met her, and she said it was too painful to talk about her childhood. She mentioned having lived for a while in the Midwest, and he could occasionally hear it in her accent, so he knew that, at least, was the truth. But she never said where, exactly. On the few occasions he dared to ask, she shut down.

Who could blame her? She'd lived a difficult life, and she didn't want to rehash it. He accepted that.

But that, of course, was before he met — and married — Allison.

She, too, had grown up in the Midwest and lived a difficult life. While she didn't want to rehash it, she did share it with him. Because that's what you do in a relationship, right? It's only natural to tell each other about the individual journeys that led to the point where your lives converged. It helps you to understand where the other person is coming from.

But Carrie was in the witness protection program, Mack reminds himself. *That's not the same thing as just having a troubled childhood.*

It would be natural for someone who had lived her formative years essentially in hiding to continue to act as though she had something to hide.

But what if . . .

What if . . .

The thought flies from Mack's head like an inadvertently released helium balloon.

He yawns, realizing that his brain is fuzzy and his limbs and spine have melded into the Tempur-Pedic mattress.

He yawns again.

Hmm . . .

Maybe the Dormipram is actually going to work.

With the house quiet and everyone — including Mack — upstairs in bed, Allison finally found a chance to get online and run Jerry Thompson's name through a search engine. It's something she's been tempted to do for the last couple of days, but she just hasn't had time.

Really? You've had time for other things. Reading two chapters in this month's book club selection, sorting through the baby's dresser to get rid of clothes he's outgrown, having lunch with Randi . . .

All right, so maybe she was trying to avoid the ugly subject.

Maybe she thought that if she ignored what had happened, Jerry would just leave her life once and for all. But somehow, with his death, he's come alive again in her head.

She keeps hearing his voice, remembering how halting it was the few times she heard him speak. She keeps seeing that vacant stare of his — not evil-vacant, the way people have described other serial killers' eyes, but more like . . .

The lights are on but nobody's home.

That's what Allison thought the first time she ever crossed paths with Jerry the handyman.

Dim-witted doesn't equal guileless, she reminds herself.

Still, having grown up fending for herself, she learned early on how to read other people, instinctively grasping whom she could trust and who might be dangerous.

Not dangerous, necessarily, in a physical sense, but dangerous to her emotional well-being. It would have been harsh enough to grow up in an impoverished single-parent household in a gossip-fueled, intolerant small town. But with a deadbeat father who walked out one day and never looked back, and a mother whose drug habit was common knowledge . . .

Yes, Allison learned exactly whom she could trust back in her hometown: not a soul.

Later, in college and in Manhattan, she did eventually forge relationships with friends and with a few men she dated. But her instincts about new people always proved to be dead-on.

How could she have been so wrong about Jerry?

How could she not have known?

Somehow, she should have picked up on something about him.

But you didn't, okay? Why is this nagging you ten years later, especially now?

You have to let it die with him. You have to.

Sitting here on the couch in her cozy lamp-lit living room, she's read everything she could find on the Internet about his suicide. She's hoping that if her lingering questions are answered, she'll be able to put it to rest once and for all.

She learned that he'd done it with poison. He'd swallowed cleaning fluid.

It's not clear how he managed to get his hands on it. One of the guards was quoted — anonymously, of course — as saying that inmates who work on janitorial duty have been known to smuggle chemicals into their cells.

But Jerry worked in the prison library. According to the guard, he wouldn't have had access to cleaning fluid.

So what does that mean? That he convinced someone to get it for him? God only knows what he had to do in return.

So what? He was an animal. He deserved whatever he got, and then some.

Another guard reported that it wasn't an easy death, or a pretty one.

Yeah, well, neither was Kristina Haines's.

Allison closes out of the last screen, leans her head back, and exhales slowly through her nostrils.

Okay.

Now she knows.

Now are you satisfied?

She listens for an answer, but all she hears is a dog barking someplace outside and the ticking of the clock in the next room. It's an antique. Mack's sister, Lynn, gave it to them when they bought the house.

"It used to be our grandmother's," she told Allison, "and then it was in our house when we were growing up. I took it when Mack and I were packing up the house to sell it. I took just about everything, because he was afraid to."

"What do you mean?"

Lynn shrugged. "Carrie didn't want old things around. I guess since she didn't have a past, she didn't want to be reminded that Mack did."

"Everyone has a past" was Allison's reply, and she was relieved when Lynn changed the subject.

She's never been comfortable discussing Carrie with anyone but Mack himself. She knows that Ben and Randi didn't like Carrie, and that Lynn merely tolerated her to keep the peace. But she doesn't intend to be one of those second wives who badmouth the first, especially since the marriage ended in death and not divorce.

What does it matter now, anyway? Carrie is gone.

So is Jerry Thompson.

It's time you let this rest, Allison tells herself, stretching.

On that note . . .

It's time you went to bed.

She closes the laptop, puts it on the coffee table, and immediately thinks better of it. J.J. will be on the move first thing in the morning.

Carrying the laptop over to the built-in shelves beside the fireplace, she wonders if Mack is still awake upstairs. She'd half expected him to resurface — or at least, expected to hear creaking floorboards overhead.

Is it possible he's asleep?

Please, please, please *let him be asleep.*

He was in such a foul mood tonight. She knows he's overtired, but sometimes she feels like she's dealing with a fourth child — one who can be even more unreasonable than the others at the end of a long day.

She usually opts to give Mack a pass when he's so obviously exhausted. Considering all that's gone on this week, he deserved one tonight. But it took every ounce of patience she possessed not to snap right back at him earlier, when they were talking in the sunroom.

Oh well. If he really does get a good night's sleep, tomorrow will undoubtedly be a better day.

Allison tucks the laptop away on a high shelf, then turns off the table lamp. She feels her way back across the pitch-black room, thinking she should have remembered to turn on a light over by the doorway, or near the foot of the stairs.

She's rarely the last one up at night. Mack is usually down here when she goes to bed, unless he's away on a business trip. Though lately, there are times when he's still at work, and she leaves the lights on and a foil-covered plate in the oven.

Tonight, the dark, quiet house isn't feeling like quite the safe haven it should be.

Reaching the front hall, Allison spots a human shadow looming just inside the door. A tide of panic sweeps her back to a Manhattan bedroom ten years ago, and a hooded figure is lunging at her with a knife . . .

She cries out and jumps back — then realizes that it's not a human shadow at all; it's the coat tree draped with jackets.

Pressing a hand against her pounding heart, she looks up the stairs, expecting someone to come rushing to her aid, having heard her scream.

Not the girls — they're deep sleepers. But Mack must have heard her . . . unless he, too, is sleeping that soundly.

Or what if . . . ?

The thought is so dreadful she can't bear to let it in.

Taking the stairs two at a time, she tries to shut out another memory trying to shove its way into her mind.

She was the one who found her mother dead on the bathroom floor in the middle of the night, having overdosed on sleeping pills.

No . . .

No, please . . .

Reaching the master bedroom, she bursts through the door. "Mack?"

No voice reassuringly responds, no one stirs in the darkened room.

She flips on the light and sees her husband huddled in the bed.

"Mack!" She moves toward him.

Still nothing.

Please, no . . .

She leans over, seeing her mother's lifeless form in her mind's eye, hearing her own shallow breathing as terror takes over . . .

And then, something else.

Not Mack's voice . . . but his snoring.

Soft, rhythmic snoring.

For the second time in perhaps a minute, Allison goes limp with relief.

He's alive. Thank God. Thank God.

Of course he is!

What the heck were you thinking? He's just asleep!

And there's no one lurking in the hallway downstairs.

And the man who tried to kill you ten years ago is dead. Okay? Can you relax now? Do you finally understand that you have nothing to worry about?

A smile plays at Allison's lips as she hurriedly strips off her clothes, pulls on a nightgown, and goes through her bathroom routine.

Yes. Tomorrow is definitely going to be a brighter day, she thinks as she climbs into bed beside her peacefully slumbering husband.

Robbie Masters's mother is always warning him that hanging around stoned outside the gas station mini-mart in Monticello will get him into trouble, but that shows how much she knows.

Talk about being in the right place at the right time.

A little while ago, when the car pulled up alongside him and the driver beckoned him over, he figured it was someone who'd taken a wrong exit off the highway and needed directions. That, or someone was looking to score some weed and wanted access to Robbie's dealer.

Boy, was he wrong.

Robbie is careful not to jostle the insulated blue bag as he carries it toward the guardhouse at the main entrance. Having grown up a mere twenty-minute drive away from Fallsburg, this is the closest he's ever come to the massive correctional facility — and he hopes it's the closest he ever has to get.

He may be a high school dropout, and he's had some minor run-ins with the cops, but he's never going to get into the kind of trouble that will land him in a place like this, no matter what his mother thinks. No way, Jose.

"I need to drop this off for one of the corrections officers," he tells the guard, who looks warily at him through the window.

"What is it?"

Robbie shrugs and holds out the bag. "It's his lunch. He forgot it. His wife asked me to leave it for him. His name's Chuck Nowak. See? His initials are right here on the bag."

"You can't just —"

"Please, sir," Robbie cuts in, because the person who's paying him to do this told him to be polite, "it's just a sandwich and a bag of chips and an apple . . . See for yourself. It's not going to blow up or anything."

"But who —"

"Look, you can give it to him or not. No skin off my nose. I've got to get going." Robbie sets the bag on the ledge beneath the guard's window, turns around, and strides quickly to his waiting car.

His heart is racing. He half expects the guard to come running after him, or the bag to blow up, even, despite what he said.

Yeah, it's a sandwich, chips, an apple, a drink. He made sure of that before he agreed to drive the damned thing up here. Still . . . you never know.

No one in his right mind pays a total stranger two hundred bucks to deliver a bag lunch — with explicit instructions for Robbie to keep his hood up and tied so tightly that his face is barely visible.

For that matter, no one in his right mind

goes around wearing a woman's clothing, a wig, and makeup.

But again, that's no skin off Robbie's nose. If Chuck Nowak the prison guard wants to pass off a freaking drag queen as his wife, that's fine with Robbie. It's all fine with Robbie, just as long as he gets paid.

He tears back down to the main road and drives a couple of miles to the secluded spot where he agreed to meet the so-called Mrs. Nowak.

The car is parked there, headlights off.

Robbie turns off his own headlights, but not the engine. Take the money and run — that's the plan. He doesn't feel like hanging around in the woods with a cross-dressing freak for one second longer than necessary.

He strides over to the driver's side of the other car, expecting the door to open.

It doesn't.

Maybe the freak fell asleep waiting.

Robbie reaches the car and raps on the window. "Hey," he calls — then realizes that the driver's seat is empty.

Maybe he . . . she . . . *it* got out to take a leak.

Maybe the whole thing is some kind of joke.

Maybe —

A twig snaps behind him.

Robbie whirls around to see the freak standing there.

But he never sees the blade that slices through the air and into his jugular vein, and he never hears the words, "Sorry, kid," whispered into the darkness before the stranger drags him deep into the woods where he'll never be found.

Frowning, Chuck hangs up — again — on Cora's cell phone voice mail. The first time, five minutes ago, he left a message.

"Babe, what's up with this lunch you left me? This is your bag. I had mine. Call me."

The second time, maybe three minutes ago, his message was terse: "Cora. Call me when you get this."

Between those two calls, and the one he just made, he called the home number, too. It went right into voice mail.

Is that because she drove out here to Fallsburg? If she had, she wouldn't be back home yet.

But Paul down at the guardhouse assured him that it wasn't Cora who dropped off the lunch bag. It was some kid who said she'd sent him.

None of this makes sense.

Chuck's heart races as he again regards the blue insulated bag that bears his initials

— and Cora's. Sitting beside it on the break room table is the identical bag he'd grabbed when he left the house.

His hand shakes as he reaches inside to remove the contents. He and Paul went through the bag down at the guardhouse, too, just making sure it really does contain food.

Now, Chuck lays it all out on the table.

First, a bottle of Poland Spring sparkling water with lemon essence — there were three left in the six-pack in the fridge back home when he packed his lunch earlier. He took one. This, presumably, is one of the two that remained.

The next two items are also duplicated in the lunch he packed himself: a green Granny Smith apple — one a day keeps the doctor away; the fridge is full of them — and a snack bag of Snyder's pretzels, which he buys in bulk at BJ's; there were at least a dozen bags left in the cupboard.

Then there's the hero sandwich.

His own sandwich is peanut butter and jelly made on Wonder bread, but this — this doesn't sit well with him.

No, not at all.

He puts the sandwich on the table and dials Cora's phone again with a forefinger shaking so badly he can barely guide it to the numbers.

This time, it rings only once before a brisk "Hello?"

"Cora!" he blurts, even though he knows in the split second he says it — even in the split second he heard the voice — that it isn't her.

"Who?"

He jerks the phone away from his ear, looks at the screen, and sees that he dialed a wrong number. With a curse, he disconnects the call. Painstakingly, he redials.

This time, the line rings several times, and it's Cora's recorded outgoing message that greets him when it bounces into voice mail.

"Please, Cora," he says hoarsely, "please call me right away. I'm . . . worried about you."

Yes. He's always worried about her, but . . .

This is different. This isn't just casual concern.

Something is wrong.

Some instinct, some sixth sense, had told him that back at the house earlier, when he felt as though he was being watched, and now . . .

He ends the call and looks again at the lunch spread out on the table; at the food; the sandwich in particular.

It looks store-bought, well-wrapped in cellophane, with what looks like meat and cheese, lettuce, tomato, and onion layered thickly between the top and bottom halves of the roll.

Yes, it must be store-bought, because none of those ingredients were in the house when Chuck left just a few hours ago, and he can't see Cora going out to buy meat and cheese. She's a vegetarian. She'll look the other way when Chuck eats meat, but she sure as hell doesn't encourage it.

Heart pounding, he reaches out and unwraps it.

He lifts the top of the roll.

At a glance, he thinks he's looking at some kind of mottled slice of meat oozing with ketchup.

Then he sees it.

CN^2.

Surrounded by a heart.

He sees it, and he knows.

It isn't meat. It's skin, human flesh . . .

It isn't ketchup. It's blood . . .

It's Cora, and the toxic horror washing through Chuck Nowak's system bubbles from his lips in an unearthly howl.

■ ■ ■ ■

PART II

■ ■ ■ ■

To die: to sleep;
No more; and by a sleep to say we end
The heart-ache and the thousand natural
   shocks
That flesh is heir to, 'tis a consummation
Devoutly to be wish'd.
                              William Shakespeare

CHAPTER FIVE

Saturday, October 1, 2011

"And then we have to go buy some new colored pencils so that I can — Daddy!" In the midst of outlining her plans for the day, Hudson breaks off with a happy exclamation. "You're up!"

Allison turns away from the cup of coffee she was about to stir and sees Mack standing in the doorway, wearing plaid boxer shorts and an old gray T-shirt.

He takes in the Saturday morning scene — Allison in her bathrobe standing at the counter, his nightgown-clad daughters with bowls of cereal at the table, J.J. in his high chair happily finger painting with goo that was once a handful of dry cereal.

Then he smiles. "Morning, guys. What'd I miss?"

Allison opens her mouth, but Hudson jumps in before she can speak.

"You missed that we're putting on a show!

I'm going to be the star and the director, and Maddy is going to be the actress, and J.J. is playing a sheep and maybe a baby. And we're making posters to put up all over town so people will come. Right, Mommy?"

"Right," Allison agrees, having long ago realized that when Hudson embarks on a creative project, it's best to go along with her in the brainstorming stage and rein her in later, when — if — logistics actually come into play.

Maddy — who learned the same thing — just smiles at her father as he bends to kiss her on the head.

"How's the Cap'n Crunch?" he asks the girls.

Maddy informs him that it's yummy, while Hudson says wistfully, "I wish we could have it every single morning."

She shoots a pointed look at Allison, who shrugs.

"Sugary cereal isn't good for you. That's why you only get it on Saturdays."

If she had her way, they wouldn't even keep it in the house — though if Mack had his, they'd all eat it every morning.

The once-a-week Cap'n Crunch rule is one of countless parenting compromises they've made over the years, many about food.

Mack has such a sweet tooth that he can't even eat an apple without cutting it up and dredging the slices in a cinnamon-sugar mixture. He's agreed not to do that in front of the girls, though, after unsuccessfully trying to convince Allison that fruit is fruit.

"They'll never go back to eating plain apples if you let them taste it your way," she said, "and you know it."

"Because my way tastes better."

"Your way isn't healthy."

"Don't be so sure yours is."

Mack was raised by a mother who did everything right, diet-wise — Maggie was reportedly a health food and exercise nut long before it became faddish — "And where did that get her?" Mack asks darkly whenever the subject comes up. "She died of cancer anyway. We might as well eat the way we want to eat. It doesn't even matter in the end."

It matters to Allison. She's the one who was raised by a woman with a death wish who considered white toast with margarine a square meal, and she's the one who's responsible for feeding three kids on a daily basis, the one who's surrounded by health-conscious mothers who wouldn't dream of putting anything into their children's mouths that isn't whole grain, organic, grass-fed, all natural . . .

Some days, she's tempted to say the hell with it all, serve candy corn for lunch, let the girls skip school, and stay up late watching cartoons. Yes, and on those days, it gives her great satisfaction to imagine the collective gasps of horror such decadence would extract from the perfect playground moms, whose advice — solicited and not — she relies upon to navigate this tricky suburban domestic landscape.

Why do the stakes seem so much higher now than they ever were in her own childhood? Is it due to geography, or generation?

All Allison knows for sure is that she's not going to botch her child-rearing responsibilities the way her own parents did. But it's exhausting, this business of trying to be the perfect mother raising perfect children.

She pours another cup of coffee and hands it to Mack. Black and strong — that's the way he's always drunk his coffee, not willing to dilute the caffeine jolt he so badly needs most mornings. It's how she's learned to drink it as well — and lately, thanks to J.J.'s early mornings, she's the one who needs the jolt.

Not Mack. Not anymore. In the space of a few weeks, the Dormipram has worked wonders. Mack is falling asleep at night and getting up well-rested in the mornings.

It's what may be going on in between that has Allison concerned.

But she doesn't want to bring that up right now. Not with the kids here.

Mack leans against the counter beside her and sips his coffee. "Other than the girls putting on a show, what's going on today? Besides more rain?" He glances at the dreary scene beyond the window.

"Errands, dance lessons, and then the party over at Randi and Ben's." Seeing his expression, she says, "Don't tell me you forgot about that?"

The Webers throw a bash every year on the Saturday closest to Rosh Hashanah, to celebrate the Jewish New Year with family and friends. They've taken it to a whole new level now that they live in a house big enough to easily accommodate hundreds, rather than dozens, of guests, from all walks of life and various religious persuasions.

"I didn't forget," Mack tells her. "I just have a lot of work to get done this weekend, and it's already been an exhausting week. I'm just not up for a huge crowd."

"I'm not, either," she admits. "We can always pretend that we're sick . . ."

"No."

Right. Mack and his pesky code of ethics.

"It's crappy weather for a party," he says, gesturing at the window. "They're supposed to have it outside. Maybe they'll cancel."

"They won't. I talked to Randi yesterday. The caterers were bringing in heated tents."

"Terrific. Tents in a monsoon." He shakes his head. "I think we should just skip it."

"Randi and Ben are our best friends. They're family, really. How can we not go?"

"We didn't last year."

"That's because it fell on September eleventh, remember? We were in Florida with the kids." And if they hadn't been, there's still no way they would have attended a party on that fateful date.

"Oh, right." He falls silent, drinking his coffee, slipping back into the shadows of September 11 memories.

Allison wishes she hadn't been forced to bring it up. With this year's tenth anniversary behind him and his sleeping patterns on track for perhaps the first time in his adult life, Mack generally seems to have turned over a new leaf.

She's the one who's inexplicably found herself brooding about the past; about the dead: Carrie, Kristina, Jerry Thompson . . .

"Mommy, is there any more Cap'n Crunch?" Hudson asks abruptly.

She blinks. "Sure. Wait — no, that was the

last of the box," she remembers.

"There's another one in the cupboard." Mack turns to open it.

"No, there isn't."

"Sure there is." He roots through the contents of the shelf. "I know I saw it last night when I was looking for — Hey, where did it go?"

All right — he just opened the door — quite literally — for Allison to tell him.

She says briskly, "Girls, if you're done with your cereal, put the bowls in the sink and go get dressed."

"But I want more," Hudson protests.

"Mommy's right, Huddy. There isn't any more." Mack turns away from the cupboard, looking perplexed.

"But I want —"

"You can have Cheerios," Allison interrupts her daughter.

"They're not even real."

Out of habit, Cheerios are what Allison calls the toasted oat cereal J.J. was munching — and is now smearing — even though it's not the brand-name kind in the yellow box she remembers from her own childhood. This is an organic version she dutifully buys at the health food store in town and feeds the kids most mornings.

Hudson shakes her blond head. "Forget

it. Come on, Maddy, let's go write our script."

"Get dressed first, okay?" Allison reminds them. "We've got about an hour before we have to hit the road."

"Okay," they say in unison, and Hudson adds, "I'll make a shopping list for when we go to the store. I'll put Cap'n Crunch on the top."

"I'll help." Maddy follows her sister to the sink with her milky bowl.

"You can tell me things, but you can't write them down. I'm doing the writing," Hudson informs her, and they head out of the kitchen.

As soon as the girls are out of earshot, Allison turns back to Mack, who's busy making silly faces at a delighted J.J., the missing cereal box apparently forgotten.

Allison hesitates, wondering if she should even bring it up.

Maybe she's wrong.

But as Mack bends over their son's high chair tray, she notices the way his stomach rounds the front of his T-shirt, and she knows that she isn't.

Mack has always been hard and lean, despite the fact that his only workout these days is dashing for commuter trains and scurrying around the city from his office to appointments.

She first noticed a bit of a paunch earlier this week, when she heard him muttering about the dry cleaner shrinking his suit pants and looked up to see him straining to button the pair he had on.

That was a day after she accused the girls of polishing off an entire bag of pretzels — which they denied — and the day before she noticed that a carton of butter pecan ice cream, which the girls would never touch because it has nuts in it, was missing from the freezer.

It had been there that afternoon. She was certain of that, because she was stuck on the phone for over an hour with her book club friend Sheila, who's in the midst of an infertility crisis. As Sheila talked on and on, Allison found herself wandering around the kitchen, opening the freezer door repeatedly, giving the ice cream a longing gaze, and then forcing herself to satisfy her craving with diet iced tea, an apple, a tub of yogurt, and, of course, the ubiquitous baby carrots.

She's been on a diet, hindered by the recent spate of unseasonable cold and rain that have kept her cooped up in the house for days now. The nasty weather is a grim reminder of the looming blustery season that is always unfairly accompanied by gravy and stuffing, eggnog and frosted cutouts . . .

But this isn't about that, or about her. It's about Mack. And ice cream, pretzels, an entire box of Cap'n Crunch . . . for all she knows, that's just the tip of the iceberg.

Food isn't even the only thing that's missing.

She can't find her good chef's knife — the one with the red handle — and a couple of bowls are gone, too. One, she found tossed in the garbage, along with soggy cereal, yesterday morning. The girls have been known to accidentally toss cutlery, but a bowl?

"Mack," she says abruptly, "we need to talk."

"About the sunroom?" he asks in a weary, not-again tone. They've been trying to come to an agreement about what should be done with the window treatments.

Tired of waiting for him to put the shades back up, Allison started to do it herself last week, then realized that the old shades look dingy next to the new paint. They've been talking about ordering new ones, or perhaps curtains or shutters, but haven't been able to find the time to agree on what they want, let alone actually go shopping or place an order.

"No," she tells Mack, "it's not about the sunroom. Although —"

"Let's not get into that now," he says quickly. "Please."

"Fine." She shifts back to the more pressing matter at hand. "Have you ever heard of sleep-eating?"

"Hmm?" Holding his fingers at the sides of his cheeks, he wiggles them at J.J. and sticks out his tongue.

"Sleep-eating. I think you're doing it."

Mack turns away from J.J. to face her. "What are you talking about?"

She quickly explains about the missing food, only to have him laugh.

"You think I ate it in my sleep? And then chucked the bowl into the garbage?"

"Yes, I do."

Before she can elaborate, he shakes his head, still looking amused. "You're the one who's on a diet, Al. Are you sure you're not just —"

"It's your medicine, Mack," she cuts in. "The Dormipram. It's one of the side effects. Didn't you read the packet that came with it?"

"Not really." He gratifies a fussing J.J. with another silly finger-waving face.

She shakes her head. Of course he didn't bother to read the packet. That's always been her department — the endless investigation into every medication that finds its way into their medicine cabinet.

"Well, I read it, Mack. Look at me. Come on. I'm totally serious here."

"So you're saying I'm . . ." He shakes his head incredulously. "I'm, what, sleepwalking into the kitchen at night and bingeing on ice cream?"

"Among other things." She nods, giving J.J. — fussing loudly now that the clown show has come to an apparent end — a wooden spoon to bang on his tray. Above the commotion, she says, "It makes sense."

Mack just looks at her, apparently not in agreement.

"You said yourself your suit pants were tight the other day," she points out.

He immediately glances down at his stomach, then up at her — still not entirely sold, but she can tell he's starting to believe it's possible.

"Some medicine causes weight gain, you know," he tells her. "Years ago, when Carrie was shooting herself up with all that medication trying to get pregnant, she gained a lot of weight. Dr. Hammond — that was our doctor at Riverview Clinic — said that it was from the hormones in the fertility drugs."

"You're not taking hormones."

"I know, but —"

"Look, Mack, it's true. You can go online and see for yourself — this medicine has a bunch of bizarre side effects. Weight gain isn't one of them. But sleepwalking, sleepeating . . . and trust me, it could definitely be worse."

Over the relentless pounding of J.J.'s wooden spoon, she tells Mack some of the anecdotes she read on the Internet last night when she did her research into the subject. People taking Dormipram have fallen down flights of stairs, made lengthy phone calls, left their homes and had sex with strangers — all in their sleep, without any recollection.

"What do you think?" she asks Mack.

"I can't even hear myself think!" Mack snatches the spoon from J.J., who immediately cries out in dismay. Ignoring the ruckus, Mack turns back to Allison. "Why didn't you tell me this before I started taking the stuff?"

Because I'm tired of feeling like I'm overreacting every time a doctor prescribes medicine.

I'm tired of this endless paranoia about drugs — justifiable, or not.

Aloud, she says only, "Because the vast

majority of people who take it never have any problems."

"Great. So I'm one-in-a-million. Next thing you know, I'll be going next door in the dead of night and crawling into bed with Phyllis Lewis."

Phyllis, who happens to be a striking brunette, can be quite the flirt, and the image is a little unsettling.

But Allison merely rolls her eyes. "Trust me, if that happens, you're off Dormipram forever."

"Are you kidding me? I'm off it forever now."

"You don't have to stop taking it." Allison wets a couple of paper towels at the sink. "You're doing great on it."

"Yeah, if I keep doing this great, I'll be able to fit into a Santa suit without padding by the time Christmas rolls around."

"At least you'll be well-rested," she quips, wiping the soggy cereal off J.J.'s hands as he wails and wriggles against the straps of his chair.

"Nope. I'm done. That's it. I'm going to flush that stuff down the toilet."

"Don't do that. Maybe now that you're aware of what you're doing, it won't happen anymore. Give it another chance. Okay?"

Mack frowns, but says nothing.

Lifting her fussy son out of his high chair, Allison says, "I've got to get moving. I'll change him and then the girls and I have to go."

"You're not taking J.J. with you?"

She stops and looks back at him. "I wasn't going to. Why?"

Why? Mack echoes silently, as their son flails his arms and legs, trying to launch himself from his mother's arms.

"You're going to be home, right?" Allison isn't about to bend on this. It's been a long week trapped indoors with the human octopus, and she needs a break.

"I am, but I have work to do, and you know how he is when you're not around."

"He's like that even when I am around. Anyway, he'll go down for a nap."

"What if he doesn't?"

Poised to tell her husband he'll just have to deal, then, Allison bites back the words when she sees the dark look in Mack's eye.

Dammit, dammit, dammit.

Things were going so well, and she had to go and ruin everything. Now he's going to stop taking his medicine, stop sleeping, and it'll be back to grumpy, overtired, over-worked Mack.

For all she knows, he's not even sleep-eating. After all, it's really just a guess.

But then, if he didn't eat the missing food, who did?

Maybe she was mistaken about it . . .

No. You found the empty wrappings and cartons and a bowl in the garbage, and crumbs and sticky smears on the counter . . .

The only other explanation would be that some intruder had crept into the house in the night and helped himself to their food.

The idea is so much more benign than the late night intruder — the Nightwatcher — who's haunted her for all these years that it almost seems laughable.

Almost.

To Allison, there's really no humor in the thought of a stranger creeping around the house while everyone is sleeping. None at all.

The experience a few weeks ago with Chuck and Cora Nowak was exhilarating, but over much too quickly. Still convinced that the most fitting punishment for the others responsible for killing Jerry will be to lose the people they love most, Jamie now understands that the task isn't meant to merely be accomplished. It must also be savored.

That means getting to know both Rocky Manzillo and Allison MacKenna very well. Getting to know their household routines, their habits, their families. Getting to know what matters most in their world — and then taking it all away.

The only way to do that is to watch them, listen to them. And that, of course, requires the proper surveillance equipment — not at all hard for Jamie to acquire or install, thanks to all those years in prison with gloating inmates willing to teach the tricks of the trade.

And so, on a rainy September afternoon, correctly guessing there was nobody home in Rocky Manzillo's Bronx row house, Jamie had broken a basement window and stolen from room to silent, deserted room installing tiny cameras and microphones. The job was done in a matter of minutes.

It was all for nothing, though. Since that day, Jamie has occasionally caught Rocky coming home alone in the wee hours to sleep until dawn, shower, and leave again. But for the most part, the house has remained empty and still.

Things have been much more interesting at the large suburban house where Allison lives with her husband and their three little children — happily ever after, Jamie realized in disgust, watching her push her daughters on their fancy wooden swing set one breezy afternoon about a week ago.

The house was unlocked, of course, and why wouldn't it be? The area couldn't be safer, a far cry from Jamie's neighborhood back in Albany, and Rocky's in the Bronx. Allison would have no reason to imagine that anyone would ever want to sneak into her house while she was right there in her own backyard.

Once inside, Jamie was tempted to linger, but didn't dare. Not any longer than it took to set up the tiny cameras and voice recorders, keeping an eye on the family out the window the whole time.

Allison had a baby balanced on her hip and took turns pushing the swings, first one and then the other, with the hand that wasn't clasping the baby. The little girls were giggling, kicking their legs as they arced through the air. It was obvious, watching them, that they hadn't a care in the world.

But just you wait, Jamie thought, giving them one last glance from the second story window of the master bathroom.

On the way back through the bedroom, there was just one last little detail to tend to. For old times' sake, because Jamie couldn't resist.

Before even opening a drawer, it was easy to tell at a glance which of the two bureaus belonged to Allison. One held on its polished top some loose change, a pocket knife, and an electronics charging station. The other, a carved jewelry box, framed family photos, and some kind of three-dimensional contraption consisting of Popsicle sticks bound together with too much colored yarn and tape.

A child's clumsy artwork, Jamie guessed. Exactly the kind of thing a mother would proudly display. Not a father.

At least, not the kind of father Jamie has known . . .

And been.

It doesn't mean Allison's husband isn't the most doting daddy — and husband — in the world, though. In fact, Jamie fervently hopes that's exactly the case.

It would mean that, unlike Jerry, Allison has everything to live for — and everything to lose.

It's only been a few days, but already, that's proven to be true.

Even better, watching and listening to the MacKenna family quickly yielded a couple of very interesting — and useful — facts. A new phase of the plan took shape almost immediately.

Now it's just a matter of waiting for the right opportunity to present itself.

■ ■ ■ ■

"Mack! Wow, look at you!"

He turns to see a female stranger who's come up beside him at the edge of the makeshift dance floor. She's standing a little too close — but then, who isn't?

Undeterred by the cold, rainy weather, the Webers had gone ahead with their outdoor party plan, instructing the catering team to cover the huge brick patio where the party is traditionally held. Lit by hundreds of votives and filled with tables, chairs, a band, and people, the heated tent — while almost circus-huge — has had Mack feeling claustrophobic all evening.

Now, he attempts to take a small step away from the woman beside him, but his back is already up against a tent pole.

Carefully balancing the nearly full martini glass in her hand, she tiptoes up to kiss him on the cheek with lips so red he's sure there will be a mark.

Instinctively, his eyes search for Allison. Not that she's the jealous type at all. Nothing like Carrie. Nothing like most women, really. He's a lucky guy.

He finds her, in a group with a couple of her friends who are doing all the talking, probably filling her head with information about building a home greenhouse to grow her own organic produce from seed or getting on waiting lists now for college admissions coaches who will help Hudson get into Harvard a decade from now, or some such nonsense.

He wishes Allison wouldn't buy into it, but she's trying so hard to do everything right with their children, and who can blame her?

Gone are the days when kids walk or ride their bikes off to school and come home to eat store-bought, preservative-laced cookies and play freeze tag with neighborhood kids till dark. That's how Mack grew up.

His mother was health conscious, yes — and look where that got her. But she didn't obsess about the ingredients of every morsel he and Lynn put into their own mouths, or whether they'd get into an Ivy League school — Mack didn't; didn't attempt to, didn't *want* to. He worked his way through a state college, had a blast, and turned out just fine.

Relatively speaking.

"I'd know you anywhere," the woman at his side informs him, and he turns back to her.

His first instinct is to politely say the same

thing, but he actually has no clue who this person might be. She's a beautiful brunette, svelte in her little black dress and heels, reeks of class — but in these circles, who doesn't fit that bill?

Maybe she's one of Ben or Randi's many cousins, he decides, or a neighbor he met at a party in years past.

She grins. "You have no idea who I am, do you?"

"Of course I . . . *don't.*" Compelled, as always, to admit the truth, he's rewarded by a throaty laugh.

"Zoe Jennings."

The name should probably ring a bell, but it doesn't.

"I used to be Zoe Edelman . . . ?" she prompts.

"Zoe?" Oh! Zoe! This lovely creature bears no resemblance to the pudgy young woman who wore glasses, had quite a knack for telling dirty jokes, and could hold her own with the boys when they all went out to guzzle beers after work. "My God . . . how long has it been?"

"At least ten, twelve years, right?"

"At least," he agrees, remembering back to the good old days when they shared a bullpen at the booming advertising agency where he began his career. "Guess we're getting old, aren't we?"

"Hey, speak for yourself."

"I am. You look great." Mack notes that she's had a nose job, and maybe some other work as well. Well below the nose — not that he's looking. But given that low-cut dress, he can't help but notice.

"You look great, too."

Yeah, right. He'd had to suck in his gut just so that he could fasten the top button of his khakis.

Sleep-eating. The very thought of it has been bothering him all day. It's unsettling to think that he's been walking around the house at night like some kind of zombie . . . though it wouldn't be the first time.

When he was a little boy, he was known to occasionally wander downstairs in his pajamas, wide-eyed but obviously asleep. According to his parents and sister, he carried on conversations, but there was a vacant look in his eyes that scared Lynn.

"It was like someone else — someone creepy — had taken over your body," she used to say. "It scared me."

It scared him, too. He hadn't thought about it in years, until this morning.

Sleepwalking, sleep-eating . . .

No, thanks.

He promised Allison that he'd give the

Dormipram another try, but he has no intention of doing that.

Certainly not tonight, with the bourbon he's had.

Contrary to his wife's optimistic belief, the party hasn't turned out to be much fun — and it's deteriorating quickly.

"So I hear you're a big shot in ad sales these days," Zoe tells him.

"*Big shot?* I don't know about that . . ."

"Don't be modest, Mack. I know the industry, remember? You're a big shot. Admit it."

"Where are you now, Zoe?"

"Do you mean, work-wise?" At his nod, she says, "I'm not. Working, I mean. I'm a stay-at-home mom. Two kids, you know the drill. I married Nate — you remember him, right?"

"Nate . . ."

"Nathan Jennings," she supplies with a smile.

"Oh, right. I remember Nathan." He does, vaguely. Nathan, Zoe . . .

Names and faces from another lifetime.

"Nate ran into Ben on a sales call not too long ago, and they caught up, and when Ben found out we just bought a house here, he invited us to come tonight."

"You bought a house *here*? In Glenhaven Park?"

"It's the place to be, isn't it?"

"I guess so. Where's your house?"

"On Abernathy Place."

"That's right around the corner from where we live — we're on Orchard Terrace."

"I know, Ben told me. Small world, isn't it? Can you believe we all wound up in the same town?"

Mack can. He and Allison may have played follow-the-leader after Ben and Randi moved up to Glenhaven Park, but ever since the recession hit, the area has exploded with their upwardly mobile colleagues snapping up McMansions — and mansions — on the market at rock-bottom prices, some even in foreclosure.

"Like you said," he tells Zoe, "it's the place to be."

She touches his sleeve with fingernails that are as red and shiny as her lips. "I heard about your wife."

"Allison. I'll introduce you. She's right over —"

"No." Now Zoe is squeezing his arm. "I meant your first wife. Carolyn, was it?"

"Carrie." He drains the watered-down remains of the bourbon in his glass and wishes a bartender would materialize with an instant refill. Straight up.

"I'm so sorry, Mack."

He never knows what to say in response to that.

I'm sorry, too . . .

It's all right . . .

Don't be — our marriage was over anyway . . .

He just nods.

"I remember you were dating her when we were working together," Zoe goes on. "She was very sweet."

You never met her, Mack wants to tell her. He's certain of that, because Carrie never wanted to socialize with people he worked with. She never wanted to socialize with anyone. And she certainly wasn't sweet.

Maybe Zoe's thinking of someone else.

Or maybe, over the years, she's talked so often about her brush with a September 11 victim that she's convinced herself, and the rest of the world, that she actually knew Carrie. Whose name she thought, until a moment ago, was Carolyn.

For months after she died, Mack ran into people who had barely known her, or people who, he's fairly certain, hadn't liked her if they did know her, because to outsiders, Carrie wasn't very likable.

Hell, Mack was an *insider* and in the end,

180

she wasn't very likable to him, either.

But those people would talk about her as if she'd been some kind of hero or martyr.

Strange how sudden death brings instant celebrity to the victim and to those left behind. Especially a death as spectacularly horrific as Carrie's.

"You must have been devastated when it happened," Zoe tells Mack, who nods, because that, at least, is the truth.

He wishes somebody would show up to rescue him. Turning his head, he spots Allison's friend Sheila and her husband, Dean, standing nearby but keeping to themselves, looking somewhat glum.

Allison told him that they're in the midst of infertility treatments — at Riverview, the very same clinic Mack and Carrie used.

Not surprising, really. The place came highly recommended; some of the best fertility specialists in the city — perhaps in the entire country — are on staff there.

Mack carries a lot of memories of those days at Riverview, located in a Washington Heights brownstone that struck him as charming the first time he ever saw it, yet gloomily foreboding ever after.

The only happy scene he recalls unfolded in a sun-splashed room at the very beginning of the journey, when Dr. Hammond told him and Carrie that she could help them conceive. On that day, parenthood was tantalizingly within their reach.

As time marched on, though, things went downhill. Mack certainly didn't relish his regular treks to the clinic's windowless room — stocked with sticky, outdated porn — to leave sperm deposits. The former altar boy in him couldn't help but find the experience somewhat humiliating. But it was nothing compared to what Carrie went through, and she never missed a chance to remind him of it.

The hormonal drugs wreaked havoc on his wife, and weight gain was the least of it. Always somewhat moody, she became downright impossible. Not a memory he particularly wants to revisit.

And so, a day or two ago, when Allison suggested, over a hurried breakfast in their kitchen, that he give Sheila and Dean a little pep talk about the infertility experience, he flatly refused.

"Nothing I have to tell them is going to make them feel any better. If anything, it would be the opposite. My experience at Riverview didn't exactly have a happy ending, remember?"

Now, he quickly looks past Sheila and Dean, avoiding eye contact.

Ben is nearby, talking to the lead guitarist of the live band. They're on a break at the moment — a most welcome one, as far as Mack is concerned.

His father had worked for a record label, and he's enjoyed music — particularly live music — for as long as he can remember. But tonight, the amped guitars and relentless percussion made him cringe, and he's not quite sure why.

All he really wanted was a quiet Saturday evening on the couch. But here he is, because this is his best friend's party and Allison, who's stuck home with the kids every day, really wanted to come. They even actually have a sitter for once, having borrowed Greta, Ben and Randi's au pair, for the night.

"Don't worry about anything," Randi told Mack and Allison when she offered Greta's services, since both her own children were conveniently invited to slumber parties. "You know she's great with kids. And if it'll give you peace of mind, you can borrow my nanny cam for the night."

"You're still using that?" Allison asked, and looked at Mack.

How well he remembered when the Webers first installed the surveillance equipment that allowed them to spy on their childcare providers, back when their children were young. Ben walked him through the house and showed him the tiny cameras hidden in every room.

It didn't sit well with Mack at the time — though of course, that was before he became a father. Now that he is, he knows how hard it is to leave your precious children with a virtual stranger. He can't blame the Webers for wanting to keep an eye on things. And, as Ben pointed out, this is the world they now inhabit.

"There are cameras everywhere you go, Mack. Seriously. Big Brother is always watching."

"In public, that's true." He'd read somewhere that since 9/11, monitored surveillance cameras are able to zoom in on anything in the city, right down to a square inch on the sidewalk. "But at home . . ."

"Wait till your kids are older," Ben told him. "Yesterday, I walk into my son's room to tell him something, and I'm wearing a towel, and then I realize that we're not alone — Josh has a video chat open on his iPad and there's some kid in there who can see and hear everything that goes on. There's no privacy anymore, anywhere — even in your own house. You never know who's watching and listening. A nanny cam is the least of it."

As a perpetually worried mom, Allison would have gladly accepted the use of the nanny cam for tonight, but Mack talked her out of it.

"It's just a few hours," he reminded her. "And Greta is trustworthy. If she weren't, the Webers wouldn't use her."

"I guess you're right."

Now he wishes he hadn't been so gung-ho on the sitter.

As Zoe talks on, speculating about what September 11 must have been like for him, Mack looks over at Allison, who — as if sensing he needs her — turns her head to meet his gaze head-on. She's lost a few pounds lately, and she looks spectacular in her own little black dress.

From where she is, she probably can't see Zoe, who has her back to her, and of course she has no idea that he's trapped in a conversation about Carrie.

Carrie, unlike Allison, would never have considered Ben and Randi friends — much less family — and insisted that they come here tonight.

Allison was right, of course. They had to come. But now . . .

Obviously thinking the same thing he is, she raises a questioning eyebrow and lifts a thumb, jerking it in the direction of the nearest tent flap.

God, yes, he tells her silently, with a slight nod.

God, I love my wife, he thinks, and turns back to Zoe Edelman — make that Zoe Jennings — to make his excuses and get the hell out of here.

CHAPTER SIX

Rocky Manzillo trudges wearily up the front steps, glad to see that there are no soggy plastic-bagged newspapers littering the stoop this time. He'd finally remembered on Thursday night — after coming home to three days' worth of rain-soaked *New York Posts* — to ask his next-door neighbor to grab the day's paper whenever it's still sitting there at noon.

The neighborhood is far from the most dangerous area in the Bronx, but it's definitely not as safe as it was when Rocky was born here sixty years ago — or, for that matter, when he and Ange were raising their three boys here twenty-five, thirty years ago. And you don't have to be a cop to know that it's never a great idea to advertise an empty house.

Then again, for all Rocky cares right now, anyone can walk right in and help himself. Material possessions? Who gives a shit about any of that?

As long as you've got your health . . .

Funny. It was Ange who always went around saying that, and Rocky who rolled his eyes about all those checkups and medical tests she wanted him to have. She worried about him.

And I never worried about anything. Ever. Not even about Ange.

But that was certainly not because he didn't love her. She was his childhood playmate and high school sweetheart; his bride; the mother of his children; his best friend. Ange is his whole world.

It's just that Rocky has never been the kind of guy who goes around worrying about terrible things that might happen. When you're a homicide detective with the NYPD, you've got your hands full enough trying to do something about all the terrible things that already *have* happened.

This . . . this is worse than anything Rocky could ever have imagined. To see his wife lying there in the trauma unit, comatose, with a breathing tube down her throat and a feeding tube in her stomach, day after day, week after week . . .

Swallowing over the lump that took up permanent residence in the back of his throat when Ange suffered her brain aneurysm in August, Rocky unlocks the door and steps into the entry hall.

Right away, he notices that the house smells funny.

When Ange was here, it always smelled like whatever she was cooking or baking, and it smelled like her freesia-scented bath gel, and it smelled clean.

Now it smells — not dirty, exactly, but dusty. Musty. Not clean. Not like food, or freesia, or Ange.

That's because Ange isn't here; hasn't been here in almost two months; might never . . .

No. Don't you dare go there.

Rocky pushes forward, through the living room, where the shades are drawn, and the dining room, where the good tablecloth is covered with a clear plastic one and a crystal vase of peach-colored silk flowers sits precisely in the center. On either side are long peach tapers set into the matching crystal candlesticks Ange's sister Carm, their doting junior bridesmaid, gave them on their wedding day so long ago . . .

Thirty-eight years. The aneurysm struck just a few weeks after they celebrated their thirty-eighth anniversary. At the time, they talked about taking a Caribbean cruise two summers from now, for their fortieth.

"Maybe we'll bring the kids along," Ange said.

"On our second honeymoon?" Rocky wondered how the heck they were going to afford a trip like that for the two of them, let alone their three sons, two daughters-in-law, and two grandchildren. "That's one, two, three . . . six extra people!"

"Eight," Ange corrected.

"Including you and me. Right. Eight."

"Ten including you and me."

"How do you get that?"

Ange smiled her slightly smug secret smile. "You forgot to count Kellie and the baby."

"Who?"

"Kellie — Donny's new girlfriend."

Their youngest, Donny, a musician down in Austin, *always* has a new girlfriend. Unlike Rocky, Ange keeps track. Kellie was the one who'd visited them in New York with Donny earlier in the summer.

"Okay, so Kel— Wait, *baby*? What baby?"

"I've got a feeling she's pregnant." Ange nodded like she does whenever she thinks she's right about something far-fetched.

Of course, she usually is, especially when it comes to her grandchildren-to-be. She had known somehow that their daughter-in-law Laura was pregnant — despite having given up hope after years of unsuccessful infertility treatments.

"She's going to get pregnant the old-fashioned way," Ange said, long before it happened. "You wait and see."

Rocky waited, and he saw.

"A cruise for ten? What am I, made of money?" Rocky grumbled when Ange made the Kellie prediction.

"It can be a cruise for nine," Ange said with a gleam in her eye, "if you don't want to go. Just think, you can have the bed to yourself, eat whatever you want, no one around to nag you . . ."

He laughed and pulled her close. "I don't mind the nagging."

"I'm going to remind you that you said that someday."

"Probably later today."

"Probably."

Dammit. If Ange comes out of this, Rocky will take the whole family on the cruise — including Kellie and the baby that she is, indeed, expecting early next year. And they won't wait until their fortieth anniversary, either.

But Ange isn't aware that her suspicion about the new grandchild was well-founded. Or maybe she is. Who the hell knows? The doctors believe she can hear Rocky talking, so he talks. He tells her everything he can think of, about the kids, the grandkids, his job . . .

Not that he's been focused on any of that lately. He goes through the motions, but all he cares about is Ange getting better. When he's not working, he's at the hospital, sitting by her bedside, holding her hand, telling her how much he loves her and wants her to come back home.

He keeps waiting for some kind of sign that she's in there somewhere, listening. A hint of her voice, or even the slightest tightening of her fingers, a fluttering of her eyelids . . .

Nothing. There's been nothing.

But there will be. Please, God.

"I'm not giving up on her," he told her neurologist, Dr. Abrams, that first day, after being given the grim prognosis. "And you're not telling me to, right?"

"Anything is possible, Mr. Manzillo, but —"

"That's all I want to know," Rocky cut him off.

It's since become his mantra.

Anything is possible.

In the kitchen, Ange's kitchen, Rocky turns on a light.

Between the hospital and the murder case

he's working on, he hasn't been home in a few days, and he can't remember the last meal he ate. His waistband is so baggy he's had to tighten his belt another notch this week. Ange would love that — she's always after him to lose weight. Funny, because she's also always after him to eat.

The stereotypical Italian wife and mother, Rocky thinks with a faint smile that fades quickly.

He has no appetite, but out of habit, he opens the refrigerator, closes it, opens it again, and stares absently at the sparse contents until an unexpected sound startles him. It's an eerie, faint wail that sounds like a baby crying, or . . .

There it is again. It's coming from somewhere beneath his feet.

Rocky closes the fridge and walks over to the tiny mud-room off the back of the house. From there, one door leads to a tiny patch of chain-link-fenced backyard; another to the basement. Opening that one, he's greeted by the scent of earthy mildew and a rustling movement below.

Man or beast? Should he go back for his gun?

Again, he hears the sound. That wasn't made by a human.

Brilliant deduction, Detective. What else do

you know?

Poised at the top of the step, he listens to whatever it is skittering around down there. Hmm. Too big to be a mouse; not big enough to be a threat to an unarmed man.

He flips a light switch, illuminating a bare bulb in the dank depths, and descends the creaky basement stairs. The floor is wet. Rain seepage has been a problem throughout all the years in this house, but they've never had to deal with squirrels or chipmunks tunneling their way into the basement.

Tonight, though, Rocky hears a large rodent scrambling in the distant, cobwebby corner behind the boys' old changing table and wicker bassinet that neither of the daughters-in-law wanted for the grandchildren, much to Ange's disappointment.

Maybe Kellie will take it for the new one, Rocky finds himself thinking. Ange will like that.

Then he remembers — Ange, in a coma. If the doctors are wrong about her being able to hear him, she's going to be in for a great surprise when she wakes up.

Then again, she probably knew about the baby even before Kellie and Donny did.

How, Rocky wonders, does Ange do it? Woman's intuition?

On the heels of that thought, he wonders whether she had any inkling that she was a ticking time bomb.

Thinking back to the hot August night she got up in the wee hours complaining of a massive headache — and keeled over on her way to the bathroom — he's overcome by a fresh wave of grief and horror.

She took such good care of him, and the boys, everyone . . .

Why didn't she take better care of herself?

Rocky realizes his vision has blurred and uses a fist to wipe away the tears trickling down his cheeks.

He turns away from the nursery furniture that reminds him of when his sons were babies and Ange was young and healthy.

Who cares about the animal lurking in the shadows? Let it make a den down here and spend the winter. Rocky isn't in the mood to —

He sees the broken window.

Frowning, he walks over to it. The glass is completely gone, every shard pushed out of the frame and lying on the damp concrete.

No animal did that.

Perplexed, Allison goes through the top middle drawer of her bureau one more time.

No. It's nowhere to be found.

The water stops running in the bathroom and a moment later, Mack appears in the bedroom wearing only boxer shorts, teeth brushed, ready for bed.

"Your turn," he tells Allison, then takes a closer look at her, standing befuddled in front of the open drawer. "What are you doing?"

"I just . . ." She shakes her head and closes the drawer, then opens the next one over. "I'm looking for something."

"What?"

"Nothing." She moves around the socks in the drawer, then closes it and opens another. Maybe she put it away in the wrong place after she last wore it, which was . . . when?

At least a month ago. Maybe two.

"Al?"

She looks up to see Mack still watching her.

"What are you looking for? Maybe I ate it while I was wandering around feasting in my sleep."

She can't help but laugh at that, and so does he.

"What is it, your cell phone again?"

That went missing earlier in the week. She found it in a bin filled with toddler toys. Still obsessed with electronics, J.J. must have pickpocketed her phone when she wasn't looking.

"Not my cell this time," she tells Mack. "You know that champagne-colored silk baby doll nightgown you gave me on our anniversary last year?"

"I thought it was beige, but champagne-colored sounds better."

"I was going to put it on and wear it to bed to surprise you . . ." She jerks closed another drawer after rifling through the contents.

"You have no idea how much I love that surprise."

"Don't love it too much, because it's not going to happen. I can't find it. It's not in my lingerie drawer and it's not in any of these, either."

"Maybe it's in the laundry."

"Can't be." She opens a drawer filled with jeans. "I haven't worn it in ages."

"Yeah, don't remind me. But I guess we both agree that I deserve to get lucky after tonight."

"Oh yeah? What do you mean by that?"

"I went to that party for you."

"Oh, come on, it wasn't that bad."

"It wasn't that good."

"Who was that woman you were talking to at the end of the night?" she asks, remembering. "The one who hugged you?"

"That was Zoe Edelman. I guess Zoe Jennings now — she married Nate Jennings. I almost didn't recognize her, though. She looks totally different."

"You means she wasn't always drop-dead gorgeous?"

"You think *she's* drop-dead gorgeous?"

Allison glances up from the drawer. "You don't have to pretend you don't think so, too, Mack."

"She was all right."

Allison rolls her eyes. "If she was 'all right,' then I'm barely adequate."

"Come on, you're the one who's drop-dead gorgeous, Allie."

"You're just trying to butter me up so that you can have your way with me," she accuses with a laugh.

"That is . . . absolutely true. But you *are* looking hot."

"How did she wind up at the Webers' party?"

"Zoe? Ben and I knew her years ago, Nathan, too, when we all worked together. I guess they just moved to town, so he invited them to the party."

"That's nice."

Nothing but jeans in the drawer she just searched. *Where the heck . . . ?*

"Whatever." Mack comes over and puts his arms around her. "Listen, who needs the nightie? Just come to bed."

She can smell the bourbon mingling with minty toothpaste on his breath and is glad she insisted on driving home from the party, and then running Greta back through the rain-slicked streets to the Webers'. The bash was still in full swing and the band was playing again, but Allison was glad they'd left early this time.

It seemed everyone she'd talked to over the course of the evening wanted to discuss the local scandal of the week: how a fellow elementary school mom had written the obligatory note for her daughter to get off the school bus at a different stop to have a playdate at a friend's house — without realizing the friend had stayed home sick that morning. Her daughter dutifully handed in the note, the driver dutifully left the child off at the different stop, and the little girl wandered the streets, lost, for a solid hour before a neighbor noticed.

The moms at the party had plenty to say about the situation: the girl's mom should have called to confirm that her daughter had safely arrived at the playdate; the sick girl's mom should have called the mom to say that her daughter would be absent and canceled the playdate; the bus driver shouldn't have let a first-grader off the bus alone, regardless of what the note said . . .

Should have, shouldn't have . . .

Lately, Allison is starting to feel like all these women ever want to do is criticize other people's children and parenting skills, the school district policies, the teachers . . .

That, and offer unsolicited advice: about the kids, the house and landscaping, holiday plans, even Allison's hair, which she's decided to let gradually go back to its natural brunette shade. The only person who hadn't offered advice at the party was her friend Sheila, who'd asked for some.

"Do you think Dean and I should start looking into adoption before we run out of money? These treatments are costing us a fortune, and there are no guarantees. At least with adoption . . ."

"Still no guarantees," Allison pointed out.

"No, I know, but the odds of bringing home a child are a lot higher. I just don't know how much more of this I can take. The hormones are making me so crazy and miserable that at this point I'm starting to think that I'll be lucky if Dean doesn't leave me."

Allison couldn't help but think about Mack and Carrie. About what Mack had said about Carrie's mood swings and volatile behavior in the months leading up to her decision to give up on trying to get pregnant . . .

At which point Mack *did* leave her.

Allison has never really found fault with him for that.

After all, as far as Mack was concerned, Carrie's giving up on motherhood was a deal breaker. Mack was meant to be a father.

But the father of my *children. Not Carrie's.*

A sudden gust rattles the window glass beside the bureau.

"Come on, Al," Mack coaxes, still wrapped around her, his body warm and aroused.

"I just want to make sure I'm not going crazy. I could swear I saw the nightgown in my lingerie drawer yesterday, because it made me think of our anniversary coming up . . ."

"You're not going crazy. But *I* might if you don't come to bed with me. It's been a long time."

"Yeah, well, that's not my fault, Sleeping Beauty," she points out as he nuzzles her neck. "You're the one who's out like a light every time your head hits the pillow. That reminds me — you didn't take the Dormipram tonight, did you?"

"Nope. I had a couple of drinks at the party. Anyway, I told you, I'm finished with that stuff."

"You promised to give it a little more time now that you know the problem, Mack. I think you should go back to see Dr. Cuthbert. Maybe he can —"

"Can we please stop talking and start *doing*?"

"Hey, that's my line," she protests, laughing as he pulls her toward the bed.

It isn't until much later — after Mack has rolled over to his side and is, if not asleep, at least lost in his own thoughts — that she thinks again about the missing silk nightgown.

Only then, listening to a steady rain pattering on the roof, watching the eerie shadow play of storm-swayed branches beyond the window, does she allow herself to consider the one thing she's been trying to keep at bay.

Ten years ago, right before Kristina's murder, there was a series of petty burglaries in the apartment building. Nothing much was stolen — other than women's clothing and lingerie.

During the trial, the prosecution alleged that Jerry was behind the break-ins and that he'd stolen lingerie, then forced his victims to wear it while he murdered them.

What if — ?

No. Jerry's gone forever, Allison reminds herself for the hundredth time. *He's not slipping into women's bedrooms — into my bedroom — and stealing lingerie.*

She must have been mistaken about seeing the nightie in the drawer. It'll probably turn up someplace tomorrow.

And if it doesn't . . .

Maybe Jerry's come back from the dead to steal your underwear.

Stroking the lace-trimmed silk in the darkened motel room illuminated only by the bluish light of the computer screen, Jamie smiles contentedly.

What a night.

Onscreen, a grainy video image shows Rocky Manzillo standing at his kitchen counter, stirring a cup of instant coffee. He just spent the last half hour on a search mission, after presumably finding the broken basement window.

Jamie couldn't see what happened down there, because there were no cameras. But they're planted throughout the rest of the house, so it was possible to watch Rocky going from room to room, apparently looking for signs of an intruder or theft. His body language revealed that he was more pissed off than frightened. That made it tempting for Jamie to go over there right now, tonight, and find out what it would take to bring that tough cop to his knees.

But that, of course, isn't part of the plan.

Anyway, things are heating up nicely over at the MacKenna house. The other image on Jamie's split screen shows their bedroom, so dimly lit that it's impossible to see what's going on. But their voices came through loud and clear.

Jamie listened with interest to the bit about the woman Mack used to know. He was trying so hard — too hard — to deny that he was, apparently, attracted to her.

Zoe Edelman Jennings.

Jamie jotted down her name, and her husband's — Nathan — just in case.

In case?

Ha. A new phase of the plan has already begun to take shape.

Jamie was especially titillated when the conversation turned to the missing nightie.

Is this what you were looking for, Allison?

Smirking, Jamie waves the champagne-colored garment in front of the screen.

You're not buying that it got lost in the laundry room or put into the wrong drawer, are you?

Oh, how I wish I could see your face right now. I know you're still wide awake, aren't you? I can feel it.

You know something's not quite right.

Maybe you even remember what happened ten years ago — the lingerie that was stolen from the drawers of female tenants . . . and then turned up on the bodies of those dead women.

Maybe you're worried that your precious nightgown will turn up covered with another woman's blood.

Hmm . . . maybe you're right.

Sinking into the pillow on Ange's side of the double bed — which is better than lying on his own, beside her vacated space — Rocky is somehow exhausted, yet not tired enough to go to sleep. His mind is numb, his body aches, his heart aches . . . but the adrenaline that began pumping through his veins in the basement a few hours ago has yet to ebb.

After banishing the stray cat that had found its way in through the broken window, he combed the house to see what the intruder might have stolen. As far as he could tell, nothing is missing. Ange's jewelry, cash, electronic equipment, the extensive baseball memorabilia collection his sons have been vying for years to claim . . .

Everything is exactly where it should be.

That's strange.

Rocky's been around long enough to know that a person who breaks into a house usually wants to take something — or leave something: say, vandalized rooms, some kind of written threat meant to scare the occupant, even illegal substances. Rocky has seen plenty of empty homes in this city used as drug drops by neighborhood dealers.

His search didn't uncover any evidence of a hidden stash — but that doesn't mean there wasn't one. And it doesn't mean that whoever broke the window won't be back.

That's why he opted to wear his holster to bed. It wouldn't be good to wake up in the middle of the night with his weapon beyond reach and a stranger prowling around the house.

Then again, it's not the worst thing a man can wake up to in the middle of the night. Not by a long shot.

He closes his eyes and the stormy chill of this autumn night falls away. He sees Ange silhouetted in the moonlight filtering through the screened window on her side of the bed; hears the old box fan humming in another window; feels the warm, humid air blowing on him.

"Where are you going?" he asks her.

"To get some Advil. I have a terrible headache."

She starts across the room, then collapses.

He doesn't see it happen, but he hears it — a terrible crashing thud. For a moment, he thinks she's tripped over something and fallen.

"Ange?" he calls, already swinging his legs over his side of the bed.

No answer.

He finds her on the floor, and he's sure she must have fainted from the heat.

"Ange! Ange!"

She never woke up.

Lying alone in the dark, reliving his worst nightmare, Rocky Manzillo cries like a baby, the broken basement window all but forgotten.

Listening to Allison's rhythmic breathing and the drumbeat of rain, Mack clenches every muscle in his body, counts to ten, and then releases, counting to ten again.

It's a relaxation exercise Dr. Cuthbert taught him months ago, long before the Dormipram. It never worked.

The Dormipram did, dammit.

Now what am I supposed to do?

Go back to taking it, even though it does

crazy things to me?

Mack realizes that his jaw is still clenched, so hard it aches.

Why does everything have to be so difficult for him?

All right, not everything. But his career, which used to be such fun, has become a dreaded daily challenge, day in and day out. His house, always a pleasant refuge, is a hodgepodge of tasks that need his attention. Even marriage and fatherhood sometimes feel like a chore lately — four more people who need time and attention he can't always spare.

The one saving grace lately has been the newfound ability to fall asleep. The most basic, natural thing in the world, something every human being is capable of doing . . .

But not me.

Not on my own, anyway.

Frustrated, Mack sits up, swings his legs over the side of the bed, and stands. Might as well get something constructive done, since sleep doesn't seem to be an option tonight.

He starts to walk across the room, trips over something — one of his shoes, kicked off earlier and left in the center of the floor — and curses.

"Mack?" Allison's voice, in the dark, is

startled.

"Yeah. Sorry. I tripped."

"Are you awake?"

He bites back a sarcastic *Of course I'm awake! I'm standing here talking to you, aren't I?*

He knows, of course, why she asked.

"Yeah," he tells her. "Wide awake. Not sleepwalking."

"Good. What are you doing?"

"Going downstairs — don't worry, not sleep-eating, either. I have some work to do."

"At this hour? On a weekend?"

He sighs, wanting to remind her that he wanted to get something done earlier in the day, but she went out and left him with J.J. He could remind her, too, that he's lucky he's got a job in this economy.

But he says nothing at all, just leaves the room and closes the door quietly behind him.

CHAPTER SEVEN

Monday, October 31, 2011

Dusk has fallen over Orchard Terrace.

On any other Halloween night, it would bring a bustle of Halloween activity beyond the hedgerow: costumed kids scuffling excitedly through fallen leaves, working their way up and down the block from porch light to porch light. Parents would trail them in couples or groups, carrying flashlights and spare jackets and baby siblings, calling, "Remember to say thank you!" and "Stay where I can see you!"

Not this year.

This year, there are no porch lights; no flashlights bobbing along the sidewalks; no streetlights. Orchard Terrace is shrouded in darkness, blanketed in the foot of snow that fell on Saturday, a freak October storm that toppled foliage-heavy trees, knocking out power and shattering weather records — not to mention the children's excited plans for trick or treat.

Halloween has been officially canceled this year; the town deemed the darkened streets far too dangerous amid broken limbs and downed wires.

"It's so unfair," Hudson wailed when she found out, and Allison wanted to cry along with her. She'd looked forward to it just as much as her children do.

As a child, she'd always considered Halloween — the candy *and* the costume — one of the few bright spots in the year. It was the one holiday that didn't really revolve around family. Thanksgiving, Christmas, Easter . . . she invariably spent those days wistfully imagining what it would be like to be gathered around a table with parents, siblings, grandparents, aunts and uncles and cousins . . .

There was none of that in her household. Before her father fell off the face of the earth, her half brother, Brett, married young and moved to his in-laws' cattle farm out in Hayes Township. So it was always just Allison and her mother, pretending — wishing — that holidays didn't exist.

But Halloween was different. Halloween was just for kids.

Allison coveted her classmates' store-bought costumes, but poverty forced her to create her own getup out of whatever she could beg or borrow and fashion into something suitably glamorous.

When she was eight, she dressed up as Marilyn Monroe, complete with water balloon breasts that, looking back, must have been incredibly inappropriate. Her mother didn't stop her, and she herself was probably too focused on the loot she collected at every door to notice any raised eyebrows.

At eleven, she was Anna Wintour, wearing sunglasses and a wig castoff from a classmate's Cleopatra costume.

"See that? You can't buy Anna Wintour in a box!" Her mother slurred her approval.

Of course no one but Mom even knew whom she was supposed to be that year, but Allison didn't care. They didn't get her style even when she *wasn't* wearing a costume.

Well, perhaps Tammy Connolly, her one true friend back in Nebraska, did appreciate it. She was always complimenting Allison on what she was wearing. One day, she even said, "You should be a fashion designer when you grow up, Allison" — words that stayed with her long after Tammy moved away from Centerfield and disappeared altogether from her life.

Allison always covered as much ground as

possible when she went trick-or-treating, returning home several times over the course of the evening to dump the contents of her pillowcase into her pajama drawer, emptied out for the occasion. Of course, she didn't have one of those coveted plastic pumpkins all the other kids carried. Either her mother didn't have the money, or she couldn't manage to get herself to the five-and-dime, or they were sold out by the time she got around to it.

But she always managed to buy her drugs, didn't she?

Oh well. Regardless of how Allison carried it home, all that candy was her own precious stash — Sugar Babies and Snickers and mini boxes of Chiclets and Charms Pops . . . She hoarded it in her room, making it last for as long as she could, savoring a sweet treat every day well into the new year.

Last week, before the storm, a note came home in Hudson's "backpack mail" requesting that parents send their children's "unwanted" treats to the school office to be distributed to charitable causes.

Unwanted? Who doesn't want treats?

There was also a reminder that costumes would not be allowed in school on Monday, and that anything remotely costumelike would be confiscated and not returned until November 1.

"A little killjoy, don't you think?" she asked Mack, during one of their harried daily phone calls while he was at work. "I feel like they're trying to suck the fun out of the holiday. Do you know what they're having as snacks for the classroom party? Baby carrots."

"You're the one who's always trying to get the kids to eat healthy food."

He had a point. Why did it bother her so much? Lately, parenting felt like an ongoing exercise in contradiction.

"But it's Halloween!" she told Mack. "Carrots?"

"Look at the bright side — at least they're orange. And at least they're having a party."

"I know, but it's just . . . things are so different from the way they were when I was a kid."

"Most of the time, that's a good thing, Allie."

"I know . . . but not with this."

She can't imagine how she'd have reacted if someone had told her Halloween had been canceled, or that she was supposed to give away all her candy to charity. Hell, she *was* the local charity case, and she never forgot it. No one would *let* her forget it while she was living in that town, and she wouldn't let herself forget after she moved away.

Memories are good for nothin' — that's the bitter lesson her mother had learned, and tried to pass along to her. But Allison refused — still refuses — to buy into the theory. Memories, no matter how painful, are good for something. Whenever she looks back at her old life, she appreciates this one even more.

You've come a long way, baby.

That was the marketing slogan for the cigarettes her mother smoked, Virginia Slims. Sometimes, Mom would say it sarcastically, usually under her breath to — and about — herself: "You've come a long way, baby."

Brenda Taylor had grown up in a well-to-do Omaha family. Her conservative, controlling parents disowned her when she got mixed up with the wrong crowd as a teenager, winding up pregnant with Brett — and no idea who the father was.

"I'd never do that to my own child," she used to assure Allison. "Nothing you ever do would make me turn my back on you."

In the end, though, was Brenda's choice any different from the one her own parents had made? She chose to leave Allison just as surely as her own mother had chosen to leave her. For different reasons, yes. But does it really matter, when you find yourself alone in the world at seventeen, how you got there?

No. But now I have Mack and the kids and I'll never be alone again.

Halloween might have been canceled by the town, but Allison is going to see that her kids get to trick-or-treat.

Earlier, she'd spotted Phyllis Lewis shaking heavy snow off the forsythia branches along the property line, and had gone outside to see if everything was okay.

"Looks like there's a lot of damage," Phyllis said, shaking her head. "Branches down all over, and an oak tree crushed the pool house out back. How about on your end?"

"The same. Except the pool house. Good thing we don't have one. Or a pool." She flashed a wry grin. "Listen, Phyllis, I know Halloween is officially off this year, but the girls have been working hard on their costumes and I was wondering if they could still trick-or-treat at your door later."

"Are you kidding? Of course they can," Phyllis said. "In fact, why don't you all come over for dinner? Or even to sleep? We have the generator now."

Bob Lewis had bought it in the wake of

the weeklong Hurricane Irene power outages, something Mack had also planned to get around to doing, but hadn't yet. Once the power had been restored in early September, it didn't seem likely that it would be knocked out indefinitely again any time soon.

Now here they are on day three without lights, hot water, heat, or communications. School had been canceled today and tomorrow, but the trains were running again this morning and Allison had been stuck alone today in a frigid house with the kids while Mack went off to work.

"Oh, it's okay," she told Phyllis. "You don't have to feed us. Or shelter us."

"I'd love it. Bob is away on business and I'm all alone here anyway. I have plenty of food and plenty of spare bedrooms."

Randi keeps saying the same thing, calling daily to invite the MacKennas to come stay. If this goes on for much longer, Allison told Mack, they're going to take her up on it. But he'd made some calls from work this morning and been told by NYSEG was that the power should be back tomorrow. One last cold, dark night in the house . . . they could handle that, she assured Phyllis.

"It would just be great if the kids could trick-or-treat at your door. Hudson will be devastated if no one gets to admire all her hard work on the costumes — not to mention, if the only candy she gets to eat is the kind I bought. I've got SweeTARTS, Red Hot Dollars, and lollipops, but no chocolate."

"Well, I've got plenty. Bring them by anytime. I'll be home all night. I promise I'll fill up their bags."

Now, as she lights a couple more candles to make the kitchen a little brighter, Allison wishes Mack would call. She's been trying to stall the girls in the hope that he'll make it home in time to go over to the Lewises with them, but he's in the midst of what he called a "manic Monday" at work, so it isn't likely.

"Call me or text me from the office when you know which train you're taking," Allison told him earlier, before they hung up. "I'm down to one bar on my cell and I don't want to use up what's left of my battery by calling you again."

"I will. But if you don't hear from me by six-thirty, just go without me, because that means I won't be home until almost eight and that's too late for the kids."

Checking the time on her watch, Allison sees that it's almost a quarter to seven. Too late.

This will be the first year he's not here to trick-or-treat with the kids. She wonders who's going to be most disappointed about that — the girls, or Allison herself. Venturing next door in the dark with the kids, worrying about dangling limbs and wires, is about as appealing as the now-congealed boxed macaroni and cheese she prepared for dinner — yes, because it's orange.

And maybe, secretly, because it's so unhealthy. Maybe some rebellious part of her longs to push back against the many perfect-mommy rules she's been trying too hard to follow.

At the table, the girls are putting the finishing touches on their costumes by candlelight. J.J. is fussing in his high chair because no one has bothered to pick up all the things he cast overboard: a wooden spatula, a couple of soggy crackers, plastic measuring spoons, and a milk-filled sippy cup that — thank goodness — has one of those no-spill stoppers in the spout.

Allison leaves it all right where it is. Throw-things-on-the-floor-and-watch-Mommy-crawl-around-and-pick-them-up is her son's latest game, and she's not in the mood to play tonight.

"How's it going, ladies?" Allison asks the girls, who are both wearing red pajamas and white face paint.

"It's going *great!*" Hudson flutters around Maddy, obediently standing statue-still on a chair. "See? Don't you love it?"

"I do see, and I do love it."

Gone are the days when Allison bought their Halloween costumes from one of those expensive mail-order catalogs that are always coming in the mail, courtesy of demographics — theirs being one of the wealthiest zip codes in the country.

One year she dressed the girls as a plush ladybug and bumblebee; another, Dora the Explorer and Minnie Mouse. Last year, Hudson was Snow White and Maddy one of the seven dwarfs — Bashful, quite aptly.

But things have changed, and it's because the girls have been asking questions about Allison's childhood, as if they've finally absorbed the realization that she was actually a little girl once, too. When the subject of Halloween came up a while back, Hudson, in particular, listened with interest to the news that Allison used to make her own costumes.

"How old were you?"

"Around your age."

"You mean your mom let you cut fabric and sew stuff? She didn't even help you?" The pathos in it clearly escaped wide-eyed

Hudson. "You were so lucky! Can we do that?"

"You don't have to, sweetie. We always buy our costumes, and you can choose anything you want."

"But we want to make them! Please!"

Taken aback by this ironic turn of events, Allison asked, "Why?"

"Because it would be so cool!"

Cool. Imagine that.

Allison had to remind herself that just because her kids *can* have fancy store-bought costumes doesn't mean they *want* to.

She agreed to the plan, impressed by her daughters' creative, independent streak. Well, it was mostly Hudson. Mild-mannered Maddy went along with it based on a single stipulation: that the costumes had to be storybook characters this year. That was fine with her big sister, who welcomed the challenge with typical gusto.

Hudson came up with a Seussian theme that even includes J.J. He'll be a miniature Cat in the Hat; his sisters, Thing One and Thing Two.

Allison loves watching her girls interact with each other, though it makes her a bit wistful, too. Her own life would have been so different if she and Brett had been closer in age — or just plain closer. Or if she'd had a sister instead of a brother, or in addition to him . . .

One night, as a little girl, she had such a vivid dream about a sister that she woke up convinced it meant her mother was going to have a baby. That was the morning she learned her father had left them — and the morning Allison's imaginary sister, Winona, came to live in her head.

That was probably a healthy thing, in retrospect. She'd talk to Winona when there was no one else around — which was most of the time. Winona always listened in silent agreement. Eventually, of course, she disappeared, the way imaginary friends do.

Oh hell, the way people do.

"We're almost ready," Hudson announces, patting the pile of fuzzy electric blue yarn into place on her sister's head. "Does this look like blue hair?"

"Absolutely," Allison tells her. She'd offered to order wigs, but Hudson declared that cheating.

"I bet your mom wouldn't have made you order a wig," she said, and Allison couldn't argue.

She's never painted a rosy picture of her childhood, but she hasn't come right out and told her daughters the harsh truth, either. They know that her parents were divorced and that her mother died young, but it hasn't yet occurred to them to ask for the gory details.

Just as well. Their own lives are safe and snug and wholesome; they simply have no frame of reference for a world where little girls go cold and hungry, or are abandoned forever by their father, or after years of disappointment and a string of broken promises, find their mother dead on the bathroom floor . . .

A mother who once told her drug counselor, "Weakness is my weakness."

Thank God. Thank God my children will never know that pain, that fear, because their own mother's motto is "Strength is my strength."

And I would never break a promise. Ever.

Ten minutes later, Allison puts out a big orange ceramic bowl of candy next to the lit jack-o'-lantern on their top step.

"What's that for, Mommy?"

"Just in case some other mom decides to take her kids out trick-or-treating."

"Even though it's against the law," Hudson specifies.

"Right." After making sure she has her house key and phone in the back pocket of her jeans, she locks the door after them.

223

"Okay, everyone . . . ready to trick-or-treat?"

Naturally, the girls are, but J.J. clearly isn't thrilled, to say the least, about his role in the charade.

"Mommy, tell him he has to leave the hat on," Hudson admonishes, swinging her own bag, mail-ordered a few years ago and embroidered with her name. Maddy has a matching one.

Allison says, "J.J., leave your hat on," because that's much easier than pointing out the futility to Hudson.

"Yeah, if you don't, J.J.," his oldest sister adds, "then you'll just be a plain old cat and it doesn't make sense. Right, Mom?"

"Don't worry, we'll put it on him before we ring Mrs. Lewis's doorbell." Allison tucks the red and white striped stovepipe hat — which Hudson fashioned quite impressively out of felt — into the pouch hanging off J.J.'s stroller.

The rest of his costume consists of an oval bib of white felt glued to his so-navy-it-looks-black blanket sleeper, and a red bow tie at his neck — also glued. Hudson enjoys glue.

Of course, she originally wanted to tie the tie around J.J.'s neck for authenticity's sake. But Allison drew the line there; she couldn't bear to think of the potential danger a necktie would create for J.J. the acrobat. As it is, she spends her son's every waking hour in a perpetual state of hypervigilance that leaves her utterly exhausted by the end of the day.

That's fine, when all she has to do after the kids are down is crawl into bed herself.

But when there's more to come — like this past Friday night — she's in trouble. They'd hired a sitter again — this time, the teenage niece of Hudson's kindergarten teacher — for their anniversary dinner at Mardino's, their favorite Italian restaurant. Allison had looked forward to it all week.

But of course she didn't want to leave the house until after J.J. was safely asleep — well after eight o'clock, which was unusual for him. He must have picked up on her extra-nervous energy, or maybe he was just teething.

In any case, Allison yawned through dinner, and by the time the dessert menu came, she could barely keep her eyes open.

"Maybe you should order an espresso," Mack suggested.

"I can't drink caffeine now. It'll keep me up all night."

He shrugged. "Take a Dormipram."

"No, thanks. That's your prescription, not mine."

He'd actually stopped taking the medication for a few nights after she alerted him to the sleep-eating, but that didn't last for long. The insomnia came roaring back with a vengeance, and he was miserable.

Now that he knew what it was like to actually get a good night's sleep — and that it *was* possible — Mack decided he'd rather deal with the drug's side effects than with chronic insomnia.

"Maybe Dr. Cuthbert can put you on something else," she suggested, but Mack balked at going back to see him, saying there's no way he can take time off from work for another weekday appointment.

He claims he hasn't had any more issues with sleep-eating, but Allison isn't so sure. She hasn't heard him getting up in the middle of the night, not that that means anything, since she sleeps so soundly she never stirred when he was doing it.

She's been hiding the sweetened cereal and other food he was gobbling down in the night, just in case — so far, so good — but she can't stash the cold stuff anywhere but the fridge. The other day, right before the storm, she was almost positive four containers of yogurt had vanished overnight, along with half a gallon of her favorite diet iced tea, yet the empty containers weren't in the trash.

Maybe she was mistaken about the contents of the fridge, though she doesn't want to do a new inventory right now — she's trying to keep it closed to prevent spoilage until the power comes back.

Or maybe a sleepwalking Mack is now going to great lengths to hide the evidence of his midnight binges.

When his sister, Lynn, called to check on them earlier today, Allison mentioned it to her, needing to confide in someone — but not one of her local friends. They all gossip, and Mack would be mortified if it got around town.

She remembered Lynn mentioning once, when they were all staying at the beach house together on vacation, that her brother used to walk in his sleep as a child. Today, Allison brought it up, asking for more details.

"It was the creepiest thing," Lynn said. "He'd walk into the room with his eyes wide open, but he was completely out of it. I'd get freaked out, but I wasn't allowed to try to wake him up."

"Why not?"

"Dr. Victor — he was our pediatrician —

told my mother that you should never wake a sleepwalker."

"Why not?" Allison asked again.

"He said the person might get aggressive and violent. Trust me, I wasn't about to take any chances with that. My brother used to wrestle me sometimes — just normal kid scuffles — and I knew how strong he was. So I'd just let him do his sleepwalking thing and stay out of his way."

"What did he do?"

"You know — just sort of walk around like a zombie, talking to himself sometimes, or to us. It was complete gibberish. Kind of funny, looking back now. But at the time, it scared the shit out of me."

"Did he ever eat in his sleep?"

"Maybe . . . I don't remember. Why? Is he at it again?"

"I think so."

"Well, don't worry. He's harmless — as long as you don't try to wake him up," Lynn added with a chuckle. "Listen, I know I can be a real chatterbox, and I don't want to keep you on the line — you said your battery is going."

She was right — It was, and Allison hung up reluctantly. She wants to talk to Mack about it, tonight, and about an idea that got stuck in her mind a while back, when Ben and Randi offered to let the MacKennas borrow not just their au pair, but their nanny cam.

Those cameras, she recalls, were so tiny and so easily concealed that no one would ever guess that they were there.

What if Allison were to set up a few around the house to catch Mack sleepwalking and sleep-eating?

She'd tell him, of course . . .

Or would she?

I don't know. It's probably a bad idea. I wouldn't want anyone keeping an eye on me, and it doesn't seem fair to do it to him.

She just wonders whether it might help if he saw himself.

As the girls make their way around downed branches toward the reassuringly lit-up house next door, Allison's cell phone vibrates in her back pocket. She pulls it out, noting that it feels sticky. J.J. got his hands on it earlier, and of course threw a full-blown tantrum when she wrestled it away.

A glance at the caller ID reveals that the call is from a private number — Mack's cell phone, most likely. It always comes up that way.

It's about time he called.

She presses the phone up to her ear with one hand while trying to keep the stroller on the sidewalk with the other hand as J.J. wriggles around trying to launch himself out.

"Where are you guys?" Mack asks, huffing a little, as though he, too, is in motion.

"We're about to ring the Lewises' doorbell. Where are you?"

"Running for the train. I'm trying to catch the 6:51."

"Okay — wait, hang on a second." Realizing J.J. managed to get his hands on the cat hat and throw it overboard, she backtracks to scoop it up, calling, "Hudson! Maddy! Wait up!"

"What's going on? Don't lose the girls in the dark. It's dangerous out there tonight."

Irked, she shoots back, "Do you really think that's going to happen? They're just a few steps ahead of me. They're excited."

And if you were here with us, you could hold their hands while I deal with Mr. Impossible.

"Just be careful. Did you take pictures for me?"

"I couldn't. The camera battery wasn't charged."

"Can you take one on your cell phone?"

"I told you, the battery is really low."

"Al, I really wanted to see their costumes."

"Then you should have been here," she snaps, and instantly regrets it. "I'm sorry. I

230

know you wanted to be. It's just . . . it's been a long day."

"Tell me about it."

Okay, maybe he's not inferring that *his* long day was somehow much longer — and thus much more difficult — than *her* long day. But that's what it feels like to her.

"I've got to go, Mack. See you when you get home."

"Have fun," he says glumly.

"We will," she returns, just as glumly.

Hanging up, she catches up to the girls.

"What's that noise?" Maddy asks, hanging back a little as Hudson climbs the steps to the Lewises' front door.

Realizing she's referring to the rumble coming from the attached garage, Allison says, "It's the generator. It's making power for the house. See how their lights are on?"

"Why can't we get a generator too?"

"Ask Daddy," Allison grumbles under her breath, reaching for J. J.

"Come on, Maddy! Mommy, hurry up and take him out and put his hat on!" Hudson commands, her finger poised to ring the bell.

"Hudson, do *not* order me around."

"I'm sorry. I just want it to be really good."

"I know you do. Don't worry. It *is* good." She unstraps the baby and plops the felt hat on his fuzzy head. He immediately pulls it off and tosses it to the sidewalk.

Dismayed, Hudson picks it up. "J.J., you have to wear it!"

"Shh, he will, just ring the bell." Allison puts the hat back on him and is gratified when it stays that way — but only for a few seconds before J.J. throws it again.

He laughs with glee as Allison bends with him to pick it up.

Hudson glares. "He's ruining everything. He just looks like a baby in pajamas."

"As far as he's concerned, he *is* just a baby in pajamas," Allison points out, her patience just about depleted. "And it's past his bedtime."

"No, it isn't. He doesn't go to bed until —"

"Hudson, please just ring the bell."

"He has to wear the hat!"

"He just doesn't understand Halloween," Maddy pipes up. She descends the steps, takes the hat, puts it on her little brother's head, and holds it there with a firm but gentle little hand. "There, J.J., see? You're a kitty cat! The Cat in the Hat! Meow, meow." The baby laughs at her cat imitation.

"Ring the bell, Huddy! Hurry!" Maddy says between meows.

Allison smiles at her middle child, so often

the lone voice of reason in this family of passionate personalities.

Phyllis Lewis comes to the door with a Longaberger basket of candy, managing, as always, to be effortlessly sexy-elegant. Tall and slender, she's wearing a snug-fitting black cashmere turtleneck with trim black pants and flats, looking like a 1960s screen siren. Her face is fully made-up and her chestnut-colored hair is short and chic and perfect, making Allison all the more conscious of her own unshowered-since-Saturday state.

"Trick or treat!" the girls shout.

"Oh my goodness!" Phyllis slaps both manicured hands to her cheeks. "What have we here?"

"We have here Thing One and Thing Two plus also the Cat in the Hat," Hudson informs her proudly. "I made the costumes all by myself. Well, Thing Two helped a little."

"Well, aren't you talented?"

"Yes," Hudson agrees immodestly.

Phyllis laughs. "I happen to love cats, so I might just have to give you an extra treat or two because of that."

She urges the girls to take lots of miniature candy bars and deposits a handful into J.J.'s bag with a wink, saying, "I'm sure someone will be able to help him eat those. Where's Daddy tonight?"

"He's still at work, unfortunately," Allison tells her, and Phyllis shakes her head.

"I remember the days of trick-or-treating alone with the kids. I dreaded taking them out without Bob, but he was always on the road when they were this age. He still is — last week, Tokyo, this week, London . . ."

"That stinks," Allison says. "You must be lonely."

"Oh, but I'm not! Not at all. Don't tell Bob," she leans forward and says, in a conspiratorial whisper, "but I actually prefer to have him gone. As long as I have lights and heat, it's nice to have the house to myself."

Allison can't imagine ever *preferring* to have Mack away from home. Yes, things change — but they aren't going to change that much in *her* marriage.

Are you sure about that? With a little twinge of regret, she remembers the way she snapped at him on the phone a few minutes ago.

"Come on, Mommy, let's go!" Hudson is already halfway down the walk, anxious to get back home and tear into her chocolate.

"I'm coming, I'm coming." Harried, she

234

bends to strap J.J. into his stroller again. "Thanks, Phyllis."

"I know it can be crazy, Allison, chasing around after little ones, but time is going to fly by. Those three will be away at college before you know it, just like mine."

Phyllis's son, Ryan, is at Brown; her daughter, Laurel, is at Cornell. Scholastic, athletic, and extracurricular overachievers, both — par for the course in Glenhaven Park.

"Enjoy every minute of this, Allison," her neighbor calls after her as she wheels the stroller down the path. "Trust me — you're going to miss it when it's over."

Mothers of older kids are always talking about how quickly children grow up. It bothers Allison that they all seem so wistful for the good old days, as though it's all downhill from here on in.

She glances back over her shoulder to see Phyllis still silhouetted in the doorway, looking out into the night. Jet black Marnie has appeared beside her, poised in profile with her feline back humped and her front paws extended toward her mistress.

It's a sight Allison quickly forgets as she catches up to her children . . . but one she will forever remember, with a shudder, whenever she thinks of what happened to

Phyllis and Marnie later on this Halloween night.

Mack expects Allison to be a bit frosty toward him when he gets home too late to even see the kids in their costumes, having just missed the 6:51 train after all. When he walks in the door, she's upstairs wrangling the kids into bed. The house is cold and lit only by a few flickering candles that cast weird shadows on the walls. He goes right up, of course, and is immediately regaled with a recap of the evening's activities by his sugar-fueled daughters.

Allison can't get a word in edgewise if she wants to — and he can't tell whether she wants to. The baby is overtired and cranky and she has her hands full.

"I left you some macaroni and cheese," she calls from J.J.'s room after Mack has kissed everyone good night, changed into a double layer of sweats to keep warm, and is about to head back downstairs.

That's a good sign.

He thanks her and goes down to look for it in the candlelit kitchen, hoping it's the homemade kind she sometimes bakes in her big blue-and-white Corningware dish.

But it isn't — of course not. It's Kraft, from a box, sitting on the countertop in a

Saran-wrapped plastic bowl. He forgot that the oven is useless without its electronic control panel. Only the gas stove burners are working.

He eats the mac and cheese cold with ketchup, standing at the counter. Then he finds a slightly wizened apple in a bowl on the counter, slices it, buries it in cinnamon and sugar, and carries it to the living room. An orange jar candle is burning on the coffee table, throwing off a tiny bit of light and a powerful pumpkin smell.

He crunches through a slice or two, caught up in his BlackBerry, which was fully charged when he left work but is already down a bar. In trying to tie up a few loose ends he left at the office, he succeeds only in complicating matters even further, and now he's worried he's going to run out of battery before anything is resolved.

This power outage is getting to him.

No, this *job* is getting to him.

Understatement. This job is killing me.

The fall programming schedule is under-delivering, not achieving the ratings estimates. The clients, furious and frustrated, are looking for make-goods, but there's no inventory for that; the ad sales team has been scrambling for ways to avoid having to return cash to them in what has become a no-win situation . . .

Hearing footsteps on the stairs, he looks up from the e-mail he's in the midst of painstakingly typing with his thumbs.

Through the archway, he can see Allison descending into the votive-lit hallway in her pajamas and a thick fleece robe. She looks like one of the girls, with her long hair hanging loose and her feet in fuzzy slippers — particularly when she stops to peruse the big candy bowl sitting on a table near the front door. After picking through it, she picks up the whole thing and pads into the kitchen with it.

A minute later, she's back, still carrying the candy, along with a glass of diet iced tea.

"Trick or treat." She offers the bowl to Mack.

"No, thanks. I've got an apple."

She looks at the plate parked next to the candle on the coffee table. Even in this light, it's obvious that the fruit slices are all but obscured by drifts of cinnamon sugar.

"There's probably more sugar there than there is in this entire bowl," she comments.

"Probably," he agrees with a shrug. "And by the way . . . we're out of apples."

"We're out of everything except candy. I have to go through the fridge and freezer and toss all the perishables even if the power comes back tomorrow."

"Well, before you go to bed, make sure you hide that bowl someplace where I can't get to it, okay? Just in case."

"What — ? Oh." She gets it. The sleep-eating thing. "Right. I will. But there's no chocolate — I didn't buy any because I didn't want you to be tempted."

"I don't think that really matters. I hate sweet pickles and you're telling me I ate a whole jar last week in my sleep."

She sighs. "I just hope you don't eat anything from the fridge that's spoiled and make yourself sick."

"I'll try to warn my subconscious mind."

"I don't think that's going to work."

"I was kidding, Allison."

"Oh. I can't see your face." She sets the glass and candy bowl on the coffee table — beyond his reach — then sits beside him on the couch, tucking her slippered feet under her and unwrapping a lollipop.

He goes back to typing on his BlackBerry, wishing he could turn on the television. He doesn't really feel like watching it, but he doesn't feel like talking to Allison right now, either.

Okay, so maybe he's the one in a frosty mood, thanks to the earlier tension between them. He's under enough pressure at work. He doesn't need her cranking it up at home.

She shivers. "It's freezing in here."

"Do you want me to build a fire in the fireplace?" he asks, hitting send and looking up from his BlackBerry at last.

"Not really," she says around a yawn and a lollipop stick. "I'm going up to bed in a minute. It'll be warmer under the blankets."

"Isn't it going to take you longer than a minute to finish that sucker?"

"I only want a few licks. I'm still on my diet. I have three more pounds to lose. I guess we probably should give all this candy away, like the school said."

"Killjoy."

She smirks. "Hey, anything for charity. So . . . stressful day at work?"

"I really don't want to talk about it."

She nods and licks her lollipop and sips her iced tea in silence as he checks to see if there's a response yet to his last e-mail.

There isn't.

"Mack?"

"Yeah?"

"Are you happy?"

Startled, he looks up to find her watching him intently. Even in this light, he can see that her blue eyes are troubled.

"You mean right now?" he asks. "Or

generally speaking?"

"Both."

He shrugs. "Things are beyond crazy at work, but . . ."

"Things are crazy at home, too. Maybe we should . . . I don't know."

His heart does a nervous little flip-flop.

"What?" he asks, reminding himself that this is Allison, not Carrie. This is a successful, solid marriage. She's not going to end it — and this time, neither is he.

"Maybe we should do something about it. Make some changes. I feel like we never get to see each other anymore, you're always working, I'm always exhausted. . . . Is this how it's supposed to be?"

"This is the life we chose, Al. The house, the kids, each other . . . what is it that you want to change?"

"Not *us,*" she says hastily, and rubs her forehead, hard. "I don't know. Maybe not anything. I just feel like . . ."

He waits for her to finish.

She doesn't.

She stands, leans over, and kisses him on the head.

"Where are you going?"

"Bed. Maybe all I need is a good night's sleep."

He used to think that was all anyone needed.

Not anymore.

Watching her go, he realizes she left the bowl of candy behind. He stands, picks it up, looks around the dark room, and walks toward the desk in the corner. The bowl is too big to stash in a drawer, but he pulls out the leather chair, puts the bowl on the seat, and pushes it back into the kneehole. No one would ever know it's there.

Not even me.

Pretty bizarre that he's hiding something from himself.

How is it possible that he wanders around the house at night and wakes up with absolutely no recollection?

How is it possible? You've been doing it all your life.

Well, when he was a little boy he did, anyway. For all he knows, he's been doing it ever since, though the sleep-eating is a new twist.

He's fairly certain it hasn't happened lately, though. Every night, after he takes the medicine, before he falls asleep, he does his best to will his subconscious mind into submission.

You will stay in bed.

You will stay in bed.

He hasn't gained any more weight, and Allison hasn't mentioned any missing food.

Wearily, he blows out all the candles, climbs the stairs, and looks in on the kids again, one by one. They're all buried beneath layers of blankets, sound asleep despite the pervasive cold.

Are you happy, Mack?

When he reaches the bedroom, Allison is either already asleep or pretending to be. You'd think the caffeine in her nightly iced tea would keep her awake, but it never seems to.

It isn't fair, Mack thinks, not for the first time, having long ago given up coffee in the afternoons on Dr. Cuthbert's advice.

She left a votive candle burning on the bathroom sink. He shakes a familiar white capsule out of the orange plastic bottle and washes it down with water. Then he blows out the candle.

Are you happy, Mack?

The question echoes through his head as, shivering, he climbs into bed. The answer manages to elude him, but sleep, blessedly, does not.

CHAPTER EIGHT

Last night, long after Mack fell asleep, Allison lay shivering on her side of the bed, having a good cry into her pillow.

It wasn't that she thought her marriage was in serious trouble.

Of course not.

She loves Mack, and he loves her. It's just . . .

They're going through a rough patch, that's all, between his job and the kids and never having time for each other. She sees that, even if he's not willing to acknowledge it, or do anything to change it.

But everything seemed more positive in the bright sunlight of Tuesday morning. Luckily, NYSEG kept its promise and restored power to the area by dawn. Allison woke up to find that the house was warm and appliances and electronics had hummed back to life.

Mack was playful with the kids and he

kissed Allison on the cheek before he left for the train.

Around noon, he even texted her to say he'd be home before seven tonight, so she decided to cook one of his favorite meals: spicy pepper steak over rice. White rice, not brown. Brown may be healthier, but it just doesn't taste as good as sticky white in this dish, and Allison is getting tired of feeling obligated to ride the health food train all day, every day. A little simple white starch once in a while isn't going to kill anyone, right?

You'd think so, listening to those super-nutritionist, super-vigilant, super-organized supermoms on the playground, at book club, at the bus stop.

She's got to stop hanging on their every bit of advice — solicited or, more often, not; putting constant pressure on herself to do every little thing perfectly. It sucks the fun right out of life.

So Allison loaded the kids into the car and went out to buy the white rice. She visited two different supermarkets in search of just the right cut of meat, loading up on fresh dairy and produce, too, with three different varieties of apples for Mack.

She'd also stopped at Target and replaced the missing chef's knife, along with a new set of cereal bowls that hopefully won't disappear into the garbage this time.

Back home, she threw away every perishable item in the fridge and freezer, and now that it's all restocked . . .

I know exactly what we have, and how much.

As always, the prospect of Mack's sleep-eating looms in the back of her mind, along with the nagging question about whether she should set up the nanny cam to catch him at it.

When the phone rings late Tuesday afternoon, she's crying.

This time, it's only because she's chopping onions.

She tosses the knife aside, quickly rinses her hands, and picks up the phone, glancing at the caller ID panel. She just hopes this phone call isn't going to be Mack reporting that he won't be home for dinner after all.

Private caller.

She answers with an expectant, "Mack?"

There's a crackling sound, and then a male voice — not her husband's — comes on the line. "Is this Allison?"

"Yes?"

"Bob Lewis. From next door."

"Hi, Bob. I thought you were in London."

"I am, but — Have you seen Phyllis around lately?"

Something in his voice ignites a spark of apprehension. "Yes, just last night. The kids trick-or-treated at your house. Halloween was canceled, but —"

Bob cuts her off, which isn't like him. He's usually exceedingly polite.

"Have you seen her today?"

"No, but . . . why? Is everything all right?"

"I've been trying to get ahold of her all day, and she's not answering the house phone or her cell, or her e-mail or texts. That's not like her."

Bob says something else, but she can't hear it thanks to J.J., babbling and banging a wooden spoon on the tray of his high chair. She steps away, into the doorway of the darkened sunroom, standing where she can still keep an eye on her son.

"I'm sorry, Bob, I couldn't hear you. What was that?"

"I said I'm just worried because she always calls me first thing in the morning — that would be afternoon for me — and she didn't this morning. I know the power was out, but she has the generator . . ."

"She does," Allison agrees, "and anyway, the power is back on again. It has been since early this morning."

"You're not having any trouble with the phone lines, are you? There's not another storm, or . . . ?"

"No, the sun was actually out all day. It's melting all this snow." Allison automatically glances at the wall of glass — still uncovered, because they haven't yet gotten around to window treatments.

In the gathering dusk, now that a couple of big branches have fallen from the trees on the property line, she has a partial view of the Lewises' big Colonial next door.

"I see a couple of lights on," she tells Bob. "Maybe Phyllis went out and didn't want to come home to a dark house."

"Maybe. But she should be answering her cell. Listen, I need to get to bed — it's getting late here and I have an early meeting — and I won't be able to sleep unless I know she's all right. Would you mind going over to check on her?"

"Not at all. I can't leave the kids, but Mack should be home in about half an hour, so —"

"Is there any way you could just run over quickly now, Allison? I'm sorry. It's just that the generator could be dangerous if she doesn't remember to keep the garage door open while it's running. I keep thinking maybe something happened . . ."

"You mean carbon monoxide?" Allison is alarmed.

"I — I don't know. You have the keys to our place, right?"

"I do." Something flashes through her brain — something she never lets herself think about if she can help it.

She had the keys to her neighbor Kristina Haines's apartment, too, ten years ago. Worried after not hearing from Kristina in the wake of the World Trade Center collapse just blocks away, she let herself into the apartment to check on her . . . and found her murdered corpse.

But this, of course, is completely different. Another place, another time, another friend . . .

Phyllis could be in trouble, though — overcome by carbon monoxide fumes. Her life might be hanging in the balance, and every second counts. Allison can't tell her worried husband, who is helpless and an ocean away, that she isn't willing to go over there and check on her because of something horrible — and completely unrelated — that happened ten years ago.

No, and that's not who I am. I'm not weak. I don't shy away from my responsibilities, not like my mother did.

"If she doesn't answer the door," Bob is

saying, "just let yourself in and make sure she's not in there and . . . unconscious or something."

"I'm on my way right now. I'll call you right back in a few minutes . . . or actually, I'll just have Phyllis call you."

With those reassuring words ringing in her own head, she hangs up the phone and returns to the kitchen.

"Girls?" she calls, trying to un-pry J.J.'s fingers from around the handle of the wooden spoon. Naturally, he screams in protest.

"Shh, J.J. . . . Girls!" she calls again.

From the living room, she hears only the murmur of televised voices and jaunty kid-show music. With no school yet again today — on the heels of seventy-two hours without electronics — she's allowed them to watch TV most of the afternoon.

"Girls! Come here right this minute!"

Now there are footsteps hurrying toward her the way they do whenever she sounds like she means business.

Maddy appears in the doorway, takes one look at her face, and immediately asks, "What's wrong, Mommy?"

Beside her, Hudson, markedly less concerned, wrinkles her freckled nose. "I smell onions."

"I need help," she tells them above J.J.'s wailing as she wrestles him out of the high chair.

"Chopping onions? Because I don't like —"

"Not chopping onions! I need you two to babysit your brother for a few minutes. Do you think you can do that?"

Hudson nods vigorously, but Maddy looks even more worried now. "Where are you going?"

"Just outside. I have to run next door, but I'll be back right away. Like, in two seconds."

"Two seconds? That's impossible. No one can —"

"Two *minutes,*" she interrupts Hudson. "Not seconds. Minutes. Okay? You can time me. Come on."

She leads the way back to the living room with the girls obediently at her heels. "I'm going to put your brother into his swing — no, his ExerSaucer." Yes, that's stationary and low to the ground, so he can't fall out of it. "Stay right here with him while I'm gone, okay?"

The girls kneel on the floor beside the ExerSaucer as she straps their squirming brother into the molded yellow plastic seat. It's completely encircled by a round red tray

251

to which all sorts of gizmos are attached — bells, mirrors, rattles, the works.

J.J. immediately cheers up, reaching with a chubby, drool-and-tears-wet hand to spin a bright blue spindle.

"There. That'll keep him busy while I'm gone." She hurriedly opens the desk drawer where she keeps the Lewises' keys, expecting to have to dig for them, but the manila envelope labeled "KEYS" is right on top. She sorts through several sets, all labeled with circular cardboard rings: "Our House (spares)" . . . "Beach House" . . . "Lewis House." Okay, so far, so good.

"Two minutes," she promises the girls again, and pats her pocket. "I have my cell phone if you need anything. The number is taped by the phone."

"Or we can just scream out the front door," Hudson points out.

"Or that," she agrees with a faint smile, and then she turns her back and is on her way, the smile gone.

It's too good to be true: Allison on her way over to check on her neighbor.

I couldn't have planned it this way if I tried.

It just goes to show that things have a way of falling into place, if one has patience and truly believes that justice will prevail. The poetic brand of justice, anyway.

Jamie's only regret is that the surveillance cameras and microphones can't follow Allison now that she's out the door and on her way to the Lewises' house.

All that's visible now on the computer screen is an image of her kids.

The girls are doing just what she told them to do: sitting and playing with the baby. He's a spoiled brat, though, that kid. He keeps throwing toys on the floor. He could use a good, hard smack — that would teach him how to behave.

Jamie's hand clenches into a fist just thinking about it.

But I'll get my chance for that. All in good time . . .

For now, it's enough just to think about what a lovely surprise Allison is about to find next door.

Coming up the Lewises' driveway, Allison can see that the garage door is open and Phyllis's Saab is parked inside. The generator is beside it, but it's fallen silent since last night.

That means Phyllis must have turned it off when the power came back, right?

But wouldn't she have closed the garage door? She never leaves it open.

Maybe the generator ran out of fuel, and Phyllis didn't realize it because the power is back.

But surely she'd have noticed the absence of that rumbling motor.

At least the open door is a good sign — it means the house probably isn't full of carbon monoxide fumes.

And the fact that the car is here doesn't necessarily mean Phyllis didn't go out. A friend could have picked her up, right? And she could have forgotten her cell phone, or lost it somewhere in the house . . .

No, she doesn't have a sticky-fingered, phone-crazy baby to contend with, but people lose their phones all the time, right?

Allison makes her way to the front door and rings the bell. She promised Bob she'd check on her, and she's going to keep that promise.

After about twenty seconds, she rings it again. Waits.

Rings it again.

Worried, she fits her key into the lock. Maybe there are fumes even though the garage is open.

Maybe that wasn't enough ventilation.

Hurriedly, she unlocks the door and pushes it open.

"Phyllis?"

The house is completely still. She sniffs the air, smelling nothing, but carbon monoxide is odorless, right? That's what makes it so dangerous.

"Phyllis!" she calls again.

Silence.

Now what?

Allison props the door open, steps inside, and opens the nearest window, letting more cold, fresh air into the house. Then she pulls her cell phone from her pocket and quickly dials Phyllis's number.

Immediately, she hears a faint ringing sound from someplace upstairs.

Okay, so the cell phone is here.

What if Phyllis is, too, and is somehow incapacitated?

"Hi, this is Phyllis. Leave me a message, and I'll —"

Allison disconnects the call and quickly dials her home number. Hudson answers on the first ring, with the efficiency — if not the accent — of a British butler.

"MacKenna residence."

"Huddy, it's Mom. Is everything okay there?"

"Everything's fine and you better hurry. You have less than thirty seconds left," she reports, and Allison can just picture her looking at her watch.

"I'm going to be another couple of minutes. I just wanted to make sure you guys were all right."

"We are. Are you going to be one more minute, or two?"

"Two. At the most." *I hope.*

"Okay. Bye, Mommy. Don't worry about us. I have everything under control."

"I'm sure you do."

Hanging up, she flips on a light by the door. The overhead fixture floods the foyer with bright, harsh light.

"Phyllis?" she calls again, poking her head into the living room, dining room, kitchen, study, opening every window as she goes.

The house, a center hall Colonial, is laid out the same way as Allison's own, but on a much grander scale. She's been here plenty of times be —

Wait a minute.

The reason she's been here is to feed the Lewises' cat.

Every time she opens the door when they're away, Marnie comes running, purring and rubbing against her legs. She's an indoor cat — so where is she now?

And where is Phyllis?

"Phyllis!"

Silence.

"Marnie!"

Heart pounding, hand clammy on the polished wooden banister, Allison starts up the steps, calling for the cat, calling for Phyllis, trying not to think of Kristina Haines.

She's never seen the second floor of the Lewis house. She finds herself standing in a wide hall lined with doors — one of which is closed. Based on the layout of her own house, she assumes it's the master bedroom.

She stands staring at it for a moment. Then she takes a deep breath and forces her feet to carry her toward the door. In her mind's eye, she's in a tiny Manhattan apartment, walking toward another bedroom door . . .

But Kristina's door was open.

This is closed.

That was then.

This is now.

Allison's hand trembles as she reaches for the knob, turns it, pushes.

Whatever she's going to find on the other side of this door isn't going to be good. She can feel it, deep down inside. Phyllis is going to be there, in her bed. She knows it.

Maybe it was carbon monoxide, or a stroke, or a heart attack . . .

But it isn't good. She only hopes there's still time . . .

Please, God. Please . . .

But it's too late for prayers. Too late.

There, on the king-sized bed, is Phyllis Lewis.

Dead.

Allison knows that as surely as she knows that it wasn't carbon monoxide, a stroke, a heart attack . . .

It was the Nightwatcher.

Mack hears the sirens in the distance as he steps off the train at the Glenhaven Park Station, accompanied by Nathan Jennings and a few dozen other commuters.

He'd recognized his former colleague when he boarded back at Grand Central Terminal. Like his wife, Zoe, Nate's experienced a physical metamorphosis since the old agency days, having grown leaner, better-looking, and — if possible — taller. Or maybe weight loss and an expensive suit can just make it seem that way. His hair is still blond, still parted in a swoop across his forehead that, should his hair grow any thinner, will officially become a comb-over.

Mack quickly took a seat several rows away, though there were plenty of empty ones around Nate. He had far too much work to do on the train to risk getting caught up in small talk. He shouldn't have left the office as early as he did, but he still felt guilty about leaving Allison and the kids alone in a cold, dark house yesterday and then missing Halloween — rather, non-Halloween — last night. He'd worked straight through lunch today, not that skipping a meal is a bad thing, since he could stand to lose a few pounds, and anyway, Allison is making his favorite dinner.

Now, as Nate talks about the freak snowstorm and power outage, Mack makes all the right comments, but the sirens have carried him back in time.

Every time he hears that familiar wail, he still thinks of September 11 and Carrie. When he inhales, he swears he can smell the acrid industrial stench of burning jet fuel, and if he were to close his eyes, he knows he'd see a fireball exploding out of the south tower, just below his wife's office.

Of course, he didn't see it happen in person that day. He was in his own office uptown, going through the motions of his job and thinking that the worst had already happened that morning, when he told Carrie he was leaving.

"I'd love to meet your wife," Nathan is saying, and for a split second, Mack thinks he's talking about Carrie. His immediate instinct is to make up an excuse for her, because Carrie never wanted to meet anyone.

But then he remembers. It's not Carrie. Carrie is dead.

Nate is talking about Allison.

"Ben says she's a great girl."

Definitely Allison. No one ever said Carrie was a great girl.

Mack forces a nod and a smile. "She is great. I'm sure she and Zoe would like each other."

Yes, Allison likes just about everyone, and vice versa.

How can one man in one lifetime have loved two women who were so very different?

But then, it doesn't even feel like one lifetime. It's as though the old Mack died on September 11, and a new Mack was born.

No . . . it's not like that, either. It's more that the old Mack died when he married Carrie — and was reborn on September 11.

He feels guilty whenever he thinks of it that way — that he'd only come alive again after Carrie died. But she'd robbed him of so many things — so many people — he'd once held dear. She'd isolated him from his old life . . .

Come on. You were a grown man. You

isolated yourself. For her sake, yes — but that was a choice. You can't blame her for everything.

Maybe you can't blame her for anything.

Again, he remembers Ben and Randi's doubt about Carrie's extraordinary past. Again, he wonders if there's a way to find out the truth.

Again, he wonders why it matters now.

"We should get together," Nathan is telling him. "How about Friday night?"

"Friday . . . uh, Fridays, I'm usually pretty useless after the work week."

"Saturday, then. Hey, this snow is supposed to be gone by the end of the week. Do you golf?"

" '*Do* you golf' isn't exactly the right way to phrase that question," he says wryly. " '*Can* you golf' would be better."

Nathan grins a familiar grin. "Got it. *Can* you golf?"

"Yes, I *can.* Do I? No. Who has time with three kids, a house, a job . . ."

"I hear you, bro."

Mack isn't big on middle-aged men who call each other bro. It's like they're trying too hard to be young, hip, casual . . .

Having known Nathan when he was — when they were *both* — all of those things, and more, Mack is only reminded that the good old days are long over. It's depressing — and his low blood sugar and those sirens aren't helping matters.

"Listen, how about Saturday night, then?"

You just aren't going to let it die, are you.

"Come on over to the house. You and Allison. And I'll invite Ben and Randi, too. Are you free?"

"I think so, but I'd have to check about trying to get a sitter. It's usually hard for us to —"

"Bring the kids! They can play with ours. Caitlin is five and Harris is two. They'll love it."

Apparently, it's all settled.

Mack isn't sure how he feels about that. He always liked Nathan — and Zoe was a great girl — but bringing new friends into the mix isn't usually his department. Allison is the keeper of their social calendar, and he's just fine with that.

Oh well. She might be open to meeting a new mom, considering that the ones she's been hanging around with lately — in the neighborhood, at the girls' playdates, and at her book club — have been getting on her nerves. Not Randi, of course — but they don't see enough of each other anymore. Randi's kids are older; she lives across town, travels in different circles.

Things change.

Sometimes for the better, but sometimes . . .

Mack leaves Nathan with a promise to talk to Allison about Saturday night.

As he makes his way to his car, he can hear a chain saw nearby; a crew working to clear fallen limbs from a neighboring street. His polished black wingtips crunch through what's left of the weekend snow as he makes his way to his car; the musty scent of fallen leaves and sawdust mingling with wood smoke.

Unless it's raining or he's running late when he leaves in the morning, he always tries to park the BMW in the farthest corner of the commuter lot. He's found that he enjoys the stroll to and from his car — even that short time somehow adding to the buffer zone between the harried world of work and the comforting one of home.

Although home, lately, has been just as harried.

Three kids . . . he loves them dearly, but they can be overwhelming.

"Do you and Allison seriously want to be outnumbered?" he remembers Ben asking him when he mentioned, almost two years ago, that they were thinking of trying for a third child.

At the time, Mack laughed.

Then J.J. came along, and there are some days that Mack and Allison seem to be outnumbered by far more than just one baby.

Not, Mack thinks hastily — and a bit guiltily — as he unlocks the car, *that I'd have it any other way.*

He rolls down the window to let the chilly air waft inside as he drives toward home, past heaps of fallen branches and toppled utility poles, and a cluster of political signs that somehow withstood the tempest. Election Day is still a week away, but with snow still heaped along the curb and shovels propped beside doors, it looks more like the holiday season. Already, several old-fashioned storefronts along Glenhaven Avenue have exchanged their rustic harvest-themed window displays for tinsel and silk poinsettias.

Mack may not have welcomed the havoc wreaked by the early snowstorm, but he isn't one of those people who consider early November much too soon to start thinking about the holidays. He's always loved Christmas — but that's not why. In his mind, the holiday season marks the end of the period that began around Labor Day with a barrage of haunting reminders of losing Carrie on September 11, and his mother the October before that.

Tonight, there are sirens, and they grow louder as he draws close to home.

It's all right. Don't get yourself all worked up for no reason.

Maybe it's just a leaf fire caused by a downed live wire — though he can't smell anything burning now through the open window.

Well, if something were wrong at home, Allison would have called him.

But then, turning onto Orchard Terrace, he sees emergency vehicles, red lights flashing, parked in front of his house.

He hits the gas, full speed ahead until a cop steps out in front of him, waving his arms and shouting, "Slow down! What do you think you're —"

"That's my house!" Mack already has the car in park and is jumping out of the driver's seat when he spots his wife.

Allison is standing with a couple of uniformed cops on the sidewalk, over by the bushes that divide the property from the Lewises' house next door. She's crying — but not hysterically. Not the way she would be if something had happened to one of the kids — a thought so horrific Mack didn't allow it to fully form until now that he knows it's not true. It can't be. The children are Allison's whole world. She wouldn't be standing there talking, because her legs wouldn't be holding her up and she'd be incoherent if the worst had happened.

Yet — something is obviously wrong.

His mind flashes back to another day when he saw her flanked by police officers, and he rushes toward her.

"Allison?"

"Mack!" She turns away from the cops.

"What happened?"

"Phyllis Lewis. Oh my God, Mack — he killed her."

"What? Who? Who killed her?"

"Mrs. MacKenna," one of the policemen puts a firm hand on her arm. "You don't —"

"*He* did," Allison is focused only on Mack. "I knew it wasn't Jerry. I knew it all along. Jerry's dead, but *he* isn't. He came back, and he killed her."

"Mrs. MacKenna, please!"

"Allison." Mack takes her hand; it's cold, so cold. "You don't know —"

"Yes, I do," she cuts in. "I do know."

"How?"

Her next words slam into him like a runaway truck.

"Because she was wearing my nightgown."

266

CHAPTER NINE

"Come on, girls, let's go show Mommy and Daddy how well you packed all your things," Randi announces loudly from the top of the stairs, and Allison, sitting in the living room, knows she's sending down a warning: *You need to pull yourself together fast so your daughters don't see you crying.*

She quickly wipes her eyes and gets off the couch, making her way to the front hall just as Hudson and Madison descend. They each carry a backpack and a favorite doll, trailed by Randi, who's toting the monogrammed quilted Vera Bradley overnight bags she gave them one Christmas. Maddy's is a floral pastel print, Huddy's, a bright yellow paisley.

In the moment before they spot Allison, the girls appear worried and vulnerable. But when they catch sight of her waiting at the bottom of the stairs, they simultaneously paste on brave smiles that tug at her heart and make her want to cry all over again.

They're protecting me, she realizes. *They know I'm upset, and they don't want me to know that they are, too.*

She'd told her daughters only that Mrs. Lewis died. They were shocked and horrified, of course, and Hudson immediately wanted to know what had happened.

Allison's gut instinct was to shield the girls from the awfulness; she lied and said she wasn't sure.

"I think it probably would have been better to just tell them the truth," Mack said when he got home.

Nerves frazzled, she snapped something about his not having been here to decide how to handle it.

"I'm sorry," Mack snapped back, "I was at work."

"I'm sorry," Allison told him quickly, and sincerely. "I'm just upset."

Mack pulled her close and stroked her hair, telling her he couldn't bear to think about what she must have seen inside the Lewis house.

Allison can't bear to think of it, either, yet she hasn't been able to stop.

"We've got all our stuff," Hudson announces.

"And she means *all* their stuff." Good-natured Randi pretends to stagger under the weight of the bags, making the girls giggle and Allison smile with gratitude.

Thank goodness for Randi, who came immediately when Allison called to tell her what happened.

"I'll take the girls home with me to spend the night. No arguments," she'd said, though Allison wasn't about to argue. She wanted them out of here as soon as possible.

Randi would have taken J.J. with her, too, but Allison was afraid to let him go. It's not that Randi isn't an attentive mother, and it's not that she doesn't have her au pair right there to help, but . . .

No one can possibly understand what a handful her son can be. Allison would never forgive herself if something happened to J.J. because she let him out of her sight.

It's hard enough letting the girls leave — though of course she knows that they can't stay here; not with cops and reporters and ghoulish onlookers encamped just beyond the front door.

"Be good," she tells her daughters with a lump in her throat, pulling them close, one at a time, for a hug and a kiss. "And make sure you help Aunt Randi around the house."

"We're going to make cookies with Lexi," Madison says excitedly.

"She has a bake sale tomorrow at school," Hudson puts in. "Right, Aunt Randi? Because her school doesn't have laws against treats like ours does."

Both of Randi's kids go to private schools, where they're apparently not as vigilant about healthy snacks.

Was it only a couple of days ago that Allison was irritated about the baby carrots that were served at the Halloween party in Hudson's classroom? If only that were the biggest worry on her mind right now.

"Where's Daddy?" Madison asks her. "We have to say good-bye."

"In the kitchen. J.J. was fussing so he went to get him some milk."

"My brother fusses a lot," Hudson informs Randi, as if she didn't know.

"Mack!" Allison calls. "Come say good-bye. The girls are going."

He comes in carrying J.J., who is furiously sucking on a plastic sippy cup.

As the girls give hugs and kisses to their father and brother — who bonks Madison in the head with his sippy cup — Allison reminds Randi, in a low voice, that they don't know what happened next door. "If you can keep them from finding out . . ."

"Don't worry," Randi says, "I'll keep them busy and distracted. You and Mack come over with J.J. when you're finished here. You know we have plenty of room for all of you in the guest suite."

"I don't know . . . J.J. would need a crib, and —"

"Ben will run out and buy a portable one."

"That's crazy."

"You're crazy, Allison, if you think you're going to be able to sleep here after what happened. You're going to lie awake all night afraid he's going to come after you next."

Randi is probably right about that. But Allison doubts she'll be able to sleep anywhere after what happened.

What happened . . .

Phyllis . . .

No! Don't let yourself think about that right now! Not while you're with the girls!

"I think I'd better stick around here for now," she tells Randi. "The police said they're going to need to talk to me again." And she knows how that goes, having once before been a key witness in a murder investigation. "It could be tonight, or it could be tomorrow — I have no idea what's going to happen or when."

"Do you want me to send Ben over? I called him at work after you called me and

271

he left right away — he's on the train right now."

"No, that's all right. I'm sure you need him at home."

"I think you guys might need him more here."

"We're okay. Would you mind getting the girls to school tomorrow, though? They've missed two days this week with the closings, and —" Remembering, she says, "Mack can come get them and bring them to school. He'll be around."

Hearing his name, he looks over. "What's that?"

"You can pick up the girls from Randi's in the morning and drop them at school if I have to . . . be someplace else."

"What's tomorrow?"

"Tomorrow . . . ? I don't even know what today is. I can't think straight."

"Today is Tuesday," Randi tells them.

Allison and Mack exchange a startled glance. She knows he's thinking exactly what she is: that things really do seem to happen on Tuesdays.

September 11 . . .

And the freak earthquake that shook Manhattan . . .

They even got the news about Jerry Thompson's suicide on a Tuesday.

Jerry.

If Jerry is dead, then how . . . ?

Stop it, Allison. He's dead. You know it.

That's what Mack had told her earlier, when he first got home and she told him about the nightgown.

Yes, he's dead. She knows. But . . .

"I can't be here in the morning," Mack is saying now. "I have a meeting."

"You're going to *work*?"

"Daddy always goes to work on Wednesday, Mommy," Hudson reminds her.

"I know that, but I thought maybe Daddy would stay home tomorrow," she says pointedly.

"Because Mrs. Lewis died? Does that mean you get to stay home, Daddy?"

"No, it does not mean I get to stay home, Huddy."

Allison shoots him an incredulous look.

Seeing it, Randi quickly defuses the tension, saying, "Well, no matter what happens with that, there's no need for you to come and get the girls to school. I'll do it, and I'll pick them up, too, so that you have one less thing to worry about. We'll go out shopping and have ice cream. Maybe Lexi will come, too."

"Randi, you don't have to —"

The girls cut off Allison, thrilled about

the prospect of an afternoon with Aunt Randi and Lexi, their own personal teen idol.

"The thing is," Allison says, "you can only pick up Madison if you have our password to give the dismissal monitor. Otherwise, they won't let you take her."

Randi nods, familiar with the preschool's many security measures. Her kids went there, too, years ago.

Long gone are the days when a relative or friend can just pop in to pick up a student if the parents can't make it due to the occasional mishap or emergency. The password system is simple, but it prevents unauthorized people — sometimes even noncustodial parents — from taking a child. Each family has a secret phrase the pinch hitter must tell them so that the school, and the child, will know that the person can be trusted and that the change in plans came from the parent.

"So what's the password?"

"Cookie Monster," Allison tells Randi. It's been in place since the beginning of the year, but they've never had to use it yet.

"But where will you be, Mommy?" Maddy asks belatedly — and worriedly.

"Don't worry, sweetie, I might have to run some errands and then I'll meet you over at

Aunt Randi's. Okay?"

Having been listening to the details and looking as though she's poised to make a to-do list, Hudson asks briskly, "Now, what about me?"

Good question.

The elementary school doesn't have a password system. Every afternoon, the big yellow bus lets Hudson off just down the block from their house, and Allison meets her there.

Remembering the bus mishap she heard about at Randi's party a few weeks ago, Allison immediately decides it's best not to tamper with her daughter's daily routine.

"How about if you just take the bus back here like you do every day, Huddy? Like I said, I'll probably be here, too, but if I'm not, Aunt Randi will be waiting with Maddy. Is that okay, Aunt Randi?"

"Absolutely."

"But we still get to go shopping and for ice cream?"

"Absolutely," Randi assures again, and Hudson asks if J.J. will be able to come with them, too.

"Probably not," Allison says quickly, thinking there's no way she'd send Randi off with all three kids — plus Lexi, whose adolescent drama queen antics can be all-encompassing.

Though she wonders whether the police will be willing to talk to her if she's got a squirming baby on her lap . . .

But Mack actually seems to think he might be going to work, despite all that's happened here, so she may not have a choice.

"Come on, Rand," he says, handing off J.J. into Allison's waiting arms, "I'll walk you guys out to the car."

He takes the two overnight bags and herds everyone toward the back door after one last kiss and hug from Mommy. Randi parked on the driveway, which is, luckily, on the opposite side of the house from the Lewis home.

Left alone in the quiet house, Allison cuddles J.J. and kisses his fine baby hair. "It's going to be okay," she whispers, more to herself than to him.

Sitting at his wife's hospital bedside, Rocky stares at her face, watching for movement.

On Saturday, when Ange's sister Carm was sitting with her, she noticed Ange's eyelids twitching. She went for the nurse, who, much to Carm's frustration, wasn't sufficiently awed by the news that one of her patients had shown signs of an impending miracle.

Well, of course not. The staff is jaded, accustomed to dismissing the claims of hovering families ever on the lookout for the slightest movement, often seeing only what they want to see.

But when Carm convinced the nurse to come into the room to look for herself, Ange moved her fingers.

The nurse began to give her instructions: "Squeeze my hand," "Bend your thumb" . . .

Ange squeezed. Ange bent. Ange really was in there somewhere, listening.

Anything is possible.

Carm had tried to reach Rocky, but the snowstorm was interfering with his cell phone signal. By the time he got the message and rushed up to the trauma unit, Ange had retreated to the still, discouraging place again. Rocky stayed with her all that night, and all the next day, and has been here as much as he can since then — but there's been nothing. Not on his watch, anyway.

The staff played down the episode Carm had witnessed, presumably to avoid giving anyone false hope.

As far as Rocky's concerned, there's no such thing. Hope is hope. As long as Ange is alive, there's a chance she'll come back to him.

Ironically, she stirred again last night, while the night nurse was in the room and Rocky was home trying to catch a few hours' sleep. Again, Ange was able to follow simple commands.

Dr. Abrams admitted that it was a good sign; that she really might be starting to come out of it.

"Should I tell my sons to come home?" Rocky was scarcely able to contain his excitement. "One lives in Texas, and the other two are on the West Coast."

"It's not as if she's going to sit up any minute now and start talking, Mr. Manzillo," Dr. Abrams told him gently. "The process — *if* that is, indeed, where we're headed — is likely to take days, weeks, even. In the best-case scenario, there would be a very long road ahead. I wouldn't disrupt your sons' lives just yet."

That was probably sound advice, though Rocky didn't necessarily welcome it, or the cautionary tone.

In the past forty-eight hours, he's gone from imagining Ange's funeral to imagining her homecoming, and he's not willing to take a step backward.

Still, the painstaking waiting game is hard

enough for Rocky, both emotionally and logistically. Ange wouldn't want him to inflict it on their sons, who have families and jobs and lives of their own that need tending.

The boys check in daily, all three of them, leaving messages on his cell phone, which is, of course, turned off most of the time, per hospital regulations. When he returned their calls last night, he told them that the doctors were more optimistic every day, but didn't give them the details.

A nurse bustles into the room, pushing a cart. "How are you tonight, Mr. Manzillo?"

"I'm fine, Judy."

"That's good."

They have the same inane exchange every evening, and Rocky suspects it's repeated in rooms up and down the corridor.

None of the family members in the trauma unit are fine. But the nurses do their best to make things — well, if not pleasant, at least they try to diminish the *unpleasantness* of the situation wherever they can.

"I need to suction her, Mr. Manzillo," Judy tells him. "Do you want to step out for a little bit?"

He's on his feet before she finishes talking. As a homicide cop, he's never been all that squeamish, but when it involves a medical procedure being performed on his wife . . .

"I'll be back, sweetheart." He presses a kiss to Ange's pale, wrinkled forehead and leaves the room.

Walking down the hall, he passes rooms identical to hers, where families of other comatose patients keep the familiar, joyless vigil. Rocky knows that, according to statistics, the majority of their loved ones will never wake up. But in his heart, he truly believes that his wife is going to.

She has to, because I can't live without her. It's that simple.

He rides the elevator to the ground floor and stops in the chapel to light a candle — a daily ritual, both here and at his home parish, Our Lady of Mount Carmel.

After a quick prayer he continues on, passing the cafeteria. Ordinarily, his stomach turns at the cooking smells evocative of steam tables bearing overcooked meat, limp cabbage, mushy grains. But right now, he finds his mouth watering.

Checking his watch, he notes that it's past midnight. When was the last time he ate something? Lunch? Breakfast? Last night?

You can't go around skipping meals, Rocco, Ange's voice scolds him as she has so many times in the past. *You get low blood sugar,*

280

and it makes you cranky.

Okay. Maybe he'll come back and grab a sandwich before he goes upstairs again. But right now, he needs to call his sons. It's getting late, even on the West Coast.

He steps out the nearest exit.

The night air is cold, and there are still piles of snow. He wishes he'd thought to grab his coat. Ange would have reminded him to.

He's spent a lot of time in hospitals over the years, courtesy of his job with the homicide squad — questioning witnesses, interviewing families of victims. Until recently, the area just beyond the exits would be crowded with hospital employees — including nurses and doctors in scrubs — gathered here under the awning on a smoke break.

Rocky always found it ironic that so many in the health care profession — people who regularly see the ravages wrought by the unhealthy habit — seem to puff away on cigarettes without a care in the world.

Then again, a certain degree of compartmentalization is necessary when you greet harsh reality on a daily basis. He should know.

Anyway, a recent law has banned smoking on hospital grounds. Now the smokers are huddled across the street in the doorway of an office building that's deserted at this hour of the night. The only people hanging around the exit are the ones talking on their cell phones.

Rocky pulls his own out of his pocket, powers it up, and is surprised to see that he's missed quite a few calls. Three, of course, are from his sons — but there's one from his lifelong friend Vic Shattuck, a former FBI profiler.

It's unusual for Vic to be calling again so soon — Rocky spoke to him earlier today, updating him on Ange's condition.

There are a couple of calls from the precinct, too, that came in both before and after Vic's.

Something must have happened.

Rather than waste time listening to voice mail messages, Rocky immediately dials the desk sergeant.

"Tommy, what's going on?"

"Where are you, Manzillo? We been trying to track you down for a couple of hours now."

"I'm at the hospital, where do you think? What's going on?" he asks again.

"Hang on. I'm going to put you through to Murph."

Rocky's longtime partner, T.J. Murphy,

picks up right away.

"Rock, remember that case you worked about ten years ago? The Nightwatcher murders?"

"*About* ten years ago? It was almost *exactly* ten years ago. The perp killed himself in prison on the ten-year anniversary a couple of weeks ago. What about it?"

"It looks like you might be wrong about that, Rock."

Blame it on low blood sugar; he can't help but snap, "I'm not wrong about it, Murph. Those murders were ten years ago — the first one was on September 12. That's why you weren't on the case with me. You were . . ."

He doesn't need to say it. Murph knows exactly where he was on September 12, 2001. He was down on the pile, digging in vain for his kid brother, Luke, one of the hundreds of FDNY guys crushed beneath the rubble of the World Trade Center.

"No," Murph says, "you're not wrong about *that.* I mean about the perp being dead."

"For the love of . . ." Rocky mutters under his breath, and rolls his eyes skyward, trying not to lose his temper. "Murph, I'm telling you, Jerry Thompson killed himself back in —"

"I know what Jerry Thompson did. But it looks like you might'a had the wrong guy."

"What are you talking about? Thompson confessed. There was a shitload of evidence. We found him with the weapon, bloodstains everywhere — and with his mother's dead body, too — right there in his apartment. We had a witness who placed him at the —"

"Yeah, about that witness —"

"Don't tell me we had the wrong guy," Rocky rants on, pacing to the end of the walkway and back to the door again.

"Okay, I won't tell you. But everyone else will, Rock, because he's at it again."

Rocky stops short. "Who?"

"The Nightwatcher. Up in Westchester County. We got a new murder, same MO, same signature — stuff we never released to the public, Rock. Stuff no one else knew because the D.A. didn't introduce it at the trial. And the finger —"

"Jesus." Rocky knows exactly what he means.

The Nightwatcher had ritualistically hacked off his victims' middle fingers, taking them as trophies. Sick bastard. The fingers were found in Jerry Thompson's apartment, along with the other evidence.

That detail was deliberately kept from the

press . . . along with another very important detail that never came out at the trial:

"And you know the song?"

The song. Rocky knows the song.

"Fallin'," by Alicia Keys. The soulful ballad was on top of the charts around the time Kristina Haines and Marianne Apostolos were murdered, and clearly had some meaning for their killer.

"Was it playing at the scene?" Rocky asks Murph.

"Looped to play over and over, just like ten years ago. And you know that witness whose testimony put Jerry Thompson away?"

"Allison Taylor?"

"Allison . . . Taylor MacKenna. Yeah. Her. She's the one who found the body."

"Kristina Haines's body, right. She was the first victim. They were neigh—"

"Nah, Rock, would you just listen? This murder happened on the heels of a natural disaster. Westchester's been devastated by that snowstorm. Power is down, communications are down, businesses are closed, people are all shook up, isolated in their homes . . ."

"Just like Manhattan after September 11."

"But wait, there's more," Murph says in his best infomercial host imitation. "You ready for this?"

"Just tell me, Murph."

"She found this one, too. Allison Mac-Kenna found the woman who was killed last night. They were neighbors, just like before."

Rocky curses under his breath.

"That's one hell of a coincidence, don't you think?" Murph asks.

Yeah. One hell of a coincidence.

Anything is possible . . .

"The way I see it, Rock, either Thompson has come back from the dead . . ."

Okay, almost *anything is possible. Not that.*

". . . or," Murph goes on, "the wrong guy confessed."

That . . .

That's . . .

Possible.

Ten years ago, Rocky honestly didn't think so. Nor did the jury.

In hindsight — remembering the blank, terrified expression in Jerry Thompson's eyes — he's suddenly not so sure.

But you don't get as far as Rocky has in the ranks of the NYPD by second-guessing yourself. There could be something else going on here, and that's his job — to be thorough and consider every remotely possible explanation.

"I'm heading up there now," Murph tells him.

"Pick me up at home on your way," Rocky says grimly. "I'll be there in fifteen minutes. Make that twenty. I just need to go back up and tell Ange I have to leave for a while."

"Tell Ange . . . ? How is she, Rock? Any change?"

"For the better, Murph. Only for the better."

It isn't until after he disconnects the call that Rocky uneasily remembers the broken window in his own basement. It's not something that's weighed heavily on his mind amid all that's gone on with Ange.

But ordinarily, he probably wouldn't have dismissed it so readily after a search showed nothing out of order.

Someone was in the house while he was away. Someone who took nothing away, and left nothing behind.

Or so Rocky assumed — perhaps too quickly.

"Here. Drink this."

Allison looks up to see Mack standing beside the couch holding a steaming mug. "What is it?"

"Tea. Herbal. It'll help you sleep."

"I don't want to sleep," she says automatically, but she accepts the mug from him.

"Ever?" He sits beside her. "Al, you have to get some rest. J.J.'s going to be up in a few hours."

She shakes her head. There's no way she's going to close her eyes for even a few seconds; knowing that the minute she closes them, she's going to see again the horrific scene she stumbled upon next door.

Phyllis Lewis lay on her side, just like Kristina. She, too, was wearing lingerie, a champagne-colored silk, lace-trimmed nightgown Allison recognized immediately, though it was heavily smeared with brownish stains; blood.

In those few stunned moments before she fled, Allison noticed a couple of other things: the dead cat, eviscerated, on the floor beside the bed, and the dozens of white candles around the room. They were mostly votives that had long since burned out, but a few were pillars that flickered still.

The scene in Kristina's apartment ten years ago had been exactly the same — not the cat, but the candles around the bed, almost as though her body lay on a sacrificial altar.

He's back.

She abruptly sets the tea aside. It sloshes over the rim of the mug and puddles on the wooden coffee table. She ignores it.

Now that she's had the time to process what happened — what she saw — there's no denying that the Nightwatcher has resurfaced. And if Jerry Thompson is dead . . .

He's dead. You know it.

Okay. He's dead.

That means she was wrong about him being the Night-watcher. And that means . . .

"We have to take the kids and get out of here, Mack."

She doesn't like the look on his face — the same expression he wore earlier, when she assumed he'd be staying home from the office tomorrow.

"Go . . . where?"

"I don't care. Anyplace where he won't find us."

"We can't just *go,* Allison."

"Because you have to work? Is that why?"

"That's one of the reasons, yes," he says evenly. "And there are cops right outside the front door. We're safe here. For now."

"You really believe that?"

He doesn't answer, just leans forward, plucks a couple of tissues from the box on the coffee table, and wipes up the spilled tea.

He brought her the box of tissues earlier,

when she couldn't stop crying about poor Phyllis.

She hadn't allowed the floodgates to open until after the girls had left with Randi. Neither she nor Mack wanted to upset them further.

Nor did she cry in front of Ben, who showed up about a half hour later, having bolted from a business dinner to get to them.

He sat with Mack and J.J. in the kitchen while Allison told yet another detective every detail that might be relevant concerning Phyllis Lewis, and the silk nightgown, and of course, the case ten years ago.

"You told your husband that you knew all along Jerry Thompson wasn't guilty?" the detective asked, apparently having been briefed by the officers who'd been standing with her when Mack arrived. "You testified under oath that you'd seen him at the scene. Are you contradicting yourself now?"

"No!" she said quickly. "He *was* at the scene. And he confessed to the murders. But before that, my gut instinct was that he couldn't be guilty."

And of course, in the end, logic overruled instinct.

She thinks back to the trial; to what she learned about Jerry Thompson's life leading up to his arrest. Raised in poverty by a single mother, abandoned by his deadbeat father, he had a couple of strikes against him right from the start.

Just like I did.

Even as she testified against him, somewhere in the back of her mind Allison found herself feeling sorry for Jerry Thompson. She knew where he came from because she'd been there herself.

Allison buries her face in her hands. She feels Mack's arms around her; hears him murmuring comforting words, but all she can think is *Good Lord, what have I done?*

Her testimony helped to seal Jerry Thompson's fate. She sent an innocent man to prison. Is it any wonder he killed himself?

And now . . .

Now the real killer has been lured from the shadows. He's been inside this house, this haven where her sweet children play and sleep. He claimed his next victim right here, right under Allison's nose, and the message is clear.

Watch your step . . . you might be next.

"Yes!" Jamie hisses gleefully, focused on the screen, where Allison sits with her head in her hands, now fully aware that her days are numbered.

Ah, but not in the way she thinks.

What I'm going to do to her is going to be so much more satisfying than what I did to Phyllis Lewis and Cora Nowak.

Those women didn't go easily, not by any means. They suffered good and long and hard. That came to an end, as all good things must.

Allison will be different.

Her suffering will have no end — not in this lifetime. She's going to be tortured for as long as she lives — preferably, to a ripe old age. She's going to wake up every morning for the rest of her life to find herself all alone in an empty house full of memories.

Ah, but she'll never truly be alone. I'll always be there, watching her. Someday, maybe, I'll take it upon myself to end her suffering, but until then . . .

Allison, who has so deftly made fresh starts twice in this lifetime — the first when she moved to New York, the second when she married Mack — has run out of chances to start over. Even the most resilient human being wouldn't recover from what's going to happen to Allison — what Jamie is going to do to her, what Jamie is going to take from her.

On the computer screen, Mack has his arms around his wife, comforting her.

Aw . . . aren't they just so sweet together, the two lovebirds. He's saying something into her hair, but his voice is too muffled to make out. He's probably telling her that he's there to protect her.

You just go ahead and keep saying that, Mack. I can't wait to see the look on her face when she finds out what kind of man she really married.

CHAPTER TEN

Mack closes the bedroom door and then, after a minute, locks it.

Just in case.

It's three in the morning, but Allison is still downstairs, despite his repeated attempts to get her to go to bed. He didn't really want to leave her there, but he needs a few minutes alone, and he'd better not count on waiting until she's asleep. That's probably not going to happen tonight.

He goes back to the bed, picks up his briefcase, and opens it. For a long time, he stares at the object he'd stashed inside earlier, between layers of papers he'd brought home from the office.

What the hell am I doing with a gun?

He knows how to shoot, but it's been a while. Years. As a kid, he went hunting with his uncle; as an adult, he did some target shooting with Ben, who wanted to learn how to use a gun after someone broke into his and Randi's apartment. Randi never knew about it, though. Still doesn't.

"She'd freak if she thought I had a gun in the house with the kids around," Ben told Mack, who admitted that he didn't think it was such a good idea himself.

"I keep it locked up," Ben assured him. "But it's good to know it's there, just in case."

That seemed to make more sense back when the Webers lived in the city than it does here in the suburbs — at least, until tonight.

"Whatever you do," Ben whispered, slipping the gun to Mack in the kitchen, "don't tell Allison where it came from. She'll tell Randi, and I'll never hear the end of it."

"Are you kidding? I'm not even going to tell her I have it. I'm not even sure I should take it."

"You should," Ben told him. "Like I said, it's here just in case you need it."

He thanked Ben and tucked the gun into his briefcase before Allison rejoined them in the kitchen.

Now, he gingerly takes the weapon from his briefcase and checks to make sure it's loaded. Yep. Ready to go, just as Ben promised.

Lending the gun was entirely Ben's idea,

and he'd reminded a reluctant Mack, "You always were a better shot than I am."

True. His uncle taught him well, as did the shooting range instructors. But clay pigeons — and even live ducks — are different from human beings. Mack isn't sure he's even capable of aiming at another person and pulling the trigger, and he said as much to Ben.

"What if your wife or your kids were in danger? Could you shoot someone to save their lives?"

Mack nodded grimly.

If it comes down to that — *please, God, don't ever let it come down to that* — he'll do whatever is necessary to protect his family.

He wraps the gun in a T-shirt and opens the middle drawer of his dresser — the only drawer that locks. When they bought the furniture, Allison had teased him that it would be the perfect place to stash his porn.

"What am I, thirteen years old?" He remembers laughing and shaking his head at the suggestion.

Now, he fishes the tiny, never-used key from the bottom of the drawer, tucks the bundle way in the back, closes it, locks it, and stuffs the key into his wallet.

That'll do for now. Chances are, Allison won't be putting away any laundry any time soon, and he'll find a better hiding place before she does.

Shaken, Mack unlocks the bedroom door, then looks longingly at the bed. All he wants right now is to escape this nightmare for a little while. He goes into the bathroom, takes a pill from the orange bottle, and swallows it quickly.

As soon as he does, he regrets it.

Is it really a good idea to knock himself out right now, leaving Allison to fend for herself should anything happen?

What's going to happen?

There are cops right outside, and it's almost dawn, and anyway, whoever killed Phyllis Lewis has to be long gone by now.

Still, Mack is unsettled as he climbs beneath the covers. He'll just rest, he decides. Just for a few minutes. Then he'll get up and go back downstairs to sit with Allison until the sun comes up, and then he'll figure out how the hell he's going to convince her that he really does have to go to work.

Riding up the Saw Mill River Parkway to visit the murder scene, Rocky has all but forgotten, for the time being, that he left his wife in an ICU trauma unit about an hour ago.

Right now, with Murph at the wheel and a cup of gas station coffee in his hand, he's living in the moment — something he hasn't truly done since Ange's fall.

He and Murph have been riding around together forever, it seems, expertly investigating horrific crimes, just as expertly breaking each other's chops. This is familiar territory for him.

The only thing that's changed over the decades — besides the potbellies that have sprouted on both of them — is that Murph's flame-colored hair has a smoky touch of gray in it these days, courtesy, he says, of having been married and divorced a second time, while Rocky wears a pair of reading glasses perched on the end of his nose whenever he takes notes.

Now, juggling the coffee with a pencil, he scribbles down everything Murph can tell him about the case so far, referring back to the old case files he pulled before he left, to refresh his memory.

His cell phone rings, and he sees a familiar number on the screen.

"It's Vic," he tells Murph, who nods. He, of course, knows Vic Shattuck; knows, too, that Vic had tried to reach Rocky earlier.

Murph and Rocky speculated that Vic was calling because the FBI had also been alerted about the apparent reemergence of the Nightwatcher. Though he took his mandatory retirement a few years back, Vic still has a way of getting wind of these things.

"Vic," Rocky says into the phone.

"Hi, Rock. I got your message."

Rocky had tried calling Vic back earlier, on his way home from the hospital, but it went right into voice mail.

"I just got off a plane," Vic tells him now.

"On the road again, huh?"

"Story of my life. Not complaining, though."

Vic's been doing some consulting and also travels the lecture circuit, promoting the book he wrote about the biggest case of his life: the Night Watchman. After disappearing for many years, the Night Watchman resurfaced a while back using the same signature.

Night Watchman, Nightwatcher . . .

The press reserves catchy nicknames for the most lethal serial killers.

Vic's book was open-ended; presumably, the Night Watchman is still out there somewhere.

The Nightwatcher, on the other hand, was presumed to be in custody — and then dead.

But now — who knows?

"I heard what happened," Vic tells him. "Looks like we might have picked up the wrong guy back in '01."

"Yeah, well, I'm not jumping to conclusions."

"I'm not, either, but . . . Listen, I know how you are. Don't beat yourself up over it if it was a mistake, Rock. It happens to the best of us."

"Tell me what you know that I don't. About the case, I mean. Not about me." Rocky never particularly appreciates it when Vic aims those well-honed psychoanalyst skills in his direction.

"Come on, Manzillo, yours is the most fascinating mind I've ever had the pleasure of analyzing."

Hearing the grin in his voice, Rocky replies, "I'll take that as a compliment. Listen, Vic, Murph's right here with me and we're in the car heading up to Glenhaven Park. Can I put you on speakerphone?"

"Go ahead."

Rocky presses the speaker button. "You're on."

"Hey, Vic," Murph says. "What'cha got for us?"

"Hey, Murph. This is unofficial and off the record, right?"

"Right," Murph says.

"So they tell me the signature looks exactly the same as the Nightwatcher's. I'm assuming you guys know that, right?"

Both Murph and Rocky confirm the assumption, and neither asks who "they" are.

"And you know that in a case like this, the MO is going to evolve — practice makes perfect — but the signature isn't likely to change."

"So I've heard," Rocky says dryly.

As Vic has told Rocky many times over the years — and memorably wrote in his best-selling book — the offender is always going to be playing out some kind of twisted fantasy, and there are certain key elements he needs in order to complete the crime.

"There's only one way to rule out a copycat and establish whether the same person committed this murder and the ones ten years ago."

"By studying the behavioral patterns." Rocky nods.

"Looks like we've established that they're the same. We've got the disaster — the freak snowstorm — that could have set him off. We've got the stolen lingerie," Murph points out, "and the Alicia Keys song, the candles, the severed middle finger . . ."

Yes. Phyllis Lewis's death certainly appears to have the same signature as the Nightwatcher murders, but . . .

"I don't know." Rocky shakes his head. "I'm just not convinced."

"Because . . . ?" Murph looks over at him.

"Because it's too soon. We don't have all the information. We haven't gotten a look at the scene. And . . ."

And maybe I just can't stand to even consider that I might have arrested the wrong damned guy ten years ago.

Before Jerry Thompson confessed — oh hell, even *after* he confessed — he blamed the murders on someone named Jamie. Rocky later learned that was the name of his dead sister.

"People don't come back from the dead, Rock. You know that, right?" Vic is talking about Jerry, not his sister, Jamie.

Either way — yeah. Rocky knows that.

"If Jerry didn't kill those women," he says, frustrated, "then who did?"

"Good question," Vic says. "Wish I could be there to work this case with you guys."

"So do I," Murph tells Vic, as Rocky stares at a distant set of red taillights on the winding road ahead, thinking back.

Forget about the murder weapon and the severed fingers of his victims, all found in his apartment. What logical explanation could there be for the wig, the makeup, and the bloody dress that were also there? Forensics determined that strands of long hair found clenched in Marianne Apostolos's fingers had come from that wig. The dress was a size fourteen — larger than the average woman; maybe barely large enough to fit stocky Jerry . . . but nowhere near large enough to fit his obese mother.

So it wasn't hers . . .

If it wasn't *Jerry's* . . .

Whose was it?

"Rock? You still there?" Vic asks.

"Yeah. I'm just trying to figure out what I possibly could have missed ten years ago. It's not like I haven't been doing this job forever, and I sure as hell don't go jumping to conclusions, or rely on circumstantial evidence . . ."

"You're as seasoned as they come, Rock. But look at the timing — you got this case a few hours after a terror attack that killed dozens of guys you knew; thousands of citizens you were sworn to protect."

"That doesn't mean I —"

"No, it doesn't," Vic cuts him off, "but you're only human. If there was ever any time in your career that you might not have been on top of your game; any time when you'd have been prone to slip up . . . that was it. For all of us."

Rocky mulls that over, remembering those shell-shocked days after September 11. The city was in ruins; the force was short-staffed; every available officer was down there on the pile, digging for survivors, digging for corpses with familiar faces, brothers, sons, sisters, colleagues, friends . . .

Did he ever truly consider, on that long ago night in Jerry Thompson's apartment, that someone else might have been involved?

Or did he take one look into Jerry's vacant face, recognize that Jerry wasn't all there, and perhaps subconsciously dismiss his trying to cast the blame elsewhere as desperate babble?

I'm a good detective. That's not how I operate.

Anyway, even Jerry's own attorney never introduced the possibility of another actual suspect, and besides . . .

"Look, the person Jerry blamed had been dead for years, Rock."

Yeah. The sister, Jamie.

How many times had he gone back and looked into the old case file just to be sure?

Too damned many. Seeing autopsy photographs of a child's bloody corpse is never easy.

Tragic end to a tragic story. She was just a kid.

A kid who beat her brother's brains out, Rocky reminds himself yet again.

But a kid who never had a chance.

At sixteen, Jerry and Jamie's mother, Lenore, had gotten herself knocked up by a fourteen-year-old juvenile delinquent named Samuel Shields. Aside from the birth certificate, there's no evidence that the father ever had anything to do with the twins — although a lone photograph discovered among Lenore Thompson's belongings might suggest otherwise.

It's a shot of Jerry and Jamie posing with a man who bears a strong resemblance to Jerry. It might have been taken not long before Jamie died, judging by her apparent age in the photo.

When shown the photograph just after he was taken into custody, Jerry shook his head and said that he had no idea who the man was. Maybe he was lying, or maybe he'd forgotten, thanks to the head injury he'd later suffered.

"Jamie Thompson is dead," Vic is reminding him, over the speakerphone.

"Yeah. I know that."

How many times had Rocky read through the reports to confirm there was no doubt about the identity of that corpse? There was none. After being stabbed in an apparent random mugging, Jamie had been a Jane Doe until forensics matched dental records and DNA samples supplied by her mother, Lenore.

DNA doesn't lie.

"Jerry Thompson is dead, too," he points out. "So where does that leave things now?"

"Someone else killed Phyllis Lewis," Murph says. "That's where it leaves things."

"Right. Someone who knew exactly how Kristina Haines died and wanted Allison Taylor MacKenna to find this body, just like she found Kristina's, or . . ."

"Or what?" Vic prompts as Rocky trails off, and Murph glances over at him, wearing an expectant expression.

Ever since he heard about that particular detail — Allison finding the body — an idea has been teasing at the edge of Rocky's mind.

"Let's say Jerry Thompson really did kill those women ten years ago," he says. "Who else would have known the exact details about the MO, the signature, the trophies . . . the stuff that the public didn't know?"

"You and whoever worked the case," Murph tells him. "The CSU guys, the

M.E. . . ."

"And Allison Taylor," Vic muses. "That what you're thinking?"

"That's exactly what I'm thinking."

Murph raises a bushy eyebrow but says nothing, looking through the windshield at a green exit sign up ahead.

"She's Allison MacKenna now; she got married." Rocky tells Vic. "So, yeah, she was at the scene of the Haines murder, found the body, called 911, and —"

"And you ruled her out as a suspect ten years ago."

"I know I did." Rocky had interviewed Allison, both at the scene and at the precinct, and had been satisfied enough to dismiss her. But now, looking back, he remembers something else he'd considered at the time.

"Theoretically, the Nightwatcher could have been a woman," he muses aloud.

"Female serial killers are rare," Vic points out now, just as he had ten years ago. "Most are white males between the ages of twenty and forty. And when women are involved, they're rarely as violent and sadistic as the Nightwatcher is — unless they're part of a killing team."

"Which is possible," Murph puts in, checking the rear-view mirror before merging into the right lane.

"Right. Anyway, I was leaning in that direction before we found Thompson — not a killing team, but a female killer — based on the long hair in Marianne Apostolos's hand —"

"It came from Thompson's wig," Vic reminds him.

"No, I know, but it wasn't just that."

"I remember. There was no rape."

"Exactly," Rocky says, "and that was unusual, because the motive was supposed to be sexual, and the scenes were staged to look romantic and sexy with the candles and the lingerie, but . . . it didn't add up at the time."

"It doesn't add up now that Jerry Thompson's dead, either," Murph mutters.

"But if we go back to considering Allison a suspect in the first murders," Rocky muses, "how do we connect her to the bloody dress? It wasn't anywhere near her size, for one thing."

He remembers her well — a tall, slender blonde who couldn't have been more than a size two back then. The dress was a size fourteen.

"I'd say that a copycat crime is a strong possibility," Vic concludes.

Possibility.

Not probability.

The probability is that Rocky missed something ten years ago and the real Nightwatcher slipped through his fingers.

"Let's just see what we can find out," Murph says, flicking on the turn signal and steering into the right lane, "because this is the exit."

Sitting on the couch with her laptop open on her knees, Allison stares at yet another decade-old deer-in-headlights photo of a handcuffed Jerry Thompson.

Fury bubbles within her.

She's angry with herself, of course, for not paying more attention to her instinct that he wasn't capable of committing Kristina's brutal murder — but she's angry with Jerry, too.

Why the hell did you confess to a crime you didn't commit?

Why did you let them — let me *— put you away for the rest of your life for a crime you didn't commit?*

Why the hell didn't you speak up in all these years you spent in prison?

She closes the laptop and rubs her raw eyes.

At around three, Mack decided to go upstairs and get some rest. He wanted her to come, too, but she wasn't the least bit tired.

Still isn't.

She has too much adrenaline — too much anger — rushing through her blood. Too many thoughts and questions careening through her head.

Why the hell am I angry with Jerry? He was as much a victim in all this as the dead women were . . .

But this — Phyllis Lewis — *this* didn't have to happen.

For ten years, the Nightwatcher was out there still, watching, waiting to strike again when everyone — when *Allison* — believed he was safely in prison. Or dead.

Phyllis was slaughtered because of that.

Because of me.

He struck as close to home — *Allison's home* — as he could.

There's no doubt in her mind that he'll return.

Not tonight. There are detectives everywhere, keeping surveillance. But they can't stay here forever.

Neither can we.

He was here, in this house. How did he get in? Through a screened window, back when the weather was warmer? It would have been so easy . . .

Easy, too, to temporarily steal a set of house keys and duplicate them, along with the keys to the Lewis home. It sickens Allison to think that they were sitting right on top in the desk drawer, in a clearly labeled envelope.

"It's never going to happen again, because we're not going to rely on keys and locks anymore," Mack informed her. "We're getting an alarm system, one with a code and a monitoring service."

The thought brings little comfort.

Things can never be the same here now.

We're going to have to —

The thought is curtailed by the distinct sound of footsteps; a sound that knocks the breath out of Allison like a sucker punch. It takes a moment for her to realize that it's coming from the second floor, where Mack and J.J. are.

Wild thoughts run through her head.

What if the Nightwatcher managed to evade the police surveillance team and climb in a second floor window?

What if he was hiding up there all along?

What if —

The stairs creak and she turns her head slowly to look through the archway into the hall, holding her breath as the footsteps descend.

311

Is it Mack?

Or is it *him?*

He moves steadily, not necessarily stealthily; he's not trying to sneak up on her. But that means little; he's proven himself to be a brazen son of a bitch, and —

A pair of legs come into view between the spindles on the stairway, and she exhales audibly, recognizing Mack's gray sweatpants.

"You just scared me to death," she calls to him.

He doesn't reply, just continues his methodical journey down the stairs.

"Mack?" Getting off the couch, moving toward the hall, she gets a better look at her husband and realizes that something is off. He's looking straight ahead, eyes wide open, and it's as if . . .

The lights are on, but nobody's home.

It's the same long-ago thought she had about Jerry Thompson, and her stomach gives a sickening little lurch.

"Mack!"

He turns toward her, looks at her — but no, not *at* her. Through her, with an unnerving stare.

Her first instinct is to go over and shake him, but then she remembers what Lynn told her. Their childhood pediatrician had said a sleepwalker who's forcibly awakened might become violent.

Allison steps back out of the way as he passes her, moving toward the kitchen. After a moment, she follows him, shaken.

He doesn't seem to know she's there, and she watches him wander around the kitchen. He opens the refrigerator, stands for a moment in front of it, and closes the door. He picks up a green apple from the full basket on the counter, puts it back. Picks up a red one, puts it back. He opens the shallow spice cupboard, closes it, turns and moves to a new row of cabinets, opens one, and stares at the stacks of plates and bowls.

"The lion is bleeding," he announces, or maybe it's "The line is reading" — as if that makes any more sense.

He closes the cupboard, stands for a moment, and then — with sudden, frenzied purpose — opens a drawer and begins to hunt through it, muttering to himself.

Chills skitter down Allison's spine as she watches. It's as though her husband — familiar, comfortable, solid Mack — has had his very soul vacuumed out of his body, replaced by this . . . this . . . robotic alien being.

All at once, he seizes something and removes it from the drawer with a flourish.

His back is to Allison; she can't see what it is.

He closes the drawer, turns, and her racing pulse skids to a halt.

Her husband is holding the new chef's knife, the one she bought to replace the red-handled one that vanished.

For a moment, Allison stands frozen.

Then she hears herself shout out, "Mack!" and finds herself moving forward, toward him, toward the knife.

As she goes, she knows that she's doing precisely the wrong thing, but she can't help it. If she doesn't stop him, he's going to hurt himself, or —

"Mack, wake up!" She grabs him by the shoulder and shakes him. "Put that down! Mack!"

Dazed, he looks at her — *through* her — wrenches himself away, and strides across the kitchen, still holding the knife.

"Mack, no!"

Abruptly, he drops it, or maybe tosses it, and it slides across the tile, the blade's point facing her like an arrow. That part is happenstance — Mack would never hurt her, ever, and it's too far away and lacks the velocity to reach her . . .

And yet, seeing it coming, she gasps in horror.

A sound reaches her ears — J.J. crying, upstairs. Her scream must have woken him, she thinks, and then she remembers that it's five-thirty in the morning and this is what time he usually gets up.

Mack keeps walking, already in the hall, going for the stairs — not, however, with any sense of purpose. His feet are shuffling along and he doesn't seem to hear Allison behind him or the baby's wails above.

She darts around him as he puts his foot on the first step. Fierce maternal instinct sends her quickly up the flight and into the baby's room. J.J. is standing in his crib, both hands on the railing, crying his eyes out — just as he is every morning of his life.

The moment he sees Allison, though, he breaks into a big, wet smile, arching his little arms toward her.

She plucks him from the crib, holds him hard against her pounding heart, and looks toward the doorway, half expecting to see Mack there.

He's not.

She can hear him at the top of the stairs, and walking down the hall, and then she hears the master bedroom door close after him.

J.J. strains in her arms and makes a frustrated grunting sound, as if to say, *Why are we just standing around? Let's get moving!*

Allison shifts him to her hip and walks with him, past the girls' open bedroom doors — an unsettling reminder that they aren't here this morning, and of the reason for that.

She passes the closed master bedroom door, reaches the top of the stairs, and then backtracks.

At the door, she hesitates, wondering what she's going to find on the other side. Flashing back to last night — outside Phyllis Lewis's bedroom door — she hastily retreats again.

This time, she goes down the stairs as J.J. babbles, happy to have the action — any action.

In the kitchen, Allison sees the knife still lying on the floor. She picks it up, tosses it into the sink, and sets J.J. into his high chair. With trembling hands, she fumbles at the straps, finally managing to get him secured as he squirms unhappily.

"Stop, J.J.!" she says sharply, and immediately regrets it when his little face contorts with an unhappy howl.

"Shh, baby, it's okay, it's okay." She presses a kiss onto his head and quickly grabs a sippy cup from the drying rack. She sets it on the counter, grabs the milk, and fills the cup. Beside it is the fruit basket, heaping with the Macoun apples she bought at the supermarket yesterday.

Mack had taken one out and put it back. Is that why he went for a knife? Was he going to cut an apple?

Probably. What did you think?

After several attempts, Allison threads the cover onto the sippy cup and hands it to J.J., who instantly stops fussing and starts gulping. She puts a handful of dry cereal onto his tray, telling him, "I'll be right back, sweetie."

Happily munching and sipping, he doesn't give her a second glance as she leaves the kitchen.

All is silent overhead. She takes the stairs two at a time. This time, she doesn't hesitate at the master bedroom door, but wrenches it open.

As she hurries across the threshold, banishing the memory of Phyllis Lewis — and of Kristina Haines — from her troubled mind, she can see Mack in the bed.

He's lying on his side, facing her. His eyes are closed; his breathing rhythmic.

She stands watching him for a long time. This man is familiar, even though he's sound asleep.

The man she saw downstairs with the

knife . . .

With a shudder, she turns away, pulls the door closed, and heads for the stairs. Her legs are liquid, her skull is in a tension stranglehold, her shoulders burn. All at once, the physical effects of last night's frantic stress — and sleeplessness — seem to have caught up with her.

I should have crawled into bed when Mack tried to insist.

Too late now.

She can hear J.J. down in the kitchen, and she can tell by the high-pitched note in his baby babble that he's on the verge of tears.

He's just a baby. He doesn't know that his mommy is a nervous wreck and his daddy . . .

Why the hell did Mack have a knife in his hand?

Gripping the railing, she descends the stairs, nearly dizzy with exhaustion and anxiety.

Deal with one thing at a time. That's the only way you're going to get through this.

Coffee. She needs good, strong coffee.

She returns to the kitchen. Seeing her, J.J. throws his sippy cup with a gleeful squeal.

She picks it up, puts it back . . . and he promptly throws it again.

Allison wearily sidesteps it.

J.J. wails.

She sighs. A new day has begun.

Ironic, because she feels as though the nightmarish old one hasn't yet drawn to a close.

Rocky shakes his head as he descends the wide stairway in Phyllis Lewis's large Colonial, thinking of her poor husband. Bob Lewis is on a plane somewhere over the Atlantic, flying home to . . . hell.

Forget the outside — the property strewn with splintered branches, lush shrubbery flattened under the weight of October snow, the roof of the pool house smashed beneath a massive oak tree. That's nothing compared to the aftermath of the storm that raged beyond the front door.

"This is some showplace," Murph mutters, trailing a couple of steps behind. "Home, sweet home, huh, Rock?"

Rocky shrugs, thinking of the well-worn Bronx row house where he and Ange raised their three boys.

That's home, sweet home . . .

But not without Ange.

The other day, restlessly sitting in the ICU waiting room while the nurse performed a suctioning procedure, Rocky picked up a pamphlet that was intended for long-married people dealing with a spouse with a debilitating illness, or facing widowhood. When he realized what it was about, his instinct was to toss it aside, but he found himself reading through it — at first relating to the advice, and then resenting it.

Basically, it was all about learning to live alone again.

Rocky, who'd gone directly from his parents' house to the army to marriage with children, has never lived alone in his life.

And I don't want to learn how.

His partner's voice jars him from his melancholy thoughts.

"I daresay that the bloodbath in the master suite takes away from the impeccable decor," Murph declares in a fake-haughty accent.

Ah, gallows humor. Whatever gets you through.

Every homicide detective has his own way of coping with the violent horror witnessed on an almost daily basis.

Murph, ever the jokester, tends to laugh it all off, or blow some steam playing practical jokes around the station house. Other guys throw themselves into sports in the off hours — running, hoops, even boxing — probably one of the healthiest ways of dealing with the stress. Many of their colleagues,

conversely, have their share of vices —
mainly cigarettes and alcohol — to help ease
the tension.

Rocky has never gone in for any of that.

All he ever needed, at the end of a grueling day or night on the job, was to come
home to Ange. And now . . .

Now you just have to bide your time until
Ange is home and things are back to normal
again, that's all.

The first floor of the Lewis house, like the
second, is humming with activity.

Uniformed patrol officers, crime scene
technicians, the team from the medical
examiner's office — some shooting the
breeze, others going about their investigative procedures, a few simultaneously engaging in both banter and business.

Early morning light falls through the
windows on either side of the front door at
the foot of the stairs. Rocky really needs to
get back to the hospital. What if Ange is
waking up right at this moment, while he's
forty minutes away? What if she opens her
eyes and asks for him and he's not there?

Again, he thinks of Phyllis Lewis's husband and he feels blessed because at least
he, Rocky, has hope.

For Bob Lewis, there is none.

A gallery of framed family photos hangs

on the wall alongside the stairway. The usual: a wedding picture, a couple of family group photos, baby portraits, grade school portraits, senior portraits, cap and gown shots. Mother, father, sister, brother. Just your average, all-American happy family . . .

Shattered by a brutal crime, and the only saving grace is that Phyllis's bloody corpse wasn't found by her husband or children.

No, it was found by Allison.

Rocky has yet to voice his suspicions to anyone but Murph, but he's about to.

Captain Jack Cleary of the local police department greets them at the foot of the stairs. Tall, lean, and handsome — with just the right hint of five o'clock shadow on his chiseled jaw — he looks to Rocky more like an actor playing a detective than the real thing.

"Looks like everything around here is picture-perfect" was Murph's response, under his breath to Rocky, when they first met Cleary on the heels of their journey through the most charming town this side of a Hollywood-manufactured Americana set.

Glenhaven Park is one of those northern Westchester suburbs you often read about in the papers — on the society pages, not the crime blotter. When the New York tabloids write about the celebrities and socialites who live there, they invariably use words like "leafy" and "tony" to describe the town.

Rocky has been around and past it, but until tonight, has never had occasion to get off the highway here. Sure, he has friends in high places — who doesn't? — but not quite this lofty.

Main Street is going to be abuzz today, that's for damned sure. Your classic case of "This kind of thing just doesn't happen here."

Oh, but it does. It happens everywhere.

And it's going to happen again, Rocky knows. Another woman is going to be found hacked to death in her bed.

Maybe not here, but somewhere. Most likely in the general area.

Maybe tonight, maybe tomorrow night, maybe next week, depending on the cooling-off period. Most likely sooner rather than later.

Unless . . .

He thinks about a case he worked years ago, one that remains unsolved. The Leprechaun Killer, he and Murph called it — but only privately, because the name stemmed from a clue that wasn't released to the press or the public.

A woman was murdered in her Manhattan apartment in the early morning hours after Saint Patrick's Day, and a short-stemmed green carnation was found at the scene. Rocky speculated that it was a fledgling serial killer's calling card and waited for the guy to strike again. The fingerprints that were lifted from the stem and petals yielded no match from the database.

As always, when the Leprechaun Killer pops into his head, Rocky wonders about the security guard. That's just one aspect of the case that troubled him for years afterward.

Around the same time the woman was murdered, the lobby guard from the office building where she worked was found brutally stabbed in Central Park, the apparent victim of a random mugging. His wallet was missing and it took more than a week to identify his body. There was no record of a green carnation at that scene — but that didn't mean it hadn't been there and been overlooked in the park foliage, or displaced by an animal.

As a detective, Rocky didn't believe in coincidences. He thought the two cases were linked, and was convinced that the killer would soon strike again.

He never did.

But this, Rocky reminds himself, is different.

This isn't the first murder, and it won't be —

"Detectives, come with me. You're going to want to hear this." Jack Cleary's brusque command interrupts Rocky's thoughts, and he waves a hand for them to follow him into the adjoining living room.

Rocky notices a big basket half filled with chocolate Halloween miniatures on a table by the front door. He tries to imagine the woman he just saw upstairs greeting trick-or-treaters just hours before her gruesome death, still alive and — and in one piece.

He saw for himself that the middle finger on her right hand is, indeed, missing. Everything, right down to the positioning of her hacked, bloody body, curled on her side, leaves not a doubt in Rocky's mind that the Nightwatcher is back in business.

The Alicia Keys song is, indeed, involved this time, but in a slightly different way. Last time, it was audible to anyone within earshot, playing over stereo speakers. This time, the body was found wearing earbuds connected to an iPod looping "Fallin' " over and over in her ears, long after she had ceased to be able to hear it.

Ten years ago, a CD player; today, an iPod

— sign of the times. Doesn't really change the signature.

There are no other songs on the iPod. Just "Fallin'."

The local detectives are looking into the registration for the electronic device but Rocky would bet it's not going to yield anything useful. This offender knows exactly what he — or she — is doing; so far, they haven't even found a single fingerprint.

Cleary closes a set of French doors, sealing them into a large, hushed room with plush off-white carpeting. He motions to a seating area, a cream-colored upholstered sofa and chairs grouped around a low glass table. On it is a perfectly aligned stack of hardcover coffee table books. The top one is on shabby-chic, cottage-style decorating — possibly just for show, judging by the elegant, traditional decor throughout the house.

Rocky sits on the sofa, feeling as though he's going to leave a smudge, and Murph, having heedlessly smudged many a surface in his day, more or less flops down on a chair opposite.

Cleary, who has undoubtedly never smudged anything in his life, takes a seat between them. His blue eyes are troubled, and he wastes no time getting to the point.

"I just talked to the CSU guys," he says, "and something has come up that we didn't expect at all."

"What's that?" Rocky leans forward, resting his stubbly chin in his hand.

"This is strictly between us. I don't want it going beyond this room. No leaks in the press. Got it?" He looks from Rocky to Murph.

"Got it," they say in unison.

"Good." Cleary nods like a preschool teacher whose students have just correctly guessed the first letter of the alphabet.

Rocky can't help but feel a little resentful, and he isn't sure why. Maybe he's just jealous of the guy's good looks. Or maybe he doesn't appreciate his slightly superior attitude — one that probably suits him well in a hoity-toity town like this.

Still, this is his jurisdiction, and there's no mistaking who's in charge here, regardless of the number of homicide cases this guy has likely seen over the course of his career here — in contrast to how many Rocky and Murph have worked.

"Compared to the case you investigated ten years ago," Cleary says, "we've got the same MO, and we thought we had the same signature, but we were wrong."

"About what?" Rocky asks.

"There's been a departure."

"You mean in signature?"

Cleary nods.

Rocky and Murph look at each other.

When you're comparing one crime scene to another to determine whether the same person committed both, the signature analysis is the key.

As far as Rocky can tell, the Nightwatcher's signature is all over this crime . . . right down to the missing finger. Although —

"Do you mean the dead cat?" he asks, thinking of the family pet that was found on the floor in a pool of blood.

Cleary shakes his head. "Not that. There happened to be a cat here, the cat got in the way, so he got rid of it."

"You're talking about the iPod instead of the CD player?" Murph asks. "Because I wouldn't say that's —"

"I'm not talking about that, either. It doesn't change the signature drastically. What I'm talking about . . . it's drastic."

"Drastic enough that you're thinking this is a different killer altogether?" Rocky asks. "A copycat?"

"That's what I'm thinking."

Rocky's thoughts fly back to Allison Taylor MacKenna. If this is a copycat crime, then she's on top of a very short list of potential suspects familiar with the details of the Nightwatcher murders . . .

Until Jack Cleary utters the one phrase that Rocky never saw coming.

"Phyllis Lewis was raped."

■ ■ ■ ■

PART III

■ ■ ■ ■

The woods are lovely, dark and deep,
But I have promises to keep,
And miles to go before I sleep,
And miles to go before I sleep.

Robert Frost

CHAPTER ELEVEN

Saturday, November 5, 2011

"Was that brutal," Randi asks Allison, "or was that brutal?" Resting a hand on her marble kitchen countertop, she pulls off her black, pointy-toed high-heeled designer pumps, balancing on first one foot and then the other.

Brutal — she's referring to the wake for Phyllis Lewis, which the four of them just attended: Randi and Ben, Allison and Mack.

Brutal doesn't even begin to describe the experience, Allison thinks as she sinks into a kitchen chair.

Standing beside the open casket, Bob Lewis and his two children were alternately catatonic and hysterical, depending on who was stepping to the front of the long line of mourners to offer condolences to the family.

When Allison's turn came, Bob fell on her sobbing, thanking her over and over. For what, she doesn't know, and she didn't ask.

"He's just grateful that you went over there to check on Phyllis for him that night," Mack murmured to her as they stepped away to kneel at the casket and say a quick prayer.

That night . . .

Phyllis . . .

Try as she might, she can't get the horrific images out of her head.

Seeing her friend's dead body a second time didn't help. Allison hadn't expected an open casket and was disturbed when she spotted the corpse from the doorway. She had to force herself to make her way over, clinging tightly to Mack's arm, reminding herself that if Phyllis's family could face this, so, certainly, could she.

She overheard several people commenting on how beautiful Phyllis looked, as people have a peculiar way of doing at funerals. But it wasn't the truth. It never is.

A high-necked, long-sleeved black dress covered the horrific wounds to her torso, her mutilated hands were discreetly hidden, and her lovely face had been unscathed. But the mortician couldn't erase the unmistakable death mask pallor Allison has seen before: on Kristina Haines, and on her own mother.

"I need a drink," Randi announces, opening a cabinet above the wet bar on the far end of her vast kitchen. "So do you."

Allison automatically opens her mouth to protest, but Randi has already taken out two martini glasses, cutting her off with a stern "No arguments."

"I'll just have iced tea." Randi thoughtfully stocked the fridge with Allison's favorite beverage when they came to stay.

"That's not going to help you. You need something stronger."

"I don't like to drink when the kids are around." She's not much of a drinker ever — and certainly not the strong stuff. Alcohol is a drug, and Randi knows how she feels about drugs, thanks to her mother.

But Randi repeats, "No arguments," and pulls a bottle of Grey Goose from beneath the bar. "The kids are sound asleep."

That's true. The first thing Allison did when they got back from the wake a few minutes ago was head up the stairs to the spacious guest quarters where she, Mack, and the children have spent the last few nights.

J.J. was peacefully snoozing in the portable crib set up beside the queen-sized bed in the larger of the two guest rooms. The girls were in twin beds in the other room,

335

snuggled beneath their new quilts — a Madeline theme for Madison, multicolored polka dots for Hudson. Randi had taken them shopping to pick out the bedding on Wednesday while Allison and Mack were being interviewed — yet again — this time by Captain Cleary down at the Glenhaven Park police station.

When Allison later saw the quilts, she was touched — and a little dismayed. "You shouldn't have!" she told Randi. "It's not like they're going to move in forever."

"I know that, but the girls should be comfortable while they're here," Randi said. "And so should you. I had a crib delivered this morning, and you and Mack and J.J. are coming tonight — no arguments."

Allison didn't argue.

She had no desire to spend another sleepless, nerve-wracking night at home.

At least Mack's little sleepwalking episode in the wee hours of Wednesday morning doesn't seem nearly as ominous, in retrospect, as it did at the time.

She was just so rattled from the murder scene that when she saw him holding a knife, her mind immediately went to a dark, terrifying place.

Phyllis had died on a Tuesday.

Things happen on Tuesdays.

Mack hates Tuesdays.
But that doesn't mean . . .

No. Of course it doesn't.

When she told Mack about the knife that morning, he laughed and said he had skipped both lunch and dinner that day, and that he was probably planning to slice up an apple and eat it with cinnamon and sugar.

"Why," he asked with a grin, "what did you think I was going to do?"

The grin faded quickly, though — either because he caught sight of the look in her eyes, or because, after a momentary lapse to normalcy, he'd suddenly remembered what had happened next door.

She never did answer his question; she doesn't ever want to reconsider, even for an instant, what she might have thought, as that bizarre moment was unfolding, he was going to do — or had already done.

She's given it very little thought since, and the past few nights in the Webers' guestroom have been blessedly uneventful — or at least, if they haven't, she's been blessedly oblivious. It's surprising how soundly she's slept here . . . but as she told Randi, it's not as if they're staying forever.

"You can stay as long as you want," Randi offered graciously.

Allison shook her head, remembering what Randi said, not long ago, about regretting having built the guest suite because her in-laws would come and stay indefinitely.

No one needs — or wants — permanent houseguests.

Sooner or later — sooner *than* later — Allison and Mack and the kids will either have to go back home or make other arrangements.

"What other arrangements? We can't just sell the house and move away," Mack told her when she said, this morning, that she wasn't ready to sleep at home yet — and might never be.

"Well, we can't just stay there waiting for him to come back and kill us all, either."

"That's not going to happen. We have an alarm system now" — he'd had it installed on Thursday, along with shades for the sunroom windows, telling her after the fact — "and the police are keeping an eye on things."

Allison was shaking her head stubbornly before he'd finished speaking. "I can't," she told him. "I just can't."

He dropped the subject, putting his arms around her and silently holding her close.

She's scared. Despite her strength, despite her resolve to never let fear get the best of her, she's terrified.

Mack is, too. He must be. He's just trying not to feed her fear; trying to be the strong, stoic man of the house. Trying not to let his guard down and reveal how he really feels, not even to her, because that's how he rolls, dammit.

And I always give him a pass, because that's how I roll.

Yes, because she knows that Mack acts out of self-preservation: always holding back at least a little piece of himself.

It's just that lately, her nerves are so frazzled, it's all she can do not to demand more from him, whether or not he's capable of giving it. She's always prided herself on being able to take care of herself and her children and any obstacle fate throws in their path, but this . . .

This nightmare has left her longing, just this once, for someone else to step in and take care of things for her. She wants someone to make it go away, even though she's well aware that nobody can do that. Not even Mack.

This morning, they watched the live televised press conference held by the local police, who have formed a task force to work on the case.

"We're following every possible lead,"

Captain Cleary said into the microphone, "and we encourage anyone who has any information that might help us to call the special hotline we've set up."

With his take-charge attitude — not to mention his manly good looks — he exuded such confidence that Allison almost fooled herself into thinking the case would be solved in no time.

That lasted about five minutes. Then the press conference ended and it was back to wondering and worrying and trying to stay calm for the kids' sake.

"Here." Randi puts a full martini glass into Allison's hand and clinks her own gently against it. *"L'chaim."*

"L'chaim. What does that mean?" she asks, having first heard the Hebrew toast last year, at Lexi's Bat Mitzvah.

"It means 'to life.' Fitting, don't you think?"

Allison nods, sips, and swallows. The drink is pure alcohol. It burns all the way down her throat and lands in her empty stomach. She hasn't eaten all day, really, and . . .

I don't drink like this.

"I know you're more of a white wine girl," Randi comments, seeing the look on her face, "but I thought you needed something stronger right now."

Allison nods, and they both take another silent sip from their glasses. This time, expecting the burn, she welcomes it and the promise of numbness in its wake. She does her best to banish the mental image of her mother, wild-eyed, incoherent, out of control . . .

I could never be like that. One drink isn't going to do that to me.

"Are you hungry?" Randi asks, and Allison shakes her head.

She's never hungry anymore. In a matter of days, she's lost the final few pounds she wanted to lose, and then some.

But she'd better go easy on the alcohol with nothing in her stomach to soak it up. Just another sip or two, and she'll set the glass aside.

A buzzer rings on their third sip, and Randi furrows her salon-sculpted eyebrows. "Ben?" she calls. "Is there someone out at the gate?"

"Sounds that way," he returns dryly from the next room, where he and Mack are settled in front of the television with beers.

Randi rolls her eyes. "Would you mind answering the intercom?"

Allison pictures Ben rolling his eyes, too, as he calls back, "Sure, no problem."

"You're not expecting anyone?" she asks

Randi, who shakes her head.

"No, and I don't like it when the gate bell rings — or even the phone — when the kids aren't home."

Both Lexi and Josh are spending the night at friends' homes. Knowing how Allison worries about leaving J.J. with a sitter, Randi had arranged sleepovers for her children so that Greta would only have Hudson, Maddy, and J.J. to watch while they were all out at the wake.

The girls, of course, were disappointed that Lexi wouldn't be here, but not for long. For all her German reserve, Greta manages to be playful, tirelessly engaging the girls even when it comes to Candy Land tournaments that go on for hours.

"Sometimes I just think the worst, you know?" Randi cocks her head, listening as Ben answers the intercom.

"I know." Allison sips her drink again, not wanting to point out that the worst can — and does — happen.

But not to us. Please, God. Not to us.

In the other room, Ben's voice and a staticky voice are conversing over the intercom.

"Who do you think that is?" Randi whispers, as if Allison might have some idea.

Allison shrugs, not caring, as long as it's not an emergency of any sort — and it doesn't sound like one.

"I'll be right back. I'm going to go see."

Randi leaves Allison to sit sipping her drink, thinking about Phyllis's family, and her own. Thinking about what it would be like for her children, and for Mack, if something were to happen to her. Thinking about what it would be like for her if something were to —

No. I can't bear to think of it. I can't.

In the hall, male and female voices mingle with Ben and Randi's, and she hears footsteps approaching.

The Webers appear in the kitchen doorway, accompanied by an attractive, vaguely familiar-looking couple.

The pale-haired man is dressed in the suburban weekend uniform: chinos, loafers, button-down, and jacket. The brunette woman, in a black coat and dress and holding a Saran-wrapped platter, could be coming from a funeral or going to a party. Her hair is pulled straight back from her face in a long ponytail, a style that would be unbecoming on a less attractive woman . . .

Like me, Allison reminds herself, thinking of all the slapdash ponytail days when J.J. was in the height of his hair-pulling phase. But the style serves to accentuate the woman's high cheekbones and large dark eyes.

Ben calls for Mack to come into the kitchen as Randi takes the couple's coats and turns to Allison.

"You remember Nathan and Zoe Jennings."

She doesn't. Should she? Is it the booze?

Crossing to them, feeling a little unsteady on her feet, she forces a smile. Her drink sloshes a bit over the rim of her glass onto her right hand as she goes to transfer it to her left, realizing the man is extending his own hand in greeting.

She quickly wipes on the side of her own black dress — as well cut as Zoe Jennings's, she's certain, yet somehow not flattering her own figure nearly as much — and shakes both her hand and her husband's.

"We were so sorry to hear about your friend," Zoe tells her.

"Thank you." Allison sets down her glass on the nearest surface, trying to place the couple.

"Zoe made some brownies. She thought the kids might want a treat," Nathan says. "But don't worry, they're the healthy kind."

"I use organic oat flour and pureed spinach. No nuts," Zoe adds. "My kids don't like them, and I figure your girls probably don't, either."

Allison's first thought is that she's right — the girls don't like nuts, but they don't like spinach in their brownies, either.

Her next thought is that Zoe somehow knows that she has daughters, that she lost a friend — and, obviously, knows Mack, because when he appears in the doorway, Zoe makes a beeline over to hug him.

"I was so looking forward to getting together tonight," she tells him.

She *was?*

"When I called Ben and Randi to invite them to join us, too," she goes on, "Randi told me what had happened. We'd heard about it, of course, but we had no idea she was your neighbor. Randi said you were staying here until . . . well, until everything blows over."

"We tried to call earlier and see if it was okay to stop by, but we couldn't get ahold of you," Nathan puts in.

"We just came from the wake." Randi puts the platter of brownies on the table and peels back the plastic wrap.

"Was it awful?"

No, it was absolutely delightful, Allison finds herself wanting to say to this Zoe person who apparently made Saturday night plans with Mack and puts spinach in brown-

345

ies and has now taken off her coat to show off a killer body. No cleavage — the dress is conservatively cut — but it's slinky enough to reveal that she's either had a boob job, or is wearing the world's most invisible bra.

Allison can't help but check to see if Mack is looking at Zoe's figure, but he's not. He catches her eye and his mouth quirks a little, not a smile, not a frown, but an expression she can easily decipher after all their years together.

Sorry about these people, he's saying. *I know you're not in the mood to socialize with strangers.*

He's right about that.

Suddenly, she longs to be home, despite everything. Home with her husband and children, where they belong. Home where she'll feel more like herself and Mack will act more like himself and everything will be back to normal . . .

Except, how can it ever be normal now?

"I'm sorry we had to meet under these circumstances," Nathan is saying, and Allison realizes he's talking to her.

"Oh . . . I . . . so am I."

"We'd still love to have you guys over," Zoe tells her, "after the dust settles."

After the dust settles — an awkward thing to say after a funeral, but the irony seems to escape Zoe, making Allison like her even less.

Again, she looks at Mack.

Reading her mind, he says, "I forgot to tell you, Al — right before everything happened, I ran into Nate on the train and he and Zoe had invited us over for Saturday night — tonight."

"That's . . . nice." *But who the hell are these people?*

"You'll have to be sure and take that rain check," Zoe says, "and I promise that when you do come, we won't just talk about old times."

"You're the one who already dug out all those old pictures to show Mack and Ben," her husband reminds her.

"I'm sure Allison and Randi want to see them, too."

"Are they incriminating?" Randi asks Zoe, and Allison notes that her martini glass is almost empty. "Because I always like to see incriminating pictures from Ben's past . . . as long as they were taken before he met me."

"Well, I'm sure Nate has a few of those. The guys used to go to all the big media parties."

"So did you," Mack tells Zoe, with a grin.

For a brief, irrational instant, Allison

resents it.

How, she wonders, can he be suddenly smiling after all that's gone on the last few days? And at a total stranger — if only to Allison — who's returning it with such ease; an outsider who came barging in at the least opportune moment, when Allison was ready to be alone with her friends and her husband and her thoughts and her good, stiff drink.

Oh please. It's not about you, she reminds herself, picking up her glass and relishing another burning sip. *Don't be petty.*

Still, she can't help but feel wistful over Mack's sudden jovial demeanor, given the darkness of his mood these last few days. Never one to share emotions — ha, understatement of the year — he seems to have retreated emotionally more than ever lately, whenever they're together.

Which hasn't been often. To Allison's dismay, he went into the office on Wednesday morning for a few hours to attend his meeting, and back again on Thursday, after taking the first part of the day off to handle the alarm installation. Yesterday, he put in a full day at work.

"I have to go," he told her when she protested, and reminded her that she and the kids are completely safe at Ben and

Randi's. The house is like a fortress. It isn't even just the house; the property is surrounded by an electronic security fence and an access-control iron gate.

"I'd feel safer with you here," she told Mack.

"Okay, but it's not like you really *are* any safer, and it's not like going to work is optional. Especially with everything that's going on right now."

He was talking about what was going on at the office, she knew — as if that could possibly hold a candle to the hell that had broken loose in their lives.

"You get personal days, though, Mack. Maybe —"

"I used them up in September when I stayed home to paint the sunroom, remember?"

"What about a bereavement day? You can take one for Phyllis's funeral on Monday morning —"

"I only get those if an immediate family member dies," he replied, and the words made her shudder inside.

"Someone *did* die. This is serious, and —"

"Allison, for the love of God! Stop! Do you think I don't know that? Do you think I *want* to go to work?"

Taken aback by his explosion, she just

looked at him.

"I'm up to my eyeballs in problems right now and heads are already rolling! I can't just take off right now because a neighbor passed away!"

"She didn't pass away — she was murdered!"

"Do you think that makes any difference at all to my boss? My job is on the line here!"

So are our lives, she wanted to remind him — but when she noticed the irate look in his eye, she was afraid to. Suddenly, she was afraid of *him.*

Looking back on that conversation — as she has done many times since — she's convinced herself that she overreacted. She used to have a corporate job herself; she knows the kind of pressure he's facing. At least, she used to know.

Mack is just doing what he has to do: going to work, earning a living. She doesn't need to make it harder for him; she's always prided herself on being self-sufficient, perfectly capable of taking care of herself and the kids — and on not being one of those wives who spends her husband's money without a care. She's not like that. She knows how hard he works.

So why did you have to give him such a hard

time? It isn't like you.

No, and Mack wasn't behaving like himself, either.

The pressure is getting to both of them.

With Allison's self-loathing over her resentment of his obligation to his job has come a hefty dose of guilt — *it's not like you're sharing the breadwinner burden* — and, more than anything else, terror.

She jumps at every little noise, perpetually looking out the windows and over her shoulder, expecting to see . . .

Him.

The hooded figure who attacked her in her bedroom that night ten years ago.

The Nightwatcher.

God help her, God help them all; it wasn't Jerry Thompson, who is safely dead and buried.

It was someone else, and he'll be back, and how can Mack just be standing here right now in the Webers' kitchen holding a beer and smiling like an idiot at this woman who won't shut up?

"I never went to the magazine parties where the guys all met the *Penthouse* Pet of the Year," Zoe is saying, ostensibly to Randi and Allison, though she's looking at their husbands, "and I wasn't even invited the time Hugh Hefner flew everyone out to the

Playboy Mansion for —"

"Whoa, easy now, Zoe," Ben cuts in with a laugh. "Randi doesn't want to hear about that, do you, babe?"

"Trust me, I don't, and Allison doesn't, either, do you, Al?"

"No, thanks," she says with absolute conviction.

Now she remembers — Zoe. She's the woman Mack used to work with, the one who got married and moved up here not long ago. Allison didn't recognize her with her hair pulled back. Mack was talking to her the night of the Webers' party, the night . . .

The night I noticed that my nightgown was missing.

She closes her eyes and swallows hard, remembering the last time she saw it — bloodstained, on Phyllis Lewis's lifeless body.

The others continue talking and laughing around her as though nothing terrible has happened, and Allison loses herself, once again, in the nightmare.

". . . just the way you look . . . tonight." Rocky finishes singing and leans over to kiss his wife's forehead. "Yeah, yeah, I know . . . I'm no Sinatra, but I'd say that wasn't half

bad, huh, Ange?"

Encouraged by the ripple of movement beneath her closed eyelids, his heart lifts another notch, buoyed by a gust of hope.

It's been happening more and more frequently today — this visible twitching of her eyes and her mouth and her fingers. Yesterday, too, according to Carm, but Rocky wasn't here much, busy with the case up in Westchester.

The news that Phyllis Lewis had been raped really threw things off for him, and instantly led to a couple of conclusions. Most importantly, he's almost positive — much to his relief — that he hadn't arrested the wrong guy in the Nightwatcher case after all.

Given the departure in signature, it looks more like they're dealing with a copycat killer — and clearly, it isn't a female, which lets Allison Taylor MacKenna off the hook. As for her husband . . . James MacKenna was there with her that day ten years ago. Not married to Allison at the time; he was just a neighbor, as was Kristina Haines.

Rocky clearly remembers interviewing him back then, and quickly dismissing him as a suspect. He was as all-American Mr. Nice Guy as they come: former altar boy and Big Brother volunteer, with a respectable family background and solid career, not an overdue library book or parking ticket to his name. Beyond that, the guy's wife had been among the thousands of New Yorkers missing in the twin towers; his alibi the night of Kristina's murder was that he'd been desperately searching hospitals and victim centers for her.

As Rocky recalls, Carrie MacKenna was one of the first names to emerge on the official lists of those who had been confirmed dead.

Later, the *New York Times* printed the "Portraits of Grief" series that captured each of the victims — not in formal obituaries, but essays about their personal lives, about who they had been, rather than what they had done. He remembers reading the one about Carrie, and noting that her husband mentioned that they'd been trying to start a family, battling infertility . . .

At the time, Rocky's oldest son, Tony, and his wife, Laura, were enduring the same grueling, expensive treatments. He remembers feeling sorry for James MacKenna, who had gone through so much already in his efforts to become a father, and in the end found himself alone and bereft.

What are the odds that the guy might emerge a decade later as a cold-blooded copycat killer?

Not nearly as high as the odds that Jerry Thompson talked in prison.

Rocky and Murph are planning to head over to Sullivan Correctional to see what they can find out. Thompson could very well have shared the details of his crimes with a since-released inmate — one who decided to duplicate the crimes for kicks, and add rape to the signature. With luck, they'll be able to pinpoint a suspect and match him to the semen collected at the scene.

But right now, with Ange showing signs of coming out of the coma, the case can wait. Rocky's been at her side since early this morning. The doctors instructed him to talk to her, so he did, and when he ran out of things to say, he started singing to her — every song in his repertoire, with repeat performances of his favorites.

"The Way You Look Tonight" was the first dance on their wedding day. He's sung it maybe ten, twelve times in the last hour or two, filling in his own words wherever he forgets the lyrics. He knows that one pretty well, but some of the others, he has to wing almost completely.

"What else do you want to hear?" he asks Ange. "More Sinatra?"

He gets through a few lines of "Mack the Knife" before faltering on the lyrics.

"Never mind," he tells Ange. "How about some pop? 'Brown-Eyed Girl'?"

She's not big on that song, but he's always loved it, because it makes him think of her.

"Okay, okay, I know — forget 'Brown-Eyed Girl.' This show is for you. I'll do some Beatles."

He remembers teasing her back in junior high when she camped out in front of the Ed Sullivan Theater with a bunch of other girls, trying to catch a glimpse of the Fab Four. And he remembers being secretly, irrationally jealous of her favorite Beatle, Paul McCartney, for most of seventh grade and part of eighth.

But Paul didn't get to give Ange her first kiss. That privilege belonged to Rocky, on the deserted playground one cold January afternoon when the sky was impossibly blue and the wind kept whipping Ange's long hair across her eyes as they talked, until he had to reach out and brush it away. He saw the expectant look in her big brown eyes right before she closed them, and he knew that she thought he was about to kiss her, so he did.

Now, looking at those closed eyes, he remembers the first thing she said when she opened them that long-ago day after he kissed her.

"Thank you."

Taken aback, he'd asked, "For what?"

"For finally doing that. I thought I was going to have to make the first move."

They've laughed about that many times over the years.

"*Finally,* Ange? You said *finally*? We were twelve years old. My voice hadn't even changed yet. What did you expect, a full-blown Junior High Casanova?"

"Well, at least you were a fast learner once you got things going."

Sitting here now, he brushes a tear from his eye, remembering that day on the playground with her. So many days on that playground with her, teeter-tottering when they were so little their legs didn't touch the ground, pushing each other on the swings while their mothers chatted, and in later years, pointedly ignoring each other during recess — Ange skipping rope with the girls, Rocky playing stickball with the boys.

There was never a time without Ange.

There will never be a time without Ange.

"Okay," he says, a bit hoarsely, "some Beatles. At least I know the words to most of those songs."

He sings "Love Me Do" and "She Loves

You." Ange's favorite has always been "Mi-chelle," but damned if Rocky's going to try that one — he has a hard enough time sing-ing lyrics in English. Forget French.

She likes "In My Life," too — it was the mother-son dance at their boys' weddings. But when Rocky tries to sing it, he only gets through the first line before his voice cracks and he can't go on.

"There are places I remember . . ."

The playground . . .

The old high school gym where we danced every dance, always . . .

Home.

He can't seem to swallow the lump in his throat.

"Mr. Manzillo?"

Saved by the scrubs-clad nurse in the doorway. She's not one of his favorites here, probably because she reminds him of Sister Margaret Joseph, a stern nun from his altar boy days. Her mouth is perpetually set in a disapproving slit and her eyes are black beads that, whenever they settle on him, make him feel as though he's done some-thing he shouldn't have.

"There's a call for you at the desk from a Mr. Murphy. He said he's been trying to reach you on your cell phone, but . . ."

"It's turned off." *See? I follow the rules,*

Sister. I mean, Nurse.

"I told him someone would give you the message but he said it's important and he needs to talk to you right away. He insisted on holding the line."

Rocky is already on his feet and giving Ange another quick kiss before following the disapproving messenger down the hall to the nurses' station. She hands him the phone and advises him to make it quick. In exactly those words.

"Murph? What's going on?"

"Sorry to bother you there. How's Ange?"

"The same." Not really — better than the same — but now is not the time for details, even happy ones. "What happened?"

He only has to wait a moment for the inevitable response, and in that moment, he guesses — correctly — what's coming.

"Looks like our friend's been busy. We got another homicide."

"When? Today?"

"No — back in September. No one linked it. And here's the kicker: the victim was the wife of the prison guard on duty the night Jerry Thompson killed himself."

Rocky sucks in his breath. "Same signature? He took the middle finger?"

"He took the whole damned arm, Rock, and served it up to her husband for lunch.

Literally. This is one sick son of a bitch. I'm headed out to Sullivan right now. You coming?"

Rocky hesitates only a moment.

He thinks of Ange — and then of a ruthless killer already trolling for his next innocent victim. Someone else's wife.

"Yeah," he says grimly. "I'm coming."

When the phone rings in the dead of night, Nathan Jennings is in the midst of a troubling dream — a nightmare, really.

Jarred abruptly awake, all he recalls is that he was running as fast as he could down a dark road.

Was he chasing someone? Or being chased?

It doesn't matter. It was just a bad dream. But the telephone ringing, at — checking the clock on the bedside table he sees that it's 2:48 A.M. — that's not a dream, and it's not good.

Sleeping beside him, Zoe doesn't even stir as he reaches for the phone. She's a notoriously heavy sleeper. When the kids were babies a few years back, she always relied on him to wake her when they cried for wee-hour feedings.

As he lifts the receiver, his mind runs through various possibilities. Wrong number? Or has something happened to his aging mother? To Zoe's aging father?

"Hello?"

He's greeted by a barely audible whisper. "Nate?"

"Yes . . . ?"

"Mack."

"Mack? What's wrong?"

"My car died. I need a ride. Can you come get me?"

Nate sits up, surprised.

It's not that he minds helping out, but . . .

It's just strange, that's all, that Mack would call Nate of all people, and at this hour. But an old friend is an old friend.

And after all, Nate did say to Mack and Allison, when he and Zoe left the Webers' earlier, to call if there was anything they could do.

"Seriously, we'd be happy to help if you need us," Zoe chimed in. "I can watch your kids while you go to the funeral Monday if you want, or just to give you a little break."

Nate could see by the slightly stiff expression on Allison's face as she thanked them that she wouldn't be calling the Jenningses for a favor anytime soon. She'd just been through hell, he knew, and he didn't blame her for not chitchatting with the rest of them as they shared drinks in the Webers' family room.

Zoe, however, had deemed her standoffish. "I pictured her differently," she said in the car on the way home. "I mean, I'm sure it was hard for her to live up to his first wife, but —"

"Give her a break, Zoe," Nate had cut in. "She looked traumatized. You would be, too, if you'd just come from the wake of your murdered friend — whose dead body you happened to discover, no less."

"Maybe," she allowed. "But she just doesn't seem like Mack's type."

Nate didn't ask who she thought Mack's type might be, afraid he already knew the answer. That Zoe had harbored a serious crush on Mack back in their agency days was no secret to anyone — except maybe to Mack himself.

Now that they're all grown up married couples, there's no reason to bring it up again. Still, he couldn't help but feel a twinge of discomfort, seeing the way his wife watched Mack.

As for Allison, he just wishes they could have met for the first time under more pleasant circumstances. He felt sorry for her and found himself second-guessing the wisdom of the drop-in condolence call, which had been Zoe's idea, not his.

"It's what you do when a friend loses someone, Nate."

"Yes, maybe we should wait a bit."

"Why?"

"I don't know — to give them some time."

"Time for what? You don't have to come with me, Nate, but I'm doing it."

When Zoe made up her mind like that, there was no stopping her.

Nate is sure the visit wasn't just an excuse to cross paths with Mack. Of course not. That would be a ridiculous assumption.

Zoe is just feeling adrift up here in suburbia, and she's eager to make new friends among the local moms. Allison and Randi are the logical place to start, right?

Of course.

"Where are you?" Nate asks Mack now, whispering as well — though he knows an air horn blast in her ear probably wouldn't wake his sleeping wife.

"Off the Saw Mill. Exit 37. You'll see me."

"How about if I just —"

There's a click, and Mack is off the line.

Nate is tempted to call him back and finish his sentence — which was going to be an offer to send over a tow truck instead. He presses the recall button on the phone, which brings up the number from which the call came.

James MacKenna, the caller ID panel reads, above the date and time stamp. About to press the button that will automatically dial the number, Nate thinks better of it.

I did tell him to call me if he needed anything. I guess I should be glad he did.

With a weary sigh, Nate gets out of bed and hurriedly starts to dress.

CHAPTER TWELVE

In the dead of a rainy November night, Sullivan Correctional Facility strikes Rocky as an infinitely dreary place. Possibly no less cheerful, he surmises, than it might be at high noon on a sun-splashed day. But now, bathed in the greenish light of low-watt LED bulbs, the small administrative room is terribly depressing. He can only imagine what it's like over on the cell block, where Charles Nowak was on duty when Rocky and Murph arrived a short time ago.

Now, as they sit waiting for someone to bring him in, a weathered-looking, heavyset female administrative assistant pours coffee from a filmy carafe into two foam cups.

"Want cream and sugar?" she asks.

"Cream," Murph says.

She grabs a tall canister, dumps a generous heap of white powder into one cup, adds a plastic stirrer, and looks at Rocky. "You?"

"Just black, thanks."

"You sure?" Looking dubious, she offers a largely unnecessary "The coffee's not that great here."

"I'm sure I've had much worse," Rocky assures her, but after a sip, decides that might not be true.

The woman lingers in the doorway. "Can I ask you a question?"

Murph nods. "What's that?"

"My cousin's kid has been missing for over six weeks now, and the cops won't help her. They think he ran away."

"You don't think so?"

"I don't know. Robbie ain't the best kid you ever met — he's a dropout and he's had some trouble with the cops and my cousin found drugs in his room — but she still don't think he'd just take off and not call her for all this time."

The mothers never think that, Rocky thinks sadly.

"Her name's Ginny — Virginia — Masters, and her son's name is Robbie. Robert Alan Masters. Can you help her out? Maybe just talk to her?"

"Why are you asking us? We're NYPD," Murph points out. "Why not —"

"Because you're detectives, and the cops she's talked to won't help her. They wouldn't even let her fill out a missing persons report right away because they said he don't qualify."

"Where does your cousin live?" Rocky asks.

"Over in Monticello."

"Sorry," Murph tells her, "that's not in our jurisdiction."

"This ain't, either," she points out with a stubborn gleam in her eye.

Before they can respond, two men appear in the doorway. One is the prison official who was sent to summon Charles Nowak from his post; the other, a tall, gaunt man in a guard's uniform, is presumably Nowak himself.

"Detective Manzillo, Detective Murphy, this is Chuck Nowak." He shoots a pointed look at the woman still waiting for help with her cousin's missing son. She grumbles something under her breath and leaves the room, followed, moments later, by the official.

Rocky puts her and the kid out of his head, sets the coffee cup aside, and reaches for his pencil and notebook.

"We just want to ask you some questions about a case we're investigating, Officer Nowak," Rocky tells him, settling a pair of reading glasses on the end of his nose. "I understand that you recently lost your wife. I'm very sorry."

Murph echoes the sentiment.

The widowed prison guard responds to their condolences and a few preliminary questions in bleak, monosyllabic monotones.

Rocky scribbles "17 years" on the notebook — the amount of time Nowak says he's been working here at the prison — and clears his throat, preparing to ask a question whose answer he anticipates as being less definitive.

Murph voices it before he can, and much more bluntly. "Who do you think was responsible for the death of your wife, Officer Nowak?"

The man visibly winces at that phrase — "death of your wife" — as though the loss is still too fresh to bear. His hands clench so tightly on the table that his knuckles are mottled white knobs.

"I don't know who did it." Nowak finally lifts his dark gaze to meet Murph's head-on. "Do you?"

"The homicide squad hasn't had any leads that I'm aware of." Murph looks at Rocky, who nods in agreement.

"But you have an idea?" Nowak's questioning glance sweeps from Murph to

Rocky. Neither of them answers that, of course.

"Tell us about Jerry Thompson," Rocky suggests, and Nowak's dark eyebrows rise.

"What about him? He's dead."

"Killed himself by sipping cleaning fluid, right?"

Nowak nods and drops his eyes again, but not before Rocky glimpses something unsettling in his expression.

Murph goes on, "Why do you think he did that?"

"Why did he kill himself, you mean? Who the hell knows?"

And who the hell cares? The second question goes unspoken, but Rocky hears it loud and clear in Nowak's tone.

The guy is wondering why they're wasting their time and his on a waste-case inmate whose life — and death — can't possibly compare to his beloved wife, Cora's.

"Did he say anything before he died that . . . raised any red flags?" Murph asks.

"About what? That he was going to kill himself?" At Murph's nod, Nowak says, "Nope."

"What about the other guys? Did he talk to them?"

"You mean, did he tell them what he was

369

planning to do?" Nowak shrugs. "I have no idea."

Again, the peculiar, fleeting expression in his eye, and a slight hesitation in his voice.

Intrigued, Rocky says, "Jerry Thompson didn't have access to cleaning fluid, Officer Nowak. Someone got it for him."

"What, you think *I* did that?"

"I think you have some idea who might have."

"Is that why you're here?"

Ignoring that question, Rocky asks, "Who was it, Officer Nowak?"

"I don't know."

Oh yes, you do.

"All right, then . . . who do you think it might have been?"

Something seems to shift in Nowak's brain, and he surprises Rocky by saying simply, "Doobie Jones."

"Doobie?" Rocky echoes, writing it down.

"Jones. Right. Doobie — that's what they all call him."

"What's he in for?"

"Rape. Assault. Murder," Nowak intones. "He had the cell right next to Thompson's, and he worked in janitorial. He could have gotten his hands on it, no problem."

"On the cleaning fluid."

"Right." Nowak shrugs.

"Why would he do that? Were they friends?"

"They talked."

"What about?" Murph asks.

"I don't know. A lot of things."

"He talk to anyone else?"

"Probably."

We're going to talk to every inmate here who had regular contact with Jerry Thompson, Rocky silently tells Murph, who nods before posing the next question to Nowak:

"So you think Jerry asked this Jones person to help him commit suicide?"

"For all I know, it was his idea."

"Jones's idea?" Rocky asks, and raises an eyebrow at Murph when Nowak nods.

"It could have been. He's a master manipulator and Thompson was one of those guys who could be talked into just about anything."

Those words settle over Rocky like a clammy cloak as he remembers Thompson's halting confession.

"You never said anything to anyone about your . . . suspicion?" Murph asks.

"No one ever asked."

"And now . . ."

"You're asking. Listen, I don't give a rat's ass what happened to Jerry Thompson or what happens to Doobie Jones. I don't even care about finding whoever . . . hurt Cora. She's gone. Nothing's gonna bring her back. I just thought . . . maybe that was why you were here. Because you knew something."

He does *care*, Rocky realizes, hearing the catch in his voice. He just can't see beyond the pain to realize that he might find some measure of peace and comfort in closure.

Rocky's heart goes out to this desolate man, just as it does to Phyllis Lewis's husband and children, and to the families of Kristina Haines and Marianne Apostolos and Hector Alveda, even after all these years.

He vows, with renewed conviction, to bring to justice the son of a bitch who killed Phyllis and Cora. There isn't a doubt in his mind that their murders are connected to the others.

Obviously following the same train of thought, Murph asks Nowak, "This Doobie Jones — was he released from prison?"

The answer isn't one Rocky was expecting: "No. He's still here. He's never getting out. Why?"

Because I thought we could button this up neatly. I figured Thompson told Jones what he did to those women ten years ago, and Jones was sprung and decided to pick up where his dead friend left off.

All right, so obviously, he didn't, Rocky acknowledges.

But someone did, and it's only a matter of time before he strikes again.

Sobbing and terrified, Zoe Jennings doesn't want to wear the pink silk teddy Jamie had stolen from Phyllis Lewis's dresser drawer. But of course, it isn't very hard to convince her to change her mind.

All Jamie has to do is show her the red-handled chef's knife, its blade glinting in the flickering light of the hastily lit votives, and remind her of her children sleeping down the hall, and she's more than willing to do whatever Jamie asks.

Which isn't much.

There simply isn't time. Jamie figures she has a half hour or so before the husband might return. Maybe longer, but she isn't taking any chances.

She gags Zoe with a wadded-up pillowcase, just as she did Phyllis. Straddling her, she reaches into her pocket with one gloved hand and pulls out the small iPod, one of several purchased on the street in New York. Stolen merchandise, of course, peddled by a pathetic junkie who, if the police ever do track him down for questioning, will be lucky if he remembers his own name.

After ensuring that the lone song on the playlist is set to repeat infinitely and that the volume is turned up as high as it can go, Jamie stuffs the earbuds into Zoe's ears and presses play.

Her body jolts at the blast of sound, and she writhes on her bed as though she's being tortured.

"Oh, honey, you have no idea," Jamie tells her, shaking her head in disgust and reaching for Zoe's wriggling right arm with her left hand as she readies the knife in her right. "Stay still!"

Zoe whimpers, trying to wrench her arm from Jamie's grasp.

"Stop that! Do you hear me?"

Of course she doesn't. She can't, above the music.

Jamie roughly yanks one earbud from her ear, pulling out a handful of her long hair in the process.

"If you don't lie still, I'm going to go get your little boy and your little girl, one at a time, and I'm going to make you watch while I use this on them."

Her body goes limp — no longer struggling, but still trembling all over, and he sees that her big dark eyes are wide, fixated on the knife. Alicia Keys sings "Fallin' " over the tiny speaker in the dangling earbud he pulled from her ear.

Jamie places Zoe Jennings's cold, quivering hand palm-down on the bedside table, beside the telephone her husband hung up less than fifteen minutes ago.

"Are you watching? Are you?"

She is, in horror.

"Good. Here we go."

The knife is getting dull. It isn't easy to get the blade all the way through layers of skin, flesh, tendon, and bone as Zoe strains and sobs and strangles against the gag. By the time the job is finished, she's passed out.

Jamie pockets the severed finger, a nice addition to the new collection that includes souvenirs from both Phyllis Lewis and Cora Nowak, whose middle finger he'd sliced from her hand out of habit before catching sight of her tattoo and being seized by brilliant inspiration.

Rather than attempt to skin Cora's forearm right there on the spot and risk ruining the exquisite artwork in his haste, Jamie opted to chop off the whole arm at the elbow. It wasn't until after she'd left the scene — with the finger, the arm, and of course the monogrammed lunchbox and

375

snacks from the Nowaks' cabinets and fridge — that she turned her attention back to the meticulous task at hand: peeling away the layer of skin and flesh that contained the tattoo that would be a telltale message to Cora's husband.

Jamie was so proud of her handiwork when she finished.

After adding the key main ingredient to the sandwich she'd bought at a convenience store off Route 86 west of Newburgh, she discarded the bloody remains of Cora Nowak's forearm in the woods, where furry predators would surely feast on it in short order.

Jamie did have one regret, though.

Because she hadn't set out to kill Cora herself — her husband was the intended victim — she wasn't able to set the stage the way she'd have liked.

No candles, no music, no lingerie . . .

And most importantly, when Cora's body was found with the entire right arm missing, as opposed to just the middle finger, no one would even grasp the significance of the crime. No one investigating the case would ever think to link it to the Night-watcher murders — despite the victim's husband's connection to Jerry Thompson. But really, that's beside the point now.

Punishing Chuck Nowak was like a warm-up for the main event.

As for Phyllis Lewis — that was far more satisfying all around.

They managed to keep it out of the press, but Jamie is certain the homicide squad made the connection. She knew it the moment she saw Detective Rocky Manzillo burst into his house early Wednesday morning, quickly change into a dress shirt and tie, grab his badge and his gun, and leave again.

Well, well, well, Jamie thought, watching the action courtesy of the surveillance cameras she'd set up in the Manzillo home so long ago. *Finally, something worthwhile to see here.*

There was no doubt in Jamie's mind that Manzillo was headed up to Westchester. Too bad she couldn't be a fly on the wall when Manzillo walked in on that oh-so-familiar murder scene and realized he'd made a tremendous mistake ten years ago.

A mistake for which Manzillo deserves to be punished.

And he will be, when it's time. But for right now . . .

"Wake up." Jamie slaps Zoe Jennings hard across the face. Out cold, she doesn't stir.

A shame she's going to miss the best part,

but time is short.

Jamie jabs the blade viciously between Zoe's large, silicon-enhanced breasts first, because that's what it felt like to Sam when Jerry was stolen away: as though someone had stabbed him in the heart.

Yes, that's what it's like to lose the person you love most at the hands of another, and you want to do the same thing to the one who stole that person away. You want them to suffer that same unbearable agony.

Zoe Jennings dies quickly.

But Jamie keeps sinking the knife into her body, over and over, eyes closed, seeing someone else bleeding, suffering, dying.

This isn't about Zoe at all.

It isn't about her husband, a total stranger whose loss couldn't matter less to Jamie in the grand scheme of things.

No, the Jenningses — like Phyllis and Bob Lewis and Chuck and Cora Nowak — are insignificant casualties in a much more meaningful game. They merely had the misfortune to cross paths with *her*, the one who is to blame.

When it's over, Jamie tosses the red-handled knife — the one that came from the MacKennas' kitchen — onto the floor beside the bed.

■ ■ ■ ■

"Allison!"

Startled from a sound sleep by an urgent whisper, she opens her eyes, then clasps her hands over them, dazzled by a blinding overhead light.

"Sorry, sweetie . . ." She hears the wall switch click and then Randi's voice saying, "It's okay now, I turned it off. Where's Mack?"

Mack?

Allison opens her eyes again, this time to shadowy darkness — and confusion.

It takes her a moment to remember where she is — the Webers' guest room — and that Mack should be here in bed with her. Yet even in the dim light falling through the doorway to the guest sitting room, where Randi is standing, backlit, Allison can see that his spot is empty

"Where's Mack?" Randi asks again, no longer whispering.

Allison's heart pounds as she sits up — too quickly; her head pounds as well, and her stomach gives a queasy lurch.

"Nathan Jennings is on the phone. He said Mack called him for a ride, but when he got there, he couldn't find him."

"Got where?" Allison swallows back excess saliva with the tinny taste of fear and vodka, trying to understand.

"Wherever Mack said he was stranded. On the road someplace, I think. Ben is on the phone with him now."

"Mack?"

"No, Nate. Here, Al, come talk to him."

Allison stands hurriedly, fighting back full-blown nausea. She remembers — and regrets — having downed in a few gulps that second, welcome, stiff martini Randi handed her after the Jenningses left.

She doesn't remember much that happened after that, not even coming up to bed . . .

And now the Jenningses . . . Nathan Jennings on the phone, looking for Mack . . . Mack not here . . .

What in the world is going on?

Hearing a rustling near the bed, she remembers belatedly — J.J. is there, sleeping in the portable crib.

Not sleeping anymore, though. He emits a sound that begins as a soft whimper and winds up an ear-splitting wail, and she instinctively bends over to pick him up. He's soaked through his terry cloth pajamas, poor thing. Did she forget to change him one last time before putting him down for the night?

Wait — she wasn't the one who put him down. She was at the wake, and J.J. was here with Greta, whom he barely knows, and now it's the middle of the night and he's wet and Mack isn't here and Allison wants to cry, too.

"Here . . ." Randi is beside her, reaching out for the baby. "I'll take him. Go talk to Nate. Ben is on the phone in our room."

"He's wet."

"I'll change him. Go ahead, Al." Randi sounds worried.

Mack — where is Mack? What's going on?

Feeling dizzy, she hurries from the guest sitting room and out into the hall. There, she makes a wrong turn and winds up at the foot of the stairs leading up to Greta's third floor quarters.

Hastily backtracking, feeling more frantic — not to mention sick to her stomach — by the moment, she finds her way to the other wing of the house. The door to the master suite is open, and she can hear Ben on the phone.

Sitting on the edge of the bed, wearing only boxer shorts and five o'clock shadow, he looks up when she enters. "Where's Mack?"

"I don't know." Taken aback by the concern in Ben's dark eyes, she forgets to be embarrassed by his state of undress. "He's not in bed."

Ben frowns and says into the phone, "No, he's not. Yes. Allison. Okay, hang on." He passes the receiver to her wordlessly.

"Hi, Allison." She recognizes Nathan Jennings's voice. "Do you know where Mack is?"

She has some idea, and shudders inwardly at the thought of him wandering around the Webers' kitchen, rummaging through the cupboards.

But she doesn't know if Mack ever confided in Ben about the sleep medication, or — if he did — about the bizarre side effects that accompany it. And even if he did, surely Nathan Jennings doesn't know.

"He called me and said his car was broken down just off the Saw Mill and he needed a ride."

"But that's not . . ."

Yes. It is. If sleepwalking and sleep-eating are possible, then surely sleep-talking — over the phone, or otherwise — is also possible.

"The last thing I knew," she tells Nathan, her stomach churning, "he was in bed."

Even that isn't the entire truth. She doesn't even remember coming to bed last night; only that Mack turned in much earlier than she did, soon after the Jenningses left. He must have been here asleep when she came up. Surely, she'd have noticed if he wasn't.

Or would she?

But Nathan doesn't need to know any of that. Her only obligation is to protect Mack from . . .

Well, she has no idea what, but her instincts are telling her to tread carefully.

"Where are you now?" she asks Nathan.

"I'm standing on the side of the road, off Exit 37, where he said he would be."

"Why would he call *you* for a ride though?" she asks, not bothering to add the *no offense* that pops into her head. She really doesn't care whether she offends this man who, with his wife, barged into her life at the worst possible time.

Remembering the way Zoe Jennings reminisced with Mack — and Ben, too, for that matter — and having picked up on her attitude of easy familiarity toward him, Allison feels the same irrational pinprick of jealousy she experienced earlier, when Mack smiled at Zoe.

Zoe, and her husband, too, had known a Mack Allison herself never had the opportunity to meet — a Mack who was young

383

and single and unencumbered by a doomed marriage, a terrorist attack, a high-pressure job . . . the weight of the world.

I was cheated, Allison found herself thinking earlier as she listened to the easy banter — a silly thought, she knew then, and knows now — but she's only human.

"I'm wondering the same thing," Nathan Jennings tells her, "and I have no idea why he called me."

"Are you sure it was him?"

"I looked at the caller ID on the phone after he hung up, and it had his name on it, so . . ."

"Oh. Well, did you call him back?"

"I tried to. He didn't answer. It just rang right into voice mail. I left a message. So you don't know where he is?"

"No. I don't. I'm sorry." Too overcome by worry and nausea to keep going around and around with him, Allison gestures for Ben to take the phone.

After handing it over, she paces across the carpet as he says into the receiver, "Nate? Ben again. Listen, I'm not sure what to tell you. I have no idea why he called or where he is, but —"

He curtails what he's saying as Allison stops abruptly in her tracks with a startled gasp.

If Mack were stranded on the side of the road, he'd have called for help from his cell phone — and that would have come up on caller ID as private, not with his name.

Their home phone, though, would be listed *James MacKenna.*

"I know where he is," she whispers to Ben, who raises an eyebrow. She hurriedly touches her index finger to her lips, indicating that she doesn't want him to let on to Nathan Jennings. She isn't sure why.

Something strange and frightening is going on, and she needs to get to Mack as soon as possible.

Please, please let him be all right . . .

"Allison! Where are you going?" Ben calls as she bolts from the room.

She doesn't answer, rushing into the adjoining bathroom and vomiting into the toilet.

Pulling into the garage back at home, Nate Jennings is aggravated — with himself, mostly, for getting caught up in this elaborate wild-goose chase when he could have been sleeping.

But he's aggravated with Mack, too, wondering what the hell is going on.

Oh well. At least tomorrow — today — is Sunday and I can sleep in, he thinks.

Then again — probably not. The kids are always up pretty early, and Zoe likes to consider those early morning weekend hours "family time."

Meaning, if she has to get up and suffer through the kids' antics, so should he.

He climbs out of the car and hits the remote twice — one button to close the garage door behind him, the other to lock the car.

It drives Zoe crazy that he does that — "Why lock the car when it's already locked into the garage?" she asked before bed, frustrated at having to come back into the house for the keys after running out to grab the purse she'd forgotten in the car.

But Nate can't seem to break the habit. Before they moved here to the suburbs, he parked on the street in their Manhattan neighborhood, where even locking the car doors didn't keep thieves from breaking into it four times.

"This is Glenhaven Park, Nate — it's safe here," Zoe told him after he — out of guilt — went back out to unlock the car and fetch her purse. "You're the one who said we probably don't even have to install an alarm system here."

"I was talking about the house, not the car."

"Right, and you could probably leave the car parked out front all night, unlocked and running, and no one would steal it."

"Then nobody would have stolen your purse, either, right? You could have left it there until morning."

"My phone is in it."

"So? Do you have a desperate need to get in touch with someone now?"

"Maybe," she said, annoyed, and he watched her retrieve the phone and start pressing buttons, probably checking for texts.

She often goes back and forth with her sister, and with the friends she left behind in the city, and with God only knows who else.

Now, stepping into the kitchen, lit by the bulb beneath the stove hood, Nate sees her open purse still on the counter, right where she left it earlier. He tosses the keys beside it, drapes his jacket over the back of a chair, and heads for the stairs.

Again, he thinks about the wild-goose chase and wonders what it was about.

In the old agency days, Mack — and Ben, too — was a practical joker. They all were. So was this some kind of prank? Was Ben in on it, too?

Nate would buy that if not for the somber

circumstances. Would Mack — a grown man now, and on the heels of a tragic wake — really have gone out of his way to do something so ridiculous?

Say he *had* actually gone to the trouble of staging a ruse that dragged Nate out into the rain in the dead of night . . . wouldn't he have jumped out of the bushes to have a good laugh at him?

The old Mack would have.

The new Mack . . . who the hell knows?

He's a virtual stranger after all these years. People change. Things change. And he's going to remind Zoe of that first thing in the morning. She'd be better served by starting from scratch here in Glenhaven Park, rather than trying to reignite old friendships . . . or anything else.

Reaching the top of the stairs, Nate is sure he left the bedroom door open earlier, but now it's closed.

Maybe Zoe got up with one of the kids while he was gone.

Who are you kidding?

She probably wouldn't hear them if they screamed bloody murder.

Nathan Jennings opens the bedroom door — and crosses the threshold into . . .

Bloody murder.

CHAPTER THIRTEEN

Bobby Silva's prison nickname, Rocky and Murph have been informed, is B.S. — and not just because of his initials.

According to the corrections officer who led them to the small room where they're conducting inmate interviews, Silva is a pathological liar.

"Don't believe a word he says," the CO advises them.

"Terrific," Murph mutters under his breath. "Why are we bothering?"

"A lot of times with guys like this, there's a grain of truth in there somewhere," Rocky reminds him.

With any luck, Silva will be more forth-coming than Doobie Jones was when they talked to him a short time ago. The guy couldn't have been less cooperative, staring through them when they questioned him about Jerry Thompson. He simply refused to talk.

"You can't get blood from a stone," Murph muttered to Rocky after Jones was escorted away, "and that was the most stone-cold SOB I've ever met."

Now it's Silva's turn to take a seat across from them as the armed CO takes up a watchful post on the other side of the glass-paneled wall. His presence was a definite comfort when Doobie Jones was in here.

But this guy isn't anywhere near as menacing. Where Doobie Jones sat stealth-still, B.S. is full of nervous energy. He's small in stature, with jet black hair, close-set black eyes, and sharp features. If he were a cartoon character, Rocky finds himself thinking, he'd be a rat.

"Do you know what time it is?" he demands, left alone with detectives.

Murph pushes up his sleeve and consults his watch. "Almost three-thirty."

"I know that!"

Murph shrugs, calmly lowering the sleeve. "You asked."

"Why'd you drag me out'a bed in the middle of the night?"

"We have some questions for you," Rocky tells him, "and we hear you're a smart guy. You know more than anyone else what goes on around the cell block."

Ego sufficiently stroked, B.S. nods in

agreement. "Yeah, that's right."

"You knew Jerry Thompson pretty well, didn't you?"

"Jerry? Jerry was my best friend." B.S. twitches in his seat. "I tried to save his life. Gave him CPR for, like, two hours, but he didn't make it."

Rocky figures that's about as likely as Jerry rising from the dead, considering that B.S. was locked in his cell that fateful night, but he commends him for his heroic efforts.

Encouraged, B.S. launches into a detailed account of the action, painting himself as a bold would-be savior who tended to his fallen fellow inmate as the rest of the prison population, staff and medical personnel included, looked on helplessly.

Managing to look duly impressed, Murph says, "Wow, you're one hell of a good friend, Mr. Silva. How did Jerry get his hands on the orange juice and the poison?"

In a flash, Silva goes from effusive to wary. "I don't know."

Yes, you do, Rocky thinks. *You know that it came from Doobie Jones, and you're afraid of what he'll do to you if you rat him out.*

Murph makes a few more futile attempts to get B.S. to reveal the truth. Watching him fidget and glance repeatedly at the door, Rocky decides it's time to change the subject before the guy clams up altogether.

"So you and Jerry were best friends," he says. "Did he ever talk to you about what his life was like on the outside?"

Still guarded, B.S. lifts his chin. "What do *you* think?"

"I think you were the one person he trusted in this place, and you were probably a good listener."

"Yeah, I'm a great listener. All the guys tell me stuff all the time, because I'm the only one they trust. I used to be a secret agent before I got here, so I know how to keep my mouth shut."

Masking his amusement, Rocky waits for B.S. to finish telling him about the government secrets he's been privy to over the years, right up to the raid last spring on Osama Bin Laden's compound in Pakistan.

"And what about Jerry?" Murph finally cuts him off. "What kinds of secrets did he confide in you?"

"A lot of stuff. You know."

"Did he ever talk about what he did to get himself in here in the first place?"

"Sure."

"What did he say?"

"He said his sister, Jamie, killed a bunch of people and he got blamed for it. He said no one believed Jamie was real. Everyone thought she was dead, even Jerry's mother and father, but she wasn't."

Rocky nods, rubbing his chin.

Yes, Jamie was dead — no dispute there.

But what if Jerry mistook someone else for her? Or what if someone convinced Jerry that she was Jamie? What if that person, posing as Jamie — a person who fit into a size fourteen dress — had committed the murders and then slipped away as the police closed in, leaving a confused and hapless Jerry to take the fall?

It would explain how the murders could be replicated now with the deaths of Cora Nowak and Phyllis Lewis.

"Did you say Jerry's *father* thought Jamie was dead?" Murph asks.

Startled, Rocky raises an eyebrow, belatedly picking up on what he'd missed.

"Jerry said it was his fault that she died," B.S. tells them. "That's what I said."

No, it isn't.

But this is even more intriguing, and Rocky raises a hand slightly, in case Murph is about to call him on the lie. Of course, he isn't. He senses, as Rocky does, that they might be on to something.

Jerry Thompson reportedly never knew his father, Samuel Shields, who was just fourteen years old when he got his sixteen-year-old girlfriend Lenore Thompson pregnant with twins.

At the time, Samuel had even bigger problems than that. His own father, a paranoid schizophrenic, had tried to kill him and later been committed to the psych ward. And Samuel himself had already been in and out of juvenile detention — with an unpromising future ahead of him as a convicted felon.

Remembering the photograph in Jerry's file — the one that showed him and his sister with a man who looked like he could have been their deadbeat father — Rocky asks B.S., "How was Jamie's death the father's fault?"

"He got mad and went after Jerry's mother. When Jerry went to help her, his sister attacked him. Then she ran away. And she was killed out on the streets after that."

The latter part of that story is undeniably true.

What about the first part?

"Do you know if Jerry was ever in touch with his father while he was here?" Murph asks.

"Nah, he didn't know where he was, he said. He never got any visitors. Me, I get visitors all the time," B.S. brags. "My family comes, and my friends, and the governor came a couple of times — he's working to get me out of here — and . . ."

The governor. Right.

Rocky and Murph exchange a glance, reminding each other that they can't believe anything this guy says.

Then again . . .

What if there's some truth to what he said about Jerry?

They do their best to glean more meaningful information from B.S., but true to his name, he has nothing more to offer.

When at last he's taken from the room, Rocky shares his latest theory with Murph: that there really might have been a Jamie: either someone Jerry mistook for his dead sister, or someone who convinced Jerry that she was Jamie.

"And you think that's the person who killed those women ten years ago?" Murph asks. "And now Nowak's wife and the Lewis woman, too?"

"It could be."

"But why start killing again now all of sudden, ten years later?"

"Jerry's death. That might be what triggered it. Nowak was killed just days after he died; Lewis about six weeks later. And when you look at the victimology . . ."

Murph nods thoughtfully. Of course he

knows as well as Rocky does how important it is to profile the victims along with their killer. You look at what they have in common, figure out why they might have been targeted by the unsub — unknown subject.

Rocky goes on, "Nowak was on duty on Jerry Thompson's cell block the night he killed himself."

"Or was murdered, depending on who you want to believe."

"Right. And Phyllis Lewis's connection to Thompson was less direct, but it's there, Murph. She lived right next door to Allison, and Allison's testimony put Jerry into prison in the first place."

Murph whistles under his breath.

"So let's say this person — someone Jerry believed was Jamie — really did — *does* — exist," Rocky continues. "If Thompson's death was the trigger, where do we look for the motive?"

"Revenge."

"Exactly. You kill Nowak's wife to get back at him. You kill Allison's neighbor to get back at her."

"But why not Nowak himself? Why not Allison herself?"

"For some people, losing a spouse is a fate worse than death," Rocky says simply. "Believe me."

"I do." Murph gives him a sympathetic pat on the arm.

Determined to focus on the business at hand, Rocky says, "Whoever killed Cora Nowak knew what losing her would do to her husband. And he maximized the impact with that gruesome sandwich delivery."

Rocky and Murph had studied the grainy surveillance videotape that showed the perp dropping off the so-called lunch that night. You couldn't make out a damned thing; just a dark, hooded figure with his face completely obscured. It could have been anyone.

"But you're talking about a wife," Murph tells him, "not a next-door neighbor. What about the Lewis case? That doesn't make as much sense."

"No," Rocky agrees. "It doesn't. Unless there was more to the relationship between Allison MacKenna and Phyllis Lewis than we know."

"They're both married with kids."

Rocky gives Murph a pointed look.

"Okay," Murph says, "anything's possible. But I don't buy it."

Frankly, Rocky doesn't, either. But you have to look at all your options.

"We've got to talk to anyone we can find who knew Jerry Thompson ten years ago, anyone who can shed some light on this.

Including his father." Rocky is still intrigued by B.S.'s mention that Jerry's father was there the night he was attacked by his sister, and by his own memory of the photograph sitting in the case file.

He quickly dials the precinct and asks Tommy, the station house desk sergeant, to put him through to Mai Zheng, one of the newer junior detectives on the squad. She's incredibly proficient when it comes to computers and records.

She answers her phone on the first ring.

"Mai," he says, "I need you to do something for me. Write down this name: Sam Shields."

He quickly tells her to look into Shields's background; find out if there was any way he had been a part of Jerry's life after all, and whether he's the man pictured in that old snapshot in Jerry's file.

"I want to know where he was in December 1991, around the time that Jamie Thompson was murdered," he tells Mai, "and I want to know where he was when the Nightwatcher murders took place — and where he is right now. Got it?"

"Got it," Mai says. "I'll get right on it."

He hangs up to see a thoughtful-looking Murph scratching his chin.

"If we go with the revenge theory, Rock,"

he muses, "then who's next? Because you and I both know there's gonna be another one."

Rocky hadn't gotten that far in his line of thinking, but Murph is right.

Promptly putting himself back into the predator's shoes, Rocky returns, "Who else do you blame for Jerry Thompson kicking the bucket?"

"Doobie Jones, if you know what we know."

"True," he tells Murph, "but chances are, the unsub doesn't, and anyway — how are you going to get to Jones in here?"

"You're not. It has to be someone accessible. Someone who has more to lose."

Jesus.

It dawns on Rocky, and he can feel the blood drain from his face.

He's up and on his way to the door in a flash.

"Rock," Murph calls, startled, "where are you going?"

Rocky manages to summon a one-word reply, and it comes out sounding strangled. "Ange."

Unnerved by a second police car that races past with wailing sirens, Allison bites her lower lip and looks at Ben, behind the wheel.

His short, dark hair is tousled from the sweatshirt he'd hastily pulled over his head, and she's sure her own hair must be completely disheveled. She didn't bother to comb it, just splashed cold water on her face, grabbed her toothbrush and scrubbed the taste of vomit from her mouth. Then she threw on the closest thing at hand — a pair of jeans from the laundry bag, and the starched white dress shirt Mack had worn to the wake earlier, then apparently tossed on the floor beside the bed.

The police car disappears around a distant corner, heading in the general direction of her house.

She looks at Ben. "You don't think . . ."

"I'm sure he's fine. Anyway, you said he's been sleepwalking lately, so maybe . . ."

Yes, she did say that, sharing just enough information with Ben about Mack's nocturnal activities — but not too much. She didn't tell him about the Dormipram, or about . . .

The knife.

Why can't she stop thinking about it?

He was going to cut an apple that night, just as she'd watched him do hundreds, thousands of times before.

Pushing the unsettling memory from her mind, she tells Ben, "If he drove in his sleep, though" — and it looks as though he may have, given that his keys and the BMW were missing — "that would be so dangerous."

"Maybe he didn't do it in his sleep. Maybe he was wide awake when he left."

"But why would he have gone? And why wouldn't he have told me?"

"I don't —" Ben breaks off at the sound of another screaming police car approaching in the distance.

They're both silent, listening as the sirens grow closer before the whirling red lights overtake them. Ben pulls off to the curb to let the cruiser pass, and Allison rolls down her window to gulp fresh air.

"Hang in there." Ben is back on the road and driving faster than the speed limit now. "It's going to be okay."

She says nothing, praying that all those police cars aren't headed for Orchard Terrace.

But when they reach it, the block is dark and quiet, and Allison lets out the breath she'd been holding. Thank God.

"He's here!" she tells Ben a moment later, spotting Mack's car beyond the hedgerow, parked in their own driveway.

Ben, too, exhales in relief.

They pull into the driveway and she jumps out of the car, making a beeline for the house. But she stops short at the front door, realizing she doesn't have her keys.

That wouldn't matter anyway, she remembers, spotting the alarm company sticker affixed to the front door.

The new system is keyless — Mack thought it would be safer not to have them floating around, so easily stolen and duplicated — and she doesn't remember the code she's supposed to punch into the panel.

Mack had called her from the house to give it to her after it had been installed, and though she dutifully scribbled it down, she didn't bother to memorize it. As far as she was concerned, that was a moot point. They weren't ever going to move back in.

Now, though, she's not so sure about that. Now, she longs to open the door and step into the safe haven this house was supposed to be.

"I can't get in," she tells Ben, and presses the doorbell a couple of times. She knocks, too, then pounds, seized by a growing sense of urgency.

When at last the door opens, Mack is standing there.

"What are you doing here?" he asks,

surprised, and she's relieved that he sounds — and looks — like his normal self. Not the least bit zombielike; he's clearly wide awake.

"What are *you* doing here?" Ben returns, as a grateful Allison grabs on to her husband and gives him a quick, fierce hug.

"I got a call on my cell from the alarm monitoring service. They said there had been a security breach and that I was supposed to meet the police here. I've been waiting, but they haven't shown up yet."

"That happens sometimes with these systems," Ben tells him. "I guess the cops got busy with something else."

Remembering the squad cars that rushed past a few minutes ago, Allison realizes that the sirens are still wailing eerily in the night. Something bad is going on out there — but thankfully, it has nothing to do with Mack.

"Did you check out the house?" Ben asks Mack.

"I did. Everything seems fine."

Allison asks, in horror, "Are you crazy? You went into the house by yourself after . . . after what happened?"

Mack shrugs. "It wasn't a big deal. Probably just an electronic malfunction. It's always happening with the neighbors' alarms, remember?"

"I remember."

I remember a lot of things. I remember that there's a homicidal maniac out there somewhere.

"But you didn't know it was safe inside when you got here," she points out. "Someone could have been waiting to jump you."

"Things are different now, Allie," he says patiently. "No one is going to get into this house ever again without the alarm code. And you and I are the only two people in the world who know what it is — so don't worry."

She just shakes her head at him, terrified at the thought of what might have been.

"Mack, listen," Ben says, "did you call Nate Jennings a little while ago and tell him you needed a ride?"

"What? Nate Jennings? Why would I do that?"

"So you didn't?"

"No. Why?"

"Either someone else did, pretending to be you — or who knows, maybe the crazy bastard just imagined the whole thing."

"What are you talking about?"

Listening to the sirens in the background as Ben explains the situation, and seeing the hint of confusion meld with the guarded expression in her husband's eyes, Allison can't help but feel uneasy again.

"I'm going to call Jennings and figure out what's going on," Ben decides.

"First," Mack holds the door open and steps back, gesturing him inside, "I need to call the monitoring service."

Ben walks past him, but Allison hesitates before crossing the threshold.

Mack touches her arm. "Hey. It's okay."

No, it isn't okay.

Looking up into his eyes, she searches for some real reassurance, but finds instead that familiar mask of emotional restraint. He's worried — he has to be — and afraid, too, but he isn't letting on.

Allison forces herself to walk inside.

Stepping into the front hall — seeing the three framed baby portraits on the wall and breathing the familiar scent — she's swept by an unexpected wave of homesickness.

Yet she can't get past the knowledge that *he* was here, whoever he is; that he violated this sanctuary.

She'll never feel safe in this house again.

Walking across the hardwood floor and through the archway into the living room, she takes in J.J.'s ExerSaucer, the children's' books lining the lowest built-in shelf, the stacked throw pillows on the end of the couch where Mack likes to lie at night . . .

With an ache in her throat, she realizes that for the first time in days, she feels comforted.

This is what's missing at the Webers' house: being surrounded by familiar things that remind her of all the good times. Everywhere she looks there are mementos and photographs of smiling faces; colorful shards of a mosaic that tells the story of their life, hers and Mack's and the kids — her hard-won happily-ever-after.

She picks up a framed snapshot of the five of them together on the beach last summer. Lynn snapped it on one of the few days Mack was able to be there with them. Sand and sea as a backdrop, smiles squinting into the sunshine — even J.J. looking alert and cheerful.

That was such a great day — and she didn't even know it at the time. She remembers feeling frustrated that Mack couldn't be there for the whole week with them, wistful every time she saw another family stroll by, intact with mother and father and children . . .

Things could have been worse for us, she tells her own image in the picture, forever frozen in a smile that doesn't quite reach her eyes. *You lost sight of that somehow. You were focusing on what was wrong instead of what was right, and now . . .*

Now, she and Mack and the kids are living in someone's guest room.

It isn't fair. This is her home, dammit. Is she really going to let fear rob her family of their Happy House?

Do I have a choice?

Yes. There's always a choice.

You can run scared, or you can dig deep for inner strength, hold your head high, and fight for what you deserve.

"Allison?"

She turns to see her husband watching her from the archway. She sets the photo back on the table. Maybe she'll grab it later when they head back to the Webers'. It would be nice to have it on the bedside table as a touch of home.

Oh hell, it would be nicer to just go home.

"Where's Ben?" she asks.

"In the bathroom."

"I thought you were going to call the alarm service."

"I am." He looks like he wants to say something else, maybe take the wall down a notch at last.

She waits, holding her breath, willing him to say something, anything, that will make her feel less alone right now.

After a moment, he takes his cell phone

from his pocket, and her hopes deflate. He just doesn't have it in him, under duress, to be that guy. He has to be the strong, stoic one.

Okay, fine.

I'm not going to be the weak, frightened one, though, from here on in. No way.

Mack presses a couple of buttons on the keypad, then frowns.

"They have their number blocked."

"Who does?" she asks, having lost track of what he was even doing.

"The alarm monitoring company. They called me and I didn't put their number in my cell yet, so I thought I could just pull it up on caller ID and hit redial, but I guess I need to go look it up. I'll be right back."

He disappears.

Allison lowers herself shakily onto the couch and looks around the living room. It seems like a lifetime ago that she and Mack were here, in this house, living their day-to-day life with the kids. Has it really only been less than a week?

Through the doorway to the sunroom, she can see the new pleated fabric shades, pulled all the way down. Is that how they're going to live from now on? In the dark, afraid to let the sun in for fear that someone is out there watching them, waiting to pounce?

In the far corner is the desk where she kept the Lewises' spare keys. She pictures him — the Nightwatcher — stealthily creeping across the carpet, opening the drawer, rummaging through it.

Is that why Phyllis Lewis became a victim? Because she had the misfortune to entrust Allison with the keys to her home, just as Kristina Haines did?

What if . . . ?

Struck by a sudden, troubling thought, Allison sits up straight.

She's the one who found Phyllis Lewis's murdered body, and she was the one who found Kristina Haines, too, ten years ago.

What if the police decide she's a potential suspect?

It was her eyewitness testimony that sent Jerry Thompson to prison. What if they conclude that she made it all up — seeing him there that night — in order to throw them off her own trail?

Jerry confessed, though. You had nothing to do with that.

Yes, Jerry confessed . . . but there was another murder after he died, and it was staged to look just like Kristina's. The lingerie, the flickering candles, the missing finger on her right hand . . .

The only thing missing was the music, and —

"Allison?"

She whirls around, startled. Mack is once again behind her.

"This is bizarre. The alarm company said they didn't call me."

"What do you mean?"

"I just got ahold of them, and they didn't know anything about making a phone call to me earlier about the alarm system." He turns to Ben, who's come up behind him. "Can you call Nate Jennings?"

Ben nods and pulls his cell phone from his pocket. Mack and Allison watch in silence as he scrolls through the numbers, selects one, and presses a button to dial the call.

It seems to ring a couple of times before Ben says, "Nate?"

Even from across the room, Allison hears the explosion of sound from the phone in Ben's hand. Nathan Jennings is screaming about something, and the blood drains from Ben's face.

Allison's heart begins to pound and she stands, crossing the room to stand beside Mack.

"My God . . . my God . . ." Ben listens for a few more seconds, then says hoarsely into the phone, "Nate, I'm so sorry. I'll be right there."

Hanging up, he turns to Allison and Mack. "Zoe . . ." His voice breaks and he tries again. "Zoe's been . . . she's been . . . she's dead. Someone killed her in her bed."

Intellectually, Rocky knows the unsub had nothing to do with Ange's condition. Even if he hadn't seen her stricken with his own eyes in the darkened bedroom that August night; even if there were some way a predator could administer some kind of drug that would mimic an aneurysm . . .

The truth is, it happened long before Jerry Thompson died in prison.

It has to be a coincidence, and nothing more.

In fact, if someone seeking revenge against Rocky had figured out that his wife is the most precious thing in his world, then chances are, the damned aneurysm very well saved her life.

But that doesn't mean that someone isn't watching at this very moment, bent on making sure that Ange never comes out of her coma, now that she's showing signs of recovery . . .

The NYPD has already sent a couple of uniforms over there, and hospital security is on alert.

Still . . .

"I wonder if I should try to have her moved," Rocky muses aloud to Murph, at the wheel.

It's been over an hour since they left the prison, headed to Ange's bedside so that Rocky can see with his own eyes that she's still hanging in there.

"I don't know, Rock. In her condition, that's probably not a good idea."

"Neither is leaving her there if someone wants to hurt her even more than she's already been . . ."

Throat clogged with emotion, Rocky can't even finish the sentence.

Murph glances over and says simply, "I know. Hang in there, Rock."

They ride on in silence for another couple of minutes, Rocky weighing the odds that perhaps karma is somehow responsible for what happened to Ange. If he is partly responsible for sending an innocent man to prison, then in the grand scheme of things . . .

What right do I have to be happy? What right do I have to pray for a miracle? What right do I have to hold out hope when —

His cell phone rings abruptly. Pulse racing, he snatches it up.

412

Braced for bad news, given the path his thoughts have taken, he gets it — but not at all what he was expecting.

Thank God, thank God, it isn't Ange.

He closes his eyes in brief, silent prayer as that sinks in — then opens them abruptly and grabs his reading glasses, a pencil, and notepad from the console.

"Okay, go ahead," he tells Tommy, the station house desk sergeant, and quickly jots down the victim's name and address Tommy provides.

Zoe Jennings . . . Abernathy Place . . .

Startled, he asks, "Did you say Glenhaven Park?"

Murph shoots a sharp, questioning glance in his direction.

"Yeah," Tommy says. "That's up in —"

"I know where it is," Rocky cuts in. "We're on our way."

He hangs up and looks at his partner.

"Another one," Murph guesses. "Same MO and signature?"

"Sounds like it."

"And it's in Glenhaven Park? So there's a connection to Allison MacKenna again?"

"Looks that way," Rocky says grimly, wondering if they were on the wrong track altogether with Jamie and the revenge killings.

He rubs his eyes, exhausted, and wishes there were some way he could just take a break to think things through. Wracked by the familiar notion that he's missing something, some key piece of the puzzle, he knows that the best thing to do is take a step back and find some downtime to clear his head. That way, he can come at it from another angle and see things he overlooked when he was in the thick of it.

But there's no such luxury on this case, on this day, with the clock ticking the way it is.

Three women have already been savagely killed. The timing between the last two murders is only a matter of days, not weeks. That means the cooling-off period before the unsub strikes again is likely to be even shorter.

There's not a moment to waste right now on sleep, or anything else.

"Don't worry, Rock."

He looks up and makes eye contact with Murph before his partner turns his gaze back to the road, adding, "You know our guys will keep an eye on Ange. They won't let anyone get near her."

"How is it that you can always read my mind, Murph?"

He expects the usual quip in return.

Not this time.

"You and I have been together a long time, Rock. You're like a brother to me, and Ange . . . nothing's going to happen to Ange."

Hearing the hoarse note in Murph's voice, Rocky turns to look out the passenger's side window, blinking away tears as they race on through the night.

CHAPTER FOURTEEN

Seated on the couch in his own living room, Mack holds his BlackBerry in his jittery hand, tapping it rhythmically against his knee as he waits.

Waits . . .

Waits . . .

It's been at least an hour, maybe more, since a uniformed officer drove him from the Jenningses' home back to his own. He was informed that one or more detectives would arrive shortly to question him.

Allison is in the house, too, somewhere — driven back separately, though. It's standard procedure, he knows, to keep witnesses apart after a crime.

Witnesses?

Come on, Mack. You're suspects — at least, you are — and you know it.

That was obvious almost from the first moment he, Ben, and Allison arrived at the house on Abernathy Place.

They were greeted by a familiar scene: squad cars, rescue vehicles, cops, reporters, curious bystanders. Just like here on Orchard Terrace the night Phyllis Lewis's body was discovered . . .

By none other than Allison.

That alone would have made the local cops suspicious — he's known it all along, though his protective instinct wouldn't allow him to say that to his wife. But tonight — surely Allison didn't miss the way the officers at the scene warily zeroed in on them both when they stepped out of Ben's car.

Jack Cleary, the police captain they'd met after Phyllis's murder, materialized immediately to take charge. One of his detectives asked a few quick questions, and the next thing Mack knew, he was in the back of a squad car being driven home.

All he wants now is a chance to clear up any misconception the police might have about his own involvement here. Whoever did this — whoever stole Allison's nightgown and the Lewises' keys, whoever lured both Nathan Jennings and Mack out into the night with those phone calls, whoever killed Phyllis and Zoe — that person knows exactly what he's doing.

But *why* is he doing it?

And who the hell is he?

Mack wishes he'd paid more attention to the voice on the other end of the phone line, claiming to be an alarm company representative.

It was a man, and the connection was brief and to the point, along the lines of, "Mr. MacKenna, I'm calling from your home alarm monitoring service. There's been a breach in the system. We're sending a police officer to the house. Can you please meet him there?"

Meet him there . . .

Wouldn't the alarm company, calling someone in the middle of the night, have assumed that the person could be found *at home?* Presumably in bed?

Whoever made that call knew that I wasn't. He couldn't possibly have known that unless he's been watching.

And if he's been watching . . . then he knows exactly where the MacKennas have been staying.

All this time, Mack has assured Allison that she and the kids are safe where they are . . . but he no longer believes it.

Yes, the Webers have a good security system. No one can get past their front gate without punching in a code, the property's perimeter is guarded by an electric fence, and the house has an alarm, also accessible only by code.

Still . . .

Police protection. That's what we need.

The sooner the cops find out that the phone calls were a setup, the sooner they can focus on keeping Mack's family safe.

And the sooner they can track down the real monster behind all this.

Mack's head is throbbing; his shoulders and neck are on fire. Is it any wonder? Stress, exhaustion, shock, fear. . . .

He thinks about Zoe.

Stabbed to death in her bed, Ben had told him. Just like the others.

His gut churns. He closes his eyes, and he can see her lying in a pool of blood, with candles lit around the room and her middle finger missing, just like the others.

The image is so vivid that he can almost convince himself that he was really there . . .

But of course, he wasn't.

No, he didn't get that far . . . did he?

Momentarily confused, he runs back through the scene that had unfolded after he learned of Zoe's murder.

It had taken only a minute or two to get over to the Jenningses' house. Ben was at the wheel, Mack beside him, Allison in the backseat. He's pretty sure none of them said a word.

The cops met them out front.

Right. Talked to them, separated them, drove Mack back here.

So he was never in the Jenningses' house.

He's just so exhausted he's losing track of the series of events.

But he'd better get them straight, because the last thing he needs is to contradict himself in front of the cops.

He yawns, going back further, trying to recall exactly what had happened earlier, back at the Webers' house.

After Zoe and Nate departed, he left Allison and Randi in the kitchen and Ben watching TV, and he went up to bed alone. He didn't take a Dormipram because he'd had a couple of beers and anyway, he felt exhausted. But that didn't matter. Without the medication, for the first time in ages, it took a long time for him to fall asleep.

He remembers lying restlessly awake contemplating taking the medication after all — what was the worst that could happen?

But he didn't take it . . .

Wait, did I?

He can picture himself getting up and going into the small bathroom to find the orange prescription bottle . . .

But that doesn't mean it happened.

He can envision Zoe's murdered body, too, but that doesn't mean he saw it.

He yawns deeply and rubs the burning spot between his shoulders, again replaying the earlier events in his head.

Okay, so he must have finally drifted off, and then the ringing telephone woke him, and —

"Mr. MacKenna?"

Mack looks up to see Captain Cleary.

The other night, the man's expression was neutral. Right now, however, it's ice-cold.

"I'm Captain Cleary." He flashes a badge. "We met a few days ago."

A police officer flashing a badge — Mack is catapulted back in time to his apartment on Hudson Street, the one he shared with Carrie. Two cops at the door hand him a packet that contains all that's left of his wife: a gold band engraved with her initials and their wedding date . . .

"This" — Cleary gestures at the man accompanying him, and Mack forces his attention back to the matter at hand — "is Detective Patterson."

Under any other circumstances, Patterson would be just an ordinary-looking middle-aged man — short and round, almost bald, with thick glasses and a bulbous nose. Next to Jack Cleary, however, he appears downright homely.

Almost feeling sorry for the guy, Mack starts to rise to greet him, but Cleary jerks a vertical palm at him, gesturing for him to stay seated.

Settling back onto the couch, Mack notes with incredulity that there's a uniformed — and armed — officer stationed in the archway, eyes trained directly on Mack himself.

They actually think he's a dangerous criminal.

He opens his mouth to start clearing up this gross misunderstanding before they waste any more time on him while the real killer is still out there. But before he can speak, Patterson motions abruptly for him to be quiet.

Mack's pity for him flies out the window, but he obediently clamps his mouth shut. The cops are hell-bent on calling the shots here — as they should be, in all fairness — and the last thing he needs is to start off on the wrong foot.

He nods when Cleary asks if he's willing to answer a few questions, wondering whether he actually has a choice. Not that it matters. He has nothing to hide. Of course he's going to cooperate.

"Would you mind turning off your phone, Mr. MacKenna?" Detective Patterson asks. "We don't want any distractions."

He obliges, grudgingly, and puts the BlackBerry into his pocket.

His thoughts race as he answers the first few questions — basic ones about where he and Allison have been staying since the Lewis murder, and how he knows Nathan and Zoe Jennings.

He knows damned well where this is leading. Maybe he should have a lawyer present.

Is it too late to ask?

He nervously bounces his right leg, heel hitting the carpet in a rapid-fire staccato — then stops when he sees Cleary and Patterson glance from his bouncing foot to each other.

"So you were out of touch with them until recently?" Patterson asks.

"The Jenningses, you mean? Until a few weeks ago. I first saw them again — well, Zoe — at a party. Nathan was there, too, but I didn't get a chance to talk to him."

"And where was this party?"

"At Ben Weber's house." He wonders about Ben, whom he hasn't seen since they arrived at the Jenningses' house. Was he also questioned?

Mack hopes so. Ben is articulate and well-qualified to vouch for Mack's character; he'll be willing to help the cops straighten out this mess.

Mack just hopes he doesn't mention the gun. He's pretty sure Ben won't — after all, he doesn't have a permit for it.

It's not as though Zoe was shot, but still . . .

It doesn't look good for him to have a gun in the house — even though it's still safely locked in his dresser drawer — and Allison will flip if she finds out.

"Tell us about your relationship with Zoe Jennings."

Caught off guard by Cleary's command, Mack echoes, "My *relationship*? I don't have a relationship with her. I mean, I barely know her — barely knew her — anymore."

"And you'd say the same thing about her husband?"

Mack nods vigorously. "The only time I've talked to him in fifteen years was the other night when I ran into him on the train —"

"Which night?" Patterson cuts in impatiently.

He's holding a pen between his forefinger and middle finger as if it were a cigarette. He's a smoker, Mack realizes, probably on edge and wanting a smoke.

His fingers . . .

Fingers . . .

Was Zoe, like the other victims, missing a finger?

He swallows hard, not wanting to imagine a disembodied finger, not just for its sheer ghastliness, but for the memory it triggers.

All that was left of Carrie was her wedding ring; how many times has he fought back the horror of imagining what might have happened to the finger it was on? To the rest of her?

"Mr. MacKenna! Which night did you run into Nathan Jennings on the train?"

"I'm sorry . . ." He takes a deep breath, trying to clear his head. "It was . . . it was the night I came home and found out about Phyllis Lewis. I guess that was . . . Tuesday."

Tuesday. Yes.

It's always a Tuesday, isn't it?

"That was the only time in fifteen years that you spoke to him?"

"Yes. I mean, until they came over to the Webers' tonight — Saturday night, last night," he clarifies, noting the chalky daylight falling through the window.

"And this morning . . . ?"

"What?" Confused, he says, "I'm sorry, I just . . . I didn't get any sleep and I guess I'm having a hard time following."

"You talked to Nathan Jennings this

morning . . . ?"

"No." Maybe Detective Patterson is the one who's confused, here. Nicotine withdrawal makes your brain fuzzy, right? "As I said, Nate and Zoe came over to the Webers' last night. They left at around ten, I guess, maybe ten-thirty."

"So you didn't speak to them or call them at all after that?" Cleary asks, and clarifies, "I'm talking about earlier this morning — after midnight?"

"Do you mean did I call to ask Nate for a ride?" Seeing the man's blue eyes narrow, Mack adds, "I know that's what Nate said happened, because Ben and Allison told me. But I didn't call him."

"You're sure about that."

Mack wants to scream. "Positive."

"And there's no way you might have, say, made the call and then forgotten about it?"

"Who forgets making a phone call?"

Who, indeed?

He tries to ignore a flicker of misgiving as he admits — to himself only — that he doesn't have a great recent track record for remembering other things he's done in the wee hours. Walking, talking, eating . . .

Captain Cleary doesn't know about that, though . . . does he?

What if he's already talked to Allison, and

she told him?

Why would she?

Then again . . . why *wouldn't* she? She's not trying to hide anything . . .

And neither are you.

Mack shifts his weight uncomfortably, wishing he could fidget with his phone, or pace, or . . .

Or light a cigarette, he thinks, watching Detective Patterson roll the pen back and forth between his twitchy fingers.

Once upon a time, Mack, too, was a smoker. It seemed everyone was, during that era in New York, when he was in his twenties and you could light up anywhere you pleased, in bars and restaurants, at the office . . .

He and Carrie quit together when they decided to start a family. But around the time that his marriage started to crumble, he went back to it. The old habit took the edge off the stress, and he kept it up for a while after Carrie died.

Then you had to quit all over again, and wasn't that fun?

Whatever. All he knows is that right now, he'd kill for a cigarette.

Kill?

Not kill. He could never — would never — kill.

Never.

This is surreal.

"A call was placed to Nate Jennings, Mr. MacKenna, at" — Cleary consults his notes — "two-forty-eight A.M. It came from your home number."

Startled, he shakes his head. "I didn't make it. I wasn't even here. Someone else must have been, and made the call. Actually —" He leans forward. "I had a call myself, right around that time, from my alarm monitoring company saying that the system had been breached."

A call the alarm company denied making — something Cleary may already know.

And now he'll either think I'm lying, or realize someone is screwing with me. With all of us.

Mack takes his BlackBerry out of his pocket, pressing the on button.

"Mr. MacKenna —"

"Wait, I just want to show you something." The device powers up, and he presses the recall button, then holds the BlackBerry outstretched toward the captain. "See? I got that call at . . ." He turns the screen toward himself and checks the time. "Two forty-nine."

Just one minute after Nathan Jennings received the call from this house.

It's obvious to Mack that both calls were placed by the same person — the murderer — and that the motive for the first call was to lure Nate out of the house, leaving Zoe alone and vulnerable.

And the motive for the second?

"He was trying to get *me* out of the house and over here," he tells Cleary and Patterson, careful to keep the note of desperation out of his voice, as they take turns glancing at the phone. "It's obvious."

Neither man responds to that.

Mack's fingers twitch, itching to hold something . . . his BlackBerry, or . . . a cigarette.

Shaken, he again reminds himself that he doesn't even smoke anymore. How could he crave a cigarette?

Come on, is it any wonder? When was the last time you were under this much stress?

Unless . . .

He's been eating at night, and not remembering a thing.

What if he's been doing other things, too? Smoking?

But where would he even get cigarettes?

Could he have bought or bummed them, and forgotten that, too?

Cleary passes the BlackBerry back to Mack.

"Look," Mack says, trying to keep his voice from quaking, trying not to think unsettling thoughts, "I know what it looks like, but I'm innocent, and I'll do whatever you need me to do to prove it. Go ahead, check my fingerprints, my DNA, whatever you need."

"Are you willing to provide a DNA sample?" Cleary asks immediately.

"Absolutely, and anything else you need."

A few minutes later, left alone again while they arrange for the DNA testing, Mack finally exhales.

It won't be long now. He just has to hang in there until they clear him and move on.

He only prays, with a growing sense of dread, that his family will be safe in the meantime, and that . . .

No. That's impossible.

There is no way — absolutely no way — he could have done anything but walk, and perhaps eat, in his sleep.

No way . . .

Staring at herself in the master bathroom mirror as she blow-dries her hair, Randi sees that the rough night is evident in the anxious expression in her eyes and in the purplish valleys beneath them. She ordinarily doesn't wear foundation on a weekend day when she's just planning to stay at home, but on this dismal Sunday, she's going to need it — and some under-eye cover cream, too.

She doesn't have much time, though, to pull herself together. Greta is watching all three of Allison's kids in the third floor playroom, and while the girls are no problem at all, J.J. is a handful. Poor baby has been up since the wee hours, when Randi summoned Allison with the news that Nate Jennings was looking for Mack.

Little J.J. wanted his mommy so desperately, straining to reach for her when she came back into the guest bedroom to change quickly before leaving with Ben. Ordinarily, she'd probably have given her beloved mama's boy a quick cuddle, but she was so utterly discombobulated that she barely seemed to notice, letting Randi hang on to him. She'd gotten sick, she said, and Randi couldn't tell whether it was because she wasn't used to drinking vodka martinis — or because she was upset that Mack was gone.

Why the hell *was* he gone at that hour?

Randi still has no idea what, exactly, went on here in the night. All she knows is that she and Allison stayed up pretty late, talking, drinking.

Randi, who with her own small stature has

a low tolerance for alcohol, was taken aback by all the confidences that came pouring out of an inebriated Allison. Some of what she said wasn't the least bit surprising — like that she resents how much time Mack spends at the office these days.

"It sucks, being alone with the kids all the time," Allison slurred.

"Don't I know it," Randi told her.

Allison delivered some bombshells as well. Like when she said she sometimes fantasizes about moving back to Nebraska, away from the cutthroat pressure of New York.

"You can't go," Randi remembers telling her, on the verge of the tears that come so easily when you've had several drinks. "What would I do without you? You're like a sister to me."

She doesn't remember Allison's reply — she doesn't remember a lot of what was said, come to think of it — but she does remember hugging her and crying, the way you do in college when you're drunk and prone not just to tears, but to emotional declarations about how much you love your friends.

Going to bed is a blur in her mind.

Then all hell broke loose at around three-thirty in the morning, and on the other side of town, Zoe Jennings was murdered.

When a traumatized Ben called her with the news, Randi simply couldn't get her head around the idea that a woman so young and vibrant, a woman who just hours ago was talking and laughing *right here under the Webers' own roof,* had met such a horrific end.

She wishes Ben would get back and fill in the details, but she hasn't talked to him since around five-thirty. That was when she took a break from pacing the floor with a miserable J.J. and called her husband's cell to make sure he was all right. He sounded harried and said he couldn't talk.

"And my cell's almost dead, so —"

"But Ben, I just —"

"I'll turn it off for now to save the battery and call you back as soon as I can," he promised.

He didn't call back.

That was about two hours ago; it must be well past seven now, probably almost eight.

She tried calling Allison's cell, too, but it rang somewhere in the guest room — she'd left it behind. Mack didn't pick up when she called his. And when she tried the MacKennas' home number, it bounced right into voice mail.

Maybe she should finish getting dressed, try to get a groggy J.J. down for a morning nap, and go out to find Ben.

But where would she even look? At the Jenningses' house? The MacKennas'? Where the heck is he?

She gives her hair one last brush-through with the dryer going, then switches it off and reaches for her cosmetics bag.

"Randi?"

She jumps, startled, and sees Ben standing in the doorway.

"Sorry — I didn't mean to scare you. I said your name a few times, but you had the hair dryer on."

"I didn't hear you. It's okay." She takes a deep breath and lets it out, trying to calm her shattered nerves.

Ordinarily, she's not so jumpy.

But when she thinks about Zoe; about what happened to her last night . . .

Now, looking at her husband, she sees reflected in his eyes the same expression she just glimpsed in the mirror.

She goes over to Ben and puts her arms around him. "What happened over there?"

He hugs her back, resting his chin on the top of her head. "She was killed in her bed. Stabbed, Nate said. He's a mess."

"I can imagine."

Sadly, that's the truth. She *can* imagine, all too well.

For the past couple of hours, ever since she got the call about Zoe, she's been haunted by the thought that it could happen to anyone, anywhere, at any time. It's frightfully easy to put herself into Zoe's shoes, or Nathan's.

Eyes closed, she holds tightly to Ben, breathing the unfamiliar scent that clings to his clothes: a hint of cigarette smoke, maybe, and outdoor air, and . . .

Death?

"Did you go in there?" Randi asks, abruptly releasing her grasp and stepping back. "Did you see her?"

"No!" He shudders. "They wouldn't let anyone in, even Nate had to stay outside, and the kids were at the neighbor's when I got there. I just talked to the police, and then —"

"You talked to the *police?"*

"Yeah."

"But . . . why?"

"I was one of the last people to see Zoe alive, Randi. So were you. They're going to want to talk to you, too."

"And Mack, and Allison . . ."

Something shifts in his gaze, and he breaks eye contact, leaning toward the mirror and rubbing the peppery growth of beard on his

435

chin. "They're talking to Mack and Allison now."

"At the Jenningses' house?"

"I'm not sure where they are. They took them away."

"Who?"

"Mack and Allison."

"No, who took them away?"

"The police."

Their gazes meet in the mirror and hold.

"Why did they do that?" Randi is afraid of the answer and not sure why.

"To question them, I guess."

A strange and terrible thought flits at the edges of her consciousness like a falling leaf fluttering on a breeze, but before she can catch it, it dances out of her grasp.

"When will they be back here?" she asks Ben.

"I'm not sure." He jerks open the mirrored medicine cabinet door, shattering their eye contact in its reflection.

"Ben?"

"Yeah?" He pulls out a can of shaving cream and his razor, closing the door but not looking up into the mirror again.

She hesitates, not sure what she dares to say, or even think . . .

But again, something teases at her brain, something that happened last night . . .

something Zoe said? Or, no, something Allison said, when they were sipping their last drinks in the kitchen . . . ?

She settles on just "I'll finish getting ready, and then I'll go down and make some coffee."

Ben nods.

She doesn't move.

Ben looks at her. "What are you thinking?"

"Probably the same thing you're thinking."

"Probably." He rubs his temples with his palms. "What the hell are we supposed to do about any of this? Call a lawyer?"

"For us?"

"Us? No! Why would we — *we* didn't do anything."

"But you think . . ." She can't bring herself to say it.

"I don't know what to think. I have a name — a defense attorney out of White Plains — but . . . it hasn't come to that yet."

"You think it will?" she asks, thinking, *Defense attorney. Good God.*

"I don't know. It doesn't look good, though, Randi. For Mack."

Ben tells her about the phone calls he allegedly made and received, and that according to Allison, he's been sleepwalking lately.

"She might have mentioned that to me, too," she says, more to herself than to Ben, trying to remember exactly what Allison told her last night, when they were having that last drink.

There was something . . .

"I could tell it bothered her to talk about the sleepwalking," Ben is saying. "And I keep thinking about the nanny cam, wondering . . ."

"I haven't used it in ages," she tells him.

Greta's been here for so long, it's no longer necessary. They trust her.

But do they trust Mack?

Randi feels sick inside. "Do you think, when he comes back, we should set it up?"

"I think . . ." Ben takes a deep breath, lets it out, shakes his head. "I think we need to rethink having him spend another night in this house."

"Mack is your best friend."

"And you're my wife, and two women are dead, and the police think there's a chance he might have something to do with it. And so do I, maybe, and admit it, Randi, so do you."

She swallows hard. "I don't know . . . when I think of Mack, I just can't imagine how . . ."

"I can't, either, but we can't take any

chances."

"So what are we supposed to do? Kick them out?"

"Not *them*."

"Just him?" She shakes her head. "Allison is never going to let that happen. She and the kids will go with him if we ask him to leave, and then what? What if —"

No way. This is crazy. She just can't fathom that Mack could hurt his wife or children . . .

Or, for that matter, anyone else.

She says that to Ben, and is troubled by his reply.

"He's been sleepwalking, Randi, remember? Maybe he's not in his right mind when that happens, and . . . I don't know. Right now, all I can do is protect you and the kids — and, if she'll let me, Allison and their kids."

"From Mack," she says flatly.

"From Mack." Ben turns away, picks up the shaving cream again, and his razor.

Feeling dazed, Randi shakes her head and leaves the room.

From the hall, she can hear the faint voices of Hudson and Madison, eating cereal down in the kitchen with Greta.

I love those sweet little girls — and J.J., too — like my own. I'd never let anything happen to them, ever. If I really thought . . .

Okay . . . does she really think it?

Ben does. He was with Mack. He knows more than she does, has seen more than she did. And yet . . .

How many times has he said that he loves Mack like a brother? They were best man at each other's weddings — well, Mack's second wedding, as he and Carrie had eloped; and they're godfathers to each other's sons . . .

Which means . . . what?

That Mack can't possibly have a dark side neither of us has ever seen?

Yes.

No.

But all those years of friendship sure as hell mean something.

As if to punctuate that thought, the girls' giggles float down the stairs. They're up there in the playroom without a care in the world — daddy's girls, Allison sometimes calls them.

"In their eyes, Mack can do no wrong," she said not long ago, with a wry laugh.

Oh, Allison . . .

What in the world is going on?

"Mrs. MacKenna?"

Sitting on the edge of her bed, she looks

up to see the handsome police officer she first met a few days ago.

"Captain Cleary. You remember — we talked down at the precinct on Wednesday?"

She stands, nods.

"This is Detective Patterson." He gestures at the stout man who steps into the bedroom on his heels, also showing a badge. With him comes the unmistakable scent of stale cigarette smoke.

Allison shakes both their hands.

"Would you mind having a seat again, please? We'd like to ask you a few questions."

She sits, sneaking a glance at the clock on the nightstand. Her girls will be awake soon, wondering where she and Mack are, and J.J. — for all she knows, he's been up all night.

Does he have a rash from sleeping in that wet diaper? Did Randi find the special prescription ointment in the diaper bag?

The female police officer who drove Allison back here and stayed with her until the detectives showed up wouldn't even let her call to check on the kids. That infuriated her. But she knew better than to defy authority and make a big deal about it then — and now.

These guys don't care that she's a worried

mother. Things will move along faster if she just tells them whatever they want to know. She hopes Mack does the same thing when his turn comes — unless he's already had his turn and is on his way back to the Webers'. She hopes so. Randi and Greta can probably use all the help they can get with J.J.

Thinking of all the potential hazards her baby might encounter in that huge house that's no longer child-proofed, Allison shudders inwardly.

"Are you cold, Mrs. MacKenna?"

"What? Oh — no. I'm just worried about my kids," she hears herself admitting to Captain Cleary, despite her resolve not to go there.

"I'm sure they're in good hands."

How the hell would you know?

She decides she doesn't like him. It's not just because he's be so dismissive of her concern for her children, but . . .

Okay, maybe it is just that.

"Would you like a glass of water before we start?"

"No, thank you. What I would like is to call and check on my children. If I know they're okay, I'll be able to focus on this."

"Go ahead and call," Captain Cleary tells her with a note of resignation in his voice.

Realizing they're going to stand here and watch her do it, Allison reaches into her pocket for her cell phone.

It isn't there. She's pretty sure it was in the pocket of her jeans when she'd taken them off; it must have fallen out, or maybe J.J. got to it.

Her heart sinks. What if her son is chewing on the phone? That can't be healthy, right? Don't cell phones give off some kind of electromagnetic field?

And just as disturbing — what if Randi's been trying to reach her?

She'd have tried the house if she needed me, she reminds herself. The phone hasn't rung at all since they've been here.

She picks up the receiver on the bedside table. About to punch in the Webers' number, she realizes there's no dial tone. Frowning, she presses the talk button a few times and listens again.

"Is there a problem, Mrs. MacKenna?"

"The phone is dead. It must not be charged," she tells Captain Cleary.

"Isn't that the charging base?"

"It is, but . . ." Simultaneously, she and the two men bend to see if the cord is plugged into the wall behind the table.

It is.

"I'll take a look," Captain Cleary says,

holding his hand out for the receiver.

Allison gives it to him and watches him press the talk button as if somehow she'd been doing it wrong.

He listens, shakes his head, and hands it to Detective Patterson with a questioning look.

"I'll be right back." He leaves the room, carrying the phone.

Left alone with Captain Cleary, Allison is uncomfortable. She plays with the ruffle on the pillow sham, feeling his eyes on her. After a minute, she looks up.

"Where's my husband?" she asks boldly.

"Don't worry, Mrs. MacKenna, he's fine."

That doesn't answer the question.

Frustrated, she rolls and unrolls the ruffled hem of the sham, wishing they could get on with the questioning.

But when Detective Patterson finally reappears in the doorway, he asks Captain Cleary to step out into the hall.

Allison strains to hear what they're saying out there, but can't make out a word. After a few minutes, they reappear, obviously ready to get down to business.

"Sorry about that," Captain Cleary tells Allison. "It looks like there's a problem with your telephone line. I'm sorry you won't be able to make that call just yet. We're having it checked out."

"A problem with the phone line? What kind of problem?"

"Why don't you tell us about Zoe Jennings?" Detective Patterson suggests.

Zoe Jennings. Yes. That's why they're here.

Until this moment, Allison has done her best not to dwell on the fresh horror — or her own role in any of this — but there's no avoiding it now.

She clears her throat. Her mouth is so dry. She'd thrown up earlier, she remembers, and now her head is pounding and she's probably dehydrated. She should have accepted the glass of water.

But they're waiting for her reply, and she doesn't want them to think she's stalling.

"There's not much to tell. I'm so sorry for what happened to her" — *sorry* doesn't begin to cover how she feels about what happened to that poor woman — "but I just met her last night."

"Tell us about that."

Allison quickly recounts the condolence call.

In the aftermath of shocking, traumatic murder, she's sick with guilt over her own alcohol-fueled reaction to Zoe and her brownies and, yes, her boobs. Not that that's any of the cops' business, and she doesn't mention it, but still . . .

"So you weren't friends?" Patterson asks.

"No. We'd just met," she reiterates, anxiously twisting her wedding ring around and around her finger, wishing they'd just let her go.

"And what was your husband's relationship with her?"

The way Captain Cleary speaks that word — "relationship" — causes Allison to look up sharply from her hands.

She holds back her knee-jerk answer — which would be that Mack certainly didn't have a relationship with Zoe Jennings — knowing it might come across as defensive.

Defensive of Mack?

Or of myself?

Both. She resents the insinuation that her husband could possibly have been cheating on her with Zoe Jennings.

Wait a minute, Allison — think about that. Is that really what they're implying? Or are you reading it that way because . . .

Because she herself suddenly doubts everything she once would have sworn was true about the man she married?

Randi's words on that long-ago afternoon, words that struck a chord even at the time, drift back to her: *We can never really be sure what's going on in someone else's head, even someone we think we know well* . . .

"Mrs. MacKenna?"

She blinks. "I'm sorry . . . my husband and Zoe were former colleagues. That was their relationship."

"So they were colleagues . . . friends?"

"Maybe back then, but I don't think Mack had seen her in years."

"You don't *think* he had? You're not sure?"

"Yes. I'm sure. He hadn't. They just moved up here — the Jenningses — and they were at a party we went to about a month ago. Mack talked to Zoe there."

"So he has seen her recently."

"Just there. I'm sorry, I didn't pay much attention to it."

"He didn't introduce you to her?"

"No." *But it wasn't like that,* she wants to add.

Like what, Mrs. MacKenna? Like your husband was trying to keep his mistress and his wife from getting to know each other?

Disgusted with the track her own thoughts have taken, Allison rubs her throbbing temples, wishing Mack were here, or that she could be wherever he is, just so that she'd feel reassured about their marriage.

His faithfulness has never been a question until now.

It still isn't, dammit. Not in *her* mind.

She trusts her husband. She's positive there was nothing going on between him and Zoe Jennings. He barely has time for her and the kids, let alone an affair.

Then again . . .

Isn't that what cheating husbands do? Claim to be working late while they're really —

Stop it! Just stop, Allison!

Mack isn't capable of hurting her that way. Mack loves her and the kids and their lives together, and he would never jeopardize that. Whatever his faults are — hiding his feelings, not reaching out for help — he's an honorable man incapable of telling a white lie. How can he possibly be living a huge one?

He can't.

He isn't.

"What about Phyllis Lewis?"

"What?" She frowns at Captain Cleary. "I have no idea if she knew Zoe Jennings."

"No, I meant — what was her relationship with your husband?"

"Oh my God! This is nuts! They were neighbors! Friends! That's all!"

So much for her resolve to play it cool.

"Why don't you just come out and ask me if I think Mack had affairs with Phyllis and Zoe and killed them both?" she challenges. "Then I can tell you flat-out that that's the craziest thing I ever heard."

Jack Cleary's reply is maddeningly calm. "Mrs. MacKenna, you understand why we have to ask these questions. Your husband called Nathan Jennings in the middle of the night, told him his car had broken down, and said to meet him off the Saw Mill River Parkway. And while Nathan Jennings was out of the house, looking in vain for his friend in need, someone who opportunistically *knew* he was out of the house came in and killed Zoe Jennings."

"But Mack wasn't even the one who made that call."

"It came from this house," Patterson points out, "and he was here at the time."

"Do you know that for sure? What time it was? Because he got a bogus call on his own phone telling him to come over here."

"And did you witness that call your husband received?"

She hesitates before admitting, "No. I was sleeping."

"In the same room? The same bed? And you didn't hear the phone ringing, or your husband talking on it?"

No, because I was passed out from drinking too much.

"I've always been a sound sleeper." Even

449

as the words come out of her mouth, she knows they sound lame, and she can tell by the looks on their faces that they agree. *They think I'm covering for Mack. I'm making things worse for him. But if I admit that I was drunk, I'll lose every last bit of credibility.*

"So you don't know for sure when the call came in," Cleary asks, "or what was said?"

"No, but I'm sure if you check Mack's phone, you'll find it."

Even as she says it — even if Cleary checks Mack's phone — she knows it won't prove anything. They'll say he could have placed that call himself, to his own phone, to set up an alibi.

"How do you know that your husband didn't call Nathan Jennings, Mrs. Mac-Kenna?"

She clenches her jaw, not wanting to answer Patterson's question, well aware that it won't help matters.

"Mrs. MacKenna?"

"Because he told me."

"You're not a hundred percent sure of it."

"I'm sure of it because Mack wouldn't lie to me."

"All right. But let's say that he himself isn't sure of it."

"What do you mean?"

"Has your husband ever exhibited any

unusual behavior in the middle of the night?"

Her heart sinks. Do they know? Or are they guessing?

She told Ben about the sleepwalking on the way over to find Mack. Did Ben tell the detectives when they talked to him?

If he did, and she denies it now, they'll know she's lying about that, at least, and they'll likely wonder what else she's lying about. They'll probably assume she's trying to cover for Mack.

Am I?

She pictures him with the knife in his hand, and the vacant look in his eyes, and she remembers what Lynn said about sleepwalkers becoming aggressive and violent if startled awake.

Mack ate while he was asleep — if the missing food wasn't evidence enough, his visible weight gain certainly was — and he didn't remember a thing about it the next morning.

Is it so hard to believe that his nocturnal activities could have included other things — darker, uglier things — and Mack would have no memory of that, either?

Suddenly enveloped in a cold sweat, bile rising in her throat once again, Allison forces herself to think it through.

Do you honestly believe Mack mutilated and killed two women in his sleep?

"Your husband's nocturnal behavior . . . ?" Patterson prompts.

With resignation, Allison admits, "He takes sleep medication. Dormipram, it's called. One of the side effects is sleepwalking."

"Does he talk in his sleep?"

She remembers the crazy gibberish he spoke in the kitchen that night. "Sometimes, but —"

Cleary cuts her off, asking, "Does he remember these episodes later?"

"No." She's not about to elaborate unless they force her.

"So it's conceivable that your husband might have left the house in his sleep and made a phone call in his sleep? One he didn't remember when he woke up?"

"I don't think that's what happened."

"I didn't ask you that. I asked if it's conceivable. That's the question you need to answer."

"I guess so," she says reluctantly. "But —"

"Thank you, Mrs. MacKenna."

Jamie's lips curve into a smile as she stares at the computer monitor.

Things couldn't be better.

The live-action image from one of her surveillance cameras shows Mack sitting on the couch in his living room, nervously tapping his BlackBerry against his knee as a police officer stands guard in the doorway.

In another screen, Allison MacKenna is putting some things into an overnight bag as a female officer waits in the doorway.

According to the conversation that just wrapped up between Allison and those cops, she's going to be driven back over to the Weber home. She asked if she could pack some spare clothing, which makes it obvious to Jamie, at least, that she's not planning on returning home again any time in the near future.

But the big question of the day is, where will her husband be sleeping from now on?

My money's on anyplace other than with his wife.

Jamie's smile gives way to a giggle at the thought — especially when she remembers the hint of misgiving in Allison's tone as she answered the detectives' questions about her dear husband.

She wanted so badly to defend him, but she couldn't.

She wanted so badly to find a reason to trust him, to give him the benefit of the doubt — and perhaps she did.

For now.
But that won't last for long.

She's soon going to find out that she married a monster capable of pure evil; a monster capable of robbing her of the very thing that matters most to her in this world. And when that happens, there will be no going back. She'll be shattered.

On screen, Allison surreptitiously wipes her eyes on the rolled-up sleeve of the men's shirt she's wearing and sneaks a peek at the policewoman to see if her tears are noticed.

"Are you almost finished?" the woman asks without the slightest bit of sympathy for poor little Allison, wife of the most notorious criminal this safe small town has ever known.

If you think that's bad, lady — that he killed a couple of so-called innocent women — just you wait.

Allison nods and takes something else from her drawer — not the one where she keeps her lingerie. Such a pity Jamie has no reason now to rummage through another drawer filled with deliciously silky undergarments.

Everything is in place for the final phase of the plan, though Jamie did hit a slight speed bump when the MacKennas moved out of their house after the Lewis murder.

The Weber home, with its sophisticated security system, provided a whole new set of complications.

But then, Jamie always did welcome the opportunity to rise above the greatest challenge, and this was no exception.

The plan hinged on finding Mack's BMW in the commuter parking lot, and there it was on Thursday afternoon, parked as always in the secluded far reaches, almost obscured by a clump of shrubbery.

It was so easy for Jamie to crouch beside it and affix a tiny camera just beneath the mirror on the driver's side of the door. The camera was trained not on the car itself, but angled to focus on a spot directly opposite the door, about three feet above the ground.

The exact height and location of the keypad beside the Webers' security gate. All Jamie has to do is watch carefully the next time Mack punches in the "secret" code.

Ha — there are no secret codes where you're concerned, Jamie silently tells Mack, who was so pleased with himself after having that new burglar alarm installed at home.

You probably should have waited to share the password with Allison in person — or at least, have whispered it into the phone when you made that call.

But I must say, I'm so glad you didn't.

Now there's just one more step to take before James MacKenna is sent off to prison for the rest of his life, and his wife is left utterly alone for the rest of hers.

But what needs to happen next won't be nearly as satisfying as what came before. There will be no wriggling, scantily-clad female begging for mercy — not a grown one, anyway, and somehow that takes the fun right out of it.

What will I do when I've won this final battle?

What reason will I even have to go on living after it's over?

Maybe I won't.

Maybe I'll do what Jerry did, and leave this miserable world behind.

On the screen, Allison picks up a framed photograph from her dresser top. Jamie can't see it clearly from here, but remembers which picture it is: the one of Allison with her baby on her lap and her daughters at her side, one cozily tucked under each arm.

A mother and her children.

Jamie watches Allison tuck the photo into her overnight bag, then zip it closed.

Ah, yes, Allison, that's a great idea. Take the picture with you. Take all the pictures with you.

After all . . . you're going to need something

456

to remember them by.

Gazing down at what's left of Zoe Jennings, Rocky feels sick to his stomach.

Not because of the badly mutilated corpse — he's all but immune to gruesome murder scenes after all these years — but because the son of a bitch got to her before Rocky got to him.

There I was paranoid about myself, worrying about Ange, and this poor innocent woman —

"Detective Manzillo?"

He looks up to see Jack Cleary striding into the room.

"I just spoke to your partner downstairs," he tells Rocky. "He said I'd find you up here."

Yeah, Murph hadn't felt the same need to hang around the dead body . . . not when one of the local uniforms had popped into the room to say that they'd just tapped a Box O' Joe from Dunkin' Donuts somewhere outside.

"I'm gonna take a coffee break," Murph decided. "Who knows, maybe there's doughnuts, too. Or fancy pastries, with these Westchester guys."

After Murph left the room, Rocky had placed a quick call to the hospital to see if there'd been any change since he last spoke to them.

"I just came on duty, Mr. Manzillo," the nurse told him, "and I heard that you're worried about some security issues. I don't know anything about that — all I can tell you is that it looks like she had a peaceful night."

Peaceful — he supposed that was good, as opposed to . . .

He looked at the body on the bed, knowing Zoe Jennings's last minutes on this earth had been anything but peaceful.

But Ange — Ange, he doesn't want to see peaceful. Ange, he wants sitting up, talking, walking, laughing, scolding him about his lousy diet.

"I expected to see you at the press conference I called yesterday morning about the case." Cleary jars him back to the moment.

"Yeah, I was planning to be there but . . . I couldn't make it. My wife is . . . she's been sick. I needed to be with her."

Rocky doesn't miss the flicker of disapproval in Cleary's blue eyes. Even then he expects the guy to say something — ask how his wife is, or express his regret that she's been sick — but he says nothing at all.

Rocky glances down at the captain's left hand and is surprised to see a wedding band. For all he knows, Cleary could be the best husband in the world — but somehow, Rocky doubts it. And somehow, that matters to him more than it should.

Cleary gets down to business, indicating the body on the bed. "Same signature as the Lewis case."

Right. Multiple stab wounds, missing middle finger, iPod earbuds hanging from her ears. There are votive candles, too. And she's wearing an ill-fitting lace teddy that Rocky is willing to bet came from another woman's bureau drawer — probably Phyllis Lewis's.

"Exactly the same signature?" he asks.

"Other than the fact that he got in through a window . . ."

Right. Rocky knows that. They found broken glass downstairs beneath one of the windows overlooking the backyard.

Clearly this time, the Nightwatcher didn't have a key. But that didn't stop him.

There was broken glass in Rocky's house, too, beneath a window.

Had he come in looking for Ange?

If she hadn't been in the hospital, would she be . . . ?

"And this time, we got the weapon. Kitchen knife with a red handle. He dropped it. No prints. But if you're asking whether she was raped, Detective Manzillo," Cleary says, "the answer is yes."

Rocky nods. He'd figured as much.

"Cora Nowak wasn't raped," he tells Cleary, then clarifies, "she's the wife of the CO over at Sullivan Correctional."

"I heard about that. Look, I don't know how it ties into this. All I know is we've got a semen sample here to match to the one we got at the Lewis place, and we've got a suspect who volunteered to provide us with his own DNA."

"*Volunteered?* Who is it?"

"James MacKenna."

Rocky's eyes widen. "Why him?"

Cleary quickly explains about the phone call that had conveniently summoned Zoe Jennings's husband from their bed in the middle of the night, Rocky hears the song he'd sung — well, tried to sing — just a few hours ago echoing in his head.

Mack the Knife.

Suddenly, it seems less a serenade to Ange and eerily like a harbinger of things to come.

But of course, that's ridiculous. He's no psychic. The song was just a coincidence. Besides . . .

"What about other prints? Not just on the knife, but . . ." The room has been dusted, of course.

"So far, it looks like he didn't leave any."

"So he wore gloves, but not a condom," Rocky says, more to himself than to Cleary.

"Looks that way."

"And Jennings is sure that it was Mac-Kenna on the phone?"

"The call came from his number."

"But the voice — he was sure?"

Cleary hesitates. "He says MacKenna was whispering, so it was hard to tell."

Rocky digests that.

"Another thing — looks like the phone line at the MacKenna house was cut sometime after that call was made."

"How does that fit in?"

"Who knows? Maybe he was trying to stage it to look like he and his family were victims, too."

"You say MacKenna volunteered his DNA?" At Cleary's nod, Rocky asks, "Why would he do that if he's guilty?"

"Because maybe he doesn't *realize* he's guilty." Cleary doesn't add a "duh," but he might as well have.

"Explain," Rocky says tersely.

"The guy sleepwalks. His best friend mentioned it earlier, and when I asked the wife about it, you could see that she didn't want to say anything, but she did. She said he's been taking some kind of medication

— Dormipram? It makes him get up in the middle of the night and do all kinds of crazy things."

"Like . . . ?"

"Like eat . . ."

"And kill women? Chop off their fingers?"

Cleary shrugs and says with exaggerated patience, "The subconscious mind is a complicated thing, Detective Manzillo."

Yeah. As if he didn't know. And so is this case.

Rocky's heard about Dormipram and its bizarre side effects. He's not ruling out that medication could trigger an otherwise sane man to commit a series of heinous murders in the dead of night, but . . .

He isn't sure he buys it.

Why not? Because you spoke to MacKenna yourself ten years ago?

Because you're feeling guilty over the fact that Doobie Jones most likely force-fed poison to Jerry Thompson?

Because you're thinking Thompson was innocent after all, and that there really was a Jamie?

Because Cleary didn't ask about Ange?

Or because he looks like a freaking movie star?

Maybe all of the above.

In any case, Rocky isn't jumping to any

462

conclusions. That might be Cleary's style, but it isn't his.

MacKenna was smart — he remembers that. Too smart to stage such an obvious ruse.

"If MacKenna wanted her alone in the house so that he could kill her, why wouldn't he just do it sometime when the husband was already going to be gone? Why go to all the trouble of getting rid of him with this elaborate scheme?"

"Who the hell knows how these sick bastards think? Looks like he wanted to do it then and there, so he got rid of the husband."

"But why make the phone call from his own house so that it could be traced right back to him?"

"Anyone who's capable of this" Cleary sweeps a hand at the bloodbath on the bed — "isn't in his right mind, Manzillo."

"Yeah, no kidding."

But what about Cora Nowak?

What about the mysterious Jamie?

"Sometimes you've got to go with your gut," Cleary says, "and when I talked to MacKenna, my gut told me he was a little too antsy. The guy has something to hide."

Fair enough.

And Rocky's gut tells him the case isn't as

straightforward as it might appear.

"Anyway, we've got a rush on the DNA results," Cleary informs him, "so we should have some preliminary results within the next seventy-two hours."

Maybe not soon enough, Rocky thinks, to prevent another murder. He asks, "Where's MacKenna now?"

"At his house."

"And what about his wife?"

"We had her driven back over to where her kids are."

"Which is . . . ?"

"They're staying with friends. The Webers. Why?"

"I'm gonna go talk to her. That all right with you?"

"Knock yourself out," Cleary tells him with a shrug. "Get the address from Joe Patterson. He's downstairs. You look like you've had a long night. Grab some coffee, if you want, or a doughnut."

"No, thanks," Rocky tells him. "I'm on a diet. My wife and I are going on a Caribbean cruise, and I'm trying to get into shape."

He dangles the phrase deliberately — "my wife" — to see if Cleary will be moved to ask about her health.

He doesn't, just gives a nod and pulls a

cell phone from his pocket, obviously having dismissed Rocky already.

Bastard.

Hudson is the first to look up from the Robert Munsch book she's reading to her little sister, spotting Allison standing in the doorway of the girls' guest room.

Madison is the first to leap off the twin bed and rush to embrace her. "Mommy!"

Kneeling to hug her daughter close, Allison can't seem to push her voice past the enormous lump in her throat.

"Aunt Randi said you and Daddy got up early and went out to breakfast." Hudson's announcement, when she gets her turn to hug Allison, bears more than a hint of reproach. "How come you didn't take us with you?"

"You were sleeping when we left," Allison manages to say lightly, and it's the truth, after all.

She pats her daughter's hair, which someone — perhaps the ever-efficient Hudson herself? — has woven into a neat braid down her back. Greta probably did it. She wears her own long blond hair the same way.

Madison is sporting the same hairstyle, and the girls are both dressed and smell of minty toothpaste and strawberry shampoo.

J.J., too, was bathed and well cared-for in her absence. She peeked in on him first and found him sound asleep in his crib, settled in for a morning nap he hasn't taken lately at home. But he obviously needs it today, what with all the wee-hour commotion.

She hunted quietly in the darkened room for her cell phone and found it on the floor beside the crib. Had she dropped it there herself in a drunken stupor when she went to bed last night? Or had J.J. gotten his hands on it again?

The tiny smudged prints on the phone seemed to be evidence of the latter, and her heart sank. She can't leave him. She just can't.

J.J., with his love of pressing buttons, had managed to turn the phone off. She checked her voice mail to see if she'd missed any calls from Mack — she hadn't — and put it into her pocket, hoping he would call.

"Where did you go?"

That question comes from Hudson, and is followed up with another from Madison.

"Where's Daddy?"

"Did you two eat breakfast yet?" Allison asks to distract them, not wanting to lie to them about anything unless she absolutely has to.

They nod vigorously.

466

"Aunt Randi sent Greta out to buy us Cap'n Crunch," Hudson reports, "since we didn't get any yesterday and it was a Saturday. She said you wouldn't be mad."

God bless Aunt Randi.

"I'm not mad. I wonder how she knew that you always get it on Saturdays and you missed it yesterday?"

"Huddy reminded her," Madison says proudly.

Allison starts to laugh, pulls them both close again, and the laughter suddenly gives way to a flood of tears. She hastily wipes them away behind the girls' backs before releasing them.

"Why don't you two go back to whatever you were doing," she suggests, "while I go find Aunt Randi to thank her for taking such good care of you?"

Obediently, the girls climb back onto the twin bed. Hudson picks up the book again and resumes reading to her sister, who becomes reabsorbed in the story in a matter of seconds.

Allison watches them for a few seconds before turning away, wiping her eyes once again.

Awash in tears and regret, she thinks about Mack who, according to Captain Cleary, was transported to the local precinct for DNA testing.

"Is he under arrest?" she asked in horror, and braced herself for the answer.

"No."

"So he's free to leave?"

"When we have what we need from him, if there's no reason to hold him, he'll be free to leave."

She was torn between asking if she could be with Mack at the station and coming straight back here to her children.

Maternal obligation — and concern — won out. But now that she knows the kids are fine, she almost wishes she'd opted to see Mack.

Almost.

She's not quite ready to face him just yet.

Now that the seed has been planted in Allison's own mind — and, thanks to herself and Ben, in the detectives' minds — that a sleepwalker might be capable of violence, she keeps wondering if Mack could possibly have committed two murders.

Not Mack, the kindhearted husband she's loved all these years, but a man under the influence of a powerful medication with frightening side effects.

She's seen firsthand the destruction drugs can wreak on the human mind. If drugs can cause a person — an otherwise loving mother — to take her own life, then surely they can also cause an otherwise sane and stable husband and father to take someone else's life.

But . . . Mack?

Her Mack?

Her partner, her protector, the love of her life, the father of her children . . . ?

We can never really be sure what's going on in someone else's head, even someone we think we know well . . .

Mack never talks about the details of Kristina Haines's murder, even though he was there that day, right alongside Allison. She always figured that for Mack, that murder was, understandably, overshadowed by the drama of losing Carrie in the World Trade Center — not that he talks about the specifics of that, either.

But what if Kristina's murder has been there all along, festering in the back of his mind? What if Jerry Thompson's death or the sleep medication somehow triggered his subconscious to reenact —

"You're back!"

Allison turns to see Randi in the hallway just outside the guest suite.

She's wearing jeans and a pristine white silk top and looks so like her usual self — hair done, face fully made-up, jewelry on —

that Allison's first instinct is to resent her.

How can Randi focus on her appearance at a time like this?

But of course, that isn't fair. The kids are fine, and Greta is here, too — Allison saw her downstairs when she came in — and anyway, Randi is one of those women who always manages to look pulled together. Even at her own father's funeral a few years ago, she was elegantly stunning.

"What's going on? Are you okay?"

Allison bites her lip, unable to reply, and shakes her head, conscious of the girls in the next room.

"Come on downstairs, Allie. I'll make you some tea."

She nods and follows her friend down the hall. Ordinarily, she thinks, Randi would already be asking more questions, but today she walks in silence a few steps ahead, all the way down the back stairs that lead directly into the big, empty kitchen.

The room, with its high ceiling, pastel walls, and custom cherry cabinetry, is large and airy enough to seem bright and cheerful even on this gray, rainy morning.

"Here — have a seat." Randi pulls out a chair, and Allison can't help but pick up on a weirdly stiff, formal undercurrent in the air.

She sits at the big round table and stares at the basket of apples in the center of it. "Thank you," she says, "for taking such good care of the kids while I was gone. They said you got them Cap'n Crunch."

Randi waves away the gratitude with her left hand, and her enormous diamond anniversary ring catches the light.

She's so lucky, Allison finds herself thinking absurdly, to be married to Ben. Ben didn't come with the baggage of a failed first marriage and a dead first wife. Ben isn't under a veil of suspicion in a murder case.

But of course, Allison doesn't want to be married to anyone but Mack. She loves Mack, and this is all just a huge misunderstanding, and any second now he's going to be back where he belongs, with her and the kids. Then they'll be able to figure out their next move before whoever really did kill Phyllis and Zoe sets his sights on them.

"Would you rather have coffee?" Randi asks, gesturing at the half-full pot on the counter. "It's already made."

"I'll just take tea, thanks."

"I figured. It'll be easier on your stomach. Is it still bothering you?"

"A little. I'll be fine. Is Ben here?"

Randi hesitates, then nods. "He'll be down soon. I told him you were back. He was just going to jump in the shower, I think."

And he's not in any hurry to talk to me, Allison realizes, reading between the lines. Maybe Randi isn't, either.

Do they actually believe Mack could be guilty?

Do I?

Watching her friend fill a red Le Creuset teakettle and set it on the enormous six-burner stove, Allison tries to see things from her perspective, and Ben's.

They've known Mack for years — much longer than Allison has, even — and they adore him. But, faced with evidence that seems to link him to a pair of murders, surely they're having second thoughts about welcoming him into their home.

Maybe they're even wondering whether he could have been responsible for the murders ten years ago.

Maybe I should be wondering that, too.

It seems preposterous now to even consider that Mack, reeling from an imminent divorce and a wife missing in a terrorist attack, could have killed Kristina Haines and Marianne Apostolos . . . and Jerry Thompson's mother? That makes no sense.

But . . .

At the trial, she recalls, an expert witness, a psychiatrist, testified that a catastrophic event like September 11 could trigger violence in a person already on the brink of a mental breakdown. That might have been what happened to Jerry Thompson, or . . .

Mack?

The truth is, it wasn't out of the question in Allison's mind ten years ago, when she barely knew him — and found herself wondering whether he might have known Kristina better than he was letting on.

Of course, she quickly dismissed her suspicions. She had seen Jerry Thompson creeping around the building the night Kristina was killed, and . . .

And you were so sure he was responsible, because of that?

He was the handyman. He was always around.

Yes, he gave Kristina the creeps, but that doesn't mean he killed her, and it sure as hell doesn't mean he was the hooded intruder who attacked Allison in her apartment.

Could that have been Mack?

She quickly dismisses the question as ludicrous.

Having turned on the flame beneath the teakettle, Randi asks, "Are you hungry? Can I make you some toast?"

"No, thanks, I'm —"

"Don't say fine, Allison. I know you're not fine."

Randi doesn't tack on her usual "no arguments," but Allison isn't about to offer one. Randi's right; she's far from fine.

"Tell me what's going on." Her friend sits across from her at the round table.

"I'm not even sure. They think Mack might have had something to do with it because someone made a call to Nathan Jennings's phone from our house. But it wasn't Mack."

There's a long pause before Randi asks, with obvious reluctance, "You're sure?"

"I'm positive! He's my husband! I know him and I know he's not capable of this."

She waits for Randi — who not so long ago reminded Allison that you never really know what someone else is thinking; Randi the self-proclaimed expert bullshit detector — to agree with her that Mack is incapable of murder.

But Randi doesn't say it. She doesn't say anything, just sits staring at the basket of apples with her chin resting in her hand, like she's waiting for Allison to go on.

Allison isn't sure what else to say — or what not to say.

She doesn't dare admit to anyone, not even her best friend, that she herself may be harboring the slightest shred of doubt about Mack's innocence.

It's not that she doesn't trust Randi . . .

Oh hell, yes it is.

How can she trust her friend when right now, she doesn't even trust her own husband?

"Allie . . ."

The invisible wall seems to crumble, and Randi reaches across the table to clasp a warm hand over Allison's cold, trembling one. "It's going to be okay."

"What if I'm wrong? What if . . ."

Don't say it, she warns herself, but her defenses are down, and the words spill out before she can stop them.

"What if Mack did it in his sleep? He's done other things . . ."

"What?"

Suddenly, Randi has gone absolutely still, staring at her, almost as if . . .

"It was just . . . talking to himself, and eating," Allison says quickly, her thoughts racing as she tries to remember whether she ever mentioned any of it to Randi. "It doesn't mean —"

"No," Randi says quickly, "it doesn't mean anything. I'm just so worried about you, Allie. And the kids, too."

Her grasp is so welcome — so reassuring

— that it takes a moment for the words to register with Allison.

"But not Mack?"

"I don't know what to think about Mack." Randi shakes her head. "You just said —"

"Forget it. Forget what I said."

"My cousin Mindy —"

"Please don't bring that up right now!" Allison wrenches her hand from Randi's grasp. "Please, just . . . don't."

She doesn't want to hear again about Mindy's encounter, years ago, with Ted Bundy.

She doesn't want to be reminded that one of the most ruthless serial killers in history was able to present himself as a charming, intelligent guy.

She pushes her chair back. "I need to . . . I'm sorry, can you . . . can I . . . can I leave the kids here just a little while longer?"

She'd just sworn not to leave J.J. again, but he's asleep, and . . .

I have to go. I have to get to Mack.

"Of course you can leave the kids here, but where are you going?"

"I just . . ." She takes a deep breath. "Mack needs me."

"Allie —"

"Don't, Randi. Please. He's my husband. He's in trouble and I've got to go help him."

"Just wait until Ben comes down. He said he knows a good defense attorney who —"

"Ben said Mack needs a lawyer?"

"Not exactly that, he just thought —"

"He doesn't," Allison tells her.

Not yet, anyway.

"Do you want me to come with you?"

"No, please just watch the kids for me." Allison tells her, already heading for the front hall where she left her handbag — with her car keys in it — when she got back here from the wake . . .

Was it only last night?

Unbelievable, how things can change so quickly. One minute, you have everything you ever wanted, and the next . . .

No.

I still have everything I ever wanted. I still have my husband and three beautiful children, and nothing — nothing — is going to change that.

CHAPTER FIFTEEN

"Fancy-schmancy, huh, Rock?" Murph comments, pulling the car to a stop at the foot of the long, winding driveway leading to the Webers' three-story brick mansion.

"What did you expect?"

"Nothing less. You think these people feel safe back in there?"

Rocky regards the looming closed iron gates. "That depends."

"On what?"

"On whether the danger is out here, or right under their own roof."

"So you think they're harboring a murderer."

"I don't know what to think, but I want to talk to MacKenna's wife."

Murph shrugs. "I still think we should talk to the guy himself."

"We will, but right now, I want to get to her, so . . ." He gestures at the keypad and intercom affixed to the stone pillar on the driver's side of the car.

Murph rolls down his window, asking Rocky, "You don't happen to know the access code?"

"Nope." But he's betting that both Mac-Kennas do, given the fact that they've been staying here. He figures the Webers might regret being so hospitable right about now.

Murph presses the call button on the intercom.

After a few seconds, a tentative-sounding female voice asks, "Yes?"

"Detectives Rocco Manzillo and T.J. Murphy. We're with the NYPD."

There's a pause. "Do you have badges?"

In silence, both Rocky and Murph flip open their badges and hold them up to the surveillance camera mounted above the intercom.

"Open sesame," Murph mutters under his breath, as the gates immediately begin to swing open.

They drive through, the tires crunching on the gravel lane.

"Think they ran out of money by the time they were ready to pave the driveway?" Murph quips as a pebble flies up and hits the windshield.

"Nah, asphalt's not classy enough. Dirt roads are where it's at with this crowd,

Murph. Guess you didn't pay enough attention in finishing school."

"Guess I was too busy learning how to curtsy."

Rocky grins at the mental image, relishing the casual, familiar banter with his longtime partner.

Grim as this job is, it's the one part of Rocky's world that's not foreign to him right now. As soon as they're done here, he's going right back to the hospital to see for himself that Ange is well-protected.

Then he'll go to the precinct to complete endless paperwork.

And eventually, he'll head home to the strangely empty house to maybe catch some rest . . .

And take a good look around, he reminds himself.

The broken window now seems like an obvious link to the case.

Is it possible that he missed something the first time? Some kind of clue left behind — maybe even on purpose?

That wouldn't be unheard of with a guy like this — a killer who goes to so much trouble staging murder scenes, taking gruesome souvenirs. He gets off on playing games with the victims and with law enforcement.

"Nice," Murph says, and Rocky looks up to see him gazing at the Webers' house. The driveway ends in a loop around a landscaped circle at the front entrance. Redbrick facade, pillars, tall windows — the place looks like the country manor of someone very wealthy.

Reading Rocky's mind as usual, Murph asks, "Wall Street?"

"Ad sales."

"We're in the wrong business, Rock."

"Don't I know it."

"Think it's too late to reinvent ourselves?"

"Hell, yeah. Look at us."

"What, you think we're over the hill?"

Rocky shakes his head wryly. "Come on, Gramps, let's get moving."

The house is surrounded by neatly pruned hedges and beds that either survived last weekend's snowstorm or have since been replanted with mums and ornamental grasses. Fall foliage clings here and there to high branches of the towering oaks and maples, and fresh splintered gashes indicate that limbs were lost, but there are no branches or even leaves on the ground — courtesy, most likely, of a hired landscaping team and not the home's owner with chain saw or even rake in hand. Not in these parts.

The door opens before Rocky and Murph

have put a foot on the bottom step, and they look up to see a man standing there. Handsome, clean-shaven, and smelling of cologne, with damp-looking short hair that probably wasn't cut for ten bucks in a barbershop, he's wearing chinos, loafers, and an untucked, but perfectly pressed, blue plaid shirt.

"I'm Ben Weber."

They flash their badges and introduce themselves to Ben and the petite, attractive, auburn-haired woman who comes up behind him: his wife, Randi. With her oversized diamond ring and obviously expensive clothes and perfume wafting through the air, she, like her husband, looks — and smells — as though she belongs here.

"Come in," she says politely.

Stepping onto the marble floor of the entrance hall, Rocky notes the oil paintings on the walls, the sweeping staircase leading to second and then third floor balconies, and the classical music playing in the background. Nice. Very nice.

"We'd like to speak to Allison Taylor," he says. "Is she here?"

"MacKenna." Randi Weber's closed lips curve into a brief nonsmile.

"Allison MacKenna, right. I . . . met her before. Years ago."

"When her neighbor was killed."

Rocky nods, wondering what else Randi knows about that — and everything else that's gone on.

"She isn't here right now." That comes from Ben.

"Aunt Randi?"

At the sound of a child's voice coming from overhead, all four adults look up to see a pair of small blond girls standing at the second floor railing.

"Do you know when Mommy will be back? We heard the buzzer and we thought that was her."

"She'll be here in a little while, sweetie."

"Do you know where she went?" The taller of the two girls seems to be the spokesperson; the younger sister just bites her lip and eyes the newcomers in bashful silence.

Ben is the one who answers that question, and he shoots a quick glance at Rocky and Murph before he does. "She went out to run a couple of errands, girls. She'll be back soon. Why don't you go find Greta and see if she'll play a game with you?"

Looking unsatisfied with the explanation for their mother's absence, Allison's daughters oblige nonetheless. The adults, heads tilted, watch them climb the stairs to the third floor. They can be heard knocking on a door up there and then talking to someone. A moment later, the door closes, swallowing the voices.

"Greta is our au pair," Randi volunteers.

"And the girls are . . . ?" Rocky asks, though of course he's already guessed.

"They're Allison and Mack's daughters."

"And Allison is . . . out?"

Randi looks at Ben.

He clears his throat. "She was headed down to the police station to be with Mack. But the girls don't know anything about — anything. We don't want to worry them."

"That's understandable."

"Mack isn't —" Randi breaks off, starts again. "He's not under arrest, is he?"

"As far as I know, he isn't," Rocky tells her.

And unless something else turns up to provide probable cause, he's not going to be taken into custody in the immediate future. He'll be free to come back here to his own family and the Webers, free to either try to put the nightmare behind him, or strike again . . .

If he's the killer.

Even now, in Rocky's mind, that's a big *if*. Things still just aren't adding up the way they should.

484

"Mind if we ask you a few questions?" Murph asks the Webers.

Rocky doesn't miss the glance exchanged by the couple. It's either a silent agreement to reveal potentially incriminating information — or a silent agreement to keep it to themselves.

He's betting on the latter.

He's wrong.

Half an hour later, he and Murph are back in the car.

"What do you think, Rock? Look at the names: James — Jamie."

"It's one of the most common names there is, though. Could just be a coincidence."

"Definitely."

"And the Webers said no one calls him anything but Mack. Still . . ." Rocky thinks about what Randi Weber told them — at her husband's urging — about the conversation she'd had with Allison late last night.

She'd admitted that they'd been drinking, both of them, and that her memory of the conversation is fragmented, which doesn't make her account entirely credible, and yet . . .

"I think," Murph says, "someone needs to find out exactly where MacKenna was the night Cora Nowak was murdered."

Rocky nods grimly.

That task doesn't belong to him and Murph — not right now, anyway. They're heading south on the Saw Mill River Parkway, back to New York at last.

But for the sake of those two little girls, he's hoping James MacKenna has one hell of an airtight alibi, because his wife told Randi Weber she'd caught him sleepwalking with a knife in his hand the night after Phyllis Lewis was murdered.

"Mrs. MacKenna?"

She looks up to see a uniformed patrol officer standing in the doorway of the small room where she's been cooling her heels for over an hour, so desperate to get to Mack that it was all she could do not to keep badgering the desk sergeant.

"You can see your husband now. Come with me."

She stands, suddenly afraid.

What if she looks into Mack's eyes and sees something . . . unexpected?

Even if she doesn't — even if he looks the same as he always has . . .

She can't stop thinking about Randi's cousin, and what she'd said about that fateful brush with Ted Bundy.

No one ever would have guessed in a mil-

486

lion years that the guy was a homicidal maniac.

She drags her way along the hallway behind the officer, who stops in front of an open door and gestures for her to step past him into the room.

Mack is sitting alone at a conference table, hands clasped in front of him. He looks up when she walks in, and in the instant their eyes collide, there isn't a doubt in Allison's mind.

He's innocent.

Conscious that the police officer might be watching — or at least listening — from the hallway, she makes her way over to Mack, who stands and opens his arms. Silently, they embrace.

"Are you okay?" she asks raggedly, when she's found her voice.

"Yeah. I just want to get out of here."

"When can you?"

"When they decide to let me go." He shoots a pointed glance at the cop, who is, indeed, watching from the doorway. He discreetly excuses himself and disappears. They hear his footsteps tap away down the corridor.

Mack pulls out a chair for Allison and sinks back into his own.

"What's going on?" she asks in a low voice.

"I guess I'm a suspect." He shrugs. "I gave them DNA. Hopefully, I won't have to wait here for the results — they said it's going to take a few days."

"What? They can't hold you here that long."

Can they?

She goes on, "Ben said he has a lawyer we can call."

She expects Mack to resent that bit of news, but he seems to welcome it. "Maybe I should."

"Well, you're innocent." She forgets to whisper, and when she realizes that, she doesn't even care. Let them hear. She and Mack have nothing to hide.

"I know, but if Ben has a lawyer —"

"You don't need one." Stubborn, irrational anger takes hold. "If you're innocent, then —"

"Allie, someone is trying to make me look guilty. I have no idea who it is, or why, but they want me to take the fall for this."

"That's not going to happen. Once they get the DNA results back, you'll be cleared."

"You and I both know that, but the cops don't. And I'm afraid that as long as they think it's me, they won't be looking hard enough at anyone else."

He's right. They stare helplessly at each other.

"So what do we do in the meantime?" Allison asks, and drops her voice back to a whisper. "Calling a lawyer isn't going to change the fact that we're sitting ducks if we stay where we are."

"You mean, at Randi and Ben's?"

She nods, and opens her mouth to tell him that she's not so sure they're still welcome there because now, thanks to her, the Webers might not be one hundred percent convinced of Mack's innocence.

Why did she have to, in that moment of weakness, let on to Randi that she, too, had doubts?

They've since been erased, of course.

But she thinks better of confessing to Mack that she'd even momentarily wavered in her trust. Right now, he needs all the support he can get — especially from his own wife.

Hopefully, Randi will keep what she knows to herself — and it isn't much. The detectives already know about the sleepwalking and the Dormipram.

In any case, the sooner Allison and Mack and the kids are out from under the Webers' roof, the better.

■ ■ ■ ■

"Sorry to interrupt . . ."

Rocky looks up from the report he was filling out to see Mai Zheng standing beside his desk. He'd almost forgotten all about his request that she look into Sam Shields's background. So much has happened since then — from another murder in Glenhaven Park to the latest cause of concern for Ange's well-being.

Though his mind is at ease, for now, in that respect.

He and Murph stopped by the hospital before coming here to the precinct. Security has been tightened and there's a uniformed officer posted right outside the door to her room; a burly guy who promised Rocky that no unauthorized person is going to get past him.

Ange's condition is the same, and her sister Carm arrived while Rocky was there. She asked about the cop outside the room, and Rocky told her it was just a precaution, due to a case he's working on.

Carm isn't the kind of person who would ask for details, and for that, he was grateful. He was also glad he didn't have to leave Ange alone. Carm promised to call him if

Ange shows significant signs of regaining consciousness.

Rocky quickly clears a pile of clutter from the chair beside his desk, depositing it onto the floor at his feet, and invites Mai Zheng to sit down.

Appearances are deceiving. With her slight build, graceful movements, exotic features, and waist-length, shiny black hair, Mai bears greater resemblance to the high school girls who congregate outside the private school across from the precinct than she does the hardboiled detectives on the squad. She even sounds like a teenager, with the upspeak inflection so typical of the younger female generation. But she's a force to be reckoned with, and Rocky has great respect for her.

"What do you have for me?" he asks, eyeing the manila folder, thick with paper, in her hand.

"First of all, that photo in the file?"

"Yeah?"

"It's Samuel Shields. I matched it to one of his mug shots — and believe me, there were plenty to choose from."

Rocky leans back and steeples his fingers. "Really."

"Really. He was in and out of prison for years — but it looks like he finally reformed, because it's been a while now. He's been a functioning member of society — up in Albany — for the past six years."

"Do you have an address?"

"Right here." She indicates the folder in her hand. Mimicking an infomercial host, she says, "But wait, there's more."

"Good. Keep it coming."

"Okay, so Sam Shields? He was between sentences when Jerry Thompson was attacked by his sister in December 1991, so he could have been there — although there's nothing in the police report about anyone other than the mother present at the scene. The sister, Jamie, ran away after she attacked her brother, and she was found dead a few days later — almost exactly at the same time that Sam Shields was arrested again."

"For what?"

"He was hitchhiking in Ohio, attacked a lady trucker who picked him up. He did almost ten years in the state pen for that."

His thoughts racing as he does the math in his head, Rocky asks when Shields was released.

Mai consults her papers. "Late July 2001."

Just a few weeks before the Nightwatcher murders began.

"He managed to stay out of trouble for

almost a year," Mai goes on, turning pages. "He was arrested again . . . the following summer."

"When, exactly?"

Mai runs a fingertip along the page, searching. "August 22."

Rocky turns quickly to his computer and opens a search engine. Within moments, he has what he was looking for.

The guilty verdict in Jerry Thompson's trial was handed down on August 20.

"Where is Shields now, did you say?"

"Albany. I have the address. But listen, while he was serving his last sentence, he was treated by a prison psychiatrist named Dr. Patricia Brady."

"For . . . ?" he asks. "Or does the code of ethics mean we can't find out?"

"When it comes to prisoners, there are limits to confidentiality," Mai tells him, and he nods, well aware that these are muddy waters. "But I managed to find out — and I can't tell you how I did, or someone's going to lose his job — that Shields was taking antipsychotic medication."

"Good work," he says, impressed. "Shields's father was a paranoid schizophrenic. Voices telling him to kill people — including his own kid — the whole nine yards."

Back when he arrested Jerry, Rocky figured it must run in the family and assumed that Jamie was part of the alternate reality caused by the disease, having mistakenly concluded that multiple personality disorder goes hand in hand with schizophrenia.

Vic set him straight on that, explaining that it's a common misconception.

"First of all, true MPD is extremely rare — and an entirely different disorder," he said. He added that delusional behavior and hallucinations — like hearing voices — is extremely common with schizophrenia.

"But you and I both know that it's a common misconception that schizophrenia is often accompanied by violent criminal behavior," he reminded Rocky.

"I know that. But it's not unheard of, either."

In the end, though, to Rocky's surprise, Jerry wasn't diagnosed with schizophrenia; nor, from a legal standpoint, was he insane.

Yet violent mental illness might very well run in the family after all — in the sense that Jerry's grandfather had passed it on to his son, Samuel.

"So, after Samuel was released from prison that last time?" Mai poses another question-that's-not-a-question, and Rocky nods, waiting for her to continue.

"He took the medication for a few years," she says, "and he had a job in a factory, paid his rent, basically seemed to have his life together. And then . . ."

"What?"

"It looks like he hasn't filled his prescriptions since mid-August, and he hasn't reported to work since . . ." She consults her notes. "About two months ago: September 12."

Walking up the front steps at home less than ten minutes after he was finally cleared to leave the police station, Mack reaches automatically into his pocket for the house keys — then remembers.

He no longer needs them, thanks to the alarm system.

But someone got past it last night; got into the house to place a call to Nate Jennings.

How?

They had to have the code. But the only two people who know it are Allison . . .

And me.

Again, the strange little prickle of trepidation.

Is there any way in the world that I drove over here in my sleep and made that call to Nate?

Is there any way in the world that I —

No!

There is no way.

"Did you tell anyone the code?" he asks Allison, who is a step or two behind him.

"No. I don't even remember what it is."

"Did you write it down when I gave it to you, and maybe lose track of it?"

"I don't think so . . . I mean, I did write it down, but . . ." She shakes her head, as though she's having a hard time remembering the details. "Maybe I did lose it. So much was going on . . ."

"We need to change the code right away."

She doesn't reply, and he's pretty sure he knows what she's thinking.

Why bother? We're not going to be staying here anyway.

She's right — for now.

Back at the police station, they quietly agreed that it's time to take the kids and get out of town for a few days.

"What about your job?" Allison asked.

"At this point, I really don't give a crap," he told her. "We're not safe around here, not even at Randi and Ben's."

"But where can we go?"

He told her that he had an idea, but it would have to wait until they got home, where they could discuss it in private.

Mack wastes no time in punching the

alarm code into the keypad mounted beside the door, feeling as though he's being watched — by someone other than his wife, that is.

It's probably true. After all, he's a person of interest in the biggest murder case to hit Westchester County in years; he has no doubt that the police will be keeping him under surveillance — as will the neighbors, and probably the media, too, once they figure it out.

All the more reason to get out of town as soon as possible.

Safely inside the house, he arms the alarm again and Allison lets out an audible sigh of relief. She moves toward the stairway, and for a minute he wonders if she's going to climb it, but instead she sinks onto a step at the foot of the flight.

"You look exhausted, Allie."

"So do you."

"Maybe we'll sleep tonight."

"Where?" she asks, looking up at him. "A hotel?"

He shakes his head. "That would be hard with the kids — the five of us in one room. I had something else in mind."

The idea had actually come to him before Zoe's murder, but he'd back-burnered it at the time, caught up in getting through the work week and Phyllis's wake first. He just knew they couldn't stay indefinitely at Ben and Randi's, and he found himself dwelling on better times, happier places.

The longing he experienced was similar to his urge to flee New York every September, when even his Happy House couldn't shelter him from the pain.

But of course, jetting off to Disney World is impractical, if not impossible, right now. He'll have to settle on the next best place.

"Where were you thinking we should go?" Allison asks.

"Lynn's beach house. There's room for all of us, there's a crib for the baby, and a kitchen. The girls love it there, we have the keys, and it'll be empty at this time of year."

"But . . . the keys. What if he copied those like he did the Lewises'?"

That gives him momentary pause.

"We can't go down there and change the locks on her house without her permission," Allison points out, and gets up to follow Mack as he strides into the living room and opens the desk drawer.

He pulls out the envelope containing the keys, and sees her shudder at the sight of it, probably remembering the last time she used the keys to the Lewis house.

Mack pulls out the set for Lynn's house

and examines the circular cardboard label. "It only says 'Beach House,' " he says with relief. "Even if someone had a copy, they couldn't possibly know where it is."

"We have pictures of the house all over the place," she points out, indicating a framed snapshot on a nearby table — the girls and their cousins, with a weathered, gray-shingled corner of the house in the background.

"Come on, Allie, it looks like any other beach house in the world," Mack tells her. "Without the address — or even the town — no one could possibly guess where it is."

Obviously skittish, but trying to warm to the idea, she asks, "How would you get to work from there?"

"I could commute if I had to —"

"From Salt Breeze Pointe?"

"If I had to," he repeats. "But I'm not going anywhere until we figure out what's going on."

"Did you ask Lynn if we could stay there?"

He shakes his head.

His sister called last week when she saw on the news that there had been a murder in Glenhaven Park, horrified when she learned that the victim lived right next door. But she doesn't know about the latest developments — yet — and Mack isn't interested in telling her.

"The fewer people who know where we are, the better," he tells Allison. "It's not that I don't trust Lynn, or even Daryl — but his kids and Lynn's ex are all involved in their lives too, and you just never know."

"You're right. We can't tell anyone."

"No one will think to look for us down there."

"But can we really just leave town in the middle of all this?"

What Allison means, Mack knows, is can *he* just leave town. He's the one who's under suspicion.

But he's not under arrest yet.

The police will be watching him, of course, and he's tried to find comfort in the thought of their constant presence. But really, it only means that they're keeping an eye on him; it's not protective surveillance. It doesn't mean they'll make sure his family is safe. That's up to Mack himself.

It won't be easy to slip away, but not impossible, either. He already has a plan in place, one that can be put into motion first thing tomorrow morning, and now he outlines it for Allison.

He'd been expecting an argument from her, but he doesn't get one.

"Right now, it looks like our only option,"

she agrees, "as long as . . ."

"As long as what?"

"Nothing," she says after a pause, and Mack wonders what she isn't telling him. "I guess I'll go pack some things to take with us."

"It's probably better if you don't," Mack tells her quickly. "We don't want anyone who's watching to get the idea that we're going away."

"You mean . . . the police?"

"Right. The police."

"And him, right? You think he's watching us, too."

"Not with all these cops around. Listen, I'm going to run upstairs and . . . change my clothes," he tells her. "And then we'll go."

"Okay. I'll change, too." She starts toward the stairs, then looks back at him. "Aren't you coming?"

"In a minute. I just want to . . . grab a book to read. It'll help pass the time."

She gives him a funny look, but continues up the stairs.

Mack goes into the living room and pretends to be searching the bookshelves for the perfect beach read.

Yeah, right.

All he wants is to stall until Allison is

finished in the bedroom so that he can go up there and slip the gun from the dresser drawer. He left it behind while they were staying at the Webers', in part because he wasn't sure there was a safe place to lock it away from the kids, and in part because their house is well protected. But at the beach house, there's no electric fence, no security gate, no alarm system . . .

Those things aren't necessary, though, because no one will know we're there.

And I'll have the gun, just in case . . .

Anyway, it's only for another day or two, and then the DNA will prove him innocent, and it will all be over.

Driving the SUV back across town to the Webers', with Mack trailing behind her in his car, Allison frets.

Maybe she should have warned him that she isn't sure they'll be welcome to spend one more night at Ben and Randi's.

He'd taken that part of the plan for granted, as though it hadn't occurred to him that even their closest friends — friends who are family — might not be as convinced of his innocence as she is.

And she is. Right?

Of course she is.

She'll just have to convince Ben and

Randi. She reaches into her pocket, pulls out her cell phone, and quickly dials the Webers' number.

Randi answers on the first ring. "Are you okay?"

"I'm fine. Are the kids okay?" she asks breathlessly, worried about J.J. on top of everything else, her chest tight with the stress of it all.

"Yes. Where are you?"

"On my way back to your house. Mack is coming, too. Is that . . . all right?"

Silence on the other end of the line.

"Randi, listen to me, please. We'll be out of there first thing tomorrow, all of us. I promise."

"Where are you going?"

She hesitates. "I can't tell you." Mack was explicit about the need to keep their destination a secret from everyone, including the girls.

"Is it Nebraska?"

"*Nebraska?*" she echoes, incredulous. "Why would we go *there*?"

"Last night, you said you wanted to move back."

"What? I never said that."

"When we were talking, before bed. You don't remember?"

"Not really." She's as uneasy with the idea

of having a conversation she was too drunk to recall as she is with the notion that somewhere deep down inside, she might actually have entertained the idea of returning to the Midwest.

You hated it there. All those years in a small town . . .

And yet, the thought of living a simple life — no rush hour or commuter trains to separate her and the kids from Mack five days a week; no pressure to be beautiful and brilliant and wealthy; no sky-high taxes and cost of living . . .

"Allison," Randi is saying, "wherever you're going, I don't think you and the kids should be —"

"It's not me and the kids. It's the five of us. Mack is innocent. If he weren't, the cops wouldn't have let him go." The floodgate in her throat gives way at last, and a sob escapes her.

"Oh, Allie . . ."

"Randi, I'm begging you as a friend, you and Ben, to be there for us. Mack would be devastated if he thought you didn't . . . I can't tell him . . . We need you."

For a few moments, she can't hear a thing but her own sobs; it's all she can do to see the road, her eyes awash in bitter, helpless tears.

Stop it! Just stop!

Getting a grip on her emotions at last, she wipes her eyes on her sleeves, glad Mack is following her and not the other way around. She wouldn't want him glancing into the rear-view mirror to glimpse her falling apart.

She has to stay strong, for his sake, for the kids — and for her own. She's been through worse than this in her life — not much worse, but still . . .

I can handle it. I can handle anything. I've never allowed myself to shrivel in the face of trouble, and now isn't the time to start.

Banishing the quaver from her voice, she says, "Randi?"

"Just let me talk to Ben for a second. He's right here. Hang on, okay?"

"Okay, but . . . we're only a few minutes away."

There's a clatter: Randi setting down the phone. She strains to hear the voices in the background, but they're muffled.

Please . . .

Please . . .

Allison prays as she drives on, keeping an eye on Mack in the rearview mirror.

She can see only his silhouette behind the wheel, not his expression, but even if she could see his face . . .

Chances are, it would be a mask of composure.

Back at the police station and again at home, she'd caught fleeting evidence here and there of what he might be feeling: apprehension, worry, frustration . . .

But for the most part, he was stoic, as always.

That's Mack. That's my husband, the man I vowed to love and honor, for better for worse, in good times and in bad . . .

She didn't take those promises lightly then, and she won't now.

She slows to stop for a light, one that has always seemed notoriously slow to turn. Today, however, it seems to go green almost immediately, and she drives on reluctantly, a good ten miles an hour below the speed limit.

Does Mack realize she's trying to stall?

Come on, Randi . . . get back on the line . . .

Come on . . .

At last, she hears her friend's voice.

"Allison?"

"Yes?" She holds her breath.

"Ben and I aren't comfortable having Mack here with . . . not with our kids in the house."

Her heart sinks and she swallows back a wail of protest.

506

She can't blame them. Really, she can't. If the tables were turned . . .

I'd do the same thing. I'd never take a chance with my children's lives, not for a friend, not for anything.

"We're going to send Lexi and Josh to a hotel overnight with Greta. Just for this one night. Ben and I will stay for . . . for you, and the kids, if you need us."

Weak with relief and gratitude, Allison says hoarsely, "Thank you, Randi. Thank you so much. I don't know what I'd do without you. I promise it's going to be okay, and I promise we'll be gone in the morning . . ."

She hears the rumble of Ben's voice in the background.

"You don't have to do that, Allison. That's not what we want. We're . . . worried. About you and the kids."

And there it is. Nothing Allison says — nothing Mack does — will convince Randi and Ben of his innocence.

"Don't be," she says in a clipped tone. "The kids and I are going to be just fine. Mack is going to keep us safe."

She tells Randi that they'll be arriving momentarily and hangs up.

Again, she glances into the rearview mirror.

Again, she wishes she could catch a reassuring glance of her husband's face.

But all she sees is the shadow of a man behind the wheel. If she didn't know who was driving . . .

He could be anyone, she finds herself thinking, unsettled. *Anyone at all . . .*

In the wee hours of Tuesday morning, Rocky Manzillo is at home in bed, trying to catch a short rest, when his ringing cell phone blasts him back to consciousness.

He fumbles for it, answers it. "Manzillo here."

"Yeah, where are you? Still up in Albany?"

He immediately recognizes Jack Cleary's voice, and he sounds rushed.

"No," he says groggily, "I drove back a little while ago and I'm on my way to the hospital in about" — he glances at the glowing digital alarm clock, which he set before sinking his head into Ange's pillow — "forty-five minutes."

On Monday, his wife continued to show little signs that she might slowly be regaining consciousness. Carm has kept a steady vigil, and Rocky was in and out of the room a few times yesterday, in the midst of investigating Sam Shields, who seems to have fallen off the face of the earth on

September 12.

So, for that matter, has the entire Mac-Kenna family. No one has seen them in about twenty-four hours, which has led Rocky to believe that Shields might have gotten to them somehow. When he thinks about those two little blond girls . . .

"Listen to me, Manzillo," Cleary says brusquely, "you can forget all about Albany. Forget all about waiting on that search warrant for Stan Shields's house because —"

"Sam Shields," Rocky corrects him, wondering why he's bothering. Cleary hasn't exactly supported his investigative efforts into Jerry Thompson's father, convinced he's looking in the wrong direction.

He may very well be, but he owes it to himself — hell, he owes it to Thompson — to check it out.

"I know which way you've been leaning in this investigation," Cleary goes on, "and I know you're not expecting this at all, but you can't argue with science."

"What are you talking about?"

"We just heard from the lab. We got the preliminary results on the semen that came from both Phyllis Lewis and Zoe Jennings."

"And . . . ?"

"And we've got a match."

"You mean the same person raped them both."

"I mean the same person raped them both, yes . . . and I mean that we know who it was. We had an exact match. It was James MacKenna."

■ ■ ■ ■

PART IV

■ ■ ■ ■

One may not reach the dawn
save by the path of the night.
Germaine Greer

CHAPTER SIXTEEN

Tuesday, November 8, 2011

Walking on the beach on this cold, gray morning, Allison wishes she'd thought to pack something warmer than the fleece pullover she's wearing. With the bracing wind off the water and the air damp with sea spray and drizzle, this is down parka weather.

Back inside the drafty beach house, which was never properly winterized, it's most definitely sweater weather.

"I'll need to go to the store tomorrow and pick up some coats for the girls and sweaters and warmer pajamas for everyone," she told Mack last night as, shivering, they made up beds with slightly musty-smelling sheets and layers of blankets they found in the linen closet.

"I'd rather you didn't go anywhere for the time being," Mack told her. "That's why we stopped for groceries on the way here. We

513

need to lie low now. We can't take any chances."

He was probably right. They certainly haven't taken any so far, and his plan worked perfectly.

Yesterday morning, Mack left in his car to catch the early train into the city — trailed from the Webers' gate, he later reported, by an unmarked police car. He left the BMW in the parking lot and was pretty sure a plainclothes officer boarded the commuter train with him.

Luckily, Glenhaven Park is one of the first stops on the line. The car was almost empty, and Mack was able to get an aisle seat right next to the door. The man he suspected was following him sat down several rows back, and was soon enveloped by the crowd of commuters who boarded at every subsequent stop. The early trains are jammed every morning, but particularly on Mondays, and Mack was counting on standing room only. He wasn't disappointed.

125th Street in Harlem is the last stop before Grand Central Terminal — which, of course, is the daily final destination of just about everyone on the commuter train.

When the doors opened at 125th, Mack stood and darted off the train.

Even if the plainclothes cop had spotted

him, there was no way he could have made it out of his seat and up the crowded aisle before the doors closed again and the train moved on.

Mack told Allison that he'd looked over his shoulder a few times as he raced through the station, and he was positive no one was following him. He made it down the block and into a coffee shop, where he quickly changed his clothes in the bathroom, pulling on the jeans and jacket he'd stashed in his briefcase and discarding his suit in the trash.

"Your beautiful suit." Allison shook her head, remembering what it had cost.

"I'll get a new one when this is over," Mack promised, and she found herself trying — and failing — to see into a future when it would be life as usual for them.

How can we go back now?

Even if they find the real killer and Mack's name is cleared . . .

She just can't imagine being able to pick up where they left off.

"We will," Mack promised in a low voice as they drove south along the shore, tracing the route they'd taken so often in happier times. "You'll see. Everything will go back to the way it was."

Is she even sure that's what she wants?

For everything to be the same?

Are you happy, Mack? she'd asked him that night — Halloween night — almost exactly a week ago.

Now she can't remember what had prompted her to ask, or what he'd said in return.

As the movement of the car lulled the kids to sleep in the backseat, Mack sat beside her in the front, recounting how he made his way across town to Broadway and boarded the subway, taking a southbound Number One train down to Penn Station.

Rush hour was in full swing and the area was wall-to-wall people, of course. Even if anyone had been dogging Mack — and he told Allison he was positive he'd shaken the tail — it would have been nearly impossible for anyone to stick with him at that point.

He walked to the PATH station, teeming with Jersey commuters, and hopped the first available westbound train. He didn't care where it was going, as long as it carried him out of the city.

It was then that he called to tell Allison where to pick him up. She, of course, was on the road already in the SUV, with the kids drowsy in the backseat.

She'd left the house shortly after Mack, and predictably, no one had followed her.

Obviously, the police were only interested in keeping Mack under surveillance, no one else.

She hadn't planned to say good-bye to Ben and Randi before she left. In fact, she'd barely seen them since she and Mack returned to the house on Sunday afternoon. The kids were in the room when they crossed paths with Ben and Randi, and of course, for their sake, no one brought up the situation at hand.

After some strained small talk, Mack and Allison settled into the guest quarters to watch a Disney movie with the girls. From an upstairs window, she glimpsed Ben and Randi leaving the house with Greta, Lexi, and Josh, who were all carrying overnight bags.

She thought she saw Mack glance out as well, but if he spotted them, he didn't ask where they were going, and Allison didn't volunteer the information.

Ben and Randi returned early in the evening with a couple of pizzas for their houseguests, but went straight up to bed themselves, claiming to have already eaten. Again, the presence of the girls was the buffer that kept anyone from bringing up what was really going on.

Allison was in the hall when the Webers

retreated into the master bedroom suite, and she distinctly heard the lock turn on their bedroom door.

She fought back a twinge of resentment.

They don't know Mack as well as I do. They're afraid. How can I blame them for fear?

But I'm not afraid of Mack . . . I'm afraid for him . . .

That was the last thing she said to Randi yesterday morning before she left for Salt Breeze Pointe.

With J.J. balanced on her hip, Allison was more or less tiptoeing down the stairs with one last bag before waking the girls, when she heard footsteps in the hall below. There was Randi, wearing a robe and also carrying a bag.

"I packed up some things I thought you could use," she said, "wherever you're going. Some cereal for the kids — Cap'n Crunch" — she flashed a brief smile — "and . . . there's something for you, too."

Allison thanked her with a lump in her throat, and they talked for a few hurried minutes before one last embrace.

"Remember what I said, Allison. Promise me . . ."

Promise me . . .

How well Randi knows she'd never break a promise.

How well she knows Allison would never take a chance with her children's lives.

She meant well, Allison knew, but she just didn't understand.

I'm not afraid of Mack.

And yet . . .

Watching a lone seagull arcing against the gunmetal sky, Allison hugs herself against the cold and wonders what's going to happen now. They can't stay at the beach house indefinitely. Not like this.

It's dim and depressing inside, with plywood covering all the windows, and they didn't dare take it off for fear that someone would notice. The rooms bear the faint odor of mildew and insecticide, and the kitchen, despite the box of baking soda sitting on a shelf in the unplugged and empty refrigerator, smells faintly of soured dairy and old citrus fruit.

The girls had been so excited yesterday when she told them where they were headed — which she didn't do until they were well on their way. She wanted it to seem like a fun adventure, and her daughters were wholeheartedly on board . . . until they stepped over the threshold.

Hudson sniffed the air and wrinkled her nose. "It's yucky in here. Where's Aunt Lynn?"

"She couldn't come this time." Mack didn't miss a beat. "That means you get to choose any bed you want."

"I don't want any. When can we ride the rides and get cotton candy?"

Allison and Mack looked at each other, and he broke the news. "The boardwalk is closed at this time of year."

"What?" the girls exclaimed in unison.

That did it.

Folding her arms, Hudson announced, "I want to go back to Aunt Randi's."

"I want to go *home,*" Madison said in such a small, sad voice that Allison wanted to cry.

She swallowed the lump in her throat and said, as gaily as she could manage, "Come on, girls, it'll be fun. We'll get settled and then we'll all play a game together."

Most of the old board games stacked in the living room had belonged to Mack and Lynn when they were children. Ordinarily, the girls overlook the damp-basement smell that wafts from the boxes, but today they complained about it. They complained about everything, and Allison couldn't blame them.

It's one thing to visit the beach house in the heat of a glorious summer, when fresh air and sunlight fill the house, and the boardwalk and beach are alive with activity. It's quite another to be here off-season, especially during the week. Not only has Lynn's house already been closed down for a couple of months, but the boardwalk attractions are shuttered and the beach itself is bleak and deserted.

Craving fresh air and some hint of normalcy, Allison jumped at Mack's suggestion that she go out for a solo morning walk, just as she always does when they're here in July. She never tires of catching the first hint of the sun coming up over the ocean, like melted rainbow sherbet pooled out on the horizon.

But there's no sun today; not even a horizon — just a monochromatic mist that makes sea indistinguishable from sky.

Still, it's so good to be outside after a week behind locked doors that she's walked farther than she should have; stayed away longer than she intended.

Slowly, reluctantly, Allison turns back toward the house, knowing she should probably get back.

So many memories flash back to her as she walks; most — though not all — are wonderful.

She remembers shelling with the girls, and splashing with them in a bathtub-warm tidal pool, and wading into the icy surf holding hands with Mack just weeks before their wedding. She remembers missing him on the beach last summer, and she remembers the lifeguards clearing the water, years ago, when a distant dorsal fin proved to belong to a shark and not one of the dolphins that liked to frolic along the shore.

Funny how she'd forgotten that incident until just now. How many times has she swum in the ocean since without giving thought to the predator that might still be lurking in its depths?

She quickens her pace and leaves the sand for the boardwalk, her sneakers making hollow thumps along the weathered wood. Waves pound and seagulls screech, and Allison wonders about her daughters, who must be awake by now.

When she left about forty-five minutes ago, they were sound asleep and Mack was trying to spoon-feed J.J., who was sitting in his convertible car seat that was now attached to a stroller base. Strapped in but fussing, the baby tried to grab everything within reach, and Allison wished she'd thought to bring along the portable high chair they'd been using at Randi's.

Maybe Mack will agree that she should run to the store back on the mainland and buy one, along with everything else that will make them more comfortable for the time being. There's a big Target somewhere in Toms River. She and Lynn make an annual sojourn to stock up on snacks and sunscreen and paperbacks to read on the beach.

Those lazy summer days seem so distant now that Allison feels as though she's momentarily regressed into a past life she isn't sure really even existed.

Making her way back along the boardwalk, she passes a lone jogger and an elderly woman walking her dog. Both are bundled against the cold, and neither gives her a second glance.

It seems to be taking much longer to get back, maybe because she's heading into the wind. She finds herself wishing she'd thought to bring her cell phone, then remembers — it wouldn't matter. She can't even call Mack — there's no landline at the house, and he insisted they both turn off their phones right after she picked him up at the PATH station yesterday, saying someone could use the built-in GPS software to find them.

"Can't we just turn off the location settings?" she protested.

"Why take chances?" It was becoming his mantra.

She picks up her pace, wishing she hadn't wandered so far. What if Mack gets worried and comes out to look for her, leaving the kids alone in the house?

No, he'd never do that. Not with everything that's gone on.

Would he?

What if he thought I was in danger?

Dammit. If only she had her phone.

But it wouldn't matter, she reminds herself again, scurrying past shuttered arcade games and boarded-up food stands, spooked by the eeriness of the abandoned carnival atmosphere.

She's almost running by the time the flat roof of the two-story house comes into view, a couple of blocks off the beach and surrounded by deserted summer rentals. She pulls the keys from her pocket, fumbling for the right one as she takes the steps two at a time.

She bursts inside, breathlessly calling, "Mack?"

Then it hits her; she looks back over her shoulder to make sure.

Yes. The driveway alongside the house, where the SUV should be sitting, is empty.

And so, a quick and desperate search tells her, is the house.

■ ■ ■ ■

Rocky sits by Ange's bed, holding her hand, singing "Angie Baby."

Another oldie but goodie. Helen Reddy. 1974. Rocky and Ange were newlyweds, expecting their first child. Whenever he happens to catch the song on the radio — which isn't often enough — he pictures his wife with long, straight hair parted in the middle, standing in the kitchen with a hand resting on the small of her back, belly huge and round in a maternity top.

As usual, he makes up the lyrics he doesn't know, but he remembers the part about her being a special lady . . . and how nice it is to be insane, because no one asks you to explain . . .

As he sings, his thoughts are on James MacKenna and Jerry Thompson and Sam Shields.

Rocky and Murph had spent all day Monday in Albany, tracking Shields's last movements. The shift supervisor at his factory job confirmed that he hadn't reported to work since September 12, and that he hadn't bothered to call in or quit or return phone calls.

No one appeared to be home at the shabby

duplex where he's been living for a few years now; neither Shields nor Roger Krock, the elderly upstairs tenant, answered the bell. Rocky tracked down the curmudgeonly landlord, who refused to talk or provide access to the place, saying only that the rent has been paid on time, as always. None of the neighbors — most of them either elderly or down on their luck — had seen anyone coming and going in weeks.

Mai had confirmed that Shields wasn't listed as Jerry Thompson's next of kin in the prison records; in fact, he wasn't listed at all, and thus hadn't been personally notified of his son's death. Chances are, he learned of it courtesy of the news media, along with the rest of the world. And right after he heard . . .

He disappeared.

A few days later, Cora Nowak was dead, and her sadistic killer delivered her mutilated remains to her husband on a sandwich roll.

Shields, with his sick, twisted reasoning, might have been prone to do that.

But James MacKenna?

Rocky shakes his head. It doesn't make sense.

Before Cleary called this morning with the news about the DNA match, Rocky was so sure he was on the right track with Shields.

Even now . . .

Something isn't adding up.

If MacKenna is behind this, then where is he now, and where are his wife and kids? Randi Weber thought the whole family had gone into hiding together, but she had no idea where they might be. She said Allison had seemed to brush off her final warning that MacKenna might harm her and the children.

"She said she wasn't afraid of him," Randi told Rocky. "She was afraid *for* him."

Ever since Cleary told him about the DNA match, Rocky has mentally gone over and over everything he knows about Mac-Kenna; everything MacKenna said to him years ago about Kristina Haines, on that awful day when he had just lost his wife . . .

Why can't I accept that the guy is guilty? Why do I feel like I'm missing something?

Rocky was on his way back up to Glen-haven Park, where the task force was waiting on a search warrant of the MacKenna home, when Ange's neurologist called to say there were encouraging signs that she might be starting to regain consciousness.

"How soon?" Rocky asked.

"There's no way of knowing when — or if

527

— it'll happen," was the cautious reply. Before Rocky could voice his frustration, the doctor added, "But if I were you, I'd come on over to the hospital."

So here he is, watching his wife's eyelids twitch, willing her to wake up.

He finishes singing "Angie Baby," and he begs God, again, to bring Ange back to him.

This time, he tacks on a prayer for Allison MacKenna and her children to be delivered safely from whatever trials they're facing.

A cart rattles into the room before he finishes praying, and he opens his eyes to see his favorite nurse.

"How are you today, Mr. Manzillo?"

"Judy! What are you doing on duty during the day? I thought you work the night shift."

"I do, but I switched today. My daughter is going in first thing tomorrow morning for a C-section and I want to be there with her."

"That's great. First grandchild?"

She nods vigorously. "Poor kids have been through so much trying to conceive. I don't think any of us believed it was ever going to happen."

"Our son and daughter-in-law went down that road, too," Rocky tells her. "They went to a clinic until they finally ran out of money — or maybe they just ran out of hope."

"You should never run out of that," Judy

says, pulling on a pair of latex gloves. "There's always hope."

She's talking about getting pregnant, but Rocky is talking about much more when he agrees, "Yes, there is. Just when you least expect it —"

"That's exactly what happened with my daughter," Judy says. "She got pregnant the old-fashioned way."

Rocky stares into space, no longer listening as Judy goes on talking about her daughter's pregnancy.

What if . . . ?

He jumps to his feet.

"Mr. Manzillo? Are you okay?"

"I'm sorry, Judy," he says over his shoulder, already on his way out of the room. "I just remembered something. I have to make a phone call."

About to pour her fourth cup of coffee after a sleepless night, worrying about Allison and the kids, Randi feels her cell phone suddenly vibrate in her pocket. She sets the pot back on the burner and pulls out the phone, hoping it's not another automated reminder to get out and vote today.

Her heart beats faster when she sees that it is, indeed, an auto-text message — but one that reads: *Signal Active.*

Late last night, her fear and curiosity got the best of her and she revisited the phone locator site Allison showed her on that long-ago afternoon in her kitchen.

She punched in Allison's cell number and the unforgettable password HUMAMA, hoping to get a location on her missing friend.

The search resulted in the message *Signal Inactive.*

Seeing that there was an option to be notified if there was a change in status, Randi punched in her phone number.

Now, she returns to the locator site and enters the password once again, then holds her breath as the search gets under way.

Moments later, she finds herself looking at a large, pulsating blue dot on a map. It's somewhere on the water — New Jersey, she sees, quickly pressing the minus sign button to scroll out on the map.

It's somewhere on the Jersey Shore, just north of Salt Breeze Pointe, where she knows Mack's sister has a house.

So what do I do with this information?

Remembering the business card Detective Manzillo handed to her on Sunday morning, she wonders whether she should call him.

The blue dot is moving really quickly.

Almost as though . . .

Is Allison being chased?

Maybe she should call Ben at work and ask him what to do.

No. He mentioned that he had a client meeting this morning. He'll never pick up his phone, and she doesn't want to wait for him to call her back.

It's all right. I don't need to ask Ben.

Detective Manzillo said I should call him if there's anything else he should know.

It's just like with the story Allison told me when she was drunk, about finding Mack in the kitchen with the knife.

I knew Detective Manzillo should know about that, and . . .

Yes. He should know this.

In the small upstairs bedroom where the girls slept, Allison finds both twin beds empty, covers thrown back.

Hudson would have made her bed. She does every morning, without fail, the moment she climbs out of it.

Racing back to the kitchen, Allison struggles to contain the fear that swept through her when she realized Mack and the kids and the car are missing, refusing to allow it to erupt into full-blown panic.

She needs to keep her wits about her.

Yes, they're gone. But that doesn't mean something is wrong.

Maybe he took the kids and went out to buy . . . cereal or jackets or . . .

Or maybe he went out looking for her . . .

J.J.'s car seat is gone — but so is the stroller base. Why didn't Mack detach it? Why take the whole thing? Did they go out walking?

No, the car is gone, she reminds herself, raking a hand through her wind-tangled hair and trying to think straight.

When she left, the stroller was parked beside the table, and Mack was sitting in a chair facing it, spoon-feeding J.J. Now she sees that the chair he'd occupied is tipped over backward, and her purse, which she'd left dangling from the stroller handles, lies beside it, the contents scattered across the floor.

Even if Mack had been willing to leave it that way, Hudson wouldn't have allowed it . . . if she had a choice.

So they left in a hurry.

Where did they go?

Allison quickly kneels to find her phone on the floor. She's going to turn it on, regardless of what Mack said, and she's going to hope he did the same thing so that she can reach him.

He wouldn't just abandon her here . . . not by choice.

The gnawing doubt of the past few days now begins to tear at her like shark teeth, gnashing jagged holes into her reasoning.

She quickly rummages through her belongings on the floor: wallet, packet of wet wipes, keys . . .

Everything that had been in her purse is here — except for her phone . . .

Where is her phone?

Did Mack take it with him?

Why would he do that?

So that you wouldn't be able to use it to call him.

But why? He'd have to know she'd be beside herself with worry, coming back here to an empty house . . .

Even if turning it on for a few minutes might send off a GPS beacon, and anyone searching might be able to find them . . .

Mack still wouldn't want me to be here alone and frantic, isolated, without a car, and unable to call him, or call for help . . .

She remembers the knife in his hand, and the empty look in his eyes, and cold dread slithers over her.

Again, she claws through her belongings on the floor, and presses her cheek to the worn linoleum to see if the phone could have skittered under the stove or refrigerator or . . .

What the hell is that?

On trembling hands and knees, she crawls toward the object that lies a few feet away, well apart from the emptied contents of her purse.

Dear God.

Dear God.

It's an empty syringe.

Allison scrambles to her feet, staring at it. Maybe . . .

Maybe one of Daryl's kids is a diabetic.

Maybe a junkie has been squatting in the house.

But that would mean the syringe was here when they arrived yesterday, and somehow they overlooked it . . .

It's lying squarely out in the open, in the middle of the floor.

And it couldn't have been there yesterday, Allison remembers, *because I crawled around looking for mousetraps and marbles and anything J.J. could find and hurt himself or choke on, and . . .*

This can't be happening.

It isn't happening, she assures herself. Her always-active imagination has gotten the best of her and she's jumping to conclusions instead of considering the possibilities.

Like . . .

Like, there's a logical explanation for the syringe, and the girls are here somewhere, playing hide-and-seek the way they do with their cousins, and Mack and J.J. are . . . are playing with them . . .

She finds her voice, shouts their names, one after another, over and over again as she races for the stairs, climbs them, runs down the hall searching room after room. When she reaches the girls' bedroom, she yanks the blankets off the nearest bed, as if she could possibly have missed someone sleeping there.

Something flies out from between the folds of the bedding, and lands at her feet.

Stricken, Allison stares at another empty syringe.

And that's when she realizes.

Today is Tuesday.

Mack knows these roads well, but he's used to creeping along them with the windows down, radios playing, the smell of hot asphalt mingling with the damp salt air . . .

That's how he's driven these roads, on lazy summer days, when traffic clogs every artery on the barrier island and you'd better not be in a hurry to get to where you're going.

Today, he's in a hurry.

Today . . .

Today is Tuesday. Always a Tuesday.

There's barely any traffic, allowing him to heedlessly barrel through stop signs and red lights as he speeds along parallel to the water.

Just ahead, the light goes from yellow to red.

Mack doesn't slow down. A delivery truck is approaching from the left, bearing down on the intersection. If Mack stops to let it pass, he'll lose time, and every second counts.

Nothing is going to get in his way. Nothing is going to stop him. Not now. Not when he's so close.

He bears down on the gas pedal. The driver of the truck doesn't glance in his direction; doesn't see him coming. Mack enters the intersection a split second ahead of the truck, swerving hard to the right to skirt around its path. He hears the blast of the horn, the screeching of tires. The truck swerves to the right, missing his door by maybe an inch.

Hearing the sickening crunch of metal behind him, he sees in the mirror that the truck has hit a lamppost. Speeding on, he listens for the sound of sirens behind him; keeps an eye on the rearview mirror for flashing red lights.

What if they materialize?

I'll just keep going.

If I stop, it'll be all over. There's too much to lose; I can't risk it.

He thinks about Allison. By now, she must be back at the house. She'll be frantic when she realizes that he and the kids are missing. He's sorry for that.

Sorry for a lot of things.

But I'm just doing what I have to do.

Jaw set, he stares at the road beyond the windshield, focusing not on what lies behind him, but on what lies ahead.

Allison races down the narrow, deserted street, turns a corner, and spots a house whose windows aren't covered in plywood. There's no car in the driveway, but maybe, just maybe . . .

Please, God, let someone be home. Please.

She races to the door and bangs on it. "Hello!" she shouts. "Is anyone here? Hello?"

No one answers, just like at the last house she tried, a few doors up from Lynn's beach house.

With a cry of frustration, she turns and keeps going, up the street, around another corner. Every house on this short block is boarded up.

The same is true on the next.

And the next.

There has to be someone here, some-where, please, please . . .

Rounding another corner, Allison spots a car in a driveway. Beyond it lies a house whose uncovered windows spill yellow lamplight into the morning gloom like a beacon. On the step: a pot of withered-looking brownish mums and a newspaper in a blue plastic bag.

Thank you, God. Thank you.

Allison runs toward the house, panting hard, already shouting for help at the top of her lungs. By the time she reaches the house, a startled-looking elderly man in a cardigan and bifocals is peering out at her through the glass window in the door.

"Please!" she calls to him. "Please! Some-body took my children!"

Looking suspicious, he shakes his head, seems to check the lock on the door, and starts to turn away.

"Please, sir! You don't have to let me in, just . . . just please call the police!" Tears roll down her face and her body sags beneath the weight of an awful reality she can no longer deny.

With a moan, she sinks onto the weathered steps, burying her head in her hands. For a long time, she sits there, gasping for breath, trying to find the strength to keep running, the strength to bear the impossible truth and the unimaginable loss.

Her babies, her beautiful babies, her girls, and her boy, and . . .

My husband.

Mack. Dear God, what has he done?

What has *she* done, trusting him with those three precious little lives?

I knew better! I did! I knew, and that's why I let Randi talk me into —

The thought is curtailed by the sound of wailing sirens in the distance.

Rocky paces the sidewalk in front of the hospital, phone in hand, willing the damned thing to ring again so that he can get back to Ange's bedside.

Maybe he should just go back up anyway.

But if he does, he'll miss the call, and too many lives are hanging in the balance.

Thank God Ange's isn't one of them. Not in the immediate moment, anyway.

Right now, she's safe and stable, and she

would want him to do exactly what he's do-ing.

Pacing . . .

Waiting . . .

Thinking about the one possible reason a calculating killer might so drastically change his signature, adding rape to the ritual . . .

Supposedly.

At last, his phone vibrates in his hand.

"I've got it," Mai tells him. "You were right. James MacKenna and his first wife did go through infertility treatments. They used the Riverview Clinic in Manhattan."

Rocky holds his breath, waiting for the rest, hoping against hope . . .

"There was a break-in at the lab they use back in October," Mai goes on, "and several sperm samples were stolen. Including James MacKenna's."

Before Rocky can react, his phone buzzes, indicating a call coming in. Frowning, he's about to ignore it — then thinks better of it. What if it's the nurse, calling from up-stairs?

He checks the caller ID.

"I have to take this," he tells Mai. "I'll call you right back."

Quickly, he disconnects that call and picks up the incoming one. "Manzillo here."

"Detective Manzillo? It's Randi We-

540

ber . . ."

Yeah. He knows.

"How can I help you, Mrs. Weber?"

"I know where Allison is, and . . . she's on the move. Really fast. I feel like something might be wrong."

Jamie clutches the wheel of the rented Jeep with gloved hands — warm knit winter gloves. They won't leave prints.

As much as she loves to wear dresses, Jamie is bundled against the cold today, wearing jeans, a sweater, a parka, boots. She even left the wig behind in the last motel room, not wanting to risk shedding synthetic hairs this time and letting the cops think anyone but Mack is responsible for this.

I don't look like myself, she thought, surveying herself in the mirror earlier. *I look like Sam.*

But that's okay. When this is over . . .

What will I do when this is over?

Do I even want to go on?

It's a question that has weighed heavily on Jamie's mind. The answer, she figures, will come to her when the time is right. It always does.

Ah, there's the jetty up ahead, jutting out into the churning gray-green waters of the Atlantic.

She'd scouted the location yesterday afternoon, driving up and down the bleak coastal island in search of the perfect spot to stage the grand finale, not sure exactly what she was looking for until she found it.

The jetty is well off the beaten path, located on a stretch of beach where there are just a few houses, all of them large summer rentals that have obviously been closed up for the winter.

"We're almost there," Jamie informs the three children in the backseat.

It would be much more interesting to talk to them if they could reply, but of course they can't. All three children are unconscious, thanks to the needles Jamie stuck into their arms. The girls are on the floor, like limp rag dolls; the baby still strapped into his stroller, which Jamie simply turned on its side and shoved sideways across the backseat.

"Your mother thinks she's so smart. But she told me exactly where to find you, did you know that? There I was on Sunday afternoon, minding my own business —"

At that, Jamie breaks off and giggles.

"All right, I was minding your parents' business. They were plotting their big escape, thinking they were so clever, talking about a beach house somewhere . . ."

A beach house to which Jamie, of course, has the keys.

"Of course I copied all the keys I found in the desk drawer way back in the beginning," she informs the sleeping children. "I figured they might come in handy at some point."

Have they ever.

Although there *was* a fleeting moment of worry when it seemed Allison and Mack weren't going to mention the exact location of the house. It would have been so bothersome to try and tail them to wherever they were going, and much too risky at this point to venture back into their house looking for clues.

But then, oh lucky day, Allison asked her husband, "How would you get to work from there?"

"I could commute if I had to —"

"From *Salt Breeze Pointe*?"

At that, Jamie broke into a delighted smile, assuming — correctly — that they were talking about the charming little town on the Jersey Shore.

There was no need to even follow them down here. Jamie meandered along later in the day, arriving just in time for darkness to settle in. Then it was just a matter of driving up and down the streets until Allison's SUV materialized, parked in a carport alongside a rambling two-story house.

Well equipped for what lay ahead, Jamie broke into the house next door and kept an eye on things until the right opportunity presented itself.

"Your mother made things even easier for me when she took off this morning all by herself, you know?" Jamie tells the children. "I let myself in with the keys — walked right in through the front door, quiet as a mouse. I bet you didn't hear a thing, did you? I know your father didn't."

Jamie spotted Mack in the kitchen with his son. He was making faces at him, and the baby was making a racket, laughing like crazy.

A nice little father and son moment, she thought, enraged. Jerry never had a moment like that, and now he never would, thanks to Allison.

"This is all your mother's fault," Jamie tells the children, wishing they could talk, sob, protest, beg, *something.*

Jamie would feel a lot better if Allison's kids were suffering the way Jerry had suffered.

"It isn't *fair!* You just get to go to sleep, and you're not going to feel a thing! Why did I take the easy way out?"

Jamie glances into the backseat. It might

be worthwhile to wait until they wake up. . . .

Worthwhile, yes. But not feasible.

Things are already in motion. It's now or never.

"I've got the kids. I've got the opportunity. I've even got this." Jamie pulls Mack's BlackBerry from the console. It's going to add such a nice touch.

Funny how things just fall into place. The device was conveniently lying on the dresser in one of the bedrooms when Jamie reached the second floor of the beach house.

In another bedroom, the girls were sound asleep. It was so easy to jab one slender white neck, and then the other, with the syringe that would knock them out almost instantly. Carrying them down the back stairs without making a sound was a little more challenging, though. They were heavier than they looked — dead weight, Jamie thinks now, with a grim little smile.

The painstaking process took much longer than anticipated, so long that it was a wonder the girls' father hadn't stirred from the kitchen, or their mother hadn't come back from her walk.

At last, the still figures lay on the floor of the Jeep.

Then came the truly tricky part.

Jamie knew it would take some kind of diversion to separate Mack from the baby. Knocking over the table in the upstairs hall seemed like a good idea — and one of the few options available — but it wasn't without risk. Had Mack decided to search the entire second floor before going to check on his daughters, whose room was at the end of the hall, he might easily have come across Jamie, hiding inside the linen closet right at the top of the stairs, a few feet from the toppled table.

But Mack didn't do that. He must have sensed that Daddy's girls needed him.

But it was too late for that, wasn't it, Daddy dear?

As Mack's footsteps pounded down the hall toward his daughters' room, Jamie bolted from the closet and raced down the stairs as quietly as possible. She grabbed the baby, stroller and all, jabbed him with the needle, and ran out to the waiting Jeep.

Driving away from the house, Jamie spotted Mack in the upstairs window, looking out. It was so tempting to give a jaunty little wave.

How does it feel to be helpless when your child needs you? How do you like it?

Jamie coasted down the street, making sure Mack got a good look at the Jeep, on the off chance that there might be other cars on the road.

We wouldn't want you to get confused, now, would we?

Mack was soon chasing the Jeep that, ironically, Jamie had rented using the desktop computer in the house on Orchard Terrace just a few days earlier. The username and password were even conveniently saved on the car rental agency's Web site, along with the credit card information.

After making the rental reservation, Jamie used the search engine to type in some information that might come in useful . . .

Not for me, though.

The computer search was strictly for the benefit of the investigators who will confiscate Mack's hard drive after this is all over — if they haven't already.

The final step, as Jamie drives the Jeep out onto the jetty, is to toss Mack's cell phone onto the floor in front of the passenger's seat, where it will be easily found later by the divers.

CHAPTER SEVENTEEN

"Calm down, ma'am. Calm down."

"I can't calm down!" Allison screeches at Lieutenant Sparks, the young police officer who escorted her away from the front steps of the old man's house. "My babies! He took my babies!"

"Who did?"

"My husband!" She clutches Lieutenant Sparks's arm. "He's . . . I don't know, he's gone crazy or something. Please. It's not him, it's the drug —"

"He's on drugs?"

"No, not like — please. You have to stop him before he hurts them. Please . . ."

At the wheel of the SUV, Mack screeches to a stop on the narrow jetty, jams the gear shift into park, and jumps out. There's barely room alongside the car for him to stand; the rocky drop-off into the water is mere inches from his shoes.

He edges past it and pushes forward.

Through the mist, he can see the car whose taillights he chased from Salt Breeze Pointe, after he realized, in a panic, that someone had taken all three of his children.

It's a miracle that he even managed to catch up with the vehicle — which he can now make out is a Jeep — considering that the driver had a generous head start.

It didn't take long for Mack to dump out Allison's purse and grab her keys, yet those were seconds that carried his children farther and farther away from him. He lost precious seconds, too, in a frenzied, futile search for her cell phone so that he could call 911, but it didn't seem to be there, and he quickly gave up.

By the time he got outside, he was shocked to see the taillights still visible down the block, almost creeping along, almost as if . . .

Several times, he almost managed to catch up to the car and then would lose it again as it raced south along the barrier island.

Now it's almost within reach, parked just ahead, right at the end of the jetty, again, oddly, almost as if . . .

As if he's waiting for me.

How the hell did he find them here at the shore anyway? They weren't followed, they told no one, and the only time he and Allison even mentioned their destination was in the privacy of their own . . .

Home.

Mack's heart sinks, remembering something Ben said to him not long ago, when they were talking about the nanny cam.

There's no privacy anymore, anywhere — even in your own house. You never know who's watching and listening.

That's it, Mack realizes. *That's how this bastard knew where to find us, and it's how he knew the alarm code. He heard me tell Allison, or he watched me punch it in. Electronic surveillance.*

As Mack races toward the Jeep, he feels in his pocket for the gun he's kept close at hand since they fled home. When they reached the Webers' on Sunday, he was afraid Ben was going to corner him and ask for it back, or that he'd bring it up in front of Allison, but he didn't.

Thank God he didn't.

Thank God I have it. And I swear I won't hesitate to use it.

As Mack hurtles himself along the jetty, the driver's side door of the Jeep opens.

A figure steps out.

Mack's hand closes around the gun and he draws it out as he runs, shouting, "Stop!"

The figure seems to ignore him, leaning into the car.

Mack raises the gun and slows his pace to take aim, not daring to take a wild shot while running and risk hitting the Jeep with his children inside.

The Jeep — it's moving again, he realizes, stunned.

The vehicle is rolling forward . . .

Toward the end of the jetty . . .

Toward the water.

Mack hurtles himself forward with a scream as the Jeep goes over the edge.

Huddled in the backseat of the police cruiser, Allison numbly watches the old man in the cardigan painstakingly adding his signature to a report attached to a clipboard. At last, he hands it back to Lieutenant Sparks, who nods and says something, then glances back at the car.

Allison quickly looks away, not wanting to meet the young cop's eyes again. Every time he looks at her, she can see what he's thinking, and she wants to scream at him that he's wrong; that it isn't like that.

Mack is a good man, an honorable man. He loves his children — and her — more than anything on this earth. He's not some horrible violent deadbeat who would ever . . .

No, never.

Not if he were in his right mind.

It's the medication — that's what she tried to explain to the police officer, but he heard "drugs" and he got the wrong idea.

Or did he?

What's the difference what kind of drug it is?

What's the difference if a doctor prescribed it?

Allison's mother took prescription medication and killed herself.

Mack is taking prescription medication, too — what's to stop him from killing himself, or —

She moans; she can't bear to think about it.

My babies.

No. Our *babies.*

Mack loves them as much as I do; he was there when they took their first breaths, their first steps . . .

She thinks of him giving the girls piggyback rides, reading bedtime stories, watching princess movies on rainy days . . .

But not lately.

That was the old Mack, the loving daddy and husband who was home more often, and wasn't always checking his BlackBerry, or looking as though he were a million miles away . . .

The new Mack is different.

But that doesn't mean he's capable of . . .

No. It just means he accepted a big promotion with a tremendous amount of responsibility, and that he's worried, in this lousy economy, about job stability and rising taxes and cost of living and dropping stocks and retirement accounts . . .

And he's stressed.

Who isn't?

But he's not a monster.

If the kids are with Mack, he'll protect them.

Longing to believe that, Allison buries her face in her hands, wiping the tears from her eyes. When she looks up again, Lieutenant Sparks is on the phone, listening and nodding and hurriedly scribbling something on the paper attached to the clipboard. He hangs up, says something to the old man, and then strides over to the car.

"Mrs. MacKenna," he gets behind the wheel and slams the door, "did you say your husband took your cell phone with him?"

She nods numbly.

"Looks like they've picked up the GPS signal in your phone."

"They? Who's they?" she asks breathlessly.

"I think the information came from the NYPD."

"The *NYPD*? But how would —"

"I don't know, I thought that was what they —" Interrupting himself, he quickly jerks the car into reverse. "In any case, he's not far from here, but he's on the move, heading south. We've got a couple of cars on the way."

"Can you . . . do you know if . . ."

"That's all I know, ma'am." Throwing an arm along the seatback, Lieutenant Sparks looks over his shoulder. The car skids backward in the sandy dirt, and then they're on their way to the scene, sirens wailing.

Clutching her cell phone, Randi sits on the edge of the queen-sized bed in the guest room, thinking about Allison and Mack and the kids and waiting for the phone to ring. Detective Manzillo promised to call as soon as he hears anything at all.

Please let it be good news. Please let them be okay. Please . . .

Randi stands, paces across the room and back again. She smoothes the quilt on the bed where she was sitting, then looks at the portable crib next to it.

She should probably fold that up and put it away.

No. Not yet.

Maybe they'll want to come back here when this is over. In fact, maybe she should change the bedding, here and in the other guest room, so that everything will be fresh and ready, just in case.

Ordinarily, it's a job she'd leave for her housekeeper, but right now, she desperately needs something to do, something other than pace or brood.

She strips the crib and the bed and carries the bedding into the bathroom. After depositing it into a laundry basket there, she notices that the wicker wastebasket needs to be emptied. It's full of crumpled tissues — probably Allison, wiping her tears. Her eyes were red and swollen this morning when she left.

On the verge of tears herself, Randi takes a plastic garbage bag from the sink cabinet and starts to dump in the contents of the wastebasket.

Something heavy falls into the bag. Randi reaches in and sees that it's the E-ZPass tag from Allison's SUV.

That means she's most likely headed south or west — there are tolls on all the bridges. She doesn't want anyone tracking her car, obviously, by checking to see where it was used, so she'll pay cash.

Randi is about to toss the trash bag aside when she spots something else that isn't crumpled tissue — something orange.

She fishes it out.

It's a plastic bottle from the pharmacy. According to the label, it contains Dormipram, prescribed to James MacKenna.

The bottle is half full of pills.

Hearing the tremendous splash as the Jeep hits the water, Jamie turns and runs, heading straight for Mack, reveling in the startled dismay on the face of his foe.

He probably thinks I'm going to jump him.

Ah, but that won't be necessary.

My work here is done, Jamie thinks gleefully.

He can see that the SUV's motor is still running. How convenient.

All Jamie has to do is jump behind the wheel, drive away from here, and abandon the car somewhere. Maybe in the driveway of a deserted house, where no one will notice it for weeks, months.

By the time anyone finds it, Mack will have been arrested for drowning his children.

Who's going to believe his crazy story about someone stealing them out from under his nose — in a car he rented himself?

Not the police.

Not the families of all those women whose bodies bore undeniable evidence of Mack's DNA.

Not his lovely wife.

It's over.

Allison has lost everything she had to lose, and as for Jamie . . .

I win.

I —

Too late, Jamie sees that Mack has a gun.

Torn, Rocky looks over his shoulder at the double doors leading back into the hospital, and then at the parking garage across from the entrance, where he left his car.

What the hell am I supposed to do now?

The case is exploding; he just got word from Murph that a frantic Allison Mac-Kenna reported to the cops down in Jersey that her husband has abducted their children, and yet . . .

Ange.

How can I leave her?

His phone, still clutched in his hand, buzzes yet again. He answers immediately. "Manzillo here."

"Jack Cleary. I heard about the theft at the clinic. Good work. We've got the lab on it, checking for chemicals that would indicate cryopreservation."

"You'll find them," Rocky says flatly.

"Even so — the theft could have been a coincidence."

"It wasn't."

"Detective, even if it wasn't, we've got the guy's own wife saying he took the kids and they're in danger."

"She said that? Are you sure?"

"I didn't talk to her myself, if that's what you mean, but she said they're in danger, and believe me —"

"How does she know?"

"That they're in danger? I don't know how she knows. But I know how *I* know. I'm inside the house right now."

"Which house?"

"The MacKennas' house on Orchard Terrace. The warrant came through a little while ago."

"Good. What'd you find?"

"For a start, we found a home computer registered to MacKenna that was last used a couple of days ago to do an Internet search on Susan Smith."

"Who the hell is Susan Smith?"

"Case down in South Carolina. It made national headlines fifteen, maybe twenty years ago? Young mother with two small boys strapped in the back of her car, says she was carjacked, but —"

"But she did it herself." Rocky remembers and his stomach gives a sickening twist. "She drowned them — drove the car into a lake."

"That's right."

Jesus. Rocky tilts his head back, closing his eyes.

"Our friend also did his homework on fast-acting sedatives," Cleary goes on, "and he set up a car rental down in Jersey . . ."

Cleary goes on, filling in with details that make Rocky's head spin with the realization that he needs to give it up and admit that for the second time in his career, his gut instinct is wrong.

Dead wrong — that's for damned sure.

Jerry Thompson is dead because he went to prison for crimes he didn't commit, and now . . .

I know I've asked you for a lot lately, Rocky prays, remembering the two little blond girls, Allison's daughters. *But please watch over those children, the girls and the baby boy. Please keep them safe from harm, and if that isn't your will, then I beg you to deliver them quickly. Please don't let them suffer. Please . . .*

Nothing is going to stop Mack from getting

to his kids in the water.

Nothing — no one — is going to get in his way.

As the stranger races toward him, he raises the gun.

Seeing the weapon in the instant before Mack fires, his target suddenly spins around. He doesn't run away; he'd have to know that would be futile. There's no place for him to go.

Instead he goes still, like a child playing freeze tag, almost as if he's waiting . . .

Bastard.

Mack pulls the trigger.

Taking the bullet in the back, his target falls to the ground without a sound.

Mack streaks past him, not caring, not seeing anything but the Jeep, still visible but already starting to tilt and submerge.

He runs straight to the end of the jetty and dives in, arching as far out as he can to avoid the cruel rocks beneath, thinking only of his children trapped inside the sinking Jeep.

He surfaces beside it, gasping for air as bracing waves wash over him. The door is still open and he reaches inside. His hands immediately become entangled on a clump of seaweed —

No, not seaweed.

Hair.

Hudson's long, blond hair.

He pulls, and the next thing he knows, his daughter is above the surface. Holding her up somehow with one hand, he reaches quickly into the Jeep again and his fingers brush more streaming wet hair: Madison. As he pulls her up, his fingers bump against something hard and round, a pole of some sort —

J.J.'s stroller, he realizes, wedged into the backseat.

He's got both girls above the water . . .

Thank God.

Thank God.

"Hudson!" he screams. "Madison!"

They need to wake up right away; need to keep themselves afloat so that he can dive down for their brother.

"Hudson! Madison!"

Mack is struggling in the water now and they're limp in his arms, both of them. Why didn't the blast of icy sea snap them back to consciousness?

Are they alive?

"Hudson! Madison!" He has to get to J.J., but he can't let go of his daughters or they'll sink.

"No!" he screams as the top of the Jeep disappears below the surface with his son still trapped inside.

Allison can see the rotating red and blue lights all over the waterfront: police cars, rescue trucks, ambulances. The jetty is teeming with uniformed personnel: cops and paramedics, and . . .

Divers.

She watches in mute horror as they approach the scene, trying not to let her mind go to the darkest place. She glimpses a pair of EMTs loading someone onto the back of an ambulance, but she can't see the person on the stretcher. The EMTs hurriedly climb in after it and the rescue truck pulls away, sirens wailing, racing north, toward the road to the mainland and the nearest hospital.

Lieutenant Sparks pulls to a stop near the foot of the jetty.

"Stay here," he tells her, gets out of the car, and strides toward the action.

"I can't." She shoves the door open.

She forces her legs to work beneath her, willing them to hold her up and carry her toward the wretched scene when all she really wants to do is turn and run away, far away, back home . . .

Home.

A sob clogs her throat. She wants so badly to be back there, back with her little girls and her baby boy, and yes, with Mack, too . . .

We're going to go home. We are. We're going to get past this, whatever it is, and we're going back to our Happy House. We're going to —

Suddenly, she sees him: Mack.

He's bundled in a blanket, talking to a pair of wary-looking cops as a paramedic takes his blood pressure.

Something flutters in Allison's heart. He's her husband. He's shivering, maybe injured, and . . .

And he's alone.

"Where are they?" she yells.

Mack turns toward her, and the rest of them, too.

Up ahead of her, Lieutenant Sparks waves her back. "Mrs. MacKenna, I told —"

Ignoring him, she screams again at Mack, "Where are they?"

His eyes settle on her, and even from here she can see that they're full of love, and relief, and she forgets.

"Allison!" he shouts, and starts toward her

The cops are on him instantly, holding him back.

"It's okay," she hears Mack say. "She's my wife, I need to tell her . . ."

"Stay right where you are," a stout man in a trench coat tells him firmly.

He strides in Allison's direction, pulling a badge from his pocket, and she braces herself.

"Mrs. MacKenna, I'm Detective Looney with the Salt Breeze Pointe PD."

"Yes. Where are my children?"

He clears his throat. "There was an accident."

Her knees buckle. She starts to go down, but is steadied by both Detective Looney and Lieutenant Sparks.

"Your children were in the back of the car your husband was driving . . ."

Were.

They *were.*

"Where are they now?" she asks shrilly, wrenching herself free.

"Your husband pushed the car into the water with the children in the backseat . . ."

"Noooooo!" she wails, and this time she does go down, sinking onto her knees. From where she is, she can see, for the first time, a pool of blood out on the jetty. Beside it is a prone figure covered in a tarp. Much too big to belong to a child, but . . .

"What happened? Oh my God, who is that?"

"Mrs. MacKenna, please try to calm

down. We think it was a Good Samaritan who must have come along and tried to stop him. Your husband shot him in the back as he tried to —"

"Mack *shot* him?" she echoes, and shakes her head. "No. He wouldn't. He *couldn't*. He doesn't have a gun."

"He does. We recovered it. He —"

"No! I just told you, he doesn't —"

"Mrs. MacKenna, we have his gun and he admitted to using it to shoot the man, okay? He confessed."

She goes absolutely still.

Mack shot someone?

Killed someone?

Confessed?

"But that . . . that doesn't make sense."

"I'm sorry," Detective Looney says quietly. "But we have word that DNA evidence has linked him to a series of murders in Westchester County, and —"

She gasps, clasping trembling hands over her face, covering her eyes, as if to protect herself somehow from seeing the shocking truth.

But it's there anyway, right in front of her.

I'm married to a complete stranger.

A few months ago, she remembers, she'd asked Randi, "How could I be such a terrible judge of character?"

She was talking about Jerry Thompson at the time — about how sure she'd been that he was incapable of violence.

Ironic that she might have been right about him after all — and wrong about Mack.

"Mrs. MacKenna?"

"Where are my babies?" she asks dully, lowering her hands and staring at the cold water.

Hudson . . . Madison . . . J.J. . . .

"Your husband, we believe, had second thoughts and pulled the girls out."

"What?" she turns back to the detective. "They're *out*? He got them *out*?"

"Yes, the girls are —"

"J.J.?" she asks frantically. "What about J.J.?"

"He was still in the car when we got here —"

"Allison!" Mack calls.

"No, no, no, no . . ." Sobbing, she shakes her head. "My baby . . ."

"Mrs. MacKenna, listen to me. Our men went down immediately and managed to get to him. He was revived, and he was in that ambulance that just —"

"He's alive? And the girls? The girls are —"

"They're all alive, Mrs. MacKenna. All

three of them."

"Allison!" Mack again. "Allison!"

Dazed, she looks over.

Tears are streaming down his face. "They're saying I did this. Please, Allie, you know me."

I don't. I don't know you at all.

She turns her back on Mack.

"Allison, please! I promise you I would never hurt them."

I promise you . . .

She remembers a string of broken promises.

Her mother's far outweigh Mack's. Maybe she's overly sensitive because of the way she was raised; maybe that's why she has a hard time forgiving, forgetting, trusting . . .

"You have to believe me, Allison. This guy — this is no Good Samaritan. He's a monster. He came into the house and he took the kids. I was trying to save them. I chased them here in our car —" He points at the SUV. "If that isn't true, then why is it here? How could I have driven two cars here?"

Allison looks at Detective Looney, who tells her somberly, "We think that he parked the SUV here earlier and then walked or hitchhiked back to the house to load the kids into the other car — it was a rental, in his name. We think he planned to use the SUV as a means of escape after he . . . uh . . . after the other car was . . . in the water."

With the children in it.

Oh, Mack.

Oh, God.

"Detective Looney, take a look at this." A crime scene technician holds out something in his gloved hand. "It was wedged in the padding of the baby's seat."

The baby. They're talking about J.J.

As Detective Looney takes the object, Allison realizes, with a start, what it is.

An iPhone.

"That's mine," she tells the detective abruptly. "It has to be. J.J. — he's always . . ." Her voice breaks.

"Allison!" Mack calls. "Please, just listen to me. I swear to you, I'm not lying. I never lie. You know that."

Mack . . .

Mack doesn't lie.

Ever.

He's a monster . . . he came into the house and he took the kids . . .

I was trying to save them . . .

Allison was so sure he'd taken her phone so that she wouldn't be able to call for help, but if J.J. had it . . .

She whirls around and asks Detective Looney, "Were there any witnesses? Did anyone actually see my husband do this? Any of it?"

"Mrs. MacKenna, as I told you, your husband confessed —"

"To shooting the man who stole our children, not to trying to hurt them himself."

"The DNA —"

"No." She shakes her head rapidly. "I don't care. I don't care what the DNA says. If no one saw —"

"Someone *did* see, and he paid with his life." Out of patience, his eyes blazing, the detective gestures at the bloody figure on the ground. "And we have some questions for you."

"I have to get to my children, but —"

"And we'll take you to your children, but —"

"Please, *just listen to me!* My husband didn't do this. I can prove it."

"How?"

She closes her eyes briefly.

Forgive me, Mack.

"I'll tell you. But first, please, can I speak to my husband?"

"I'm sorry. Not now."

She nods. She'd expected as much.

"Mack!" she calls. "I love you! No matter what. I love you, and I believe you. I do."

"Thank God." His voice is ragged. "I love you, too, Allison."

She swallows hard and turns back to Detective Looney. "Let's go. I need to get to my children."

"Mrs. MacKenna —"

"I know. The proof. I'll tell you on the way to the hospital."

No longer able to stand waiting outside for his cell phone to ring with news of the MacKenna family, Rocky finally called Murph and made him promise to ring the nurses' station if he hears anything at all.

Now, stepping off the elevator, eager to get back to Ange, he sees one of the nurses come flying at him, and his heart stops.

"Mr. Manzillo! There you are! Dr. Abrams is looking for you!"

Rocky immediately breaks into a run, down the hall toward Ange's room. He bursts through the door to see the neurologist bending over his wife, with several nurses gathered around the bed.

"What's going on?" he asks breathlessly — but he sees for himself, before anyone can reply.

Ange's eyes — those beautiful brown eyes

he was terrified he might never see again — are open.

Even lying in a big white hospital bed with her scraped head bandaged, Hudson has an invincible air that fills Allison with a tremendous sense of relief the moment she catches sight of her.

"Shh, Mom, Maddy's sleeping!" her daughter cautions as Allison gingerly gathers her into a hug, and she points to her sister in the adjoining bed.

Allison smiles and leans over Madison, kissing her forehead and stroking her hair for a moment before turning back to her firstborn. "How do you feel, Huddy?"

"Great. But I don't know what time it is. Do you know where my watch is?"

"I don't, but I'm sure we'll find it."

"Okay. What happened?" She sounds more curious than upset. "How did I get here? The nurse said you would tell me."

"You were in an accident in the car. Do you remember?"

"No. I thought . . ." Hudson frowns. "All I remember is going to bed last night."

As helpful as it might be if Hudson could shed some light on the chain of events, Allison knows it's better this way — better that whatever was in those discarded syringes spared her children the horror of the truth . . .

But, thank God, not the worst truth imaginable.

Hudson looks over at her sister. "Was Maddy in the accident, too?"

"Yes."

"Is she going to be all right?"

"Yes."

"What about Daddy and J.J.?"

"They're going to be all right, too," Allison promises her. "I'm going to go see J.J. again now." She's been with him for the last half hour, ever since she arrived at the hospital. He's still in serious condition, but stable now. It wasn't easy to leave him, but of course she wanted to see the girls, who had both been sleeping when she arrived at the hospital. She had asked one of the nurses to summon her if either of them woke up.

"Will you tell Maddy I was here," she asks Hudson, "and send the nurse back to get me when she wakes up?"

"I'll tell her. Take your time, Mom. Maybe you can look for my watch out there."

Allison smiles and kisses Hudson's bandaged head, then Madison's again, before slipping out the door to get back to J.J.

Unlike his big sister, he looks tiny and

vulnerable, with tubes and wires connecting him to machines that monitor his vital signs. The doctors are fairly certain there's no permanent damage — although there's no way of knowing just yet.

A young blond nurse with a round face smiles at Allison as she settles back into the chair she vacated at her son's bedside. "He's a tough little guy, isn't he?"

"He is." Allison nods, smiling, remembering.

"Your girls look a lot like you," the nurse tells her. "But not him. He must look like his dad."

"Yes. He does."

The nurse doesn't know.

Hopefully, she never will. Hopefully, Mack will be cleared any second now.

The nurse slips away, and Allison leans back to wait.

Holding Ange's hand, looking into her eyes, Rocky can't seem to stop smiling — or chattering, filling her in on everything she's missed in the past few months.

"Mr. Manzillo?"

His one-sided conversation interrupted by a nurse, Rocky reluctantly breaks eye contact with Ange and turns around. "Yeah?"

"I'm sorry — I have a message for you

from a T.J. Murphy."

His heart skips a beat. "What is it?"

"I wrote it down. Here, I'll read it to you. *Allison and kids are safe. 10–22. P.S. You were right about Shields. He's 10–84.*" She looks up from the paper in her hand. "Does that make sense to you?"

"It does. Definitely. Thank you."

Rocky breathes a sigh of relief.

Ten–84: the police code for DOA.

And 10–22: take no further action.

Smiling to himself, he turns back to see Ange's eyes tracking the nurse leaving the room, then making contact again with Rocky's gaze.

Such a simple thing — but it means she's in there, paying attention.

"That was about a case I've been working," he tells her. "Anyway . . . where was I? Oh, that's right — so, listen, I told you about this when you were asleep, but just in case you missed it — you were right."

If she could, he knows, she'd say, *What'd you expect? I'm always right.* And then, after waiting a beat, she'd ask, *About what?*

Someday — but not soon enough — she should be talking again. Maybe walking, too. Dr. Abrams was cautious in his prognosis, but even he wore a jubilant expression when he shook Rocky's hand and told him he'll be back later.

Rocky thanked him.

After all these torturous weeks, months, of praying, hoping, waiting . . .

Ange talking.

Walking.

Laughing.

Living.

For now, though, it's enough to see the flicker of pleasure — yes, and triumph — in his wife's eyes when he tells her, "Donny and Kellie — they're expecting a baby. Just like you said. You're going to be a grandma again."

For now, it's enough to feel the warmth of her hand in his.

And, most importantly, it's enough to know that he won't have to learn how to live without her after all.

"Allie? Allie . . . wake up."

Morning . . .

Already?

She groans in protest, but Mack is shaking her gently. "Allie . . ."

"Not yet."

It was so nice back there in the dream she was having . . .

I want to go back . . .

Back . . .

Home . . .

"Allie!"

Her eyes snap open. It's not morning. She's not home in bed . . .

She's in a chair in a strange room.

A hospital room . . . ?

J.J.!

She turns to see that his little chest is rising and falling rhythmically, reassuringly, then swivels back to see her husband standing over her.

"Mack?"

"They let me go. They said . . ." He takes a deep breath. "His name was Samuel Shields."

His name was Samuel Shields.

His name was Samuel Shields.

It doesn't make sense. What — who — is Mack talking about?

"He's the one who did this, Allison. He killed those women, and he set me up, and he took the kids."

"But who — why —"

"He's — he *was* — Jerry Thompson's father."

Allison gasps.

"They have video evidence of him in the beach house," he goes on, "and they said . . . it was because of you. You set up cameras . . . ?"

She swallows hard. "Randi's nanny cams. She gave them to me when I left . . ." *Was it only yesterday?* "I told her I didn't want them, I didn't need them, but . . . you know, 'no arguments.' She was worried, because . . ."

She takes a deep breath. This is the part that's hardest to admit.

"That night I had too much to drink, I guess I told Randi about you sleepwalking with the knife. I wasn't going to use the cameras, but she made me promise, and I did, because . . ."

"Because you didn't trust me," Mack says quietly.

"I'm so sorry. There was just a part of me that —"

She hesitates.

There's no other way to say it. He's right. You might as well own it.

"No, Mack, I didn't trust you. I knew it was just the medication, but I couldn't take a chance with the kids that —"

"You weren't the only one, Allie."

"What? What do you mean?"

"I didn't trust myself. For all I knew . . ." He shakes his head. "I felt like I was losing my mind. Between the stress at work, and not sleeping when I didn't take the Dormipram, and then, when I did take it, I couldn't remember for sure what I had done, where I had been . . . That's why I threw it away."

"Threw what away?"

"The Dormipram."

"You stopped taking it?"

"A few nights ago. I don't care if I never sleep another wink for the rest of my life. I was afraid it might have made me . . ." He squeezes his eyes shut for a moment, as though he can't bear to imagine it. "But it wasn't me. And if you hadn't set up those cameras . . . I might have believed the evidence myself."

"They said — back home — there was DNA."

"There was."

"The test was wrong?"

"No. It was my DNA — stolen from the Riverview Clinic. He found out, somehow, about that. About a lot of things."

"You killed him — that was him, down on the jetty?"

Mack nods grimly. "The last thing that son of a bitch did was turn around so I could shoot him in the back. He knew that it would look like —" He shrugs. "I guess it doesn't matter now."

"You had a gun." She still can't believe it.

"Yes. To protect you and the kids. I got it —"

"You can tell me later." Allison stands up. "Or — you know what? I don't even want to know. All that matters is . . ." She chokes up, unable to finish, but looking into Mack's eyes, she can see straight into his soul at last.

He gets it. He knows.

"I love you, too, Allie," he whispers, opening his arms, welcoming her in.

Alone in her living room the next morning, a middle-aged woman stares at the television with more than passing interest in a morning news program.

"A bizarre twist in a case that was thought to be solved a decade ago," the reporter announces, standing on a sidewalk in front of a two-story Colonial-style home, white with dark green shutters, set back beyond ivy-covered trees and a tall hedgerow. "In 2002, handyman Jerry Thompson was convicted for a series of murders that took place in New York City in the immediate aftermath of the September 11 attacks. Sentenced to life in prison, Thompson committed suicide on the tenth anniversary of the murders. Now, it appears he may have been an innocent man, convicted of crimes that were, in fact, committed by his own father."

The scene shifts from the news desk to a mug shot superimposed with the name Samuel Shields.

The reporter goes on to talk about how Shields killed several women in "leafy, tony Glenhaven Park," a New York City suburb.

Glenhaven Park.

That's where Mack lives now, with his children and his new wife, Allison.

Now the television is showing a montage of small-town scenes: diagonally parked cars along a bucolic main street, briefcase-toting commuters boarding a train, children laughing on a playground . . .

"James MacKenna had moved to this idyllic town to escape the horrific memories of September 11, having lost his first wife in the World Trade Center . . ."

The reporter goes on talking, describing how Samuel Shields framed James Mac-Kenna in the latest series of murders.

The woman on the couch has stopped following the story.

All she can do is stare at the photograph now on the screen, the one labeled Carrie Robinson MacKenna.

A familiar name to go with a familiar face.

The same face, though now weathered with the lines wrought by sorrow and age, that the woman glimpsed in her own bathroom mirror just ten minutes ago.

". . . and the good news this morning is that all five members of the MacKenna family are safe and sound and looking forward to getting back home, where they will finally be able to put this nightmare behind them. I'm Mary Lindsey reporting live from Glenhaven Park, New York."

With a trembling hand, the woman who once called herself Carrie Robinson MacKenna aims the remote at the television, turns off the program, and closes her eyes, lost in memories, deciding it might be time to go home at last.

CPSIA information can be obtained
at www.ICGtesting.com
Printed in the USA
FFOW021018160513